Picking Up His Pieces

By: Nikole Morgan

www.nikolemorgan.com

Picking Up His Pieces

Nikole Morgan
www.NikoleMorgan.com
Greenville, SC

ISBN: 978-1-4675-4534-1

Printed in the United States of America

10 9 8 7 6 5 4 3 1

WWW.NIKOLEMORGAN.COM

Acknowledgements

I thank God for being the driving force that pushed me into my destiny. I thank Him for his Holy Spirit that is a precious gift to me. He led me all the way. I give Him all the praise. This is His ministry, not mine. I was just an instrument He used.

Thank you to my mom, Evelyn Butler. You are truly my 'ride or die chick'! As a single mother you raised me and my two sisters to be strong and confident. You've always had our backs.

To my husband, Cedric, and my children, Dre, D.J., Christian, and Shekinah who put up with me during this journey through the late nights, the traveling and falling asleep at my computer. You guys are the best. Thank you for allowing me the time to be a writer when you needed me to be mommy and wife. I'm still learning how to balance these rolls.

To my Pastor, Curtis, and First Lady Johnson; thank you for believing in the gift that God gave me. Your teaching has equipped me and given me a Kingdom mindset.

Hugs and Kisses to my sisters Tjuana Purry, Crystal and Victoria Butler whose support and love goes beyond measure. You ladies are my rocks! To the best grandparents in the world, Furman and Liz Hallums thanks for just being the remarkable supporters you are.

Diane Westmoreland, you are a "Precious Jewel." Your support of me and my family over the years is something I can never thank you enough for. I love you from the bottom of my heart.

Thank you, thank you, thank you to Dennis Chappell and Vonda Simmons who were the feet and the Spirit of this book. You made it move, and because of you, many people will know Christ.

Karen Richmond, I could not leave you out, your motivational speech one day changed my life. If it hadn't been for you my twenty year old dream would still be a dream. Thank you for pushing me out there.

To my writing coach, Jennifer Tardy, thanks for holding me accountable, keeping me on task and encouraging me to go get it.

Special thanks to my consultant Tweedy Poole who believed this project would change the world of writing and take it to new heights. There is nobody I know who would have made the sacrifices you made, you are my hero.

To my Editors Debra Jonahyak and Jill Callot, you guys made me look good. Thanks for your hook-ups and belief that this project was a keeper.

Big hugs and kisses to my readers: Yasmine Kearse, Nikkii Harris, Debra Valentine, Katina Williams, Pastor James Irby, Pastor Wendell Jones, Pastor Wilbert Simpson, Tatia Merrill, Kesha Good, and Alison Foster. Your feedback helped me tremendously.

To my street runners, Big shout out to you guys, Mahalia Hamblin, Tracey Downs, Eric Smith, Aaron Nicholson, Tangela Harris, Theresa Dowling and every beauty and barber shop that allowed me to hang up my posters all over 10 states and cities. You guys are the bomb.com.

To my Aunt Patricia Ballentine and cousins Jemine and Jennifer, thank you for showing up at one of the most difficult times in my life. Your presence was priceless.

And last but not least, to my late father, Mr. William Arthur Smith. You always told me that I could do anything I want to, if I put my heart into it. I did it Daddy – I did it!!!

Dedication

This book is dedicated to my three sons, Lavadre, Devante, and Christian, all of whom grew up without their farther. Although I couldn't teach you how to be a man, I trust that God will mold you into the men that he desires for you to be. No matter where you are in life, whether physically, mentally, or spiritually, you have the power to move forward. Behind every thought success was that they could succeed.

And to my brother, Jason Jefferson and every man young or old: I encourage you to never give up. Although in life you go through plenty of adversity you should always remember God designed you as an image of strength. He anointed you to overcome.

Chapter 1

Introducing Ivy James

Young Ivy sneaked into the aromatic kitchen while his momma answered the phone in the next room, to pinch off a small piece of fried chicken sitting on a platter. He wanted so badly to lift the top off the crock pot so he could stick his finger in the ham hock and pinto beans to suck that seasoned juice, but he didn't know how much time he had before Momma returned. He stared and licked his lips at the lightly browned corn bread where it sat atop the stove. Hearing his mother's bedroom slippers sliding across the old wooden floor warned him that he'd better get out of there quick. He gently replaced the glass top on the old silver pot so it wouldn't make a sound, and licked his fingers as he whisked by his mom, smiling.

"I don't know why people would call your house and hang up," JoAnn said, wiping her hands on her cotton print apron.

"Just don't have anything better to do," she sighed, snuggly re-pinning her long loose strands neatly back into a bun.

She glanced at an eight-year-old girl standing at the sink, busy peeling potatoes.

"Courtney, baby, you're cutting the potatoes way too big." JoAnn frowned as she took the dull knife away from her daughter. "You gotta cut them up small so they won't take so long to cook."

"Courtney!" Jessie roared to life from his broken tan recliner in the living room that sat in front of the old RCA television. "Can you bring Daddy some iced tea please?"

The girl looked over at JoAnn timidly as her mother selected Jessie's favorite jug from the dish cabinet.

"Take this to your daddy, baby," JoAnn motioned as she handed her the jug. "Go on now," she smiled. JoAnn leaned back a little as she watched her baby girl walk into the next room.

"Here Daddy," Courtney said in her still, sweet voice.

"Come here, squirt," Jessie smiled.

"Sit on Daddy's lap," he said, patting his knee. Courtney climbed up into the chair with him, and started to laugh as her dad tickled her.

"Come on now, Courtney," JoAnn stepped into the room.

"We've got to finish making this good ole potato salad," she smiled briefly, pushing a dark curly tendril from her damp forehead.

"Okay, Momma." Courtney quickly slid off her father's lap. "But Momma, I don't want to cook no more," she whined. "Can I go outside and play with my friends?" she pleaded.

JoAnn put her hands on her generously curved hips. "Some kind of helper you are," she grinned.

"Go on," she gestured, waving her hand for the girl to scoot.

Courtney raced out of the kitchen with a whoop. Jessie James stood at the screen door watching his daughter and her friend play jacks on the sidewalk. He loved his wife and kids. Courtney, the splitting image of her momma, was the smartest in her class at school. His good-looking, active son Ivy, on the other hand, only liked school for two reasons: lunch and recess. Jessie hauled off trash from neighboring lots and curbs to take care of his family, but most of the time that didn't cover the bills. His number hustle compensated for the shortfall and enabled them to even have a little extra now and then for the movie theatre or bowling alley.

Contrary to the average man, he struggled tremendously at trying to be a decent husband and father; his demons made sure of that. Like the Apostle Paul, even when he wanted to do right, he still couldn't stop sinning. The more Jessie tried to suppress his demons, the more they clamored to be fed.

"Hey JoAnn, I'm going out for a little bit," he said, stealing a piece of the golden fried chicken.

"Give me some of that sweet brown sugar," he kissed her neck.

JoAnn smiled and frowned simultaneously. "But Jess, dinner will be ready shortly. I've got a few more pieces of chicken to fry. Aren't you hungry?" she asked.

"I'll be back, sweetheart. I've got to go see a man about a mule," he joked as he pushed open the screen door.

JoAnn's sister-in-law Sheree whipped her Ford Escort into the driveway at 2775 Laredo Avenue. Working on her second pack of cigarettes, she took the last drag of her Salem Light and stared at the license plate on JoAnn's Toyota Corolla. She didn't see Jessie's truck in the back yard and wondered where he could have gotten off to so quickly. She had just called fifteen minutes ago and heard his voice in the background before she hung up on JoAnn without saying a word.

Needing more than a cigarette to calm herself down, she tried her husband Russell's part-time job office one more time, when he didn't answer after the fourth ring; she didn't bother to leave another message. She'd called him seventeen times in the last two hours and left three messages. Sheree knew that fast receptionist was on the other line running her mouth spreading gossip instead of doing her freaking job. The longer she sat in the driveway, the madder she got. She hopped out of the car, slamming the door, and walked toward her brother-in-law's house. JoAnn met her at the screen door with a pleasant expression as the irritated light-skinned petite woman stomped up the concrete steps. Sheree didn't smile as JoAnn opened the screen door.

"Hi Sheree; where's Kevin and Kimme? I've got dinner fixed," JoAnn said, with a concerned look. "Are you okay? You look funny, is something wrong?"

Sheree met her sister-in-law's concern with an angry tone. "No! I'm not okay. We need to talk," she began.

JoAnn led her to the kitchen table where both women sat down. Feeling uneasy and puzzled, JoAnn smoothed out the wrinkles in her apron, and re-tied the string on her small waistline, before fidgeting with the pocket. Sheree jumped right in.

"When I asked you to keep the kids for Russell and me while we worked the graveyard shift, it was because I felt like we're family, and where I come from, family is supposed to stick together."

Jo Ann nodded.

"My kids love coming over here to visit with their cousins. Russell and I enjoy having Ivy and Courtney come to our house. We would never put your kids in harm's way, ever. Last week when Kimme cried not to come over, I didn't understand why, and she wouldn't tell me. All she would say was she didn't want to ever come here again. I assumed maybe she and Courtney had gotten into an argument or something; you know how they do."

Sheree began to cry. "Now I think I know why."

JoAnn shifted nervously in her hard wooden seat, not knowing what to think. She slowly rubbed her thick thighs. Sheree spoke again, choosing her words carefully.

"I was separating clothes to put in the wash today, and found something disgusting."

JoAnn stared intently at her sister-in-law. The irate mother slammed her daughter, Kimme's blood-stained underwear on the kitchen table with so much force that the salt and pepper shakers toppled to the floor.

"And she hasn't started her period," she shouted, "so how did this happen?"

JoAnn stared in disbelief.

"Now, I pray for you and Jessie's sake that this ain't nothing like it looks."

Sheree stood up from the table, ready to hurt someone. She hoped JoAnn's tears were not an answer to her question.

"Oh, my God!" JoAnn held onto her heart like she was about to pass out. "I'm so sorry!" she cried, jumping up and running out of the kitchen in tears. "I didn't know he got to her! I swear to you, Sheree, I swear!"

Sheree raced behind her. "What the do you mean you didn't know he got to her?"

JoAnn was crying hysterically as she turned to face the other woman. "I made sure he stayed out of the girls' room. I watched him like a hawk. I'm telling you the honest-to-God truth. I promise you I didn't know!"

She took a hankie from her apron pocket and wiped her eyes. Sheree felt light-headed. She had wanted to believe she had been wrong, but her assumptions and worst fears were now confirmed. She stood there a moment in total disbelief.

"Has he touched Courtney too?" Sheree yelled.

JoAnn dropped her head in admittance. "No!" Sheree screamed, jerking her head away as though to avoid the sight of sin.

"His own daughter!"

'It was only once, and he didn't go all the way, JoAnn reasoned to herself as she ran to Sheree to calm her down.'

"What kind of mother are you?" Sheree pulled back and slapped JoAnn in her face as hard as she could.

"How could you let that bastard touch our babies? For God's sake, JoAnn, what the hell is wrong with you?"

JoAnn's tears continued freely down her cheeks. "I've been praying, asking the good Lord to help him fight this sickness."

JoAnn touched Sheree's hand searching for compassion. Sheree jerked away. "Get your damn hands off me. Both of ya'll are sick, you and Jessie. I don't know whose worse, you or him. You all up in church every week praising Hallelujah while your husband out here molesting kids."

Sheree looked back at JoAnn and lost it. When she thought about Jessie pressing his two hundred pound body on her innocent baby, it was too much to bear. There was no telling what he'd said to Kimme to make her not tell. When she thought about how scared her baby and niece had to be, her emotions threatened to surge out of control. Sheree lunged at JoAnn, swinging with all her might. She wanted JoAnn to feel as much pain as she did. JoAnn didn't even try to retaliate. Her shame and guilt wouldn't let her protect herself.

"Where is that no-good S.O.B.?" Sheree punched JoAnn in the face. "Where is he," she shouted, placing her hands around the other woman's neck.

JoAnn struggled for air. "I...can't..." She coughed and sputtered.

Sheree loosened her grip around JoAnn's neck. "I don't know," JoAnn gasped, breathing heavily.

"I'm telling you the truth," JoAnn panicked. "Please...." she tried to reason with Sheree.

"We need to get him some help. He's a good man. It's just the devil won't let him be."

With another hard slap Sheree replied, "We don't need to do a nothing. How dare you say something so ridiculous!"

Sheree looked at JoAnn as if she didn't recognize her. She couldn't understand how in the world JoAnn could protect a monster like Jessie. A small part of her felt sorry for the other woman. Was she that desperate to hold on to this man - or just stupid?

"If he makes it to jail, he'll be lucky," Sheree yelled before storming out the door.

Reeling from the blows Sheree had rained down on her, JoAnn tried to stand up, wiping her bloody nose. "Sheree, wait!" she cried, rubbing her aching body.

"You best make funeral arrangements!" Sheree screamed back at the house. "Because, when Russell finds out his brother molested our daughter, Jessie's a dead man."

"Sheree!"

JoAnn tried to run toward Sheree's car, but it was too painful to move. She grabbed the door handle to regain her balance. Sheree was backing out of the driveway, burning rubber by the time JoAnn struggled to the porch. JoAnn fell to her knees, heart pounding, with bloodstains covering her white apron. She didn't know what to do. A few minutes passed. JoAnn was still on her knees on the porch's wooden floorboards. Suddenly she panicked. She had to find Jessie and warn him. If Russell found Jessie before she did, she knew it would be bad.

JoAnn got up and hurried inside to the degree she was able, which wasn't very fast. She grabbed her keys and headed to Ivy's room, where she banged on the door. The boy's face paled when he saw his mother bloody and appearing to be in pain. Jumping up, he put his Atari game controller to the side and threw his headphones on the floor. He ran to his mother, crying. "Mom, what happened?"

JoAnn spoke slowly. "Listen to me carefully, Ivy. I need you to find your sister," she said as she changed into some comfortable shoes and made her way back to the kitchen to get her purse.

Ivy was close on her heels, wondering what in the world could be going on.

"Your sister was supposed to be outside playing, but I don't see her. I need you to find her quickly."

She grabbed her son by the shoulders and looked into his fearful eyes. "I'm okay, baby," she said, wiping a tear from his eye.

"I've got to go out and find your daddy. Bring your sister back here; I want you to lock all the doors. Don't let anybody in the house, especially family. If your daddy gets here before I do, hand him this note."

JoAnn turned to find a pen and some paper to write on. Scribbling a warning to her husband, she handed Ivy the torn piece of paper. "Make sure to lock all the doors when you and your sister are safely in the house," she said, moving from the kitchen.

The loud sound of something breaking caused JoAnn and Ivy to jump. Fear relaxed from their faces once they saw the shattered ceramic bowl of freshly made potato salad scattered all over the spotless floor. The pounding in their chest was deafening as they both breathed a sigh of relief.

Getting into the car, JoAnn's search for Jessie began. She drove past his friends' houses, the bars he went to, the number joints, and even the hoochie momma strip club he visited on Wednesday nights while she was at Bible study. He couldn't be found anywhere. She'd been driving the streets for hours in search of him, and even considered driving by Sheree's house just to see if the police was there, but decided against it. JoAnn felt nervous and jittery and wished this was all just a bad dream. She imagined her husband and children, along with her, sitting at the dinner table eating fried chicken, pinto beans, macaroni and cheese, potato salad and corn bread.

While stopped at a red light, JoAnn poured out the contents of her purse in the passenger seat, trying to find her address book to call some of Jessie's friends, but it wasn't there. She didn't have time to worry about finding it. She quickly pulled her car into the parking lot of the supermarket on the corner of Purry Street and Madison Avenue. Searching through the seat, she looked for the loose change that had fallen from her purse. She must call and check on the kids to make sure everything was okay on the home front. Just as she turned to open the car door, she looked up and saw Jessie's black pickup truck stopped at the red light facing her. Jumping out of the car, she waved her hands in the air frantically.

When the light turned green and his truck approached, she noticed he had a passenger. When he passed, JoAnn looked harder to see who was inside. She started to hyperventilate when she saw Courtney beside him. JoAnn jumped into the car and turned the ignition, but it was already still on. She threw the car in drive and made a quick u-turn from the corner. She tried her best to catch up to them. There had to be close to ten cars between them, but she didn't panic; she could see them clearly since Jessie's truck sat up much higher than all the other vehicles.

Jessie turned down a side street and parked his truck in the dirt behind a tree at the Eastway Community Park. Watching the pickup turn into a drive, JoAnn knew exactly where he was going. The old park had been abandoned for years. She honked her horn angrily, caught by the traffic light; Jessie was up to no good. Tears streamed down her cheeks. Yes, it was true she knew that Jessie had violated their daughter once, but it was different now. She was about to catch him red-handed. Anxiety flowed through her body like a flooding river. How in the world could she have allowed this to happen? She should have spoken up a long time ago; instead she had chosen to be stupid, acting like the problem would just go away on its own.

"What kind of mother am I," she thought. Sheree was right, she was no better than Jessie. She was just as much to blame as he was, maybe even more. At least he appeared to be sick, but she had no excuse. When JoAnn pulled up behind Jessie's truck, she saw a monster. There was no way that man could have been her husband. She watched his face turn toward the child, smiling with excitement as he leaned back against the driver's window to pull down his pants.

It was at that moment she felt no hurt, no pity, and no reasoning, just pure rage. Her fury was fueled as she thought about her baby in that truck. If this was how Sheree had felt, she didn't blame her sister-in-law for beating the crap out of her. She wanted to kill that monster. JoAnn jumped out of her car, her still-aching body not protesting as she rushed as fast as possible to save her baby.

The loud sound of JoAnn's car door slamming didn't interrupt Jessie's pleasure. Jo Ann swung open the passenger door with bloodshed in her eyes. When Jessie's glance met hers in shock, she leaned into the truck and started punching with every ounce of strength. Once he leaned backward to dodge her fists, she pulled her baby by both arms and slid her from the seat, never taking her eyes off Jessie. She cursed him more these few seconds than she had in the last 14 years of their marriage. Until now, she had never hit Jessie or showed any disrespect, nor had he ever laid a finger on her, but at that moment, if she'd had a gun, he would surely be smelling like smoke.

JoAnn looked down at her child, only to realize it wasn't Courtney. She didn't know the child by name, but she recognized her from somewhere.

"How could you, Jessie?" JoAnn yelled.

"You're sick…sick, sick, sick! Get your bag of toys out of his truck, sweetie, and go sit inside my car," JoAnn told the little girl.

"Make sure you lock the doors."

Tears the size of pennies filled the little girl's scared face. She quickly grabbed the bags from the toy store containing her brand new baby dolls. Jessie pushed open his door and jumped out, running around his truck in a heated burst of anger to reach JoAnn, but he slipped and fell face-first in a muddy track. His madness erupted as he quickly stood to his feet.

"What the hell are you doing!" he screamed as he raced toward JoAnn and swung, hitting her twice in the chest.

Wrestling her to the ground, he started choking her. JoAnn tried to fight back, but his blows were too powerful. All she could do was hope he'd get tired or she'd just die, whichever came first. When Jessie stared down at his wife, he noticed JoAnn's bloody apron, which caused him to stop beating her. The evil beast in him looked toward JoAnn's car that held the desires that could satisfy his hungry flesh, but the loving man in him began to surface.

Taking those same hands he had used as weapons, he held and comforted the woman who loved him in spite of the monster within him, the woman who protected him from himself, who supported his dreams and encouraged him to be a better man. She made him feel at times like he could overcome anything. He remembered her telling him that everyone struggles with good and evil. She had said the stronger of the two will always win, but it's up to you who you feed most, because the best-fed desire will always succeed.

Jessie thought about her words as he sat there, holding her in his arms. She'd told him a long time ago in bed, late one night, about the Lord, and how to pray. All he had to do was tell God what was on his heart, good or bad. She'd told him God didn't look at the outward man like people did, but that God looks at a man's heart. He sat in the grass, holding his wife, filled with shame and guilt. He said a lot of things in his heart and mind, but never once opened his mouth.

Picking up his weakened wife, he headed toward her car. When the little girl saw him approaching with the nice lady in his arms, she felt scared and helpless. Jessie hit the car door with his foot, signaling her to open the driver's door. She looked out the window into his eyes and saw a different man; it was still Jessie's face and body, but his face looked lighter than before. The little girl felt an odd, unexpected sensation, something she had never experienced before: a spirit of peace. She unlocked the door and pushed it open. Jessie placed JoAnn in the driver's seat. He unlatched the seat and laid it back so she could lie back.

Jessie wept as he looked at what he'd done to his wife. JoAnn squeezed his hand and gave him a little smile. She tried to speak. "Don't talk, honey. Just nod if you want me to take you to the hospital."

JoAnn shook her head 'no.'

"I love you, JoAnn. I love you so much."

She squeezed his hand again. Kissing his wife on the forehead, Jessie then kissed her cheek. JoAnn looked into his eyes and smiled. "I can see God...," her voice was low and sweet.

"No! JoAnn, don't talk like that, you're not going to die," Jessie pleaded.

"I can see God in you," she whispered.

"I can see him in your eyes," she said again.

Jessie kissed his wife one more time before closing the car door. He looked at the little girl with tender embarrassment. "Lock the door, baby," he said.

Though he felt stronger and surer of his faith than ever, he still couldn't quite trust himself. Jessie went back to his truck and started the ignition. He drove off down a side street and parked. He made sure he could still see JoAnn's car, although she couldn't see him. After several minutes JoAnn finally started her car and drove away.

"Thank You, God, for answering my prayers to heal her weak body and my filthy soul."

A plan began to evolve in his mind that it might be best for him to go away for a while to pull himself together. He didn't know how he'd be able to face his wife at home after what had just happened. Should he even say goodbye to the kids? Maybe it would be best to just start the car and drive far, far away. JoAnn rolled down her window to get some air. Her chest and limbs were still sore and aching, but miraculously she was able to drive.

"I'm taking you home, honey." JoAnn said, after asking for directions.

"It won't be long now."

JoAnn could only imagine what was going through the child's head. The poor little thing had to be pretty well shaken up. She made small talk to make things feel a little normal while they drove. She found out the little girl's name was Sweet Pea, and she was second to the youngest of three sisters and two brothers. She was a third grader at Briar Elementary School, which explained where JoAnn recognized her from. That was the school where JoAnn worked as a cafeteria clerk.

The old, dingy white house looked abandoned as they pulled into Sweet Pea's dirt driveway. The glass on the front door window was cracked, and the rest were boarded up with a wooden square. The grass in the yard was a few inches from being knee-high, and a small, "Do not Disturb" sign hung on the door knob. JoAnn wrestled with whether she should get out of the car. It would probably be safer for her if she dropped the child off and drove away, but since Sweet Pea knew her from school, she thought taking her to the door would be the smartest thing.

JoAnn had already been beaten twice today; she was certain she couldn't handle another confrontation. If Sweet Pea's parents wanted answers, JoAnn had made up in her mind that she would tell them she had just been driving by and saw a man trying to take advantage of their daughter, and she had run him off. Sweet Pea sat perfectly still, staring at JoAnn as though she felt sorry for her.

"What's your name, lady?" Sweet Pea asked sweetly.

A bit reluctant, JoAnn softly answered. "JoAnn, honey – my name is JoAnn. Why do you ask?" JoAnn said holding the child's small hand.

"You're a real nice lady. Are you God's wife? I've seen you before in my dreams."

JoAnn smiled at Sweet Pea's question, but she felt relieved that the child must not have realized she was the school lunch lady.

"No, I'm not God's wife," she giggled.

"I'm one of His children, just like you."

With an urgent expression, Sweet Pea looked into JoAnn's eyes. She began to cry. JoAnn hugged her.

"It's okay, Sweet Pea; everything is going to be all right."

"I want to be like you when I grow up. I want to save people, like you saved me."

JoAnn grinned and wanted to cry, too. The little girl's words were the best thing she'd heard all day. It touched her heart to know that someone saw the good in her.

"You can be anything in this world that you want to be, my little Sweet Pea," JoAnn rubbed her cheeks.

"Just learn to trust God for direction. Always remember that."

JoAnn got out of her car, not knowing what to expect. She was sure that Sweet Pea's parents were going to want detailed answers. Her heart started racing as they slowly walked up the squeaky wooden steps. Sweet Pea seemed reluctant to keep going. JoAnn felt sorry for the child. She knew the girl would need some type of counseling to help her cope with all the drama that had taken place. Knocking softly on the door, JoAnn felt nauseated. After waiting a few seconds, she knocked again.

"Don't you see the damn sign on the door!" someone yelled from inside.

"Momma, open the door! It's me, Sweet Pea."

"Girl, you know the rules when you see the sign on the door. You and Mr. Jessie sit tight for a minute. I'll be right there," the loud female voice yelled.

JoAnn squinted, bewildered. Sweet Pea's mother (knew) Jessie? What was going on? She stood on the porch by the door while Sweet Pea sat on the steps playing with her new dolls for nearly ten minutes. She pondered leaving, but curiosity overwhelmed her; now *she* needed answers. At last the front door flew open. JoAnn moved to the side so the elderly man could get past her. He stepped over the threshold looking guilty. A woman with greasy hair walked out behind him, folding up several bills of money and putting the wad in her bra. She stood on the porch and watched the old man hurry down the street as though sneaking off.

"Who are you? Where is Mr. Jessie?"

Before JoAnn had an opportunity to reply that she was Jessie's wife, Sweet Pea's mother snatched the child off the top step. The child's white baby doll tumbled down every single step until finally hitting the concrete at the bottom.

"What the hell did you do, girl? Where is my money?"

The little girl's eyes filled with tears and a look of fear.

"I didn't get it, Momma. Something happened at the park and...."

The brassy woman jerked around toward JoAnn for answers. "Who are you, lady? If you want a piece of anything in this house, its thirty dollars, and if it's under the age of ten, it's fourty dollars."

She stood on the porch with her hand stuck out, palm up. JoAnn's nausea grew worse. She wished she hadn't taken off her apron; she could have vomited in it. Without a word she walked over to embrace the child. She held onto her a long moment, their eyes deadlocked to one another as she bodly spoke words of life, intended to reach her soul and broken spirit

"That will cost you two dollars!" The girl's mother rolled her neck.

JoAnn ignored her and kissed Sweet Pea on the cheek before turning to leave, as the child sobbed lightly.

"Oh no," Sweet Pea's mother headed toward JoAnn.

"Don't put your lips on my baby. Ain't nothing around here free, nothing. You owe me five dollars, lady, and I expect to get paid."

JoAnn kept walking, but she glanced back at the girl. Sweet Pea was waving goodbye, her eyes full of tears as she clasped her baby doll for dear life. Sweet Pea's mother ran down the steps after JoAnn, demanding her payment. JoAnn turned toward her and yelled, "I rebuke you, Satan, in the name of Jesus!"

Lifting her hand toward the house, JoAnn prayed that God would bless and protect every child under that roof. "I speak life, love and strength to the helpless children living in fear here, and I command the Spirit of Peace to hover over this place as long as they dwell here. Spirit of God, be with them, save them, and lead them to everlasting life."

Sweet Pea's mother didn't utter another word as she watched JoAnn start her car. Her shame felt magnified at the mention of God and His Spirit. Pulling away with a heavy heart, JoAnn watched Sweet Pea as she wept and continued to wave goodbye. JoAnn wished she'd never taken the child home.

JoAnn was exhausted. She wanted desperately to get home to Ivy and Courtney. She yearned to hold her precious babies, nothing else mattered anymore. Steering the car with her free hand, JoAnn wiped away more tears, using her shirt sleeve. If only today could have been a dream, she'd be eternally grateful. However, when she turned onto Laredo Avenue (which was usually a quiet suburban street of neatly kept middle class homes) the screeching sirens, blue lights and crowd of neighbors confirmed she was experiencing a living nightmare. She couldn't get anywhere near her house as police cars were everywhere. JoAnn had to park her car at the end of the street and run down the hill to her house. She could only speculate about what might have happened. She hoped Russell had only beaten up Jessie and that no one was seriously hurt, but she panicked when she saw the fat white man pull out the yellow crime scene tape to rope off the perimeter of her house.

Someone was sitting in the back seat of a police car that was parked in her driveway. She couldn't tell who it was. Russell's motorcycle was parked in the driveway behind Jessie's truck. Frantically, she wondered where her children might be, JoAnn worried they might have gotten in harm's way. She brushed past all the nosey neighbors, trying to push her way to the front porch. A policeman struggled to hold her back as she squirmed and then screamed hysterically. "This is my house!" She pushed the officer's arm.

"Let me in! Where are my children? What happened? Tell me! I need information!" She pushed him again.

"Do you hear me?" she shouted as he tried to constrain her.

"Ma'am, you need to calm down. I can't talk to you if you're screaming. Now settle down, okay?"

Her struggles ceased. She nodded limply.

"Are you Mrs. James?" the policeman asked.

Another officer approached and whispered something. He nodded as the other man walked away. "Ma'am, is your husband either Russell James or Jessie James?"

"My husband is Jessie James," JoAnn began to cry. "Please just tell me straight….Where, are my children? Are my kids okay?"

JoAnn started shaking. Trying to break away, JoAnn wanted to run through the roped off area, but he pushed her back.

"Ma'am, please, I need you to cooperate with me. I will explain everything."

JoAnn tried to calm her nerves.

"First of all, Mrs. James, your children Ivy and Courtney are safe. They are sitting with a detective close by."

The heavy officer gestured toward a vague direction to the left. "But Mrs. James, there has been a...."

Before he could finish his sentence, Sheree rushed up behind them, breathing hard as though she'd just run a marathon. She pushed to get through, but more officers dashed over to detain her. She was strong as an ox. Three officers were holding her back. "What happened?" she stopped pushing. "Is Jessie dead? Is that Russell in the back of the car over there?"

She tried to move that way. Gripping her arm, a burly officer said firmly, "Ma'am, no. Please just stay right here, Mrs. James," he continued. "There has been an altercation. We are still in the process of getting all the details."

As he continued to speak, JoAnn prepared herself for the worst. In her heart she knew Jessie must be dead. As she looked toward the house, she saw people bringing out a body on a stretcher. The body was covered with a white sheet. Small specks of blood were beginning to soak through. Sheree let out a loud scream. "Oh, God, I need to see my husband! Where is he? Oh, God! Oh, God, please!" she pleaded.

Sheree looked intently at JoAnn. "I told Russell what Jessie did. I begged him to call the authorities and let them handle it, but I couldn't stop him. He took my car keys so I wouldn't follow him. I had to get my neighbor to bring me over here...I tried calling, but no one answered. So I just called the police."

Neither woman took their eyes off the white sheet. Sheree's fear gripped her like a prisoner and she suddenly wished she could start the day all over again. She wanted Jessie to hurt but she wasn't convinced she wanted her brother in law dead.

"Mrs. James?" A detective came toward them.

"Yes!" both Sheree and JoAnn answered.

Sheree saw a chance to break through. She took off as fast as she could, JoAnn running right behind. A tall, lanky officer chased both women, but he couldn't catch either of them before they made it to the body. Determined, Sheree snatched back the white cloth. She stood still, looking over the body once, twice and a third time. Not wanting to believe her eyes, she lifted up the sleeve of the black, long sleeve shirt that Russell put on that morning exposing the tattoo with her nickname, "REE REE."

She screamed a high-pitched, "No-o-o-o! Russell, wake up!"

Her legs felt weak and her breathing grew faint as she fixed her eyes on her husband's lifeless body, remembering how just hours ago he had been so full of life. She cried onto his smooth, freshly shaved face, wishing she could once again gaze into his cocoa brown eyes. His perfectly-trimmed mustache now contained small specks of blood. JoAnn stood behind Sheree, frozen in disbelief. Her mind couldn't register that it was truly her brother-in-law instead of her husband. She had prepared herself to see Jessie's body lying beneath that sheet.

Sheree cried loudly as the paramedics lifted Russell's body into the ambulance. Her sister and her mother were now there to console her aching heart. JoAnn could only imagine what she was going through. She had no answers about Jessie, and hoped he wasn't still in the house. If the police brought him out in handcuffs, Sheree would likely lose all self-control.

"Mommy, Mommy," the sweet, familiar voices rang like bells in JoAnn's ear.

Turning around, JoAnn embraced her babies, never wanting to turn them loose. Both shivering children were wrapped in bed sheets. JoAnn's heart went out to them. Lord only knew what they had just witnessed.

"Mommy, Daddy said he loves you," Courtney said.

JoAnn had trouble hearing her as the other ambulance drove by.

"I said Daddy said he loves you," she yelled at the top of her lungs.

"I know, baby," Jo Ann said. "He told me."

"How did he tell you, Mommy?" she asked.

JoAnn hugged her tightly.

"Uncle Russell and Daddy had a bad fight, and Uncle Russell got shot."

Her eyes were round, pupils dilated, as though she were in shock. "I know, baby. I know Uncle Russell is dead. Where is your daddy? Is that him in the police car, or is he still inside the house?"

"No, Mommy, that's Mr. Billy, the neighbor in the car. They were asking him questions about what happened. He was looking through the side window."

JoAnn's confusion didn't last long as she stared toward her house. Two men were carrying another body out on a stretcher.

"Lord have mercy!"

JoAnn shook her head, moaning. "Jessie's dead, too!"

JoAnn was empty. She felt absolutely nothing: no pity, no sorrow, no pain...nothing. She couldn't even cry. There were no more tears left. She reached out for her children to embrace them, holding onto them for dear life.

The next day two detectives from Richmond County Law Enforcement showed up at JoAnn's house. They introduced themselves as Detective Simmons and Detective Daniels. They had asked to question Ivy and Courtney the day before, but JoAnn had refused. She said they had been through enough trauma for one day, and the Lord knows she had been through hell, as well.

Courtney and Ivy sat on the plaid sofa, side by side, holding hands for support. JoAnn stood beside them, not wanting to hear the story again that they were about to tell, but she had to endure it. She had to be there for her children.

"Take your time, honey," Detective Simmons told Courtney.

"If you need to stop you can. Detective Daniels and I are in no hurry," he said compassionately.

Courtney took a long, deep breath before she re-lived the events that would haunt her for the rest of her life. Jessie had walked into the house very quietly, and sat down in his favorite recliner. He had started telling God he was sorry for hurting all the people he loved, and asked God to forgive him for being a double-minded man. He asked God to take away his sickness, and everybody's sickness that was like his. He prayed for little girls like his precious daughter and niece whose daddies, uncles, and cousins had taken advantage of them. He explained to God that he didn't want to do the bad things he did. He asked God why He would make him that way. He didn't want to be attracted to children. He wanted to be a normal man, but he couldn't fight off his desires.

Courtney and Ivy had come into the living room and stood silent while Jessie talked to the Lord. JoAnn had always taught them to never interrupt someone who was praying. After Jessie had said "Amen," he asked the children to come closer. Ivy handed his father the note their mother had left for him, but Jessie never opened it.

"Daddy has to go away for a little while," he said, as they both approached tentatively, unused to seeing their father in this pensive mood.

"Come sit on Daddy's lap," he patted his knees for Courtney.

Sensing her reluctance, he added, "It's okay, baby. I know I haven't been a very good daddy, but I'm going somewhere so someone can teach me how to be better. What I did was wrong. No father should ever, ever do something like what I did to my child."

He paused, looking deeply into Courtney's eyes, as a father did who loved his child. "Can you forgive me?"

"Yes, Daddy," Courtney smiled, no longer uncomfortable by his touch.

Courtney sensed the loving spirit of a real father. "I love you, your mom and your brother," he said, reaching for Ivy's hand.

"I don't want to *ever* do anything to hurt any of you."

Courtney grabbed her daddy around the neck, squeezing him tight. She felt something pure and innocent coming from her father. She loved that feeling and never wanted it to end.

All of a sudden Russell stormed through the door with fire in his eyes. When he saw Jessie embracing Courtney, although it was innocent, it didn't look that way to him. "Get your filthy hands off her!" Russell snarled.

Jessie took a long, deep breath, somewhat confused. He didn't think JoAnn would have told anybody about what happened in the park, but maybe she had been so angry that protecting him was no longer a priority to her.

"Ivy, take your little sister in the other room and play or watch TV. Daddy needs to talk to your Uncle Russell," Jessie said calmly.

Neither Ivy nor Courtney wanted to move, both sensing that something wasn't right. Ivy ran to his father and hugged him around his waist.

"Uncle Russell, can you please just come back when Momma gets home?" Ivy said tearfully.

Russell smiled grimly. "It's okay," he said for Ivy's benefit. "Your dad and I just need to have a man-to-man talk."

Ivy looked up at his father who stood three-and-a-half-feet taller than he did, pleading with his eyes to agree and send his Uncle Russell home.

"Go ahead and scoot, son. We'll only be a little while," Jessie answered soberly.

As the children quietly left the room, Russell stared rigorously into his twin brother's face, wondering how someone who looked so much like him could be so different.

"All I want to know is one thing," Russell said, angrily in a low voice. "Is it true?"

Nervously choosing his words, Jessie knew his secret had been exposed. He tried to explain to his look-alike that he had been fighting this problem for years. Jessie told Russell that he knew that he needed professional help, and he stressed how sorry he was. However Russell wasn't impressed with his brother's new efforts at being righteous.

"Just answer the damn question," Russell shouted. "I want to hear you say it! I want to hear you tell me you touched my baby! Say it, Jessie! I said, say it!"

"Russell, man," Jessie shook his head. "I don't want to be like this. I keep asking God why He would make me like this. I don't want to be this way, man. I don't."

"Didn't you hear what I said? I said, say it, little bro," Russell demanded.

Jessie cracked a hint of a smile, knowing every time Russell got mad he brought up the fact that he was forty-six seconds older.

"Well, I'll tell you what, you sick pervert. I'll beat an answer out of you!"

Russell rushed Jessie, and both men wrestled until they fell to the floor. Even though Jessie had won the high school wrestling championship for Reidville four years in a row, he no longer had the strength that he had once had. The beating continued relentlessly. Jessie's left eye was swollen nearly shut. He was missing a front tooth, and his right arm wasn't broken, but he could barely move it.

Broken glass lay everywhere, and the living room furniture had been turned upside down and sideways. When Russell finally let up on Jessie, he was more than exhausted, and his head was spinning. He continued cursing at his only brother, calling him every name he could think of. When at last Russell got up and turned to walk away, the 38 special he had tucked in his pocket fell to the floor, making a loud thump. Russell had only brought the gun as a scare tactic, in case Jessie got the best of him. The plan was to do exactly what he did- beat him to a pulp. However, when Jessie saw the gun lying on the floor, he panicked. Both men raced to retrieve the weapon.

Jessie grabbed the gun clutching it tightly in his hand, holding on with all that remained in him. Russell grabbed Jessie's arm while Jessie yelled for Russell to let go. This time Jessie couldn't let his big brother get the best of him. A gun was involved, and he didn't want anyone to get hurt. They struggled, leaving Jessie face up on the floor, pleading with Russell to release his hands. At the same time Russell yelled for Jessie to give him the gun. When the weapon accidentally went off, Russell fell flat on his back with a bullet in his chest, gasping for breath.

"Oh, my god...Daddy!" Courtney screamed, as she and Ivy jumped out of the hall closet they were peeping out of, drenched in sweat and fear.

"Ivy, call an ambulance!" Jessie yelled, "Hurry, Son, hurry!" he pleaded in a panic.

Ivy quickly dialed 911 and waited for the operator to get on the line. Jessie sat beside Russell on the floor. "Hold on, man," Jessie cried as he rocked his brother in his arms.

"I didn't mean to! The gun just went off! I'm sorry, Russell. Why didn't you just give me the gun, man?" Jessie sobbed.

Seconds ticked slowly past.

"I love you. Don't you…," Jessie paused, not even wanting to say it. "You should have just shot me and got it over with. This should be me laying here… not you, Russ."

The 911 operator told Ivy that help was on the way. She asked the boy to put Jessie on the phone, but Jessie refused to leave his brother. As long as he knew the ambulance was coming, he wasn't about to waste precious moments talking to the dispatcher. He knew there wasn't much she could do. Russell's chest began to rise and fall more slowly. Blood oozed through his teeth and mouth. A teardrop rolled down his cheek.

"Hold on, Russ. The ambulance will be here soon. Don't worry about nothing. I'm right here. I ain't going nowhere."

He continued to rock his brother's body in his arms. "You're going to be fine."

Russell's face turned pale. He was barely breathing.

"Lord Jesus, please have mercy! Please God, just let him be all right," Jessie yelled at the ceiling and closed his eyes.

He looked down at the motionless man. His heart began to mourn. He watched his brother's life slowly fade away. Lifting Russell's ear close to his mouth, Jessie whispered life changing words. Russell used the last ounce of strength he had to squeeze his brother's hand. Jessie couldn't bear the fear he saw in his brother's eyes. He turned and looked the other way.

"Don't you be afraid, Russell. We've got to believe. Can you believe with me?"

With barely any strength and his eyes now closed, Russell tried to squeeze his brother's fingers.

"It'll be all right," Jessie kept repeating over and over again.

He felt no movement from his brother's hand, but was too scared to look down. Courtney's scream caused Jessie to open his eyes.

"Daddy, he's not moving at all," Ivy cried.

Jessie looked down at his brother's closed eyes and continued to rock him back and forth, still mumbling, "It'll be all right."

Ivy tried handing Jessie the phone by stretching the cord from the wall. The operator insisted that she speak to him, but Jessie refused.

"Hang up the phone, son. Just hang up the phone," Jessie whispered.

Ivy placed the receiver on the hook in compliance with his father's orders. He stared at his dead uncle's body in disbelief. Jessie gently laid Russell's limp form on the aged carpet. Standing over him he whispered, "I'll see you in a minute."

He turned to his upset children and explained to them that it had been an accident. "The gun just went off," he said in a low voice.

"We know, Daddy," Ivy said.

"We saw the whole thing through the closet door."

Jessie walked over to the front door and locked it. He turned to his daughter with loving, compassionate eyes, picked her up, and walked toward the chair JoAnn had given him as an anniversary gift so many years ago. He took a deep breath and exhaled with resignation. "I love you, tough stuff," he smiled at Courtney.

"I meant everything I said earlier. I meant it from the bottom of my heart. Give your ole man a big hug."

Courtney wrapped her little arms around his neck and squeezed as hard as she could. "I love you, Daddy," she said as she started to cry, sensing that this terrible day was about to get worse.

"I love you, too, tough stuff." Jessie briefly enjoyed the moment of having his daughter's loving arms around him. Knowing she trusted him totally was a feeling he'd longed for. In that precious instance he actually felt like the father he was supposed to have been.

"You tell your momma I love her, too," he squeezed back.

"Okay, Daddy," she cried, clinging to him.

"Thank you for forgiving your daddy," he said.

"I hope God will be as forgiving as you are."

"Come here, squirt," he motioned for his weeping son.

"I love you, man." Jessie hugged him tightly.

"You take care of your momma and your sister for me."

Shrill sirens filled the street. Jessie knew he had few options. His mind was made up, and he had to hurry. He gently put his daughter down, stood up, and lifted his son from the floor. Looking the boy dead in his eyes he said, "Son, I pray this demon didn't pass on to you, but just in case it did, will you promise me one thing?"

Ivy shook his head to signify "yes."

"Don't you let this demon destroy you, you've got to kill it! Don't allow the monster to destroy your life. Now y'all go open the door and let the police inside, and don't look back," he said with fatherly force.

Ivy and Courtney stood still for a moment, never taking their eyes off their father. Jessie returned the stare. No one moved or said a word. Loud voices outside the house caused Jessie to turn away.

The children moved toward the door. Jessie sat down to take his last breath. In that same breath he hoped that earlier in the park God had heard his sinner's prayer of repentance, as well as the one he had whispered in his brother's ear, for the good Lord to save Russell's soul.

The loud banging of the police on the door and the explosive blast of the gun went off simultaneously. When the police officers stormed inside, Ivy was standing nearby, holding his sister in his arms, shaking. Russell's lifeless body lay on the floor, and Jessie sat slumped over in his favorite reclining chair.

****

First Lady, Yolanda James, painfully watched her husband of ten years toss and turn in their king size European bed. No matter how much she shook him, he'd never wake up until in his dream he was somewhere in a peaceful place. The trauma he'd witnessed as a ten-year-old boy had haunted him for the last twenty-six years: a constant reminder that some things you never forget.

As she listened to her husband quietly weep, she knew this monotonous dream was near its end. She waited patiently and prayed for God to give him the strength to get rid of his perpetual nightmare. Finally, his soft weeping ceased.

"Honey, wake up, you're dreaming again," she nudged him, lightly.

Ivy's eyes opened; he was a bit disoriented. His wife's loving smile comforted him. Her beautiful, loving spirit was a treasure he didn't deserve, but surely cherished each day of his life. The sweet scent from her body reminded him that he was at home in his castle, and there was nothing to fear. Pulling her close, Ivy inhaled the pure redolence of her freshly shampooed hair. He looked out into the pitch black room, wishing his nightmare had been just a dream, and that his father's generational curse wouldn't have passed down to him. Unfortunately, neither was true.

Chapter 3

Introducing Raymond Durrant

Raymond J. Durant stood up from the heavy oak table to face Judge Susan Dicapio. Shifting nervously, anxiety soared like butterflies in the pit of his stomach. His large hands and shiny bald head sweated profusely as he prepared to brace himself for the judgment that would alter the rest of his life. The sweet aroma of his wife's enchanting 360 degree perfume distracted him momentarily as it lingered throughout the courtroom. His wife Donae knew he worshipped that fragrance. She was guaranteed just about anything she wanted whenever she wore it around him. It was immortal nectar to his nostrils. Today she purposely wore it to torment him, he thought. Nevertheless, the scent reminded him of happier times and heart-warming memories.

Donae's sun-streaked shoulder length hair accented her cocoa skin perfectly. Her make-up was flawless and her size 10 designer mini-suit flattered her voluptuous curves in just the right places. The suit had been a gift he'd purchased for her nearly four years earlier on her thirty-first birthday. What better way to antagonize him than by showing up in one of his favorite outfits, smelling like a princess from heaven. She'd only worn the outfit twice, once to her only brother, Levi's initial sermon, and once to the party of all parties, celebrating a promotion at the office. She had said to him that this outfit was much too special, and held too great of sentimental value, to wear any day.

Today must be one of those special days. Too bad her special day was ironically his Doomsday, since they were minutes away from terminating an eleven year marriage. The sound of the chair scraping the polished wooden floor seemed amplified as Donae backed away from the table that sat adjacent from that of Ray and his attorney, Bill Caldwell. Ray's thoughts echoed as though floating inside a hallow tree as he watched his precious sweetheart stand to her feet. Her unsuccessful attempt to be strong and fearless was instantly sensed by Ray. Like blood to a hungry, wild animal, he could taste her weakness.

Donae's knees nearly buckled as she smoothed out the wrinkles in her snug-fitting skirt. The fear of being in a courtroom for the first time was enough to make the woman want to run for the border. This scene was nothing like it looked on television. She could now imagine how a criminal felt standing there, not knowing his or her fate. It was too frightening to even imagine.

Ray stared at his beautiful wife one last time as if to say, 'Please baby, don't do this.' He had called her nine times the night before to beg her to reconsider, but she didn't answer or respond to his text messages. He honestly felt in his heart that she still loved him, in spite of everything. Her pure and innocent beauty softened his glance, nearly causing him to tear up, but he vowed to hold it together until he reached the car. At that point he'd be at liberty to exhale and cry like a crack-addicted baby, but for now he had to "man up," as his boys would say.

Donae glanced over at him, but then quickly turned away. She had promised herself the whole trip into court that morning that she wouldn't look into his eyes. For the last eleven years those light brown eyes and long eyelashes had drawn constant surrender from her. His built frame and baby face were any woman's dream, but right now, her only desire was for this divorce to be over and done with so she could move on. At least, that's what she kept telling herself. She could feel her body slumping. Immediately she stood tall and pulled back her shoulders like a soldier at attention, hoping and praying to dear God that Ray wouldn't spill the beans: that a few too many glasses of Moscoto mixed with a little love, years of history and a tempting moment of weakness had allowed him to gladly unlock her chastity belt four months earlier. To Ray, that interlude had offered a glimmer of hope, but to Donae it was undoubtedly a fatal move against her plans, since in the state of Virginia a husband and wife had to be legally separated for twelve months or longer with (no conjugal visits), in order to be granted a divorce.

Everyone knew Ray did not want to divorce his wife. What he wanted was his family back. For the last three-and-a-half months she had tried to persuade him to let go because she was certain he had every intention of trying to save their marriage. All his friends encouraged him to fight the divorce, when at times he felt like giving up. Every attempt he made at reconciliation, Donae rejected with a vengeance. Three weeks ago he had stopped by the place he loved to call home, unannounced as always, disregarding Donae's request of calling before showing up, which infuriated her. Because of the temporary court order for him to continue to pay the mortgage, he felt like it was still his house. Although technically, he hadn't lived there in over fourteen months.

He kept a pair of boxers and a wife beater t-shirt hidden in the garage inside a storage chest, in case she broke down again and decided to help a brother out. Maybe the next time, if he was lucky, he could actually stay and eat breakfast with her and the kids... maybe joke and laugh about silly things instead of being rushed out of the house at five a.m. after Donae sobered up and found herself in what used to be her favorite place in the world, curled up between those big ole guns. His muscular arms had always been a safe haven where she could find peace and security.

Ray's plea bargain visit weeks before was one of many desperate attempts to change her mind about the divorce, but like every other attempt, he left frustrated and angry because he couldn't get through to his wife. In the beginning he figured he'd give her some time to cool off. If she was playing hard ball, maybe she'd just go stay a few days at her sister Jazmine's house to make him suffer. Instead, he ended up at a hotel, and she changed the locks. Ray signed a lease on a month-to-month basis on a little one-bedroom apartment, not realizing he'd be there over a year.

Fighting tooth and nail, Ray did everything possible to stop the progression toward divorce. He begged for marriage counseling, this time suggesting one of the Christian counselors from her church. He wasn't too keen on having those church folk all up in his business, but he had to do what he had to do. Unfortunately, Donae was exhausted from this emotional merry-go-round. Her needs had not been met for far too long. Yes, she knew her husband loved her; he never stopped. There wasn't anything he wouldn't do for her or their children. All they had to do was ask, and sometimes not even that.

Ray was a kind and generous man, loving but aggressively ambitious. The one thing he wouldn't give her was the one thing she needed most: quality time. This seemed like a small thing to ask for, or so she thought. She desperately needed and wanted her husband to be there for her and with her. No matter what she said or did, it always reverted back to the same issue, "pride of life."

A fanatical workaholic, if Ray wasn't making money, he wasn't happy. If he lost $5.99 in stock, he had to make it back, or more. He sought the finer things in life for himself and his family-luxury cars, a large home, private school for the kids. It was all about the status quo. So what if he had to work 80 hours a week to obtain it?

Donae, on the other hand, was stylish but simple. Her 9-to-5 career as a pharmacist was satisfying, and she was totally content with her Nissan Maxima until Ray pitched a fit, and she traded it in for a Lexus. Classy things were nice, but they didn't define her: Donae was comfortable in who she was. She was tired of her and the children coming second to a job and material possessions. They deserved so much more than that. The children needed a father, and she needed a husband. Actually she felt nothing like a wife, more like a single parent with benefits. Every night Ray would drag into the house, late and exhausted. He'd speak with the kids a mere five or ten minutes, eat dinner in front of the computer, and every couple of days whenever he needed to relieve some stress, he'd throw a few charity pumps her way, then off to sleep he'd go.

The arguments about his spending time with the family were null and void. He always said, *"Let's plan something in a few weeks."* Everything had to be scheduled with him, whereas Donae liked to be spontaneous. That required dropping a few details and just going for it, which wasn't Ray's style. Nothing would ever change. Sometimes if she made a big fuss, he might feel compelled to pretend he really wanted to go along with a family activity, but if he was with them; his mind was on work wondering how he could impress some senior manager and move up the corporate ladder. Donae wondered what was the use of even trying?

As a professional woman, she didn't see anything wrong with a person wanting to be successful. For Ray it was constant drive, ambition, and zeal. To her, it was flat out obsession. She was completely finished competing with his job. His career with Zanderbilt Industries was the god he loved and worshipped. He lived, breathed and moved Z.I. Ray was the first one there in the morning and the last to leave. His superiors had to notice his hard work and dedication. Saving the company millions in cost savings, they were the #2 manufacturers of fuel engines, and were quickly approaching the #1 spot currently held by the top competitor, Drexelle Engines, Inc. Ray had been working day and night with engineers for the last two years to come up with a top notch cost effective engine that burned less gas. Sadly, his obsession for money and power fueled him into a forbidden direction to obtain more success.

The affair with his boss was the straw that broke the camel's back. Donae struggled for years with his uncanny work ethic, but once he gave another woman something that belonged to her, that's where she had to draw the line. It took months and months of counseling to deal with the major trust issues. The hurt and pain felt like an eternal sickness that only death could cure. Donae lost weight and patches of her hair started falling out due to the stress. The effort to rebuild their marriage required severe effort from both of them. Her faith in him had to be restored. It was tough for Ray as well, since it meant he had to sacrifice a lot of himself to please his wife, but to him she was worth it. From the day they had first started dating while at Virginia Tech, she had treated Ray like royalty. So now it was his turn to show her, and not just tell her, that she was his queen.

In counseling, a lot of inner turmoil that Ray had been dealing with since childhood emerged. His dad's lack of work ethic had kept Ray's family doing without. They never had enough, and nothing in the home ever worked. They had to flush the toilet with a wire hanger and the kitchen sink was always stopped up. Ray and his three sisters and brothers wore dirty clothes to school because there was no soap to wash laundry.

If it hadn't been for the next door neighbor, Ms. Kitty, some nights they wouldn't have eaten. When his dad started drinking more and more, going from job after job, and coming home less and less, they found out he was living with a woman and her children in West Virginia. This turned out to be a blessing in disguise. Ray's mother Catherine was able to obtain welfare and food stamps after her husband completely abandoned them, and life began to get a little better. Ray got a four-year scholarship to Virginia Tech, and earned his bachelor's degree in engineering.

When Donae got pregnant after graduating from college, he decided to pursue an online master's degree, which he successfully achieved. Ray promised himself that he would always take care of his family, and would never be the deadbeat his daddy had been. He vowed to never let his family go hungry or lack anything, which was the reason for much of his drive.

After months of counseling sessions, Donae decided to reconcile. Learning about Ray's past she found a soft spot in her heart for him. He had never talked about it before. She was grateful to the counselor for bringing that hurt in him out into the open where it could be dealt with. It was also revealed that Ray had slept with his boss, Amanda, the regional manager and overseer of Zanderbilt Industries, in order to receive the promotion she had promised him as Director of Operations. As counseling continued, Ray discovered a lot of things about himself that he didn't like. He was obsessed with his career, and he needed balance in his life before he found himself alone.

Now in his new position as Director of Operations, he had a lot more leeway. He was in a position where he could delegate tasks more freely. So he started making time for activities other than work. He began attending church again with his family, and some Sundays he actually listened to the boorish preacher whoop till he couldn't breathe.

Finally, life began looking up for the family. Donae was happy, the marriage was healing and their family was getting stronger each day. Ray was home daily by six o'clock, eating dinner with his wife and children. It tickled Donae pink to hear her husband talking to the kids about their day at school. He was even thoughtful enough to send his teenage daughter Ramona flowers to school when the boy she liked found interest in someone else. And to see Ray

Junior explain to his father how great his field trip to the science center had been. Donae almost cried when Ray offered to be a chaperone on the next field trip, and their son's eyes lit up like lights on a Christmas tree.

Life was total bliss. She was back to that "in love" stage again, something she hadn't felt since Ray had begun working at Z.I. nearly seven years before. As time went on, she began to let her safety net down. Even their intimacy had changed. Ray was more in touch with her, he took his time, he caressed her gently - looking into her eyes intensely. The warmth of his body and his muscular embrace caused her to melt. He tasted her tears, because every time they made love, she cried.

It seemed like all the energy and time he had put into his career were now channeled toward her and the kids. Her only wish now was that it would never end. She also hoped that his relationship with the Lord would blossom just as beautifully. One evening they cuddled in bed in each other's arms, absorbing the essence they had created. Ray smiled.

Donae said, "It feels good, doesn't it?"

But what came out of his mouth stunned her. "How would you feel if I asked you to quit your job and be a stay-at-home mom?"

Donae rose from his grip. "Where on earth did that come from, honey?" she said bewildered.

Ray pulled her back to her safe haven, squeezing her. He closed his eyes and inhaled the precious love in their room. "Donae, I want another baby," he whispered.

Donae paused for a long minute. "Ray, I thought we always said we wanted two, a boy and a girl, and the Lord gave us exactly what we asked for," she said nervously.

"I just want another love child," he said with a Cheshire cat smile.

The thought of having another child made her sick to her stomach. He wasn't about to stick her with another baby to care for while he tried to climb that ladder again. She had to be smart. Although a new baby around the house would be nice, she had to be sure he wasn't going to revert to his old workaholic routine.

"Baby, I'll think about it," she said, "but don't get your hopes up."

She patted his hairy chest. "Let's get some rest."

As Ray drifted off to sleep, Donae slipped into panic mode. She had planned on discussing a tubal ligation so she wouldn't have to worry with birth control anymore. The pills were making her nauseous. The shots made her gain weight. Ray hated condoms. There was some issue with every birth control method she tried. Her restless nights continued for months. Ray didn't pressure her about quitting her job, but he kept the heat on about another child. He even went as far as telling the kids about it, which really upset Donae. The more she said "no," the more he'd try to "discuss" it. Finally she had to flat out say "Heck no! It's not open for discussion," and that was it. So, instead, they got a dog. At least that made the kids happy. Ray had to admit, Duggie the Shih Tzu was adorable, and the kids seemed excited to come home every day and play with him. One day Donae walked into the house after work, and Ray and the kids had a pull-up on Duggie as a joke. Even Donae had to laugh at that one.

****

It was the night of a grand party at Zanderbilt that had Ray dancing around the bedroom like David Ruffin from the Temptations as he got dressed in his tux. Ray said that rumors had been floating around the plant that big announcements were about to be made. He had no idea about the unveilings, nor did he really care. Knowing his boss Amanda would have informed him of any major changes. His only concern would be if the plant was moving overseas. He didn't know what the night was going to bring, but he was ready to enjoy the evening with his beautiful wife, and he was in the mood to dance. Donae was excited, too. All the head honchos were expected to be there with their glamorous wives, mistresses, and dates. This was the second time in twenty years that the company had held the party in Virginia. It traveled from plant to plant, state to state, and country to country each year. The plant that made highest yearly profits for that year hosted the party in their location at the grandest hotel. So this was a luxury event and a tremendous accomplishment for Zanderbilt Industries.

Donae knew Ray was being overly modest. She sensed he was proud of his achievements, and rightfully so. He worked hard for that company, and it had nearly cost him everything he loved. But God's grace and mercy had seen them through. Donae's excitement, however, was more on the devilish side. She was anxious to finally meet Ms. Amanda Sheridan face-to-face. She couldn't wait to flaunt her man in Amanda's face. She'd seen flabby and homely looking Amanda a time or two when she stopped by the office on occasion. Neither had acknowledged the other, except for a partial smile (or more like a grimace) from Amanda.

Donae conducted herself like the lady she was. However, she was tempted to sink to a lower level and beat Ms. Sheridan down. In spite of her instincts to protect her own interests, Donae remained cool and sophisticated. Tonight was her night; she couldn't wait to cuddle up to those guns while Amanda watched. It had been a long time coming, and she was ecstatic to show Ms. Sheridan that these guns belonged to her!

On the night of all nights she needed a few extra minutes to make sure everything was in place. Her hair and makeup had to be flawless, but here came Ray requesting a quickie.

"Come on, baby," he whined.

"No, Ray," Donae squirmed away from his embrace.

"I've got to take a shower and shave. Six-thirty will be here before you know it, and we need to be at the Westin promptly at seven. You know how I am about being on time."

"Come on, Donae," Ray pleaded, "real quick. I mean a quick quickie," he said, pumping the air with his groin.

The two of them faced off, smiling Ray shifted from side to side while Donae did the same. Ray waited on her to make a move. Donae stood still, and then began shifting quickly, trying to decide if she would head left or right. When she raced left, all he caught was her towel falling off as she dove into the bathroom.

"Nah, nah, na, nah, na," she sang as she slammed the door.

"You not right, girl," he yelled. "I need a piece of you."

"I promise, I'm going to give you a big piece when we get home tonight. It might even have a cherry and whip cream on top," she called from the shower.

Chapter 4   *Raymond*

The Durrant's pulled into the valet parking area of the Westin Hotel. Ray's black Range Rover boasted magnum wheels that shone like brand new dimes.

"Look, baby," Donae whispered.

"You left your office light on."

The plant was in distant view from the hotel. All the lights were out in the offices except for Ray's and another one three windows down.

"Maybe the clean-up crew is working late tonight," he gave a half-smile, knowing she always stayed on him about turning lights off at home and work.

"I'll shoot over there and turn them off before we leave. I know how you are about saving trees," he smiled, patting her smooth thigh beneath her sleek skirt.

"You look beautiful, baby. Are you sure you're okay?" Ray felt a twinge of long-lost guilt.

"I'm okay, sweetie," she replied.

"You sure, 'cause we can bypass the ballroom, go get a suite and have our own private party," he said raising his eyebrows mischievously.

"Ray, I'm fine, honey. That boss of yours isn't going to ruin this night. I've been itching to finally meet the heifer!" Ray laughed out loud.

"Be a good girl, okay?" he said feeling a bit uneasy about the two of them formally meeting.

Donae smiled, "Everything is good: Now let's do this," she held up two peace signs.

"You're a nut, girl," Ray said, as they walked through the double glass doors.

Inside the hotel ballroom, several men dressed for the occasion walked up to Ray and started talking. Ray introduced his lovely wife to his colleagues, some of whom were already in good spirits. Zanderbilt had held back no expense. Everything was decorated beautifully, and the catered food was out of this world. There were chefs at various stations throughout the banquet hall, each with tempting entrees. Mini-carts rolled around to each table taking beverage orders for wine, champagne, mixed drinks - whatever a person could ask for.

The Durrant's sat at a cozy table close to the rear of the huge ballroom with finance team leader Evan Hyatt and his wife, Celeste.

Also joining them were Mitch Caldwell of Engineering, his wife Tameka, and Luke Zerrico, computer programming analyst, with his wife, Gretchen. Donae gave Ray a half-smile. He knew what she was thinking. Luke Zerrico was in his late forties while his wife, Gretchen looked youthful enough that the maître'd should have checked her I.D. before serving her any alcohol.

"I love your outfit," Gretchen commented.

"Thank you," Donae smiled.

"It was a gift from my husband."

"He picked it out?" Gretchen asked.

"Yes, believe it or not he did," Donae replied with a warm smile at Ray.

"Wow! He has excellent taste."

Donae chuckled, "don't tell him that. I believe he just got lucky on this one." They both laughed.

"Baby, you want a drink?" Ray interrupted, but the ladies kept giggling.

"You want a drink?" he asked again, knowing the answer.

"No thank you, sweetie – one drink will just about knock me out, and I'll be deranged."

The truth was that a wine cooler could put her in la-la land.

"I know," Ray looked at her devilishly.

"We'll have to grab you one to go later."

Celeste chimed in, "That's okay, Donae, the rest of us will drink enough for you," as she held up her fourth vodka and cranberry juice.

"Cheers!" she bellowed, as they all laughed.

The chandelier candles above twinkled like stars as the ballroom lights dimmed following the meal. Ray and Donae danced for hours to the lively jazz band that had been hired for the event. Donae truly felt comfortable mingling with Ray's colleagues. They were downright hilarious, motivated by a little alcohol. After dancing and working the room by catching up with some of the employees she knew, Donae's three-inch heels started to limit her mobility. She excused herself from her husband as he conversed with some of the company brass and made her way to the table where the other three wives sat toasted with a capital 'T'.

The conversation changed once the men were gone. Tameka complained about everything but the kitchen sink. She felt as though Mitch should have been promoted. He had been doing the same job for the last five years, and she was tired of his complaining about being overlooked for promotions. Celeste whined that Evan had been stressed so much lately that his hair was beginning to fall. He had missed a couple of project deadlines, and there was talk he might be demoted.

Donae had never realized how cut-throat business could be until these housewives enlightened her. Gretchen didn't say much. She didn't really care if Luke was stressed or not as long as she could shop and go on vacation whenever she wanted. Checking the time, Donae noticed about forty minutes had passed. Ray had been mingling awhile. She spotted him here and there laughing with someone or another. She only hoped he was as entertained as she was.

"There she is, *Ms. Hatchet*," someone said from a table nearby.

Donae and the ladies at her table all looked toward the ballroom entrance but didn't see anyone familiar. "Oh, wow, I love the pink dress that woman's wearing," Gretchen nudged Donae, getting the feeling that Gretchen was into designer clothes.

"It is lovely," Donae agreed.

"She is *wearing* it, too, isn't she? I wonder who she is?"

"She has to work out all day to have a figure like that," Gretchen said.

"I agree," Donae commented.

"I need to find some more time for going to the gym."

"She must have a personal trainer," Gretchen exclaimed as she stared.

"She might even be one. She's beautiful," Tameka chimed in.

"Sign me up to wherever she goes," everyone laughed in agreement.

Mitch came up to the table to grab Tameka.

"Come on, baby, Amanda Sheridan is here. I want you to meet her."

Tameka rolled her eyes as she tried to stand up. "Yeah, I want to meet this famous person. From what I've heard, she's a homely, ugly wench anyway," she murmured.

"Um, Mitch...you might want to revisit that idea. I don't think Tameka is in any condition to meet anyone, especially your boss." Donae said with concern.

Mitch took a good look at his wife's rumpled demeanor and quickly concurred.

Gretchen whispered to Donae, "You might have just saved his job," she giggled.

"I know," Donae whispered back.

Talking to a few other tables of the good-spirited wives produced the same result. Everyone basically said the same thing.

Just about every wife had some horror story to tell about how Amanda Sheridan had made their husbands miserable. Donae quickly realized her motives. She was a dictator. If she didn't like you, you wouldn't go far at Zanderbilt Industries. Her uncle, Blake Sheridan, was the only reason she held such a prestigious position. Now that was information that Ray hadn't shared. This caused Donae to raise an eyebrow. She'd have to drill him on this Blake Sheridan character later.

Donae secretly took a long swig of Celeste's eighth vodka and cranberry. After the nasty taste in her mouth dissipated, she began to search the room for her husband. Her feet felt a little better, and she was ready to slow dance. She spotted Ray near the dessert bar, engaged in conversation with his good friend, Ralph. Ray appeared to be trying to escape. Ralph had a tendency to go on and on about nothing.

Finally Ray managed to break away, heading toward Donae. When Ms. Pink Dress cut him off, Ray gave her his business hug, which Donae and he often teased about being a sideways church hug, with minimum physical contact. Tonight Donae was grateful for it. She didn't want him smelling like any other woman's perfume but hers, and by the way Ms. Thang was wearing that dress with no ring on her finger, nor a date, she definitely was looking for someone tonight.

Donae didn't get alarmed until she noticed Ray looking kind of nervous. He kept fidgeting with his tie and glancing around the room. She laughed to herself because she knew Ray realized she was watching him. He probably thought Donae was getting jealous for the woman's beauty was enough to intimidate the finest of women. However, he should have known his wife wouldn't sweat it. After all they had been through, Pink Dress was the last of her worries. She just couldn't wait to see that hideous Amanda.

Donae politely slid her feet inside her heels, excusing herself from the table. She strutted toward her husband with a bright smile. "Hi honey," Donae sweetly spoke, as she waited behind Ms. Pink Dress.

"Donae," Ray smiled uneasily, "I'd like you to meet Amanda Sheridan."

Amanda turned to face Donae with a handshake. Feeling kind of woozy, Donae tried to hold it together for appearance's sake.

"Nice to finally meet you, Donae," Amanda offered a fake smile.

"Likewise – Amanda I didn't recognize you. You've lost a lot of weight, and did you color your hair or something? You don't look like the same person I saw before."

Donae looked at Ray, chastising him with her eyes for not informing her of Amanda's transformation from ugly duckling to swan.

"Yeah, I wanted cornrows, but I had to settle for color this time, had to hide these gray streaks. While I was at it, I got a little tuck here and there," she laughed.

Ha, ha, hell, Donae thought.

"I've been working out with a personal trainer at my home to get toned up, so I've lost about forty pounds. It fell off the right places, thank goodness. Everyone's saying I look ten years younger. What do you think, Ray?" Amanda asked.

No, this tramp didn't. Donae felt the blood fill her cheeks.

"This is a great party," Ray changed the subject.

"Everyone seems to be enjoying it"

"You have a remarkable husband," Amanda grinned.

"He's such a huge asset to this company. Personally, I don't know what we'd do without him. He's such a good boy," she said patting him on the back.

Donae breathed slowly. "Yes, Amanda, I certainly do agree, *my* husband is a remarkable man. He takes pride in everything he does, especially when it comes to his family. We come first in everything. I guess I can thank you for enabling him to realize that."

At that moment Ray wished he had never been born. He thought for a moment that maybe he should pretend to see a colleague and move on, but Donae would kill him if he walked away.

"Well," Amanda cleared her throat, "I certainly can't take credit for that, but I guess the happier the man is, the better he performs at work. So you just be sure you keep him happy at home, and I'll make sure he's smiling while he's here."

Amanda threw her imaginary sucker punch. "It's been my pleasure to meet you, Donae. Forgive me if I have to run: I have to keep them all happy," she smirked.

"Oh, please," Donae quickly responded, "you can call me Mrs. Durrant."

Amanda walked away without a word, but her smirk left Donae feeling uncomfortable, as though she held a trump card that no one knew everyone had forgotten about. Thankfully, the D.J. slowed things down a notch, and Ray breathed slowly again. He grabbed Donae by the hand.

"Come on, lovely lady, I want to hold you close to me."

Although Donae was fuming, she couldn't resist the urge to rub a slow dance in Amanda's face, because she knew the woman would be watching. The Durrants danced like two teenagers who were ready to test the waters for the first time. Their bumps and grinds were slowly crossing from PG to creeping on the verge of x-rated. There were many drunks on the floor, and no one probably even noticed, but Donae was sure Amanda did. Thus, her mission was accomplished. Donae had to admit her performance left Ray ready to get a room upstairs. He was about to burst a head gasket.

They hurried back to the table to say their goodbyes. The two of them were as hot as dogs in heat. Once Amanda noticed the couple appearing to leave, the music stopped and everyone looked toward the stage. Amanda stood on the podium, asking for everyone's attention.

"I'd like to thank you all for coming out tonight to help celebrate this wonderful milestone in the history of Zanderbilt Industries. It has been a remarkable journey, and I thank you all sincerely for your hard work and dedication. I realize many of you have sacrificed a great deal of time away from your families to invest in the soaring of this company. So please join me in a toast," she held up her glass of champagne.

"To Zanderbilt; with great things to come."

Everyone joined in the toast, with several employees cheering loudly. Amanda tried to talk over the cheers, but it was nearly impossible. So she stood there and waited for the rowdy bunch to calm down so she could continue.

"I'd also like to congratulate the following on well deserved promotions."

1. Chad Gillman as V.P. of Operations (Switzerland)
2. Billy Dimsdale as V.P. of Operations (China)
3. David Miller as Director of Operations (Japan)
4. Richard Reeves as Director of Operations (U.S.A. Virginia)
5. Marnisa Jennings as V.P. of Operations (U.S.A. Texas)

"Congrats to these V.P.O.'s and Directors on jobs well done." The crowd lit up with excitement.

Ray looked mangled and confused. He struggled to keep his composure. *Did she just give Richard Reeves my job*, he thought. *What is she doing?*

Donae smiled, having no clue of what had just transpired. She cheered with the rest of the crowd as Amanda called out the promoted names. She had no inkling of Ray's job title. She stopped clapping when she saw the disgust in her husband's face.

"What's wrong, honey? You look like you've just seen a ghost."

"I think I just got demoted," he said.

"What?" Donae looked puzzled. "I know she wouldn't do that after all your hard work."

Donae looked over at Tameka as if she were about to catch a charge for assault. Amanda calmed the crowd once more.

"You people sure are a rowdy bunch," she laughed.

"Do you guys always act this way when you come out to play? With pleasure I'd also like to congratulate Clint Reeves as P.M. (USA - New York) and Raymond Durrant P.M. (USA - Virginia)."

The drunken crowd went wild again. Ray was in shock.

"What's P.M.?" Donae shouted over the screaming crowd.

No one answered her. She could have sworn she saw Amanda wink at her but she wasn't sure.

Tameka rushed over, her excitement was obvious. "Thank you Lord! Maybe my husband will get a promotion now."

"Somebody please tell me what P.M. is!" Donae shouted.

Tameka calmed down to explain to Donae that her husband was now the plant manager of the company he worked for. Donae's head began to spin like a whirlwind. Ray's eyes lit up. She couldn't remember seeing him so happy. Many of his coworkers were bombarding him with questions and congratulating him on his promotion. Donae couldn't get to him to say a word. She noticed that some of the women were crying, but she couldn't tell if it was from excitement or if they didn't want to move to a different state or overseas. She didn't want to think about moving to another country. At last Ray made his way through the crowd and picked up his wife, twirling her around.

"Honey, I did it – I did it, baby."

"Ray, when did you apply for a plant manager position?"

"I didn't, baby." Ray tried to talk over the screaming crowd. This is just as much of a surprise to me as it is to you. Aren't you happy for me?" Ray asked.

"I guess I'm trying to absorb what this all means," Donae cracked a half-smile.

"Baby, look, don't worry. Everything will be fine, trust me. Do you trust your man, Donae?" Ray asked.

"Yes, honey, of course I do," she admitted.

Ray pulled her into a private area inside the hotel lobby where they could talk alone.

"Baby, are you really okay?" he asked.

A tear fell from Donae's eye. Ray wiped it away with his finger.

"You're so beautiful," he murmured.

"Listen, I promise, you and I will sit down at home and discuss this. I have two weeks to accept or decline the offer. We'll make this decision together."

Evan rushed through the area and interrupted. "Excuse me, Ray, man; they're calling for you and Clint Reeves to speak."

Ray looked to his wife for permission, praying for a glimmer of hope. Donae nodded with a hint of a smile.

"Ray, I don't think I feel well. I may take a cab home."

"Honey, please," Ray begged.

"Don't leave. I need my favorite girl here with me."

"Okay," she said reluctantly, "I'll hang around. I just know it's going to be forever now, especially after hearing that big announcement. If I start feeling worse, I'll text you to let you know I left."

Ray's face was instantly concerned. "Are you feeling that bad, baby? We can leave if you are getting sick."

"No, no, Ray. I'll get some orange juice to settle my stomach. I'll be okay. You go ahead, baby. It's just nerves, I guess."

"You sure, honey? You know you come first. They can announce that I had to leave, and we'll split."

He waited anxiously for her reply, not really wanting to leave. Donae seriously considered throwing Ms. Amanda a monkey wrench by getting Ray to go now, but she loved him too much to steal his moment. She nodded her head in agreement. Ray kissed his wife after signaling the waiter and requesting some orange juice. Then he walked back into the ballroom with Evan, feeling like a million bucks.

Donae sat in the chair, unsure what to think. She knew if he accepted the position, their lives would change drastically. Ray would have to travel a great deal, which meant more time away from their family. She started to get nervous. Standing up, Donae began walking, not knowing exactly where she was going. Her mind couldn't consume all the thoughts that were racing through her mind. One minute she thought about Ray and his promotion; the next it was the great times they'd shared during the last few months. She thought of how happy the kids were to have him home with them, and she wondered if this would be the beginning of the end. By the time she realized where she was she was outside strolling with no destination. The 3 inch heels she wore started screaming for help. Flagging the taxi down, she decided home was her next stop, she would text Ray once she got there. What a night, she pushed herself back in the hard leather seat and glanced through the window.

"Wait! She yelled for the taxi driver to stop. You can let me out here." She handed him a generous amount for a three minute ride and told him to keep the change.

Donae faced the security entrance of the Zanderbilt Building. She looked up and saw Ray's office light on, and smiled.

"Good evening, Mrs. Durrant," the security guard Steven said.

"Hello, Steven. I'm heading up to my husband's office to clear my head. Is that okay?"

"Yes, ma'am, Mrs. Durrant, go right up," he answered, "but be careful, third shifters are coming in. I'd hate for you to get run over."

Donae stepped into the elevator and pressed "6." By the time the elevator reached the designated floor, she had decided to thoroughly support her husband's promotion. This was what he'd dreamed about. She wouldn't let him down. She'd just have to adjust.

Chapter 5

Introducing Malcolm Stuart

Telese Stuart steered her Cadillac Escalade into the garage of her home, forgetting to turn the ignition off. She just sat there. The urge to light up a Newport was beginning to win the battle in her mind, but she remembered what her Pastor had said on that attention-grabbing Sunday about her body being the temple of the Holy Ghost. That Scripture had convicted her so much that she hadn't smoked a cigarette in eighty-six days. She figured since the Holy Spirit had lived in her the four months since she'd been saved, He probably couldn't breathe for all the smoke floating around in her body. So she'd stop smoking to make Him more comfortable.

Stress, fear and exhaustion were her emotions. She had come this far, and was determined that if Malcolm hadn't killed her, cigarettes were definitely not going to take her out. Adjusting her rearview mirror, she took a long, hard look at her face. Her tear-filled light brown eyes didn't come close to expressing the depth of her sorrow. Tired of being identified as the big girl with the cute face, the struggles with her weight caused her to have insecurities. At 201 pounds she often thought she had no right to complain about the fine man she was with.

Lord, what did I do to deserve this? Why does my life have to be so screwed up? Why can't I just go back in time and do this "thing called life" differently?

Unfortunately she'd called in sick to her job at Chesterfield Memorial Hospital where she earned a hefty-sized living as the Director of Nursing. More than seventy employees answered to her, and an impressive, sometimes overwhelming, stack of responsibilities rested on her shoulders. The good thing about it all was that most of the time, if everything was delegated properly: she had the pleasure of working from home. She thanked the Good Lord for that precious luxury, since it saved her plenty of embarrassment. Feeling self-pity wash over her, she stared into her red, puffy eyes and promised herself that she would trust in the powerful words of a famous singer, *"What don't kill you will only make you stronger."*

The loud knock on the lightly tinted window startled her. She unrolled the glass.

"Hey, my beautiful wife, you gonna turn the car off?"

Malcolm leaned his tall, muscular body through the window to steal a peck, but Telese veered to the right to escape his chocolate brown lips and closely trimmed goatee.

44

"Are you okay?"

"Yeah, Malcolm," she rolled her eyes.

"I'm just peachy," she snapped, turning the ignition key backwards.

"Baby, you don't look like you're okay," he replied.

"And why would I look like I was okay?" she asked.

She removed her sunglasses so he could get a clear view of the burst blood vessel in her left eye. "What did Dr. Jordan say?" Malcolm asked sympathetically with a huge load of guilt.

She constrained herself from yelling the truth that her family doctor of twenty-five years, Dr. Arthur William Thims, had aggressively encouraged her to pack her stuff and leave.

"He told me it might take weeks to heal. Now I have to work from home again."

"Baby, you know I'm sorry," he said, dropping his head.

"Yeah, Malcolm, I know you're sorry. If I don't know anything else, I know how sorry you are. Can we ever get past the point where there isn't a need for you to be sorry?"

Malcolm tried to change the subject. "Your boy is fighting tonight," he smiled, knowing her passion for the boxing profession.

Shabazz Duke was her favorite lightweight fighter, and he was scheduled to fight Markus Jones tonight on cable television.

"One of my buddies said he heard that T.C. Evans was trying to make a comeback in the heavyweight division."

"I wish Shabazz would gain about twenty pounds and go heavyweight. That's where the freakin' money is," Telese said, glad to know the fight was going to be broadcast.

"Mommy…you're home!"

The sweet voice of their six-year-daughter was like a melody to her ears. "Guess what, Mommy," Layla danced, "we're making sugar cookies after dinner tonight. Are they still your favorite of all time?"

"Yes ma'am, little Layla," Telese pinched her chubby cheeks.

"Sugar cookies are and always will be Mommy's favorite. You could have made your favorite chocolate chip cookies, and Mommy would have been just as happy," Telese said, getting out of the car and lifting her daughter up to eye level.

"We're baking chocolate chip, too," Layla smiled. "KJ wanted some, too," she said with a mischievous smirk. The child leaned toward her mother's ear.

"He likes a girl at school," she failed in her attempt to whisper.

"He's taking her some cookies tomorrow. Daddy stopped at the store, and KJ bought her a pink teddy bear with the money you gave him for doing stuff. It's a prettiful teddy bear, Mommy. It has little red hearts and a candy necklace."

By this time Telese had set her little girl down and was walking into the house, with Malcolm trailing behind. Every inch of her still ached with pain from the tussle the night before. Her long, layered hair swung from side to side as her pony tail bounced as she walked through the door.

"Hey Momma!" KJ came rushing down the stairs.

"Well, hello, Mr. Casanova. What's this I'm hearing about a teddy bear?" Telese smiled. "I don't think I like the idea of my ten-year-old son having a girlfriend."

KJ flinched, "Kayla, you need to stop running your big mouth, you little snitch!"

"All right, rug rats," Malcolm interrupted.

Layla pulled her mother down as though to whisper in her ear. Jumping into her arms she squeezed Telese's neck tight while wrapping her short legs around her waist and sticking her Tootsie Roll flavored tongue out at her brother.

"Hey, Mommy," Layla smiled.

"I'll put your cookies beside the biggest cup of milk. Then I'll pour the chocolate syrup in and stir it all by myself. But you have to eat all your food first, right Daddy?" she looked to Malcolm for confirmation.

"Daddy said you don't have to cook. He's ordering us Chinese food," K J. jumped in.

KJ felt the need to attest that they wanted her to relax.

"Well," Telese smiled. "I feel exceptionally special."

She made her way to the kitchen, kids in tow, as Malcolm tagged along.

"Am I the goodest helper?" Layla cheerfully asked.

"You sure are, Princess. You are Mommy's perfect little helper." Telese set down her purse on the counter.

"Look, Mommy," Layla said, pointing to the kitchen floor.

"Daddy scrubbed the blood off, and it all came out this time, not like before when Daddy broke your arm or that time in the laundry room when Daddy…"

"Let's show Mommy her surprise," Malcolm quickly interrupted.

"Oh, yeah, Mommy," Layla bounced up and down, "we got you a surprise!"

Layla raced down the long hallway, pulling her mother. When Layla turned the curve, she stopped and giggled.

46

"Go ahead, Mommy," she cheered, standing in front of Telese's bedroom door.

Telese opened the door and Layla rushed in. "Look, Mommy, it's that picture of the old fighting guy you like. Remember when you and Daddy went to some place and you wanted to get it, but it cost too big of money? Daddy got it for you with his whole check and some he borrowed from Uncle Googie."

"You are a little snitch, aren't you," Malcolm laughed. "Can't talk too much around you, I see."

Telese stood frozen in front of one of the most captivating portraits she'd ever seen, leaning against the pine chest of drawers. She had to wonder how in the world Malcolm had gotten possession of something so priceless. She knew he couldn't afford a luxury item of this magnitude on his income: His technician position at the cable company rarely enabled ends to meet. More often, they just waved distantly to one another. The painting at the gallery had been well over $65,000.

"Malcolm...how?" Telese looked shocked.

"It's not the painting from the gallery," Malcolm calmed her fears.

"My friend Christopher has a brother-in-law who can paint his behind off. He painted this oil painting for me, baby."

"Wow," Telese whispered.

"He is freakin good. It looks authentic, to say the least."

"It might not be the real thing, but I tell you this, that sucker didn't come cheap."

Malcolm felt the need to emphasize that he'd spent his entire paycheck and more to get it for her.

"It was supposed to be a present for your birthday next month, but I couldn't wait."

He stood behind her with a pleased smile on his face as the children beamed. The painting of an exhausted boxing champ standing over his opponent depicted a magnificent scene. Malcolm had the painting elegantly framed and placed on an easel. The painting was, hands down, one of a kind. It captured the essence of the heavyweight title fight, the determination in the Champ's eyes as well as the agony of defeat in his opponent's bowed head. Excitement on the faces of the onlookers revealed pure amazement. Even the referee, standing between two great fighters and waving his hands in the air, signaling the fight was over, portrayed a glorious image.

Under different circumstances, Telese would have been ecstatic. It was no secret that she absolutely adored the Champ. She held near and dear to her heart several autographed collector's items, having accumulated memorabilia since high school. Whenever she saw something with his picture on it, she had to buy it. Telese had videos of all his fights, which she loved to watch over and over again.

"Aren't you happy, Mommy?" Layla excitedly giggled.

"I don't really know what to say," Telese gave a partial smile.

"I guess I'm speechless."

"We figured you would be," Malcolm sneaked a side hug.

"Let's give Mommy a few minutes to take a shower and get settled."

Malcolm lifted his chunky baby from her feet. "How about we call and order dinner?" he suggested.

Layla seemed disappointed to break up the excitement until Malcolm mentioned cutting up the cookie dough. She quickly perked up. "Hurry, Mommy!" Layla exposed her two missing front teeth.

"I figured after dinner the two of us could watch the fight together." Malcolm added a questioning smile.

"Mommy will be there in a minute."

Telese didn't reply to Malcolm's comment. She watched Malcolm and Layla walk down the long hallway, holding and swinging hands. Relieved to have a moment of solitude, Telese closed her bedroom door three-fourths of the way and dived backward onto her plush, feather top mattress. The cool breeze from the overhead fan felt good as she gazed at the cathedral ceiling. She felt tears beginning to rise, but the soft knock on the door kept them from falling.

Drying up the watery residue, she softly said, "Come in."

"You okay, Mom?" KJ came in and sat beside her on the bed.

"Yes, baby," Telese rose slightly and smiled, "don't worry about me."

KJ looked at his mother's bloodshot eye and then glanced away.

"Does it hurt?" he whispered.

"No, sweetie, it doesn't hurt. It looks a lot worse than it really is."

"Momma, what if…" he paused, unable to get the words out.

"KJ, I'm okay," Telese said, looking into his water-filled eyes.

"Everything is going to be all right. Trust your mom, okay?" she asked, heart aching for her son.

"I do trust you, Mom," he hesitated, "but…I just don't want you to…" KJ dropped his head and paused.

"You know," he said.

"What's going to happen to Layla and me if you…" He spelled the letters aloud: "…if you D-I-E?"

Telese felt her heart flutter.

"I'm not going to D-I-E," Telese spelled the word too, trying to make light of it. "Don't worry."

She turned her face away before taking a long, deep breath. KJ's tears caused her eyes to fill. It was crushing her inside to hear her son in agony like this. He was terrified that one day Malcolm would kill her. He hadn't actually seen Malcolm touch his mom, but he'd heard the loud thumps, screams and arguments through the years that would sometimes leave Telese bruised and broken-spirited. He wasn't concerned about his own safety. Malcolm would never hurt his children. He'd only dished out a handful of spankings throughout their lives. Neither KJ, Layla nor his oldest daughter Crystal, who he'd adopted with his first wife, ever feared being harmed by their dad in any way.

Although KJ never felt threatened, he felt helpless and afraid for his mom. The abuse she'd endured over the years had caused a lot of animosity and strain between Malcolm and his only son. Their relationship wasn't healthy, to say the least. In fact, there definitely was no love lost on KJ's behalf. He didn't really care if his father was around or not. Lately he found himself wishing his dad would get hit by a Mack truck. Malcolm, on the other hand, loved his son. He'd tricked himself into believing that since the boy never actually saw any physical abuse, he didn't know. However, deep down inside, Malcolm knew that was not true.

Telese turned toward her son and embraced him tightly. Kissing his forehead, she poured affection into his broken spirit. "I love you, KJ," she said aloud.

"I love you, too, Momma."

He squeezed her hard. His love was evident, and it made her heart smile. At the sound of his father's footsteps, KJ pulled away. Malcolm peeked through the door.

"Hey, squirt. You okay, son?" he spoke in a concerned tone.

"Yeah, I'm cool," KJ quickly bounced off the bed.

"Dinner has just arrived," Malcolm smiled.

"You guys ready to eat?" he tried not to look into his son's glossy eyes.

"Your impatient sister couldn't wait on the rest of us. She's so anxious to bake cookies afterward."

KJ gave a partial smile. "I'm not really hungry," he said, sliding past his father.

"Are you sure?" Malcolm asked, hoping for a different response.

"I ordered the sesame chicken you love."

"No, thanks," KJ replied.

"But, ya'll can wrap me up some cookies to take to school tomorrow.

His statement made Telese perk up and smile. "I guess you really do have a sweetheart."

Somewhat embarrassed, KJ grinned boyishly.

"Do you want me to take you shopping after dinner?" Malcolm asked.

"We can get a box of candy to go with that teddy bear. I have to go to store anyway."

"No thanks: cookies will be okay," the boy yelled halfway down the hall.

Taking a long, deep breath, Malcolm softly shut the bedroom door. He held his hand on the door knob and didn't say a word. He was certain the conversation he had interrupted was about him. Inside, he felt like a big jerk. Telese didn't have to wonder what was on Malcolm's mind. She'd seen that pitiful look more times than she could count. Walking into the adjoining bathroom, she stood in front of the oversized mirror, pulled out the prescribed eye drops from her designer purse and began to read the instructions.

Malcolm stood in the bathroom doorway, watching his beautiful wife through the mirror. Her dark eyes stayed focused on her image rather than his.

"Telese, honey, I didn't mean to hurt you. I never do. I know you're angry and disappointed again. I never should have lost my temper last night. I'm an idiot, and I don't deserve you. This time I really see what you've been saying all these years; I do need help."

The battered wife never mumbled a word. After tightening her pony tail, she tilted her head back and inserted two drops into her left eye as the directions instructed.

"Baby, please forgive me," Malcolm asked in a low voice.

Telese stared through him as though he wasn't even there. She'd heard this all before. He was supposed to have gotten help years ago, but he hadn't even made it to the first session. Her lack of response made Malcolm uneasy. Normally Telese would say something to make him feel like the scum he felt like he was. He struggled inwardly, not knowing what was going on in that pretty head of hers. He had to wonder if she had reached her breaking point. All he could do was wait.

"I've already called to get some help," he said breaking the long silence.

"My appointment is a week from today with Dr. Manning. You can call to verify my appointment in the morning. Here's his office number."

He set the white business card on the bathroom sink. Malcolm's eyes were soft and tender. The guilt on his face could be seen for miles. Everything inside her wanted to rear back and slap him, but what good would that do? Enough violence had already taken place.

"Telese," Malcolm asked, "can you please say something?"

"Something," Telese said with attitude.

"Mommy! Daddy! I'm done eating. Can we make the cookies now?" Layla yelled at the top of her lungs from the kitchen.

"Just a minute, sweetie," Malcolm yelled back.

"Can you watch cartoons until we get there? Mommy and Daddy are talking."

Malcolm could hear her disappointed sigh down the hall.

"Telese, please," he begged, "can you come and sit beside me?"

He patted the cushion on the loveseat beside their bed. Telese walked toward him but stopped at the painting on the way.

"It's a work of art, isn't it?" Malcolm smiled.

"It's breath taking," Telese admitted, admiring its beauty.

Malcolm felt a huge sense of relief when she finally spoke.

"I guess this is supposed to make up for last night?" Telese looked at him blandly.

"No, baby, it's more like a peace offering," Malcolm replied.

"I just want to see you smile."

"It's bittersweet," Telese replied.

Frustrated with herself for allowing her children to witness domestic abuse, she asked Malcolm a question.

"What am I supposed to do...? Let you kill me? I can't go on like this."

"Last night when my co-worker Justin came over to the table at dinner, I was so embarrassed by your actions. All he did was stop to say hello. You read into his friendliness something that wasn't there. You shouldn't have acted so territorial and jealous. I knew when we got home last night it was going to be crazy. I was praying the argument would stop in the car, but somehow I knew we'd be having this conversation today."

Malcolm tried to be calm.

"I saw the way he looked at you, Telese. He couldn't look me in the eye, he was so busy trying to look you up and down. I'm a man, and trust me, a man knows when another man wants what he's got. He even had the nerve to say in front of me how great you look.

51

You don't disrespect a man in front of his wife like that- like I ain't nothing. He better be glad his damn lips aren't wired shut today," Malcolm said heatedly.

"So instead I had to take a trip to my family doctor," she said, throwing her hands in the air. "And besides, nobody wants me."

"We're not going to discuss this anymore. I can't stand to go through Round Two tonight, and neither can your son," she said sternly.

Telese's words burned Malcolm like fire. Deep down, he knew she was right. KJ despised him and wanted nothing to do with him. As much as he hated to admit it, the truth was that Malcolm realized he had been acting like a jealous fool. Malcolm grabbed Telese by the hand. Her reluctance wasn't a surprise, but he continued.

"Number 1... You are not fat! I love you just the way you are and number 2... You don't hear me complaining. I know I can't make up or take back what I've done over the years. I don't blame you or KJ for how you both feel. You've probably thought about leaving me because you don't think I'll change, but..." he paused, aware that his apologies seemed redundant.

"I love you. If I lost you, Layla, KJ or Crystal, I don't know what I would do. You guys are my life," he said teary-eyed.

Telese spoke softly. "Malcolm, when you're not angry, you're one of the most gentle and sweetest men I know. You're good-hearted, caring and compassionate. Most of the time, you're funny and outgoing. I love being with you when you are like that, but when you get angry, you turn into somebody else, someone I can't stand to be around. Your fits of jealousy are unjustified. Sometimes when we go out, I'm actually nervous that if a man looks at me too long. You are like a ticking time bomb. Who wants to live that way?"

Malcolm sat quietly, head bowed.

"The simple fact that you and your best friend, Morris, hasn't spoken in five years should be a clear indication that your jealousy is absolutely ludicrous. Your accusations about him coming on to me were absurd. He had been your best friend for the past twenty years, Malcolm, twenty years," she echoed.

The melancholy in her voice matched the sadness in her heart.

"Morris was the only person who could settle you down when you went berserk. If it wasn't for him who knows if I'd even be here right now?" Telese began to cry.

Malcolm sat on the love seat and listened like a school boy, not making a peep. He listened to his wife as she poured out from her heart what she had been feeling for years. Then he gently pulled Telese close. He stood up so he could look down into her face. Her pink eye reminded him of the man she couldn't stand to be around. Malcolm tried to kiss her, but she pulled away.

"No, Malcolm," she cried, "making love isn't the answer this time. We always make love afterward. We act like it never happened, but it did. We can't keep doing that. Sometimes you have to face what you've done and try to change what you can. You have to, at some point admit to being who you are and take the necessary steps to becoming the man you want to be. I can't help you do that, Malcolm; only you can do that, you and God."

Telese walked into the bathroom to get a tissue. She grabbed her cell phone from her purse that still sat on the bathroom counter, and pretended to look at it as if she had a missed call. Scrolling through her settings she touched the silence mode, then dialed a 9 and then a 1: She held onto her phone tightly, not knowing what to expect. So she felt it best to be prepared for the worst.

"Malcolm, I love you, but I can't keep doing this. Look at the message we're sending to the children by all the violence. I have to look at the message I'm sending by staying in this boxing ring and allowing this abuse to go on. Malcolm, you need to take some positive steps to take care of yourself."

Malcolm's heart began to flutter as he listened to Telese speak. She continued by saying she also needed to take some steps to care for herself.

"I'm miserable living this way. I want to be happy and feel safe in my own home. The Word of God says you're supposed to be my protector and my provider, not my attacker."

She pressed the button on her phone so the keys lit up. She found a tiny bit of comfort in seeing the 91 that faced her from the blue screen. Taking a deep breath before exhaling she dialed the other 1 and stared at the send button before speaking those dreadful words Malcolm had never wanted to hear.

"Malcolm, I think we should separate."

"No!" Malcolm jumped to his feet.

"I told you I have an appointment to get help. I really do - for real, Telese. I'm not joking, I'm serious."

She gave him a pitying glance.

"I believe you, Malcolm. I'm glad that you are seeking help. I just think right now that you need to work on yourself without me. Once you get yourself together, then maybe we can come back and talk about us…"

"Telese - what do you mean 'maybe'? Give me another chance," he pleaded.

"I promise we can make this work. I can't do it without you. I need you, baby."

Her eyes opened wider.

"You don't need me, and if you do, you shouldn't. I should be a want, not a need. Never put all your trust in another person, because people will disappoint you, even me." She said, not fully admitting her own shortcomings.

Malcolm looked at her as if she were crazy.

"Telese, are you serious?" His voice elevated enough for Telese to be concerned.

"You're really going to leave me? I didn't mean to hurt you, baby."

Telese said nothing, just shook her head in disagreement.

This will never happen again."

"You've got to believe me!" Malcolm was desperate and yelling.

"I can control myself. I know I can. Please Telese, don't do this to us. I'm telling you I'm trying…"

Malcolm could see the fear in his wife's eyes. He had to find a way to make her understand that he really meant what he said this time. He wasn't trying to buy time. He was sincere. She had to understand that he was committed to making their lives better once and for all.

Telese tried to shift toward the door but Malcolm blocked the way. His voice was loud, and he began pacing the floor, talking to himself. She froze, watching his every move. She didn't know what to do. Malcolm didn't lunge at her as he usually did, so she didn't know what was coming. Should she try to run or press send? She thought

"Malcolm," Telese cleared her throat.

Her voice and hands were shaky, but she spoke calmly.

"You're scaring me."

"I'm not trying to scare you, baby. I'm trying to freak'n understand. Why can't *you* understand, Telese?"

He quickly walked toward her, not to hit but to hold her. He thought maybe if they hugged, she wouldn't be afraid and the tension would fade. But when Telese saw him approaching, she panicked. She hit the corner of the nightstand and the phone fell from her hand.

She screamed, "Malcolm, please don't hurt me!"

"I'm not Telese," Malcolm said calmly. "I'm only trying to talk to you, baby, that's all."

"No Malcolm!" Telese screamed.

"Please just let me out the door. All I want to do right now is leave. I don't want any trouble. Please Malcolm, just let me leave, that's all I ask," she wept in fear.

All of a sudden they heard something popping. It sounded like firecrackers. KJ stood in the doorway with his BB gun, yelling, "Get away from my momma, Daddy!"

His face was drenched in tears. "Leave her alone!"

Malcolm and Telese looked at their son in total shock. A moment passed and nobody moved. Malcolm's eyes met his son's. Malcolm would never be able to erase the fear there. Telese ran to the doorway and embraced her son. He dropped his BB gun on the floor and cried uncontrollably in his mother's arms.

"I don't want you to die, Momma," he said, hiccupping between words.

Malcolm felt ashamed as he watched his son and wife embrace. Telese was holding onto the boy for dear life. Although he had no intentions of harming his wife, he could see what his actions over the years had led to. What he felt at the moment was too much to bare. Everything in him wanted to join them in that embrace, but he knew he wasn't welcome. So, for the first time in a long time, he made the right decision. Malcolm walked over to the closet and pulled down his overnight suitcase. Telese watched a little surprised that he'd given up so easily. She had to admit that seeing her son so upset was enough for her. At that point she was certain that she'd made the right decision.

"Momma," KJ cried.

"I keep dreaming about your funeral. You're lying in a casket and I can't wake you up. Can we please just move away?"

"No, son," Malcolm answered.

"*I'm*" leaving," he nodded. KJ looked up from the grip of his mother's arms to notice the suitcase in Malcolm's hand.

"One of these days you'll be proud to be my son. I know today isn't that day, but I look forward to when I can put a loving smile on your face, regardless of what anybody thinks," he said lifting Telese's face by her chin.

"I love y'all more than anything."

Malcolm stepped around them into the hallway. Reaching the living room his aching heart adored his beautiful baby girl, and he bent down to kiss Layla, who was on the chase lounge fast asleep. He momentarily watched her, thinly smiling once he saw the roll of cookie dough fall from her hand. Walking to the door he whispered into the air, "I love you, Daddy's little princess. Watch over everyone until Daddy comes home."

Chapter 6   *Malcolm*

Malcolm clocked in at the Joyner Cable Company nearly 45 minutes early. He was so used to dropping the kids off at school in the morning; he found it difficult to change his normal routine. It had been nearly a month since he'd left the house, and he missed Telese and the kids terribly. He'd finished loading up his cable truck early with all the necessary equipment for the five scheduled installations. His plan was to finish up well before 4:00 p.m. in order to keep his third appointment with Dr. Manning at 4:30. Strangely enough, he eagerly looked forward to continuing his anger management classes: The sooner he got this problem under control, the sooner he could be back with his family.

He'd call Telese and the kids to check on them each day, just to let them know even though he wasn't there, he had every intention of coming back once he took care of business. Most days he'd talked to Layla for the majority of the conversation. KJ conveniently was always busy, which he had pretty much anticipated. Telese was cordial, even tender, but he didn't expect anything less. At times she could be a little sassy, but for the most part she was sweet as candy.

Malcolm was grateful that she seemed genuinely concerned for his well-being and ultimate success. He felt frustrated with himself, as a lot of men do whose wives earn considerably more income than they do. At times he felt inadequate. The only time he really felt competent was when he was laying it down in the bedroom, but after she was satisfied, then what?

Telese and the kids seemed happy enough. Ironically, that made him sad, mainly because they were content without him. He hoped after a few weeks of his being away that Layla would come through for him and start pitching a fit because Daddy wasn't home. Despite his many faults, her love held no boundaries. He wished somebody missed him, but who was he trying to fool? His family certainly didn't need him for much of anything. Telese's income exceeded six figures while his small change only paid the utility bills and his car note. Luckily, he had a wife who didn't hold his shortcomings or short change against him. All the money went into the same pot; and she didn't complain that she contributed $149,000 to his $33,000 a year.

Slammed with a reality check, Malcolm now faced, as his great-grandma Nanny used to say, not having a pot to piss in, nor a window to throw it out of. Something inside kept telling him everything was going to be all right. The longer he was out on his own, the more he realized he didn't want to be. Any other man in his position, whether he wanted to be back home or not, would most likely have taken advantage of the opportunity, and as his great papa used to say, to go out and get some strange. But not Malcolm, there wasn't a day that went by that he didn't wish he was snuggled up in his bed with his wife. It would be great if she called just to say she missed "Mr. Harding," as she called it. She always said that Mr. Harding stood at attention every time she walked by. Hell, truth be told, this was going on his fourth week without her 38 DD's to tempt him, and frankly, Mr. Harding was tired of seeing his five fingers every three or four days. He could hold out. He wasn't one of those brothers who just had to have it all the time. He didn't want to go anywhere else. He was happy with his wife.

Malcolm had always taken pride in being a faithful man, never having the desire to step out of his committed relationship. Just like a dog with his master: as long as you feed him and treat him right, he wasn't going anywhere. He couldn't wait until his therapy session was over today so he could let Telese know about his progress. He'd learned quite a bit in the past weeks. One of the most important things was that anger is an emotion. He never really thought of it that way, but then, he never took time to think when he was angry. Anger was just anger. Whenever rage peeped its evil head up from his soul, something had to show it was there. He had to punch a wall or a door, break a table, or hit something. Unfortunately, who or what was making him angry had to pay, too. But after listening to Dr. Manning, he learned how the emotion of anger could be controlled, just like anything else.

At first Malcolm thought taking time to cool down and count backward from ten was a bit juvenile, but what the exercise did was give a person time to think, which was exactly what he needed. If he had taken a moment to think about possible consequences of acting like a fool, maybe he wouldn't have been so eager to act out his frustrations. He knew he had a long way to go yet, but at least he was moving forward.

"Malcolm!" Mr. Riley, his boss, yelled from his office. "Good, you're still here," he said, hanging up the phone as he saw Malcolm turn in his direction.

"What's up?" Malcolm answered, stepping into the doorway.

"David Lee just called in sick for the rest of this week. I need you to take his installations."

"Aw, man," Malcolm replied.

"I'm sure I can handle it during the rest of the week, but today I have an appointment at 4:30, and it's important. Can you find somebody else?"

"No."

Mr. Riley picked up the phone and started dialing.

"You've only got five stops today; everyone else has eight or nine."

"There's a reason I scheduled just five," Malcolm shifted his weight.

"I have to be somewhere."

"Well, give them a call and tell them you won't be able to make it today. This isn't open for discussion. I'm not asking you, I'm telling you," he said before speaking into the receiver.

"Hi, honey. What time does Billy's game start?"

Mr. Riley ignored Malcolm who was still standing in the doorway. Malcolm turned with his back to Mr. Riley and stood there quietly for a second or two. His fists started to ball as his head shift from side to side. *Ten.... Nine.... Eight.... Seven.... Six... five.... Four.... Three.... Two... one...* he counted slowly.

"That's all, Malcolm," Mr. Riley laughed into the receiver.

"How about closing the door on your way out, boy?" he laughed hysterically into the phone.

His rude tone echoed in Malcolm's head as he got heated to the tenth power. Standing in place, he counted again slowly, but by the time he got to four, he was standing over Mr. Riley's desk, panting like a deer. Mr. Riley had his back turned, facing the oversized window overlooking the parking lot where the company trucks were parked. Malcolm remembered how he had gotten fired from his last job for calling the supervisor a dumb punk and then threatening to join him in the parking lot after work to "talk" about it. He recalled the baby steps of progress he'd recently made. If he were to lose his job now because he got into it with his boss, how could he ever explain that to Telese?

Mr. Riley swirled his chair around after ending the conversation with his wife. He was startled to see Malcolm standing in front of him, hunched over his desk. Malcolm cleared his throat.

"Mr. Riley," he said.

"Do us both a favor and PLEASE don't call me 'boy'. I'm 6'3", 235 lbs. of man. I'd hate to have to prove that."

Immediately Malcolm regretted his last sentence, but it was too late to unsay it now. It was all up to how Mr. Riley was going to take it.

Getting to his feet, Mr. Riley laughed it off.

"My bad, brother-man" he said, before patting Malcolm on his shoulder.

"I forgot, the guys said you were quick tempered."

Mr. Riley walked out of his office to go to the restroom, fully aware that he had intentionally ticked Malcolm off. After all, David Lee was off sick, and he really did need the boy.

The best thing for Malcolm to do now was to pack up his truck and get off the property. He was fuming mad, and if he thought about it too long, Mr. Riley would be taking an involuntary ride in an ambulance. Malcolm didn't have any money for bail, so he figured it'd be best to separate himself from a potentially destructive situation – as Dr. Manning would say.

After locating the extra materials he needed from the parts department to complete all the additional installations, Malcolm called Dr. Manning's office and left a message with the answering service about cancelling his appointment. From the looks of his schedule, he'd be working long hours for the remainder of the week. He made a mental note to schedule future appointments on his day off so he wouldn't have to choke anybody.

An hour later after loading and gassing up the truck, Malcolm pulled up to the Starbucks drive-thru and ordered his favorite latte'. Telese had gotten him hooked on the coffee and cocoa, and now he couldn't stop, but he wasn't complaining. For some reason every time he drank one, it seemed to calm him down, and calm was what he needed right now. Almost spilling the latte' in his lap, Malcolm retrieved his ringing cell phone from his pants pocket. His sister Lauren had been blowing up his cell phone for the last week, but he wouldn't answer. He knew what she wanted, and he didn't want to hear it.

"Hello," he set the phone on speaker mode.

"What the heck is wrong with you, boy?" Lauren was unable to suppress her anger.

"And good morning to you, too," Malcolm said. What's up with everybody calling me 'boy' today? I'm a grown man."

"Right, good morning, Malcolm," she snapped.

"I know you've seen that I've been calling you."

"Yes, Lauren, I've noticed you called a few times. I've been busy."

"Liar!" she blurted.

"You haven't been a bit busier than the man in the moon. You just don't want to hear what I have to say. I see you can't seem to keep your hands to yourself again. Malcolm, are you a freaking idiot? She left your butt this time. You've really messed up now. I told your butt to get some help last time, but no, you couldn't listen to me, Mr. "I got this." I can't believe you hit her like that. Her eye looked a damn hot mess when I saw her at the nail salon nearly a month ago. You ought to be ashamed of yourself. Everybody was staring at her like she had some kind of disease or something. I was embarrassed to say you are even my brother. I don't know what's wrong with you."

She barely took a breath before plunging onward.

"Telese should have put a frying pan upside your head. That would make you think twice. Malcolm, you know better, after all the times Daddy used to hit Momma in front of us. You remember how we felt so helpless because we couldn't help her? I never would have thought you'd mimic him." Lauren began to cry.

"Momma didn't raise you like that. That's the reason she left Kenny Stuart and never looked back. Don't turn into our daddy. Please, Malcolm, stop this!"

Malcolm didn't say a word. He let Lauren rant and rave. He knew she was right. Deep down inside, a part of him held great respect for KJ; showing up with that BB gun to protect his mother was honorable, something he wished he'd had the courage to do as a boy. When face-to-face with the hurt in his son's eyes, he remembered his own pain while watching his momma fight an abusive husband. Malcolm had turned into the man he said he would never be.

"Now when she goes out and finds herself a real man, your going to be sick," Lauren said, sucking her teeth.

Malcolm could feel his skin starting to crawl. Her smart comment had him wanting to leap through the phone, but he had to keep his cool. He was on a roll today with managing his anger, so he took a big swig of his latte' and reminded himself that he and Lauren had the same momma and daddy.

"Are you finished?" Malcolm said after she finally paused for breath.

"Yeah, I'm finished," she snapped, waiting for his reply.

"Yeah, I messed up royally," Malcolm agreed.

"My son made me realize some hard truths, so I moved out. I'm getting it together now and when I do, I'm moving back…end of discussion," he declared.

"Uh huh," Lauren answered.

"And just how are you, quote, unquote, getting it together?"

"If you must know, I'm going to anger management classes over on Alexander and Downs Boulevard with Dr. Manning."

"Is that right?" she didn't sound convinced.

"Just so you are aware, I talked to Telese about 20 minutes ago. She asked me to babysit the kid's tomorrow night for a few hours. She mentioned the doctor's office called and said you cancelled your appointment, and they wanted to know when you wanted to reschedule. Why in the world didn't you give them your cell phone number, instead of your house number? Now Telese knows you're full of it, and those were her exact words."

"Damn!" Malcolm yelled loudly, hitting the steering wheel of his truck.

"My sentiments exactly," Lauren agreed.

"What else did she say?" Malcolm asked.

Lauren paused for several seconds.

"She's done, Malcolm. Honestly, I think she really means it. I've never heard Telese talk like that before. If you want to know my opinion, whatever happened with KJ and the whole incident when you all got into it has caused her to, as she said, assess the situation."

"She really said she was done?"

"Yes! Malcolm, I'm afraid you're going to lose her this time."

Lauren didn't mention Telese's comment about finding an attorney. She hoped if she scared Malcolm enough he could somehow go over there and work his magic, like he always did.

"Malcolm, I'm telling you, you need to make that appointment today, and you need to let your wife know that you went. You've got too much riding on this."

"Okay, thanks, Lauren. I gotta go," Malcolm tried rushing her off the phone.

"All right, Malcolm, you got to get this straightened out. You've got a great wife. I don't want to have to remind you of that train wreck of an ex-wife you had before."

"Please don't even mention Sydney," he sighed.

"Trust me, I got this. Telese ain't going nowhere, she loves Big Daddy."

"Okay, Big Daddy," Lauren giggled.

"I guess I'd better let you get to work so you can plan your magic comeback."

She paused and then added hurriedly, "Is Telese letting you take her out for her birthday tomorrow?"

"Dang it!" Malcolm hit himself in the head.

"I know you didn't forget," Lauren said.

"Sis, I've been so preoccupied with this counseling and trying to get back home, it completely escaped my mind. I did give her an early gift last month," he said in his defense.

"Now I have to work late all this week. That's the reason I canceled my counseling session."

"Well, you figure something out, and quick. There's nothing worse than for you to dis' your wife on her birthday. I love you, bro, and good luck. Better yet, I think I'll pray for you on this one."

Malcolm laughed. "I think I'll take my chances with luck, because there's no way God is going to let *you* get a prayer through."

Lauren laughed. "Bye, boy!"

"I told you to stop calling me that," Malcolm laughed.

"I love you, girl."

"Love you too, bro," she said, hanging up.

Malcolm jumped out of his truck. He would work as quickly as he could to get finished and make his appointment. He called the doctor's office back to say he would make his appointment after all. He tried Telese on her cell phone but got her voicemail.

"Hey, baby girl, it's me. I hope y'all are okay. I'm missing y'all like crazy. I'm working late this week, but I wanted to see if you'd like to hang out with your husband tomorrow night for your birthday. It's not every day you turn thirty-five. I hope you're still enjoying your painting. I'll call you this evening once I leave my doctor's appointment. I thought I was going to have to cancel because that a-hole David Lee called in sick again, but your man is going to work it out. This is too important to us. I love you, and I'm trying, baby. Bye."

Malcolm worked like a maniac, going from house to house. He knocked out his first five jobs by 1:30. On his next job he wasn't so lucky. His customer followed him from room to room, trying her best to hold him hostage. She had a single daughter with two kids, and she was trying to find them a daddy. No matter how many times Malcolm told her he was happily married, the woman wouldn't take no for an answer. Her response was, *"We can work around that, sweetie."* Her gabbing was slowing him down, and he came close to telling her to shut the hell up, but he needed a good rating on his customer service survey. Those surveys determined how big or small his bonus check would be at the end of the year, so he always tried to keep his customers happy.

Finally he took her daughter's number just to shut her up. After finishing the job, he felt hungry, but he wasn't about to stop now. He reached in the glove compartment to grab a pack of crackers and a bag of peanuts he kept to snack on. He got to his next job by 3:00. He still had four more jobs to go.

"Shoot," he shouted.

"I won't make it." *Think, Malcolm, think*, he said to himself.

Pulling out his cell phone, he called Telese once more, but she still didn't pick up. That wasn't like her not to answer her phone. He felt relieved when his phone rang in his hand.

"Hey, baby, where you been, girl? Did you get my message?" he said cheerfully.

"No, Malcolm, it's not your precious Telese."

The sound of his ex-wife Sydney's voice made his smile disappear.

"What's going on, Sydney?"

"The light bill, that's what's going on. Can I borrow $150? They're going to cut our lights off if I don't pay the bill by 5 p.m."

"Sydney, I don't have any extra money. What are you doing with your income?"

"I spend it on your daughter," she pouted.

"Yeah, right."

"And what is that supposed to mean?" Her tone was defensive.

"Nothing, Sydney. I ain't got time to argue with you."

"No! I want to know what you mean by that."

"Okay, how come every time I see you, you are always dressed to impress with a brand new hair weave, and my child looks jacked up?"

"That's a lie, Malcolm, and you know it!"

"Whatever, Sydney," Malcolm snapped back.

He just wanted this conversation to be done.

"I didn't call to argue with you, but I really do need the money, or we'll be sitting over here in the dark."

"Sydney, you get a child support check every week. You should get one today, so pay it with that."

Sydney smacked her lip, "I have to pay the water bill with that."

"Well, Sydney, I can't help you. I have my own problems right now. You need to learn how to budget your money. Besides, Crystal told me that one of your ex-boyfriends is staying there. Why can't he help pay your bills? Don't you think you need to tell him if he wants to play, he needs to pay?"

"It ain't even like that. Tony is an old friend from back in the day. He is here temporarily, just until he gets back on his feet. We are just friends."

"Whoa, whoa, whoa; it doesn't matter to me what your relationship is. My only business is Crystal. As long as she's straight, I'm good. But I think you and Tony need to figure out how y'all gonna keep the lights on, 'cause in a few weeks your child support checks are about to be reduced."

"What the hell do you mean 'about to be reduced'?" Sydney got louder.

"With all that money you and Ms. Moneybags got rolling in? I don't think so. Our daughter deserves to live good, too."

"Get used to it. I'm broke."

Sydney laughed. "Malcolm, please, you live in a quarter-million-dollar home. You and your fat ass wife drive nice cars. Our daughter deserves to live just like KJ and Layla."

Sydney began her fake crying act.

"I guess since you all high class now; you want to forget about Crystal. I don't think so. She's your oldest child, and I'll be damned if I'll let you kick my baby to the curb."

"Sydney, it's your problem you can't pay your light bill. I don't have time for this nonsense. I've been taking care of Crystal even before you asked me to adopt her, so don't try to make this about me not taking care of my child. All I'm saying is that things are a little rough right now, and I need a few months to get some stuff straight."

"I'll be damned!" Sydney was agitated. "She kicked you out, didn't she?"

"Sydney, how about you need to mind your own business, and stay out of mine?" Malcolm roared.

"When you're messing with my money, it is my business, boo! I suggest you go crawling on your hands and knees to your plus-size diva, because I will tell you this – if Crystal Stuart ain't eating shrimp, then Malcolm Stuart will be eating oodles of noodles behind some steel bars, and I mean that!"

Malcolm pressed "end call" on his cell phone while Sydney was still babbling. He knew if he stayed on the line with her a minute longer he really would be eating oodles of noodles. Sydney had a way of bringing out the worst in him. If he could get away with it, he'd put a hit out on her and be done with it. Her perfectly-shaped lips, hips, and finger tips enabled her to get just about anything she wanted from a man. Her beautiful smile and long, wavy hair, not to mention her perfect hourglass figure, hypnotized her victims. His attraction to Sydney was strictly physical. They had nothing in common. She liked to shop and watch figure skating. He preferred old antique cars and boxing matches.

When the two of them were together, Malcolm worked in a manufacturing plant as a maintenance worker making pretty good money. At that time, he had it going on. When he and Sydney met, she was already pregnant. She didn't want to know who the father was. Raped and left for dead in an alley, she woke up in the hospital severely beaten, infected with a venereal disease and pregnant by her rapist. She had been told years prior that she wouldn't be able to have children, so she decided not to terminate the pregnancy in an attempt to carry the fetus full-term to have a chance at motherhood. Crystal had inherited her natural beauty. She was simply Sydney made all over again. Hopefully she would not inherit her mother's attitude of entitlement..

Months after Crystal's birth, Malcolm proposed to Sydney, and they married shortly thereafter. However, her concern for her new baby to share the same last name was a major issue. After voicing the idea of adoption to Malcolm, he didn't think twice before signing on the dotted line, making Crystal an official Stuart. Malcolm loved his little bundle of joy, with her cute little birthmark in the palm of her hand. He always said it was good luck.

Despite his shortcomings, he gladly raised Crystal as his own. His love for her was unconditional before and after his and Sydney's marriage. You'd have never known that Crystal didn't come from his loins. His family welcomed Crystal with loving arms, but love didn't live in their hearts for Sydney. Not one female in his entire family took a liking to her. Not even his grandmother, and his Grandma Tricia loved everybody.

Grandma Tricia said she discerned the spirit of some woman in the Bible named Jezebel when it came to Sydney. She said whenever she hugged her hello or goodbye, she could sense a manipulative and controlling spirit inside his wife. Most of the time Grandma Tricia's predictions were right on the money. If Grandma didn't care for you, you could pretty much hang it up when it came to the rest of the family. His sister Lauren considered her to be whorish, and his momma said she was sneaky. But Malcolm didn't care. In his eyes, she could do no wrong.

Malcolm's love didn't turn to hate until her true colors were revealed while he was in prison. She had talked him into making a run to Florida for her cousin, Travis. All he had to do was drive the car there and back for an easy $5,000 a trip. He averaged two trips a month, sometimes three, if Travis sold enough drugs. Malcolm kept this side job for nearly four years and stacked up mounds of cash. When he got busted returning from a routine trip one night, the kilos he had hidden perfectly inside the lining of the seats were instantly sniffed out by the K-9 unit. Malcolm had a gut feeling that somebody had snitched, but who? He didn't go out much, and he lived low key. However, the police found out. He got 15 years at the Jones County prison.

Sydney flipped quicker than a pancake. She served him divorce papers in prison on the grounds of abandonment. She never once visited him, nor did she bring Crystal to see him the whole time he was there. She didn't accept any collect calls and didn't send one cent of the $50,000 he had stashed in a safe in the basement.

Malcolm promised himself not to kill her when he got out. Crystal did send him pictures that she had drawn at school and homemade cards saying her daddy was #1. Her letters made his day. If it hadn't been for his mom and sister, he didn't know how he would have survived. Somebody in Heaven must have been looking out for him. Louise, his mom, paid another attorney to actually defend his case. The lame lawyer he had originally hired couldn't even remember his name. The new attorney got his time cut to nine years of which he served five.

It took Malcolm 3 months to track Sydney down before showing up at her apartment unannounced to see Crystal. The dumbfounded look on Sydney's face was priceless. When she and her boyfriend came to the door and saw Malcolm, Sydney didn't know whether to run or scream. They thought Malcolm would beat the brakes out of them, but were shocked when he just kindly asked to take Crystal out shopping and to go get ice cream. Sydney couldn't take her eyes off Malcolm. Her boyfriend had to be ticked that she was staring at him like he was filet mignon. Malcolm looked better than he ever had. His chocolate muscles bulged through his tightly fitted spandex shirt. He knew she was trying to figure out how he got released so quickly and from where his money had come. She was simply unaware of the other stash Malcolm had kept at his mom's house.

When he took Crystal home later that evening, they carried bags and bags of new clothes and shoes into the house. Sydney answered the door wearing hardly anything. She'd gotten rid of her boyfriend and thought Malcolm was about to become her dummy again. But Malcolm and Telese had already been dating a month, and he was in love. He had paid cash for a SUV he had purchased from her through a newspaper ad, and they had been inseparable ever since. He purposely had Telese on the phone, making preparations to pick her up for dinner and a movie after he left his daughter's house. He made sure to say "baby" and "sweetheart" several times within Sydney's earshot.

"Sure you don't wanna come in for a while and maybe have some coffee or something?"

Her attempt at coyness seemed almost pathetic.

"No thanks, I really have to get going."

He wasn't ever going to get caught up in her web again.

Malcolm's heart raced with anxiety, it was quickly approaching 3:45 and he was running out of time. After finishing his next job he knew it would be impossible do get done in time, he had to think fast. He had three more jobs to do but no more time to do them. Sydney had called three times and left two nasty messages about Crystal being in the dark. He figured if he could get in touch with Telese, maybe Crystal could come and stay at the house with them for a couple days until Sydney got her stuff straight. He wouldn't feel comfortable with his daughter staying at the hotel with him and he didn't want her to see him living so low.

Malcolm sat in the parking lot of Dr. Manning's office waiting on 4:15 to come. He hadn't taken a lunch break, so this would be it. It would take longer than his usual thirty minutes, but that's just how it had to be. He called his customers to let them know that he was running about an hour behind, and no one complained. He tried Telese once more, and finally she picked up.

"Dang girl, where have you been? I've been calling you all day. Did you get my message?"

"Yes, Malcolm, I got your message. Sorry I didn't call you back. I've been tied up most of the day, trying to take care of some business."

"Okay. Hey, I've got a favor to ask," he cleared his throat.

"What kind of favor?"

"Well, Sydney called and said her electricity was going to be cut off. I don't know how true it is, but I was wondering if Crystal could stay with you and the kids for a couple of days. I really don't want her to stay at a hotel with me, and besides, I'm working like crazy. I had to take my lunch break now just so I could keep my doctor's appointment. I'm out here in the parking lot, waiting on 4:30."

"Oh wow, that's good for you. They called this morning and said you cancelled."

"Yeah, but I worked it out."

"That's good to hear. You really need to stay with it, Malcolm. I want you to get yourself together, not for me, but for yourself and your kids."

"I understand, but I want to do it for you, too," Malcolm added. "I love you, baby, and I can't see my life without you in it."

Telese didn't respond.

"Hello?"

"Yes, I'm here. I won't be in town this weekend. I'm actually leaving for Atlanta tomorrow. The kids are going to be at my sister's until I get back."

"I thought Lauren was going to keep the kids."

"I asked her this morning, but that was before I decided to go out of town for the weekend. I'm sorry I can't help you. Is Crystal okay?"

"Yeah, she's fine. What's going on in Atlanta?" he tried to keep irritation from his voice.

"I was invited by a friend to celebrate my birthday there. I figured I could use a little getaway trip with everything that's been going on lately." she sounded nonchalant.

"Wow, I see." Malcolm wanted to ask who her friend was, but he didn't want to seem nosey or jealous.

"Well, there go my plans for taking you out to dinner tomorrow. I really wanted to spend some time with you. I miss you and the kids so much, baby. I want to come home."

The silence on the phone was awkward. Malcolm sensed something wasn't right.

"Telese, is something wrong?"

"Huh uh," she replied, seeming a little preoccupied.

"What are you doing?" he asked.

"Trying to decide what to pack," she said.

"I like you in that crème-colored pants suite with the grey scarf. You look so beautiful in that."

"I was thinking about my red dress," she answered.

"Yeah, that looks good on you, too, but it's formal. Where are you going there?"

"I don't know the plan yet. I'm just taking plenty of outfits just in case."

Malcolm didn't like the vibe he was getting. He wanted to give her the third degree, but that would not help his cause.

"It's almost twenty after," Telese reminded him.

"I know. I have a few more minutes," he answered.

"How late are you working tonight?"

"I'll probably be finishing up around 7:00."

"Okay, what are you doing after work?" she asked.

"Nothing as usual. Go and grab a burger and lay across that hard mattress to watch television."

Telese laughed. "I'm sorry. I shouldn't have laughed. Do you think the two of us could meet for dinner at Winnebago's tonight?"

"Are you serious? Hell, yeah," he smiled.

A huge weight lifted from his heart. "We can meet around 8:00. That way I can go to the hotel and change first."

"That will work," she answered.

"Call if you're running late."

"Are you bringing the kids?" Malcolm could not wipe the smile off his face.

"No it will be just me and you," Telese answered.

"Okay, baby. Let me work on getting myself together so I can get home soon. I will see you…. tooooo-night!" he sang.

Malcolm walked up to the receptionist's window to let her know that he was there for his scheduled appointment. The sign on the window read. "Dr. William Arthur Manning's appointments are cancelled indefinitely." Malcolm wondered what the heck was going on.

"Excuse me, Miss. I had a 4:30 with Dr. Manning today. Why are his appointments cancelled? Do I need to reschedule?"

"Dr. Manning was pronounced dead at 1:30 today. If you'd like to schedule with another of our counselors, you may."

The shock on Malcolm's face was evident. The receptionist looked like she had been crying and really didn't need to be working. Malcolm's mouth flew open and his eyes doubled in size.

"I'm sorry. They just decided a few minutes ago to cancel all appointments. We are about to close. If you want to call back on Monday, I'm sure we can set you up with another counselor and group." She said, wiping her red nose.

"Okay." Malcolm said slowly. His heart was heavy and his curiosity was overwhelming. He'd grown very fond of Dr. Manning. The brainy guy has taught Malcolm how to make better choices, ones with consequences that weren't so harsh. Malcolm couldn't help but wonder what happened to the poor guy. He seemed pretty healthy. Was it heart attack or an accident? He wondered. Being in such shock, it slipped his mind to ask. Learning of this tragedy put a damper on Malcolm's mood. His heart went out to Dr. Mannings wife and children, whom Malcolm distantly felt like he knew. For the last month he had been looking at pictures of Dr. Manning family on the wall, imagining that could one day be him and his family. Malcolm made a mental note to find out the funeral arrangements so he could at least pay his respects.

Malcolm went back to work to finish his last few jobs quickly. Although Dr. Mannings death was hard to shake, he tried to get it off his mind. Singing in the shower "Love and Happiness," he was grateful to his lovely wife for wanting to spend time with him; it was like a dream come true. He prayed to God that his night would not end with him going back to the hotel alone.

Stopping by the store nearly an hour and a half early, Malcolm read just about every birthday card they had on the shelf. He couldn't find one to say it all, so he ended up buying three. The 18 yellow roses and vase he purchased were sure to make her smile. He could not wait to see Telese. He texted her cell phone at 7:15 just to let her know he had gotten there early. It was a good thing he arrived early because, the waiting list was an hour long. After putting their last name on the list, he walked outside to escape the crowd. He noticed the single ladies checking him out and whispering. He smiled and nodded as he walked back to his car to get the roses and cards. He couldn't understand why she hadn't chosen a more intimate restaurant, Winnebago's was always so crowded, but if that's what she wanted, so be it.   He was happy to spend time with her, and that's all that mattered.

By the time Telese arrived, Malcolm was already seated. He stood up to greet his beautiful wife and was pleasantly surprised to see how good she looked.   She had lost a few pounds since he had seen her last. Handing her the flowers, he kissed her rosy cheeks.

"Wow!" Malcolm said.

"Who is this? You look like a million bucks, baby."

"Thanks," she shyly smiled.

"I've lost almost twenty pounds."

"In a month?" Malcolm questioned, "Is that healthy?"

"Yes, as long as you exercise and eat less. I'd like to lose twenty-five more."

"You don't need to lose that much, Telese.   You look damn good just the way you are!"

"Thanks, but we both know I needed to lose some weight."

"I love every curve on your body. You never heard me complain."

Telese laughed at Malcolm's comment.   It was true; he had always loved her feminine curves.

"I ordered you some iced tea," he smiled.

The over friendly waiter came to the table and asked if they were ready to order.

"Do you want your usual?" Malcolm asked.

"No, not tonight.   I'm going to try the seafood salad with no bread and light dressing, please."

"And for you, sir?"

"I'll have the chicken cordon bleu with mashed potatoes, and broccoli with butter," Malcolm said.

Malcolm took a sip of his soft drink.

"Girl, you look so beautiful! How was your day?"

"It was okay," she replied.

"Your son and his girlfriend are driving me nuts. I get up in the middle of the night to use the bathroom, and Mr. KJ is on the phone with his little sweet thang at 1:00 in the morning. Needless to say...," she folded her arms.

"He's grounded for a week, with no video games and no phone calls."

Malcolm tilted his head in amazement.

"Wow! I guess he really is growing up. Crystal started high school this year, and Sidney said boys have been calling left and right. I don't know what I'm going to do with our kids. They're just growing up on us."

"I know. I can only imagine what's next," Telese laughed.

"How did your therapy session go today?"

"Oh, man, baby, you are not going to believe this," he said, putting the buttered bread in his mouth.

"I walked in the office after we got off the phone and there was a big sign on the receptionist's window that said Dr. Manning's appointments had been cancelled indefinitely."

Telese raised her eyebrows.

"Really? Why?"

"The girl at the desk said he died at 1:30 today. She didn't offer any details but said they were working on getting his patients new counselors. I'll reschedule with another therapist on Monday."

"Oh, my goodness, Malcolm, that's awful," she looked concerned.

"I know, baby, that's what I said. I still can't believe it. Mr. Manning was all right with me, he taught me a lot. I'm sure we will find out the details later; just keep his family in prayer."

The waiter brought over the food and set it in front of them while they continued with small talk. Malcolm gobbled down his food so quickly, Telese felt compelled to remind him he was no longer in Jones County prison.

"You want some of my salad?" she asked.

"No, baby, I'm good. It's just that all I ate was a pack of cheese crackers today. I skipped lunch trying to make it to my doctor's appointment. Mr. Riley dumped David Lee's work on me unexpectedly, and I was stuck trying to figure out how I was going to do it all."

Telese lightly chuckled.

"I see David Lee is still trying to push your buttons."

"He seems to get worse. It's like everyday he tries to take it a little bit further."

Malcolm seemed agitated just talking about him.

"Boy!" Telese chuckled again.

"He just doesn't know who he's messing with, does he?"

Malcolm smiled, "No, I'm changing baby. I try not to let him get under my skin, and I'm progressing," he reasoned.

"Can I interest you folks in a desert menu?"

The waiter refilled their drinks for the third time.

"None for me."

Telese sat back and rubbed her belly.

"I don't need a menu," Malcolm said.

"I want to know if you have chocolate cake."

"We sure do, the best this side of Virginia. You want a scoop of ice cream to go with it?"

"Sure," Malcolm smiled.

The waiter scurried off. Telese excused herself from the table and headed to the restroom. Looking around the restaurant at all the smiling faces, Malcolm hoped his night would end with such joy and laughter. Telese returned and sat down, taking a deep breath.

"Malcolm, I invited you to dinner tonight because I need to discuss our marriage."

"Okay, baby," he said, taking a sip of his beverage.

"Here you are, sir, one chocolate fudge cake and ice cream. I brought two spoons, just in case the missus would care to indulge," he grinned.

"Don't tempt me," Telese groaned to the waiter.

"It looks scrumptious."

"Are you talking about me or the cake?" the waiter teased.

"The cake," Malcolm interrupted, annoyed.

Sensing Malcolm's frustration, the waiter left the check and rolled his eyes, certain he wasn't going to get a tip. Grabbing one of the spoons, Telese tasted a corner of cake and a dab of ice cream.

"I wish you would've never ordered this. Now I'm going to go over my limit of calories," she said, taking another bite.

"It's delicious. Aren't you going to eat some?" she asked, as Malcolm sat quietly.

"So, what do you want to talk about, baby?" Malcolm pushed through a smile.

His stomach was in knots, and his hands were beginning to sweat. Telese laid her platinum visa credit card on the table gently.

"Put that away, baby," Malcolm felt insulted.

"It's your birthday dinner. Since I can't be with you tomorrow I figured we'd celebrate tonight."

"Aren't you going to read your cards?" Malcolm placed some cash on the table for the check.

"I'd rather read them at home." Telese grabbed both of Malcolm's sweaty hands.

"Are you okay?"

"I don't know yet," he answered.

Her eyes looked glossy as she dropped her head. "Malcolm…," she hesitated.

"You want a divorce, don't you?" he said with a grim look on his face.

"Yes," she replied bluntly.

"You haven't given me a chance, baby!"

He looked around, realizing that his tone had elevated. At least now he knew why she had picked a crowded restaurant.

She sighed.

"So much has happened over the ten years that we've been together. These past few years have been hell. I don't want to be your wife anymore."

"You don't love me?"

"Yes and no. How can I love a man who doesn't care about hurting me? I have to love myself enough to say 'No more.'"

"Is it just the fighting, or is there someone else?"

You know there's no one else. It's the fighting, Malcolm, I can't take it anymore."

Malcolm struggled to contain his anger. He didn't want to make a scene, so he listened, nodding briefly.

"I spoke with an attorney today," she said.

"I assume that's the reason you didn't answer your cell phone earlier."

Telese didn't reply.

"He said if you don't contest it, we can have the divorce finalized in forty-five to sixty days."

"What!"

Malcolm couldn't contain his rage. People in the restaurant started looking at him. Telese dropped her head, embarrassed.

"Malcolm, honey, please calm down."

"I am calm," he said, talking with his clinched teeth.

"My friend told me we have to be separated a year," he debated.

"My attorney said that there are ways around that," she confirmed.

Malcolm shook his head in disbelief. Did she want out of his life so bad? She wanted it that quickly?

"Telese, a lot of married people are not in love. Can't we at least try to work on getting the love back? I know in time you'll love me again. You just need to know that I won't hit you anymore, and baby, I promise you I won't."

"I'm sorry. I can't do this to myself or the kids anymore. I've tried for ten years."

Malcolm's face went blank. If he opened his mouth, things would get out of hand. Telese pulled her attorney's card from her purse and slid it across the table over to Malcolm.

"If we can come to an agreement, we can put all this behind us. I'm not asking for any child support. I just want out."

Malcolm started counting backwards from ten under his breath.

"Did you say something?" Telese asked, hearing him mumble.

Malcolm shook his head, 'no.'

"Just consider it, Malcolm. I think it's best this way."

"What about the kids?" he said calmly.

"Once you get settled in a decent place, you can see them whenever you want. I'd never keep them away from you."

"So that's it. You want me out of your life?"

"I didn't say that. I just can't be married to you anymore. We can still be friends. We have children together."

"Do I look like I want to be your friend, Telese? Malcolm exploded.

"Malcolm, people are staring at you."

"You think I care! Let them stare all they want."

"Malcolm, please don't make a scene."

The restaurant manager walked over to the table.

"Is everything alright?" he politely asked.

"Yes, we're fine," Telese answered as Malcolm fumed silently.

A few minutes later, Telese's sister walked up to the table. "Hi, Malcolm," she said, not waiting on an answer.

"Ready to go, Telese?"

"Yes, I'm ready," Telese said as she grabbed her coat.

"I'm sorry, Malcolm," she started to cry.

"I've tried for so long. I'm just tired," she hurried out of the restaurant behind her sister.

Malcolm sat in the booth, alone with his thoughts. After he composed himself, he motioned for the waiter to come over.

"Can I get you something, sir?"

"Yeah, bring me a beer," Malcolm said.

"What brand?" the waiter asked.

"It doesn't matter. I don't like any of them."

The next morning Malcolm hit the time clock without a minute to spare. He starting loading up his work truck right away. He hadn't slept a wink all night. Instead, he had continually fought back tears. He still couldn't believe Telese didn't love him anymore. That was a big blow to his ego and a bigger blow to his heart. She had sent him a text late last night saying how beautiful the cards were, and that they had made her cry.

"I'm sorry for the way things have turned out between us, and I hope one day after everything is over that we can still be friends," she'd wrote.

Malcolm was relieved that the rest of his week wouldn't be as busy for him as he had anticipated. David Lee happened to show up. At least now Malcolm could finish his handful of jobs and go back to his room to contemplate suicide. He spotted a newspaper lying on the counter in the supply room as he walked by and picked it up. Malcolm stared at Dr. Manning's picture on the front page. Beneath his photo the article described how Dr. Manning and his wife had been involved in a domestic dispute that left Dr. Manning shot to death from a single gunshot wound to the chest. His wife was being charged with murder.

"Wow, Dr. Manning."

Malcolm felt defeated. You just never know. David Lee tried to pass Malcolm in a hurry.

Malcolm said, "Glad you made it back."

David Lee answered, with a smirk "Your wife couldn't get enough so I had to take a day off to keep her happy.

Malcolm yelled "ten" before punching David Lee in the face.

At "nine" he punched him again. With "eight" he slammed him to the ground. On "seven" he hit him in the stomach, and on "six" he added another blow. Three employees ran in and pulled Malcolm off of David Lee as Mr. Riley came to see what was going on.

"Malcolm, you crazy SOB, get the hell out of here; you're fired!"

Malcolm removed his tool belt and threw it toward Mr. Riley.

"Here, boy, you can have this damn job and furthermore…"

"Five!"

Malcolm punched Mr. Riley right between the eyes.

"*Thank you,*" Kerri the supply clerk secretly whispered as Malcolm stormed out the door.

Chapter 7   *Raymond*

Relieved to be away from the rowdy celebration Donae slipped into Ray's office and rushed over to his bathroom to tinkle. She washed and then dried her hands on Ray's monogrammed towels that she'd purchased for him as a "just because" gift. Although he hated surprises, he loved that his wife was so thoughtful. Laughing loudly at herself as she started undressing, leaving on her purple lace thong and matching bra. Grabbing her clutch purse, she touched up her make-up so she'd look irresistible from head to toe, and sprayed dabs of perfume in Ray's favorite spots since he was a fragrance fanatic. Strolling around his office in her sexy undies, she admired the photos of their children on his desk. Both were the splitting image of Ray. Often she thought that the only part she played was in the fun of making them and the pain of having them. Aggressively Donae studied their photos for a sign of her DNA, only to rediscover the one thing they inherited from her was her gleaming smile.

Spotting a photo of herself, she giggled at the snapshot Ray had taken of her with a huge afro. She'd just taken her braids out that day. Her hair was tightly crinkled, and she was picking it out when he snapped the picture. Although she hated that photo, he loved it, always saying it captured her natural beauty. Donae wondered if all the pictures on his desk of her and the kids provided an escape from a stressful day. She wondered when Ray had experienced any of those hectic days some of the management wives had been referring to earlier.

It was at that moment when Donae realized how truly blessed she was. She loved her life, her husband, her job and her children, but most of all her God for spilling so much favor into their lives. Donae was so grateful for everything the Lord had brought them through and thanked Him for giving her such a great man. Ray was an awesome protector and provider. Tonight she had celebrated his dream, and on this night, not only one dream would come true, but two. Making a pit stop by the waste can, she made it official, and then excitedly raced to the restroom to grab her cell phone from her clutch purse. Once she was pleased with her seductive allure, she struck a pose on his soft leather sofa and snapped the shot, certain that the picture mail would speed him considerably.

The text message under her picture read: *Congrats 2 U Mr. Plant Manager!* I'm turning ur lights off. Ur quicke is waiting 4 u -

HURRY☺.   Before she pressed "send," the sound of whispering voices outside Ray's door sounded an alarm for her to hide. Racing to the bathroom, she quickly closed the door leaving only a small crack. Donae was certain that whoever was with Ray would soon be rushed out once her French manicured nail hit the "send" button.

Ray rushed into his office nervously. Behind him was Amanda, almost on his heels. "Amanda! Why did you follow me here? I just came to grab my brief profiles. Ray sniffed the air.

"What fragrance are you wearing?" he asked inhaling the sweet familiar scent.

Amanda patted his behind and squeezed softly. "Hush with the nonsense, silly. Are you happy now, "Mr. Plant Manager?" she giggled.

Ray smiled a boyish grin. "Hell yeah!" he fist-pumped the air.

"But why didn't you tell me about this before now? All the other guys said they knew of their promotions two weeks ago."

"Yes, honey, it's true. They knew, but I wanted the surprise element for you! You've been running from me ever since your wife found out about us, but she can't give you the power and success that I can. Now, be a good boy, come to momma and show her how appreciative you are."

Amanda slipped off her pink dress and tossed it in Ray's face, making her way to the beige leather sofa. "Ray," she whined as he stared at her in shock.

"Those old crackling hens can only entertain Donae…oh excuse me, Mrs. Durrant, for so long before she starts wondering where you are," she devilishly grinned.

"Please, Ray," she begged.

"I've needed you so badly. I don't want to dream about you any longer. I want the real deal again, and again, and again."

Donae had been peeping through the cracked door with the lights off, not making a sound. She prayed silently:

Dear God, please give my husband the strength to resist the trap that the enemy has put before him. I bind the spirit of lust and power that hovers over him now. Lord Jesus, give him a way of escape, and I pray he chooses the right path. In Jesus' name I pray. Amen.

Ray stared at the beige sofa as if in deep thought. He never looked at Amanda, but more like *through* her. He thought about how great his life was, how God has brought his marriage back together. He stood there frozen in place for a few seconds. Dropping his head, he turned in the opposite direction, now facing the restroom. In his thoughts he could almost smell Donae's perfume lingering in the room.

"Come on, baby, I need you to come through," Donae began to shake.

"Come on, Raymond," she cheered him on inside.

"Please baby, don't destroy what we have again."

It took everything in her to stand there and watch. Her heart raced like a horse running a championship race. The anxiety built up in her eyes and before she knew it, tears were falling. Never bothering to wipe them, she watched fearfully. Her legs felt as if they were about to give out until she heard Ray's deep voice soaring through the quiet room.

"I'm sorry, Amanda, I can't do it. I love my wife. I can't lose my family. It's not worth it. You're a beautiful woman, but what I have at home is priceless." He couldn't even look at her.

"I can't give you what you want."

YES! Donae whispered inwardly. *Thank you Lord. You gave him a choice, and he chose to do the right thing. That's my man!*

Donae's heart began to dance, and a smile gleamed across her face. They had won. No one could come between her and Ray. At that moment she fell in love all over again, knowing that earlier she'd made the right decision in supporting her man's dream. She contemplated opening the door fully, walking out in her undies, and making love to her husband on the floor. After, of course, letting Amanda know she wasn't wanted. Before she could move, Amanda arose from her spot heated, but she restrained her temper tantrum to take a different approach. Moving closer to Ray, she grabbed hold of his hand and turned him around to face her. She wanted to look into his light eyes and see him struggle to resist her.

"But you can give me what I need, Ray," she said.

"I want you. I always have. I can give you everything your heart desires. I can make you a powerful man." She paused for this to sink in.

"Plant Manager is only the beginning. If we play our cards right, you could be C.E.O. one day."

Amanda knew offering him power would appeal to his weakness. She rubbed his bald head and then pulled him closer to her. Holding his hand she guided him back toward the plush leather sofa. Standing in front of him she squeezed him tightly, swaying her body from side to side remembering how he'd just slow danced with his wife. She held onto him as if her life depended on it. Inhaling his mesmerizing scent, her body started soaking from the expectation of what was to come. She could almost feel him inside of her, touching her soul. She had been in love with him since the first day she saw him. She didn't care if she had to share him for now. Once his wife was out of the picture, he would be her husband and the C.E.O of the company, but for now she'd settle for just a piece of him. When Ray didn't push her away, she smiled inside. Amanda took it as a sign that he was getting weaker; he'd soon be putty in her hands, but she had to be smart and feed off his weakness. As long as she kept Donae off his mind, she'd surely get what she had come for.

Pulling him toward her, she backed toward the sofa and stretched out cozily after removing the midsize pillow, while Ray stood over her, looking at her sexy body- a new body he'd never seen before. She thought her recent plastic surgery, breast implants, and tummy tuck were about to pay off. Ray bent down slowly and kissed her glossed cherry blossom lips. She removed his suit jacket and unloosened his tie. Ray unbuttoned his shirt and tossed it to the floor. Amanda smiled as she pulled his tight body on top of her.

"We've got to hurry," he said.

"I've got to get back to the party soon. Donae will be looking for me."

"Calm down, silly. I saw her leave in a taxi. I guess all the excitement was too much for her."

Relieved to hear that calming information, Ray sighed softly.

"She must have gone home. She said she might."

Suddenly Ray's cell phone beeped twice, indicating he had a picture mail with an attached message.

"That's her. I know it," he said, quickly leaning over to pick up his cell phone off the floor.

Retrieving the message, he stared at the picture of his beautiful wife, wearing his favorite color undies, purple. Her smile enticed him. But the photo of her sitting on his office leather sofa confused him. He rose up from Amanda's clutches and sat on the edge of the homemade love bed.

"What's wrong, Ray?"

Holding up his hand for her to be silent, he scrolled down to the text message. After reading it, he immediately jumped to his feet and bent down to pick up his starched shirt.

"What's going on?"

Ray didn't move from his spot on the floor. Now he knew it wasn't his imagination. He did smell Donae's perfume, and the scent got stronger as Donae slowly approached him. As Amanda saw Donae advancing in her underwear, she tried to spring up from the sofa, but her blonde hair got caught in the Velcro holding the cushions in place. She yanked her hair from its grip, but her ocean blue eyes didn't look in Donae's direction. Amanda grabbed her pink dress and frantically searched for her shoes.

80

With tears the size of hail, Donae whispered in the quiet room. "So what does it profit a man to gain the whole wide world and lose his soul?"

Waiting for an answer, Donae kept silent. Tension filled the room like smoke in a burning house. Ray finally spoke after buttoning up his shirt. "Donae, baby, I'm sorry. I made a horrible mistake."

"You love me, huh?" Donae cried.

"You're pathetic, Ray," she wept. "I TRUSTED you, AGAIN!" she shouted at the top of her lungs.

"You're so freaking money hungry and power driven that you just sold your soul to the devil!"

She pointed toward a shaking Amanda. "I hate you!"

Donae tried her best to hold it in, but the tears overwhelmed her. They began to flood her cheeks like a stream overflowing its banks. She tried to speak, but no words would come out. Amanda attempted to slip out, but Donae had the door blocked. Suddenly Donae lunged at Amanda with both hands aimed at her neck. Amanda screamed and dropped the one shoe she could find before racing out the door, barefoot.

"Baby!"

Ray grabbed her and held her in his arms. After a few minutes of tussling, she surrendered from exhaustion, collapsing in his arms and weeping uncontrollably. Ray sat Donae down, placing his suit jacket over her shoulders. He walked over to grab her skirt, blouse and jacket off the bathroom hook. On his way back he scooped up her heels and gently set them near her. Donae's soft sobbing made his heart ache. Without any resistance, he lifted her midsize body off the couch and sat back down, holding her in his arms as he rocked her like an infant. Kissing her forehead, he squeezed her gently, weeping a little himself. As he closed his eyes to inhale her, fragrance, his tears now dropped to her face. He rubbed his eyes with her long, silky hair that tonight smelled like vanilla.

Raymond knew very well this meant the end. With his eyes closed, he silently and sincerely prayed that God would help him to become a better man and pick up the pieces of his shattered life. It was at that very moment he realized that nothing or no one was worth losing his soul. Donae felt like a stranger in what used to be her favorite place. Being in his arms no longer meant anything to her. The truth was that those manly biceps could be sold to the highest bidder in exchange for money or power, or both. She wondered why God had allowed this to happen, knowing she'd end up hurt again. It didn't seem fair.

81

Holy Spirit, I thought you were my friend? Couldn't you have warned me of this shipwreck?

Steven, the security guard, knocked softly on the door.

"Mr. Durrant, its security. May I come in, sir?"

Donae made an attempt to move, but Ray held on to her even tighter. "Please baby," he begged.

"Don't move, this moment is all I have left."

Ray made certain Donae was completely covered by throwing the couch pillows over her freshly shaven legs.

"Yes, Steven, come on in," Ray said.

"Mr. Durrant, I apologize for disturbing you. Is everything alright? There was a complaint about some yelling."

"Everything is fine," Ray answered, continuing to rock his sweet wife.

Steven motioned toward the bottom of the curtain and pointed at Amanda's shoes. Waiting for the signal from Ray that it was okay, Steven quickly tiptoed in to retrieve them.

Back at the door, Steven softly said, "You all have a blessed night, sir."

"Steven," Ray whispered before Steven had completely shut the door.

"What you may or may not have witnessed or heard here tonight is a private, personal, matter, never to be discussed. It would be very unfortunate if MBK security were to lose the contract with Zanderbilt due to a misunderstanding. Do I make myself clear?"

"Yes, sir, Mr. Durrant, perfectly clear."

Ray watched Steven close the door. He held on to his wife as if it were the very last time. Once she was no longer in his clutches, Donae quickly dressed. She requested that Ray make accommodations for her a taxi ride home. She insisted that Ray not come back to the house until some arrangements could be made concerning his lodging. Without hesitation, Ray regretfully complied. He gazed through his office window to watch as Steven helped his wife into the taxi. You'd have thought Donae had just finished a boxing match. Her hair was now pulled into a ponytail, her puffy eyes and her red nose justifed Ray to feel like the despicable man he'd become. His injudiciousness had surely cost him the only woman he'd ever really loved. He had hurt her again. How could he have been so foolish?

Chapter 8   *Raymond*

'Again...again...again'...Ray uttered the word over and over. Donae's voice echoed through his heart, taunting him miserably. He dropped his head in disbelief at the night's events. The evening had been unmistakably bittersweet, and just when he thought things couldn't get any more bitter, he noticed something familiar in the trash next to his desk. Seeing the small, oval-shaped object caused his heart to drop, and he felt short of breath. He opened Donae's birth control packet, staring at the perfectly lined circle of pills, noticing that she hadn't removed any in the past four days.

Ray fell back into his office chair, laughing, because it was more ironic than anything. He truly wanted to cry. Sitting there, he felt self-disgust well up in his soul. His life had suddenly fallen into total disarray. Tonight he had been given a prestigious position with a top-notch company, but there was no one to share his victory with. A light knock on the door interrupted Ray's pity party. He wasn't in the mood for visitors. The congratulations and butt-kissers could wait. If he couldn't be with his wife, he would rather be alone.

"Not right now," he called.

"Okay, Mr. Durrant, I'm sorry to disturb you."

"Steven... is that you?"

"Yes sir, Mr. Durrant, it's me," he answered.

"Come in, Steven."

"Mr. Durrant...."

Ray sighed. "Steven, you don't have to call me Mr. Durrant. You can call me Ray or Mr. D."

"Okay, Mr. D, I just wanted to let you know that your wife made it home safely. I asked her to call security and let us know."

"Thank you, Steven. You're a kind man."

"She asked me to bring this to you," Steven partially smiled.

Taking a deep breath, Ray mumbled, "Let me have it."

With much regret, Steven handed him the white, sealed envelope. Once he held the envelope in his hands, Ray knew from the way it felt that it was Donae's opulant wedding ring set, which sparkled like brilliant stars at midnight.

"I'm sorry, Mr. D."

Ray groaned. He got up and walked over to the window, chuckling as he observed his colleagues staggering to their vehicles. Even those who weren't intoxicated seemed to be cheerful. He wished he and Donae would have been leaving the same way.

"Steven, how old are you?" Ray asked, still looking out the window.

"I'm thirty-six."

"You married?"

"Widowed. My wife and six year old son were killed in a car accident."

Shocked, Ray murmured, "I'm sorry. I didn't know."

"It's okay, the Lord brought me through that tragedy."

Steven's tone was calm and even. "So, you believe in God?" Ray asked.

"Oh yes, without a doubt, tried and true."

"So, you're one of those holier-than-thou brothers, huh?" Ray asked.

"No, Mr. D, I wouldn't say that, but I will say this: I love Him, and I wouldn't trade my relationship with Him for anything in this world."

"Why do you love Him so much?" Ray released the breath he unknowingly had been holding. Steven exhaled, too.

"Because, He put up with me. When I gave up on myself, He still had faith in me."

"Can I ask you something real personal?" Ray said slowly.

"Did you ever cheat on your wife?"

"Not with a woman," Steven replied.

Ray turned from the window and raised his eyebrows in Steven's direction. "I know you aren't, well, you know," Ray said, perplexed.

"Nah, man," Steven smiled.

"I ain't got that issue. My mistress was alcohol, and boy did I love her," he said, shaking his head.

Ray laughed. "Whew! You had me nervous there for a minute."

"Everybody has their own struggle. I won't judge the man who struggles with that particular issue. We all do something that's not acceptable to God. Your sin may not be my sin, but we all got something we're struggling with."

Ray took a deep breath. "I really messed things up with my wife. She'll never forgive me."

Steven paused before he spoke. "She still loves you. I could see it in her eyes. As long as you've got love, you've got something to build on, but even if you didn't have love, God can do all things."

Ray looked up at the man. "You really do believe that, don't you?" he sounded convinced.

"There is nothing too hard for God," Steven replied.

"Do you think He can fix this?"

"I know He can. He's God, but sometimes He has to work on us first," Steven said, pointing to himself.

"God wanted to heal me, because the man I was before was ready to self-destruct. He knew I could be a better man."

Steven's words echoed in Ray's heart like a boomerang.

"A better man..." Ray said, remembering his words to God while holding Donae.

"But, man," Ray said as he paced the floor.

"Being saved is hard. I remember when Donae got saved, everything changed. She stopped going to the club, drinking, all the freaky stuff we used to do. She shut it down, man. I mean the change was good to some extent, but I liked the old Donae, too." He said with humor

Ray paused. "There are so many rules: you can't do this, you can't do that. This church she goes to said she couldn't wear pants or make-up."

Steven laughed. Ray was in rare form. "I understand what you're saying, Mr. D. It sounds like she just needs to study the Word a little more for herself and find the right church.

"Holiness is not just about wearing makeup, pants, clothes, music, or hanging around saved people or not. It's about a lifestyle, a personal relationship. God doesn't care about what people look like. He cares about their heart."

"So, in other words..." Ray grinned.

"He's not focused on the outside of a person. He's focused on the inside."

"There you go, man," Steven smiled.

"I like this side of you, Mr. D. You're okay with me."

Ray said, "I do have a less civilized side. I seldom show it, but trust me, it's there. Please, Steven, I'd be offended if you call me anything other than Ray."

"Are you sure?" Steven smiled.

"Mr. D, I'd hate for your company to lose its contract with Zanderbilt," he said in his baritone voice.

Ray chuckled. "I did go there, didn't I? Sorry, man."

"It's cool, Steven said.

"It's not that serious. I don't take it personally."

Steven was honored that Ray had opened up to him. He really was a nice guy.

"So, tell me, Steven, what do I do next?"

"God is the answer, no matter the question. Give it to God."

"Come on, Steve. Man, I can't get saved. I'm not ready yet. I still curse a little, drink a little, lie a little, I'm a cheater, I'm a cutthroat, power-driven, money hungry, selfish...."

"Yeah, yeah, Ray. I know," Steve smiled.

"But we're the ones He loves to transform: us jacked-up jokers."

Ray's ego, self-confidence, and pride dropped into the abyss of shame. Humility overshadowed him. The room fell silent. The only thing heard was Ray's sobs. Steven didn't speak. He gave Ray his time with God. Several moments later Ray looked up.

"I'm going to church Sunday to get saved. Where is your church?"

Writing down the name and address Steven's heart fluttered. "I'm proud of you, man. This is the best decision you could have ever made, but can I enlighten you?" he continued as Ray nodded.

"You don't have to wait till Sunday. You can be the King's Kid right now."

"Really – this minute?" Ray seemed surprised.

Steve nodded and he stood behind Ray's chair. They dropped their heads as Steven prayed aloud. "Father, we humble ourselves before You now. We honor You Lord for who You are. You're a God, who is gracious and merciful. We ask You today to forgive us of our sins and we ask Jesus to come into our hearts. We acknowledge Jesus as the Christ, the Son of the living God and that He died for our sins. We thank You for the blood of Christ that was shed for the remission of sin and we thank You Lord for saving us. In Jesus name we pray, Amen."

The new friends hugged one another. Ray smiled, and he felt good, as though a weight had been lifted off his shoulders. He knew he had a long road to travel, but he was ready for the journey.

"Now listen, Ray," Steven began.

"We're not perfect. We're men saved by grace. It's important that you find a church that walks in truth. You need to be fed the Word of God so you can learn and grow. That's important. I want you to take all that drive, power, energy and zeal you have for business and success, and use it to glorify God," he paused briefly and then smiled.

"Remember, temptations will come, so be prepared. Resist the enemy, and he will flee. You can do this, bro. I need you to survive, so let's strive to be better men, allow God to build the new man one piece at a time. It's a process, not a quick fix"

Ray nodded. "Thanks, Steven. Just pray for me and my family. I got to get this right."

"I'm praying for you, brother. We're going to get through this together. God can do anything but fail. I know this for sure."

They shook hands, and Steven left. Ray talked to God for a few more minutes. He felt like a new man. Ray never thought that would have been possible tonight. He dialed the number to the Westin Hotel to reserve a room. Then he grabbed his suit jacket, his brief profiles, and left his ego and his pride on the floor of his office. He laughed a little before turning off his office light: *Got to save them trees, baby!* Opening his office door, he froze instantly. He closed his eyes and opened them again to see if he was dreaming.

"What are you doing here?"

"Finding out how appreciative you are, Mr. Plant Manager," Amanda winked.

"You didn't think I'd let you get away, did you?"

"Amanda, go home. It's been a long night, and I can't take anymore. This is going to stop... tonight." Ray rushed by Amanda.

"Ray!" Amanda yelled at his back.

"Ray!" she yelled again, beginning to start a tantrum

Ray continued to walk without looking back. He shook his head in amazement, understanding the words that Steven had just spoken. The devil must have really been furious, and he sure didn't waste any time bringing on those temptations...

****

Judge Dicapio glanced through the papers that had been set before her one last time.

"Is there anything else before I make my ruling?" she asked the attorneys.

Against his better judgment, Donae's attorney Bryon didn't ask for spousal support, pension, 401-K savings or anything else. He had educated her to the fact that she had grounds for adultery, which were means by which she could take Ray to the cleaners, but Donae knew that whether they were together or not, Ray would make sure she and the children were well provided for. She didn't see the need to drag him through the mud. Both attorneys nodded in agreement that the information was complete. Ray became fidgety at the thought that this was really it. His heart started pounding, and he began to perspire heavily.

The judge looked down through her gold-rimmed glasses and began to state her decree.

"I hereby grant dissolution of marriage to Donae Elaine Durrant and Raymond Justin Durrant on this day, August 15th."

Ray felt faint as she continued.

"Full custodial rights of the two minor children, eight-year-old Raymond Justin Durrant II, and thirteen-year-old Ramona Michelle Durrant, are awarded to Mrs. Durrant until the minor children reach the age of eighteen. Weekend visitations are hereby granted every other weekend to Mr. Durrant, alternating holidays between both parents...."

She continued issuing her ruling, but Ray heard nothing beyond her granting dissolution of marriage. He slumped back in his chair as the judge kept talking. Ray's attorney Billy asked if he was all right. His demeanor had changed. Ray looked pale, his nose started bleeding, and sweat was pouring down his face.

"Is he okay?" the judge asked, concerned.

Ray's queasy look alarmed her, and she stood up.

"Can we get some water over here?"

Billy looked around for help.

"Something is wrong with him."

Donae rushed to his side, remembering how, many years ago, he had a similar episode after a college basketball game.

"Ray, honey, what's wrong?"

Donae teared up, removing her Gucci scarf from her neck to stop his bleeding nose. The bailiff dashed in with bottled water. Ray now had an audience as they watched him gulp down the whole eight ounces.

Judge Dicapio sat back down once Ray appeared stable, but she carefully observed the situation that swiftly unfolded before her. She watched Donae closely as she gently comforted Ray. Her tender touch and genuine affection deeply moved the judge. She saw Ray whisper something to Donae. Although Donae said nothing with her lips, her heart spoke eloquently through her eyes. The judge sensed the two of them were concealing something intense. In her twenty-eight years on the bench, she'd seen and heard it all. She certainly had the ingenuity to read between the lines when it came to discerning the truth. She was eagerly about to shed light on a buried treasure.

"I think he's okay," Ray's attorney said.

"It's probably his nerves. He got warm, and it caused his nose to bleed."

"Mr. Durrant, are you o.k.?" the judge asked.

"Yes and no, your honor, but I will be alright."

"May we please continue?" the Judge inquired.

"Mr. and Mrs. Durrant, please have a seat," the judge smiled.

Donae got up to move to the other side of the room near Byron, who seemed shaken.

"No, Mrs. Durrant, please, have a seat beside your husband," the judge pointed.

Donae complied with perplexity as she looked to her attorney for answers. He shrugged his shoulders, baffled.

"I need to ask the two of you some questions, and I demand that you answer them truthfully," Judge Dicapio sternly commanded.

"Mrs. Durrant, I will start with you."

Donae sat next to her soon to be ex-husband, shaking. The judge's tone was making her uncomfortable. Her legs wouldn't calm down, fear gripping her whole body.

"Have you given yourself adequate time to decipher your feelings?"

Donae didn't say anything, but a tear fell from her eye.

"Do you still love your husband and want your marriage to remain intact?" the Judge asked sympathetically.

Tears now uncontrollable, Donae didn't answer as she watched the officer approaching with a box of tissues.

"I see," the judge commented.

"Mr. Durrant, it's your turn," the Judge smiled.

"Do you still love your wife?"

"Yes, Your Honor, I do with all my heart."

"Do you want to preserve your marriage?"

"Yes ma'am, Your honor. I would do anything for that opportunity."

Judge Dicapio sighed heavily. "Have you known your wife in the last twelve months?"

Fully understanding her question, Ray knew the judge meant in the sense of Adam knowing Eve. He had learned that in Bible study months before at Steven's church.

"Do you understand my question, Mr. Durrant, or do I need to elaborate?"

"I understand your honor." Ray paused and breathed deeply.

Before he spoke, he stared at Donae. Her glossy, beautiful eyes were filled with hidden love, fear, anger and anxiety.

"Mr. and Mrs. Durrant, please face me," the judge spoke compassionately.

Both attorneys' eyes were fixed on Ray. He'd never felt this much pressure in his entire life.

"Yes, your honor, I have," he admitted, exhaling deeply.

"Your honor," Donae interrupted to her defense.

"I was drinking the night it happened."

"So are you honestly telling me you were in a drunken state, unaware of what was taking place?" the judge asked.

Donae dropped her head in shame, especially since the truth was she was nowhere near drunk. She had just wanted Ray to think she was. She drank half a glass, but poured the other two glassfuls in the sink. While he didn't know that, she was too full of pride to admit that she wanted to make love to him because she was lonely.

"No, your honor, I was aware of what I was doing," Donae admitted, blushing.

Well, shame on your attorneys if they didn't disclose this information, which I am more than confident they have done so, but in the state of Virginia, to be intimate during a legal separation, renders the separation null and void. Thus, I'm ruling against a divorce decree at this time."

Ray's heart danced as he secretly praised God in his heart. He gave silent thanks for this second chance. He knew it was God who had made this miracle happen. He also thanked God for giving him a nosebleed and some acting ability.

"Mr. and Mrs. Durrant, I'm recommending that the two of you to go through six months of counseling. If at the end of counseling you still want to pursue this divorce, you will have to file another legal separation. Mr. Durrant, you will still be obligated to comply with the temporary child support order and to pay the mortgage payments of the home in which your wife and children reside for an extended twelve month period. As stated prior, if at the end of the twelve months, one or both of you wish to proceed with the divorce, I will grant it pending that you've not been intimate with one another. Do I make myself clear?" she looked over her rimmed glasses.

Ray and Donae nodded in agreement.

"This is my ruling," she smiled, as she slammed her wooden gavel on the desk.

"I wish you blessings," she smiled at Donae.

"Good day."

After the whirlwind shock, both attorneys asked their clients to keep them informed of updates.

"I won't need to update you, Byron," Donae told her attorney, appearing to have gained some backbone.

"I will comply with the judge's order. However, I want to proceed with the divorce twelve months from today."

She spoke firmly and rushed out of the building. Ray started behind her, but stopped. He realizing it may be best to give her some time.

Byron shrugged his lanky arms, looking directly at Ray and Billy.

"Oh, well, fellas, I guess I will see you in twelve months."

He shook hands with Billy and Ray, and slowly walked away, as if in a daze. Ray and his attorney walked together through the double doors. Outside, Ray handed his lawyer a small yellow envelope and stated.

"This is for your wasted time."

Opening the envelope addressed to him, Billy gave a wide grin.

"You were going to tell it all along, weren't you?"

Billy looked incredulous.

A man's gotta do what a man's gotta do," Ray shrugged.

Billy put the five one hundred dollar bills in the wallet inside his suit pocket. "Thanks for the tip, Ray, but it wasn't necessary," he said.

"Oh yes it was," Ray disagreed.

"You didn't know it, but God used you today as my supporting actor."

Billy laughed, not really knowing what Ray meant. "Well, Ray, you've got 365 days to change your wife's mind. You better try to drop it like it's hot, as my niece says."

"Every chance I get," Ray smiled.

Ray sat in his Range Rover, thanking the good Lord. In all his thirty-eight years on earth, he had never kissed and told, but he'd never been as happy as he was today to tell he'd gotten some "nookie," to good purpose.

Chapter 9   *Ivy*

My God, why in the world would you open this door for me? I'm terrified to walk through it. You know my struggles, God, I just don't know if I'm ready, and I know me. I'll disappoint you. I don't want to abuse mercy, and I don't want grace to get tired of covering for me. Help me, Lord. Every time I think about how you didn't expose my dirt, my awful weakness, it reminds me of just how wonderful you are. Your patience in allowing me time to get my mess under subjection and your love reminds me how special I am to you, no matter how undeserving I am.

People have a way of reminding you of who you once were even when you would rather forget. The truth is you can never really escape your past. Ivy thanked his Heavenly Father for being a God of second, third and fourth chances. He promised God that once he conquered his issues, he'd teach other men the way to conquer theirs. At times like this he often wondered why God wouldn't remove his temptation. His desire to please God and the desire to feed his flesh were in a daily battle of internal conflict. He often thought of the Apostle Paul's "thorn in the flesh" and was grateful to not be the only believer who struggled with sinful desires.

During these times of reflection, Ivy had to admit that when he had stepped foot in the church over nine years ago, he wasn't looking for God. The church had needed a musician, and after graduating college he could use the second income of $300 a week to help pay for his student loans. When he started out at Mt. Calvary Baptist Church, he was only supposed to play back-up on the keyboards, but once they found out he could sing, too, it turned into a full-time job as Minister of Music. He was young, educated, good-looking, but single, and the women at the church sure were pretty. His anointing alone attracted all the eligible women (along with a few ineligible souls), and his genuine effort to do the right thing in the eyes of the Lord didn't always prevail.

After years of indulging his passion with more than a few young ladies in the church, he and Bishop Boozer had to have a man-to-man talk. Bishop strongly encouraged him to consider seeking a wife with which to settle down. His exact words were the following:

"Son, you don't want to play with God, and as faithful as you appear to be, I refuse to allow you to come in the house with which God entrusted me and play 'house' with my daughters in Christ."

Bishop Boozer's words rang true. Ivy's conviction about his "double life" had started long before he and Bishop had their conversation. In all honesty, some of the strippers he gave dollar bills to at the downtown club on Saturday nights were coming to church on Sunday morning, placing the bills back in the collection plate. It was at that point when the spirit of God gradually started working on his heart, forcing Ivy to realize that deep change was needed in his own life before he could truly help others.

Once Bishop Boozer noticed God tugging at Ivy's heart, he watched the Music Minister for a while as he continued to grow in Christ, remembering how he, even as senior pastor, likewise lived by grace. He took Ivy under his wing and began mentoring him in the ministry with activities like breakfast Bible studies and church men's golf outings. He encouraged Ivy to study God's word daily and pray for direction and understanding, which wasn't so farfetched for Ivy to accept, since JoAnn, Ivy's mother, had raised him and his sister, Courtney, in the church. Ivy knew the path to salvation and traveled it, but he sometimes took shortcuts that always got him lost. He would have to discipline himself in order to stay on the straight and narrow.

Bishop Boozer discovered as the years went by that there was much more to Mr. Ivan Jessie James than met the eye. He had a higher calling in his life that simply needed cultivating. Being a Minister of Music would come secondary to his anointing as a minister of God's word. As trifling as the boy was, he could preach his heart out. The more Ivy studied God's Word, the more he understood and was able to apply it to his life. The Holy Spirit gave him insight far beyond his years. The manner in which he ministered to the congregation was raw and uncut. The more he remained honest and transparent with the congregation, the more found their way to Christ. He pushed aside the rules and religious rituals, and encouraged the members to just attend weekly services. He let them know that although God had saved him at the age of eight, God was still saving him every day. At times Ivy considered his anointing a gift *and* a curse. Although he had an awesome ability to preach and sing praise, he still possessed a profligate generational curse that he just couldn't shake.

Every now and then he dabbled discreetly behind Bishop's back with women who flat out refused to let him live right. Absurd as it may sound, it was true. Every attempt he made at rejecting their advances, the flirty women kept dangling their wiles in his face, literally. Women sat in the front pews, having left their unmentionables at home, with short skirts on, trying to persuade him to pursue his desires. His struggle to do right often took a back seat to his flesh. He wasn't proud of the fact that sometimes he won and sometimes he lost, in spite of his valiant effort to live a Godly life.

When Yolanda Harris stepped foot through the doors of the sanctuary, seeking salvation for her wicked ways, he was certain he could assist her in walking down the path of righteousness. Ivy recognized Yolanda instantly. He could never forget the radiant beauty and those deep eyes that drew him in, and the lovely smile that oozed pure joy. Her newfound love for God helped *Him* want to become more committed. Whenever he was around her in Bible study or church dinners, he wanted to be a better person. He had known after only five minutes of talking to Yolanda that she was going to be his wife. His deep love for her, along with her vow of celibacy until her wedding night, had Ivy down on one knee opening a ring box after twelve weeks of dating. Needless to say the engagement lasted only a short three months.

Ivy had to hire security to be at the church on the day of their wedded bliss. Several women he had been sleeping with wanted to mug him once they realized they weren't going to share his last name. Ivy purposely asked Bishop Boozer to leave out the part during the ceremony where he would ask if anyone objected, in fear that it might incite a riot. He swept Yolanda off her feet with fine dining, lake cruises and picnics in the park. He treated her like a princess and promised she'd never want for anything. After they married, he continued to keep that promise.

It was a dreadful scandal that caused uproar in their lives. Ivy still didn't understand why sister Sheppard had lied about him by telling the church that he had fathered her unborn child. He swore he'd never had anything to do with her but have a few friendly conversations. Unfortunately, by the time the truth came out, the damage was done. The hurt and pain were intolerable because some church members actually believed the lie that came from this woman who'd only been a member of the church for two months. The ridicule he received Sunday after Sunday was nearly impossible to work through, not to mention the unfair treatment Yolanda received after taking a stand to support her husband against the brutal accusation.

It was when Bishop Boozer asked Ivy to step down as Associate Pastor that crushed him the most. Ivy questioned if his decision had anything to do with his latest teachings. He'd discovered some things in the word of God that contradicted the churches way of doing things. Bishop expressed it was only to allow some of the negative publicity to die down, but Ivy wasn't so sure he believed that wholeheartedly. He felt it may be a mixture of the two. It depressed Ivy miserably to know his Bishop, mentor, and friend had no faith in him. Especially since in this instance, he really was innocent. Yes, it was true that during his first years in ministry he had made some bad mistakes, but he had matured now, had grown in the ministry and was proud of how close to God he'd become. It was also true that he still struggled as an imperfect human, but the flesh's victories were becoming fewer, and his spirit had blossomed into a willing vessel sought to be used by God.

Although his position was reinstated shortly after a paternity test proved 99.993 percent that he was not the father of Phoebe Sheppard's child, the church had nearly stoned him. His wife Yolanda did sneak in a few little pebbles only because even she inwardly harbored a small doubt that Ivy was telling the truth. As he thought about it, the truth was that he really couldn't blame anyone for feeling the way they did. His past recklessness had fueled many doubts, and Yolanda, aware of her husband's deep-rooted issues, had every reason to believe that Ms. Sheppard's accusations could very well have been a possibility.

It seemed bittersweet, when months later; Bishop Clarence Monroe called Ivy from his hometown of Richmond, Virginia to ask him to consider interviewing for a pastoral position at Mt. Emanuel Ministries. Coming back to his hometown of Richmond to pastor a church was the last thing Ivy would have chosen to do, but he sensed it was God's leading. The scandal at Mt. Calvary had left him frustrated and disillusioned. A change would be good and was much-needed for him and his family. He would be lying if he said he had never thought of one day pastoring a church, but he knew that when that day came of course, he would be ready. However, a move back to Virginia would cause him to face his past – a past he had tried so desperately to forget. He had to make some wrongs right. He had to seek forgiveness. He was fully aware it wouldn't be a stroll in the park, but God had opened the door. With much reluctance, Ivy would fearfully walk in.

Ivy flew down from Maryland to Virginia three times to meet with the trustees and deacons and to preach a sample sermon. Once they heard him preach, the decision was nearly unanimous. His next two visits were to negotiate a salary and find a house to purchase. There were a few good reasons to move back. He could now spend more time with his mother, JoAnn, who had recently been diagnosed with Alzheimer's disease, as well as enjoy an opportunity to finally spend more than a few random days with his five children who lived there. He was grateful to two of his children's mothers for allowing his oldest son, Nicholas and his middle daughter Ebony to come down on Holidays and summer vacation.

Ten weeks after his move from Baltimore, Maryland, Pastor Ivy stood in the prayer room of his beautiful new home in the wee hours of the morning with closed eyes and a heavy heart. The flickering light from the cucumber melon scented candle lit the small, pitch black room intimately. A soft melody played peacefully in the background as Ivy slowly swayed back and forth. He reminisced about how the mercy of God had carried him through some of the most trying times in his life. Even when he wanted to give up and go back to his worldly ways, God had to continue to show him grace.

Kneeling, Ivy prayed until it was time for the sun to come peeking through the window of the room. His mind had tossed and turned most of the night. His nightmares kept him up. He even considered asking the doctor for a prescription for sleeping pills. His nerves were beginning to get the best of him. Anxiety had a grip on him that refused to let loose. Meanwhile, his bowels had no grip, keeping him sprinting to the bathroom. He would have to get it together. This Sunday morning kicked off the first day of the men's conference. The women were welcome, too, of course, but the rest of the week was closed off to the ladies, reserved only for men thirteen years and older. The conference speaker was Apostle Dexter Reed, an exceptional evangelist with a ministry based out of Orlando, Florida, that aired on primetime television.

Ivy's cousin and armor-bearer, Kevin, his late Uncle Russell's son, had picked up Apostle Reed from the International Airport the previous night and safely escorted him and his traveling companions to their deluxe hotel accommodations. Pastor Ivy invited them to dinner at one of Apostle's favorite upscale restaurants and the men enjoyed a pleasant evening of fellowship and relaxation.

Apostle Reed shared with Pastor Ivy that the Lord hadn't allowed him to rest for the last three days in preparation for the men's conference. He'd mentioned that the Holy Spirit had been showing him faces of men and women whom he did not know, which was unusual for God to do. He said he was excited about how God was already working in his heart and soul for the men of Pastor Ivy's congregation. Pastor Ivy shared the excitement and a little bit of anxiety. He knew this man of God only through word -of -mouth and from watching his ministry on television. Ivy could only pray that he was bringing Mt. Emanuel good news as opposed to a word of rebuke, but whatever the word was, he couldn't run from it.

Ivy lathered his hands and rinsed the white suds off with lukewarm water. He tried not to wake his son Bryson or Yolanda as he tiptoed back toward his prayer room, but when Ivy heard the sound of the shower spraying from the master bathroom, he got excited. He quickly stripped off his boxers and white t-shirt and eagerly made his way to the locked door. "Dang it!" he shook his head, admitting defeat.

He twisted the knob again, but it refused to turn. "Yolanda," he knocked softly, but hard enough for her to hear.

"Have you stepped in the shower yet, baby," he asked, hoping she was standing on the other side of the door in all her glory.

"Yes, Ivy," she answered.

"I'm already in."

"Why did you lock the door on me?"

"You know why, Pastor," she shook her head and thinly smiled.

"Come on baby, just a little bit more before we head to church."

"Ivy – for goodness sakes."

Yolanda hurried to wash all the critical areas.

"You woke me up in the middle of the night to play. I need to get breakfast started before Kevin gets here. I asked him to join us for a nice, home-cooked meal before service."

Ivy stood at the door, in his birthday suit. Not wanting to give up that easily, he grabbed a blanket off the arm of the chair, wrapping it around himself. Quickly he raced to the laundry room to grab a screwdriver; rummaging through the tools he looked for something he could use since he didn't see the tool he needed.

"There you are, you little rascal."

His frown turned into a smile as he spotted the shiny metal object in the back of the toolbox. Determined to get into the shower before she got out, he twisted and turned the knob until he heard it pop. His smile went from thin to all dimples as he opened the door and walked in. But then his smile faded when Yolanda whisked by him, covered in her pink terrycloth robe. Ivy didn't say a word, but he grabbed the bottom of her robe and squeezed as she walked by.

"Do you have on panties?" he followed her into the bedroom.

"Absolutely," she smiled, loosening her robe to reveal her granny panties and bra.

"God is good," he said.

"All the time," she answered, relieved to have escaped his clutches.

"You've gotten crafty," he said as he followed her to the stairway, contemplating whether to yank off her bath robe.

"I have to be," she said.

"I'm married to a sex-craving maniac," she laughed.

97

Yolanda's soft, downy robe flung open like a cape as she glided down the stairs to put on a pot of coffee, leaving Ivy upstairs to cool his heat. The Lord knew she adored that man, if she'd have realized eight years ago she'd be considering purchasing a padlock for her bathroom door, she might have re-considered marrying him. Ivy was about to drive her crazy. She tried hard to be a good wife, which included forgiving past infidelities. Knowing his addiction to sex, she vowed she'd never deny him something that was rightfully his, so she guaranteed him at least one round whenever he wanted it.

Ivy sat at the kitchen table enjoying his freshly-brewed coffee. His cheesy eggs looked almost as tasty as his wife did sitting across from him with her cinnamon glossed lips. He loved the way she rocked her short spiked hair. Everything about her turned him on.

"So Pastor," Kevin took a bite of his jellied toast.

"I've got a feeling we're in for a treat this year. This men's conference has been the talk of the town," he smiled.

"I believe you may be right. I'm looking for some lives to be saved," Ivy replied happily.

"So how did dinner go with Apostle Reed last night?" Yolanda chimed in.

"Oh, it went well," Ivy answered.

"He seems like a very down-to-earth guy, given he has a congregation of over 13,000 members."

"Man, that has to be awesome," Kevin grinned with excitement.

"I'm sure it is," Ivy responded.

Switching tracks he said.

"I don't understand why you didn't interview for the pastoral position. You're just as qualified as I am, and you've been at Mt. Emanuel forever."

"Don't start that again, cuzzo," Kevin replied.

"I'm content being a minister. I'm not ready to be a pastor and probably never will be. Right now I'm waiting on God to send me a wife. I'm not stepping into that fire," he laughed.

Yolanda chuckled. "Wow, Kevin, it takes an extremely humble man to admit that and turn down such a prestigious position."

"Maybe," Kevin shrugged.

"But, I just know I'm not walking through any doors that God doesn't open for me. Too many people get caught up in the glitter and the gold. He's delivering me from pride and being puffed up. I have to stay behind the scenes, or I'll let people pump me up or worse, I'll pump myself up."

"That's doesn't seem like you Kevin," Yolanda seemed surprised.

"I've learned not to let people tell me who I am or who they think I should be because when or if I disappoint them, the same people calling you 'pastor' will be picking up bricks to throw."

"Preach, preach, preach, preach!" Ivy nodded in agreement.

Kevin's words rang true. He definitely had matured over the years. Ivy was proud of his younger cousin. His love for the Lord shone out of him. Ivy remembered him growing up as an arrogant little snot.

"Well, might I say, I celebrate your growth with you," Yolanda said.

"I'm going to see if our son is ready before his breakfast gets cold," she pushed away from the table.

"Did Steven call you last night?" Kevin asked.

Ivy admired his wife from behind, loving the way her tailored skirt clung snuggly to her wide hips, while her silk crème blouse accented her pecan-colored skin, and those bedroom eyes of hers…

"Ivy," Kevin tried interrupting his pastor's stare.

Ivy didn't answer but kept watching Yolanda until she turned the corner to go upstairs.

"Ivy," Kevin spoke a little louder.

"Huh?" Ivy answered, somewhat in a daze.

"Did Steven call you back about adding more security?" Kevin asked.

"Oh, yes," Ivy answered, with his mind back into the conversation.

"I told him we had more than enough security. Apostle Reed's posse rolled deeper than P. Diddy after Biggie got killed."

Kevin chuckled at the analogy, which hit home nevertheless.

"What did he say?" Yolanda asked Kevin as she turned the corner behind a sharp dressed younger version of Ivy.

Kevin repeated Ivy's comment, still chuckling.

"You're a nut," Yolanda shook her head after tossing her crumpled paper napkin to the trash and missing.

"I'm serious," Ivy explained.

"He had four cars full of nothing but security."

"Did they come later?" Kevin asked.

"I only saw three men at the airport."

"Yes, three car loads showed up as we were finishing up dinner."

"Wow," Yolanda bent over to pick up the napkin off the floor.

Kevin laughed aloud as he watched Ivy smile and stare at his beautiful wife's backside.

Ivy shrugged, admitting to being busted.

"What can I say…? I love my wife."

"Pray for me," Yolanda pleaded with Kevin, this time not missing the trash can.

"If you only knew the half of it."

"I ain't mad at you Pastor," Kevin smiled.

"Love your gift from God. I can't wait till he sends me mine."

"Finally, someone who agrees with a brother!" Ivy said.

"He that finds a wife finds a good thing…. Lord have mercy," Ivy stood up and shouted, giving his cousin a high-five.

The First Lady stood near the table, shaking her head at two grown men acting silly. She praised God in her heart that today she could at least laugh, because sometimes she just wanted to cry.

Ivy whipped the Mercedes Benz into the parking space that read "Reserved for Pastor James." Yolanda smiled at her handsome husband. He looked polished in his tailor made suit. She was proud that Ivy, now a pastor, had faced his fears. She understood his dilemma of returning to a place that held so many memories of a past full of pain and mistakes, but his transition with the church seemed to be working out smoothly. The majority of the members welcomed him and his family with loving arms, and the couple felt confident that God would one day soften the hearts of the ones who didn't.

Yolanda jumped right into the women's ministry. It desperately needed some help. The group wasn't getting much participation, especially since the former First Lady had passed away, and her husband, the former Pastor Franklin had fallen ill with prostate cancer. After those events, several congregational members left to visit other churches and never came back. In the short few months that Ivy and Yolanda had been there, participation had started picking up.

Wednesday night Bible studies were slowly growing, and the choir sounded exceptionally well with the few members they had. Once Pastor Ivy got on the keyboard and sang a few melodies, people started joining left and right. Word was getting around about Mt. Emanuel's new pastor. More and more locals were coming to check him out. Pastor's unorthodox way of preaching ministered to many middle-aged and young adults. For the last few weeks the twelve hundred seat sanctuary was close to being filled.

This morning's service was no exception. Gentlemen had already given up their seats to women and children, and were standing against the walls of the church nearly forty-five minutes before church started. The overflow rooms were filling up fast. Deacons had placed big screen television monitors in the study rooms for those who couldn't fit in the sanctuary.

"My goodness," Yolanda smiled in appreciation.

"Did Apostle Reed bring his whole church?"

"I doubt that," Ivy gave her a wide eyed grin.

"He has over thirteen thousand members and counting. I don't think this many people would travel from Florida. One thing's for sure, all these guests didn't come to hear me preach," he laughed.

"Now this is what we like to see," Deacon Norris bellowed through the corridor. Yolanda politely spoke and whisked away.

"Yes, Lord," Deacon Willis came from behind him to agree.

"Now Pastor, this is how we need to see God's house, packed to capacity."

"Well, I suggest the two of you stay on your knees praying for God to enlarge our territory," he answered.

"I agree with one thing," Deacon Bailey chimed in, as he walked up behind the three men.

"We certainly do need the church packed to capacity every Sunday to pay for your ridiculous salary and vehicle," he added curtly toward Ivy.

"Good morning, Deacon Bailey," Ivy answered respectfully.

Deacon Bailey gave a wry nod.

"Deacon Bailey, shame on you. This is your pastor, and you should address him as such. He is the shepherd of this house," the other Deacon frowned.

"I beg to differ," Deacon Bailey retorted.

"You old farts are the ones who insisted on hiring him. I voted strongly against it. I'd rather have a real man of God with integrity! A man is only as good as his word, and his word ain't worth...."

"Excuse me, gentlemen," Pastor Ivy kindly interrupted.

"I'm going to check on Apostle Reed. Service should be starting soon."

Pastor Ivy escaped the brewing fire beneath Deacon Bailey's breath, offended by his unfair accusation that he was overpaid. He had accepted the offer the church made and hadn't ask for a cent more. They were paying him a few more dollars than they had paid the former pastor, and Ivy felt that was fair. Deacon Bailey's deep rooted grudge against Ivy was like a migraine that never went away. The man was angry because Ivy had impregnated his only daughter, Alisha, years ago, never marrying her as promised, and leaving her to raise his grandson without a father. This was nearly a deadly mistake that almost got Ivy killed. Had it not been for JoAnn pleading for his life, Ivy might not have made it to his next birthday.

"Everything, okay sweetie?" Yolanda asked, concerned.

"I saw Deacon Bailey had you hemmed in over there."

"Yes, dear," Ivy answered, "He's just being Barry Bailey."

"Don't fret, Pastor." Yolanda reminded him who he was.

"God is still in control, and He put you here. There isn't a devil in hell that can change that."

The loud sound of the keyboard and bass guitar filled the sanctuary, causing First Lady to quickly make her way to her seat. The praise and worship team did an awesome job of ushering in the presence of the Lord. Spiritually hungry men and women seeking

God praised him in their own unique ways, with worshipful hearts and minds cleared of earthly concerns.

Ivy closed his eyes inhaling the sweet aroma of the spirit of praise, thinking how heavenly it was and how it must delight God. Taking his mind off his insecurities, he allowed this moment to be about God, giving God what He rightfully deserved, the praises of his people. His heart grew tender at the thought of the goodness and mercy of the Heavenly Father, and all that God had seen him through. Walking over to the keyboard, he grabbed the mic and began to sing a soft melody.

First Lady stood to her feet, waving her hand in the air. Every time Ivy opened his mouth to sing praise unto the Lord, it touched her soul. She knew how much her husband cherished his relationship with God. Knowing how Ivy would beat himself up at times about his imperfections, she teared up too, not only for him but for herself. She remembered the trespasses God had forgiven her, recalling a time when she was only attracted to drug dealers and powerful men with money. Now to see her man praising God, not afraid to cry out because he loved the Lord just that much was a precious sight in her eyes, and she found it very alluring.

Looking around the sanctuary, she couldn't find a dry eye in the house. People were slumped over, giving God everything they had from the deep pits of their souls. Apostle Reed walked onto the platform, hardly able to speak. His eyes were as pink as everyone else's. He addressed the women first.

"My fellow believers, I feel so at home. There is nothing like authentic praise. It's priceless to God. I thought I came here to give you the word, but I received something, too. I've fallen in love with Him all over again."

"Ladies, I want you to hear me," he paused.

"God is about to do something this week in the lives of men in this house and those under the sound of my voice. He is about to reconstruct this house."

"You don't understand," he said.

"Your men are about to arise. Your men will never be the same after this conference. You've fasted and prayed for a change; well, change is here. God is rebuilding this house, but he has to start with the men."

Loud screams came from women who caught hold of the word, and the sound filled the crowded room with gladness. A spirit of joy hovered over the place, and the Shekinah Glory rested there.

"Men.... Men.... Men, listen to me," the Apostle whispered.

Shaking his head he put the microphone down and lay his head on the podium while sobbing lightly.

"God has chosen this house to start an awakening in the hearts of His people. He wants you to know something, my sons."

He paused several moments.

"Thank you, Lord," he said aloud, as if someone was talking to him.

"God wants you to know, He sees you trying, and He says, 'Son, if you don't give up on Me, I won't give up on you.' He says He knows your struggle, but listen....," he sounded excited and began to shout.

"You're going to win! Win! Win! Win! I said, WIN! And trust me, sons, He's not only talking to you, He's talking to me, too.

"I know you've come here expecting me to whoop and holler, and make you feel good and encouraged in the Lord. Trust me; I had planned to do that. I'm sorry, I had one plan, but God had another. God wants his children to be delivered and set free today. Is that all right?" he asked the congregation.

In unison the congregation shouted a heartfelt "Amen! Apostle Reed jumped down from the pulpit and walked out into the aisles of the church, his ministry team behind him. He walked up to a young curvy woman in a dark purple dress who was bent over, wailing.

"Miss," he said.

She slowly looked up.

"Didn't God tell you, 'That was then; this is now'? How many times does He have to remind you that He doesn't erase your future because of your past? Let...it...go...!"

Once his confirmed words settled in her spirit, she couldn't contain her joy. She rushed into a corner and hid her face in her hands, crying uncontrollably. Walking up to a man in his seat with his head buried in his collar, the evangelist asked him to please stand up. The man got to his feet. You could see the sadness in his troubled features and bent frame shrouded in a wrinkled brown suit.

"Before you got here, you weren't looking for God, were you?"

The man nodded in agreement.

"Hold out your hands, son," the Apostle commanded.

"These are not your problem," he said still holding onto the man's hands.

"The Bible says in Proverbs 18:16, 'A man's gift makes room for him and brings him among great men.' God is placing you among champions. Embrace it. It's for the glory of God, son. I realize right now you may not understand fully, but you will," he said, squeezing the trembling hands he held.

"Don't allow this chaos to be a distraction to you. If they walk away, so be it. God has something wonderful in store for you."

The gentleman looked the man in his eyes, neither backed down from the stare, and amazingly, neither man felt uncomfortable. Both felt only cool relief flooding into their spirits. The man was so far down in the dumps; he needed desperately to believe. It was true he hadn't come there to find God. He came in search of a certain woman, hoping she would be there. When he didn't see her, his plan was to leave, but he couldn't. God had such a hold on him, he couldn't get out of his seat.

"What the enemy tried to use against you…"

Apostle dropped his head and jogged up the aisle a few feet, leaving the man as he watched, "Is the same thing…," Apostle jogged back toward the man.

"You're going to use to destroy HIM!"

As Apostle Reed embraced the figure before him, the man held on for a few seconds as if it was God himself. He didn't want to let go of the word.

"Let me explain something to you, people of the church. Just because I prophesied that Word to him doesn't mean it only applies to him,"

Apostle smiled, voice raised. A woman started praising God.

"Hallelujah! Glory, glory to God!"

"You see, she just got it," he said, glad that someone heard him in the spirit.

"A word from God is a word from God. He is no respecter of persons. So if something in your spirit stirred when the Holy Spirit said it to him, you grab the word and run with it too. The Holy word of God just fell on good ground in your heart, because it's His word. It WON'T come back void."

The atmosphere in the sanctuary couldn't be explained. You had to experience it. God was truly pouring out His spirit on men, women, and even children, all of whom were being filled. Walking up to another person, the Apostle motioned for an attractive young gentleman with worry lines around his eyes, wearing a white and blue shirt, to come forward. The man quickly excused himself to get out of the pew.

"Is that your wife?" He pointed at the woman sitting beside him.

The man shook his head affirmatively.

"Ma'am, can you please join your husband?"

The woman got up and made her way through the pew to the aisle.

"Sir, God says only one thing to you. God says He'll make your name great."

The man felt as though his knees were about to give out on him, but he tried his best to stand. How could this man have known to say those exact words? He could have used anything, but that. The Apostle had just confirmed a true word from God, leaving the gentle husband in total adoration of the power of God.

Looking to the man's wife, the Apostle said, "Ma'am," as she started to cry.

"God said if you'll give Him (God) one more chance…hear me, ma'am, God is saying not the person, but Him, just give Him one more chance."

The woman looked up at the ceiling as her chest breathed in and out. Her husband grabbed her as she cried in his arms.

"What God joined together let no man put asunder, not even you," he looked sternly at the woman in tears.

The women fell back in the pew, rocking in her seat, her husband kneeling down beside her, overwhelmed. Never in a million years would she have guessed this could be happening. Apostle Reed continued giving several people prophecies from God as the instrumental music played softly behind him. Several members of the congregation he walked up to and just whispered something in their ears, and then walked away. But whatever he said must have been true, from the way each one responded.

Finally he made his way back to the pulpit, exhausted. Everything that God had poured into him over the last three days was nearly gone, but he was determined to leave that church empty when he walked out those doors. God would pour more into him later, but he refused to let a drop of this anointing return to a hotel room with him. God wanted every bit to be left with His people.

"Where are Pastor James and First Lady James?" he asked.

First Lady made her way to the front while Pastor Ivy came down from the pulpit to join her.

"First Lady Yolanda," he sighed.

"You and I both know, I don't know you or Pastor James from Adam, but I want you and Pastor to confirm if the words coming out of my mouth are not from God. For You, Lady James, God said he knows you're tired."

First Lady fell to her knees. Ivy picked her up and held her close.

"First Lady, your situation should not change your praise, but your praise can and will change your situation. God is able, First Lady. His ears have been near to your heart."

Yolanda squeezed Ivy's hand. She had felt for many years that God didn't hear her cry. Her husband's sex addiction had stripped away every desire she had to be intimate. Making love was more like a job she worked seven days a week, and all she wanted to do was rest. Instead of fussing about it, she just gave in to keep the peace, but only the Lord Almighty knew how tired she really was of trying to keep her husband satisfied.

"Pastor?"

He looked at Ivy, who had a slight sense of fear. He didn't doubt for one second that what was about to come out of the other man's mouth was true.

"I'm going to say this, and then I'm headed back to my hotel room," he smiled.

"Things you can't fight in the flesh, you have to fight in the spirit. God said he told you when you were a boy, if you don't kill it, it won't die."

Ivy dropped his wife's hand and put his palm on his forehead. He reached up to the ceiling as tears fell from his eyes. He didn't care that he was the pastor of this big church. It meant nothing to him what anybody might have thought about him. This moment was between him and God. Nobody knew those words had come out of his daddy's mouth but his little sister Courtney and his late father. Ivy wept until he had no tears left as Yolanda rubbed his back lovingly.

Apostle Reed gave hardly any effort for the altar call; people were already heading toward the altar. He called out for salvation, rededication and prayer. The flooded altar embraced men and women from every direction. Even some children felt compelled and came forward in their innocence, heads solemnly bowed. He asked for the persons to whom he had given prophetic words to come to the front of the altar. Most were already there. He asked the congregation to stretch out their hands.

"What's your name?" he asked as he went down the line.

The lady that had darted away stepped to the mic first.

"Apostle, my name is Vanessa Reardon."

The couple introduced themselves as Raymond and Donae Durrant.

A man stood beside the Apostle, shaking. Apostle Reed held his hand tightly, for he had just given his life to Christ.

"My name is Malcolm…Malcolm Stuart."

Jada Butler, Harry Fulton, Sonya Garrison, Kollette Price, Angela Lewis, and Dwayne Smithfield were names of those called to the front row. Several others were identified as the church members uttered a corporate prayer. Over three hundred people gave their lives to the Lord, and more than one hundred told God they were coming back to Him. The Apostle looked out into the congregation to ask a question.

"Can I tell you what God wants you to know?" he smiled.

"God said for those of you who really want more of Him, He really wants more of you. He is about to show you just how good He is. Now for those of you who don't believe, that's up to you. You can believe this is just hype if you want to. It's your choice, but to those of you who do believe, I need you to believe on the word of the Lord and remember, His word will not come back void."

Instruments were played softly as the minister of music played melodies to sooth your soul.

Those that could, made their way from the altar. Ivy's eyes met Deacon Bailey's as Ivy stood from a distance and watched Lester Wilkins, a longtime friend of the Deacon as he helped carry him to his seat. People were still at the altar full of the Holy Spirit long after Apostle Reed gave the benediction.

Chapter 11   *Malcolm*

Malcolm's stomach was turning cartwheels, he was so hungry. He had been job hunting all day, starting at an agency and then stopping by a few better known companies that he hoped might have an opening. The one interview that he did get was one he wasn't feeling good about. Once he explained his past drug charge, most companies tried to shoo him away like an annoying fly. The unemployment office had penalized him for six weeks because he got fired, and Mr. Riley was pulling all the strings to extend the delay even longer.

To put the icing on the cake, his precious Telese had flipped on him, pulling out almost all the money in their account. Then his mother Louise called last week and said some court papers had come in the mail. When he made it to her house to read them, he was disappointed to find that Telese hadn't kept her word. She was ticked that Malcolm wouldn't agree to a forty-five day divorce, and filed for a temporary child support order for Layla and KJ The courts weren't concerned that Malcolm didn't have a job. He was ordered to pay $600 a month in child support for Layla and KJ in addition to the $450 a month he was already providing for Crystal.

It became clear that Telese was determined to get a quick divorce, but Malcolm couldn't understand what the freaking hurry was. She stopped paying half his car note and cancelled the insurance on his vehicle. He called several times to try and get her to be reasonable, but she refused to discuss the terms that she had insisted upon. It was like she had become a different person, one that he barely knew and didn't much care for, although he still loved her deeply.

The measly sum she'd left in the account would be gone by the end of the week since he had to pay for living expenses at the extended stay hotel he'd rented from week to week. He didn't like the idea of living in a hotel, but the lights, water, and phone were included. It was all he could afford. With the exception of the time when he had been incarcerated for that brief period in his past, Malcolm was at his lowest point. However, whenever he started to get depressed, he recalled what Apostle Reed had said about his gift making room for him and sitting among kings. Something inside Malcolm wanted to laugh, wondering if the Apostle's words could have been foolish, but he couldn't. He knew the words spoken to him nearly two months ago had to hold some truth. How could Apostle

Reed have known that Malcolm really didn't come to church that Sunday looking for God?

The truth was he entered the sanctuary looking for Telese. She had been attending Mt. Emanuel for some time, and frequently bragged about Ivan James, the new Pastor. Malcolm figured at the time Telese would be back from her Atlanta trip in time to attend service since she hated to miss church on Sunday. He hoped if she saw him there and realized he had gotten saved, she would believe that he really had changed and would be patient while he got himself together. When Malcolm realized his wife wasn't there, his plan was to leave, but something wouldn't let him get out of his seat. He was rivetted by the worship, and his heart started softening as he thought about how messed up he really was. He'd tried to pull himself together, but it wasn't working. Maybe he really did need Jesus. He felt sorry for himself and desperately wanted to change.

Malcolm made up in his mind that he would give faith a try. Nothing had ever made him feel like he did that day, when he left the church. Although his situation was still the same, he felt a renewed sense of hope, and even joy. Malcolm couldn't believe that he was now a saved man. He still cursed at times and had many ungodly thoughts, but he promised God at that altar that he would at least give it a shot. If Apostle Reed hadn't exposed his wrong motives that day, Malcolm probably wouldn't have believed a word that came out of the man's mouth. He wasn't sure how this prophecy was going to pan out, but one thing was for sure: he needed to believe in something bigger than himself. If Jesus was now his big brother, he definitely needed to get a hook up.

Malcolm's mentor, Steven Hill, was an awesome man of God. Steven had been a mentor for five years now, and was a security guard at a plant called Zanderbilt Industries. He was nothing like them suit wearing, Cadillac driving, so called men of God. He appeared to be just an ordinary man, but whenever Steven opened his mouth, love poured out of him. Listening to everything Malcolm had to say and never judging. He spoke life into every situation, and after talking with Steven, Malcolm always felt better. One particular thing Steven said that struck Malcolm was to do what he could and let God do what he couldn't.

Even when Malcolm told him about his anger issues and the physical abuse directed at his wife, Steven still didn't judge him. He saw the good in Malcolm in spite of his dreadful past. When Steven had called the previous evening and asked to meet, Malcolm had been feeling anxious. He really needed some encouragement. Steven mentioned he had some good news, and Malcolm had to admit for the last few months, all he'd heard was discouraging. Something good would surely be a blessing.

A short time later Malcolm pulled up at Moe's Family Restaurant. Moe's home cooking reminded both single men of the meals their wives used to cook for them. The food was great, and the owner, Moeisha Dillard, was known around the city for her friendly nature and motherly love. She ran the restaurant with her teenage sons. Moeisha's ex-husband had left her years ago for another woman. She said she put all her anger and hurt into her creative, tasty recipes and dishes. Now her restaurant was a thriving business to which people came from miles around for a taste of her home-cooked offerings. She had the best sweet potato cobbler this side of Virginia.

Malcolm, already seated, flagged Steven as he walked into the restaurant. Seeing Steven was like a breath of fresh air, and Malcolm felt the stress just roll off his broad shoulders. Steven walked up to the table wearing Levi jeans and a white T-shirt.

"What's going on, my brother?" Steven said as Malcolm stood up and gave the new arrival a friendly hug.

"I've had better days," Malcolm smiled at him warmly.

"How did your interview go today?" Steven asked, picking up his menu and opening it.

Malcolm shook his head. "It didn't go well. That felony drug charge is like a dark cloud hanging over my head."

Steven glanced up and smiled. "It's okay. God is showing His might. Try this temporary agency, I know the owner," Steven handed him a card.

"Thanks," Malcolm said.

"I'll try anything at this point."

"Just believe," Steven smiled.

Malcolm looked confused as Steven smiled. "Hold that thought," he answered his Gospel ringtone.

"Hello," he said, holding up his index finger as Steven looked over Moe's mouth- watering menu.

"Malcolm Stuart, you're starting to piss me off. I haven't gotten a child support check since who knows when," Sydney yelled.

Malcolm sighed, wishing he had looked at the caller I.D. before answering. "I don't have a job yet, Sydney. How many times do I have to tell you that? When I get a paycheck, you'll get your money. I can't give you what I ain't got. I'm barely making it."

Sydney smacked her lips. "You better use some of your old resources and get some fast money. This is ridiculous!"

His brows lowered. "No, you're ridiculous. I ain't going back to jail for you or nobody else!" Malcolm started to get loud.

"How am I supposed to feed your daughter?" She said angrily.

"You're a deadbeat!"

"Whatever, Sydney! I ain't got time to argue with you."

Steven politely continued studying his menu. "Well, whatever time you have you need to spend on finding a job. You already got child support reduced, and you can't even pay that. You are so pitiful!"

"No! Pitiful is a woman who sits around waiting on a check."

"Excuse me!" Sydney screamed in his ear.

"I work every day. At least I got a job!"

Malcolm rubbed his cheek, truly angry now. "Well, you don't act like it, the way you keep sweating me every time one don't come in the mail."

"You ain't even a real man! I don't know why I wasted my time with you. I don't need you, punk! I got a man!"

"You trifling ass…" Malcolm caught himself.

Looking over at Steven, Malcolm felt ashamed of his choice of words. Although Malcolm was heated, he held it together. He ended the call and glanced up. The look on Steven's face seemed to say "royally embarrassed." The diner's customers were staring in his direction as they listened to Malcolm lose his cool.

"I'm sorry," Malcolm said to Steven as he looked around, embarrassed.

"It's okay, Malcolm," Steven said with a smile.

"The storm will be over after a while," he laid aside the menu, ready to order.

"Come on man," Malcolm said, annoyed.

"You keep telling me that God is going to make a way and all that, but damn man," Malcolm caught himself.

"I'm sorry, but dang, man; I ain't got a job and won't have a place to stay after this week. Maybe Sydney is right. Maybe I do need to go back to slinging dope."

Steven looked at him sternly. "Is that what you really want? Why can't you just trust God? You've got power living inside you now, and He can teach you how to walk in your anointing. Inside your anointing is everything you need."

Malcolm grunted in exasperation. "Well, can this anointing get me a job?"

Steven laughed. "God can do anything but fail."

Just then Raymond Durrant walked into the diner, smiling at Steven as he approached.

"What's up man," Ray said excitedly.

"Nothing much. Raymond, you remember Malcolm from the men's conference a few months ago?"

"Yeah man, how could I forget what God said to you?" he smiled at Malcolm.

Malcolm stood up and shook Ray's hand, but Ray embraced him warmly with a hug. "So, Ray," Malcolm said, "how have you been?"

"Man, I'm doing great. God is really showing Himself mighty."

"I'm glad He's moving in somebody's life."

"Hey," Steven said, "none of that negative energy in here." He nudged Malcolm.

Moe sauntered over to their wooden table in her black apron. "Hi, guys! What can I get for three of my favorite customers?"

She sounded as comfortable as she looked, with a broad smile and twinkle in her eye. "I already know I want some sweet potato cobbler," Ray sang out, as he slid into the booth beside Malcolm.

"Me, too," Malcolm chimed in.

The three men ordered their hefty meals and continued talking as they waited for their food to arrive, knowing it would be fresh and piping hot, as always.

"So, Ray, how are Donae and the kids?" Steven asked.

"They're doing great," Ray smiled.

"I've got some even better news," he paused.

"Well?"

Steven gave him a serious look, waiting for Ray to say something. "I might be moving back home in a few weeks."

"What!" Steven sounded ecstatic.

"Were y'all separated long?" Malcolm asked cautiously, not meaning to pry.

"Yeah, we were actually in divorce court about to make it final, but God showed up."

"Wow," Malcolm said, giving Ray his full attention.

"I hope he does the same for me."

"Trust me, Malcolm," Ray looked serious.

"God can do anything; just trust him."

"I just told this man the same thing," Steven grinned, nodding in agreement.

Moe approached their table, carrying food on a platter. Everything looked steaming hot and completely delicious.

"Here you guys go."

She set down their plates before the men, smiling as they eagerly grabbed forks and knives.

"I'm about to starve," Malcolm said, taking a bite of the golden fried chicken.

"Looking for a freak'n job all day will wear a brother out."

"You're unemployed?" Ray asked, after swallowing a mouthful of some of the cheesiest macaroni he'd ever had.

"Yeah, I'm between blessings," Malcolm replied, taking another bite of chicken. He looked over at Steven.

"There you go," Steven smiled, about to sample his pot roast and mashed potatoes.

"Man, this is great," Ray said, savoring his meal. "What kind of work do you do?"

Malcolm looked up from buttering a golden yeast roll with a pat of whipped butter. "Any and everything," he replied.

"My last job was a cable installer, but I've done it all."

"You have any experience in manufacturing," Ray asked.

"As a matter of fact, I do. I was working for a manufacturing company before I…"

Malcolm stopped himself.

"Yeah, I got experience."

Ray speared his fork into a fresh side salad and brought a bundle of lettuce, radishes, tomatoes, onions and cucumbers bathed in savory dressing to his lips.

"You ever heard of a company called Zanderbilt Industries?"

"One of my buddies has been trying to get on out there for years. I applied, but they just ain't looking to hire a brother."

Malcolm consoled himself with a hefty bite of creamy cole slaw. Ray smiled as he chewed the last of the salad from the fork.

"Well, you and your friend go out there and put in another application. Call me once you hand it in."

Shaking his head, Malcolm said with a resigned air. "Okay. I appreciate it, brah, but I've got some stuff on my record. I will give it to my homeboy. His record is clean."

Steven didn't say a word, but the smile on his face was as wide as a river as he scooped up a forkful of green beans and ham.

"What you smiling at, Steven?"

The man looked like he had something up his sleeve. "I'm just listening and watching God do what he does best."

Ray smiled, too. "So what's on your record, if I'm not being nosey."

"Nah, man, you good. I served eight years in Jones County for felony drug charges."

He looked slightly embarrassed, keeping his head down as he pushed the glazed carrots around on his plate.

"Okay, but I think you should still apply," Ray said, pulling out a business card from his wallet and handing it to Malcolm.

Malcolm stuck the card in his shirt pocket without looking at it. Moe was headed their way again. "Can I get you gentlemen anything else?" she smiled.

She had already left the desserts without being noticed since the men were so busy chatting. "How was the sweet potato cobbler?" Moe asked all three men adding a gleaming smile.

"Ms. Moe, everything was great. I wish I could take you home with me," Steven said.

"Don't tempt me," Moe chuckled.

Malcolm swallowed his last bite of desert and looked out the large, wall size window casually. "Hey, Ray, can you let me out for a second?" he seemed anxious.

"Sure, man, that iced tea goes straight through me too," he laughed.

Malcolm raced out the restaurant door, pounding his fist in his hand. "So I guess this is why you want a forty-five day divorce, huh?"

Malcolm stood in front of Telese at the door of her car. Morris, his ex-best friend from years before, looked horrified as Malcolm came lunging toward him. "I knew you were trying to get with my wife, you no good SOB. I'm going to kill you!"

"Malcolm…no!" Telese jumped out of the car.

"Stop, Malcolm, you'll hurt him!"

"That's exactly what I plan to do!" Malcolm yelled as he punched Morris to the concrete.

"You back-stabbing bastard!"

"Stop!" Telese cried.

"Somebody help!" She cried in a panic.

Ray and Steven stormed out of the restaurant and raced toward Malcolm.

"Malcolm…man, come on. It's not worth it."

Ray tried to pull Malcolm off Morris, who was now bleeding from his mouth. Steven tried to pull him up.

"Malcolm, that is not the way to handle this, man of God, you're better than this."

Malcolm didn't hear a word either of them said. He kept punching because it felt so good to finally vent the anger, bitterness and disappointment he'd been holding back for months. Ray and Steven joined forces in trying to pull Malcolm off Morris, but Malcolm was as strong as an ox. They finally managed to pull the two apart. Telese rushed over to Malcolm and pounded his chest. Malcolm reared back to slap her, but Steven caught his hand.

"No, brother, this is the old you," Steven said, looking into his eyes.

Malcolm looked back at him, his hand still high in the air. Steven's words slowly sank in as his hand began to relax and fell to his side. Telese ran over to help Morris up, he could barely walk. Once she got him in the car she sped off, leaving skid marks in the asphalt road.

"I can't believe her," Malcolm said angrily, pumping his arm to restore circulation.

"Come on, brah, calm down," Ray urged.

"People are staring man. Get yourself together. You don't need to do this. You're better than this. Remember what God told you. You're going to sit among kings." Ray's tone was low and consoling.

Malcolm looked at Ray with water filled eyes. Ray's eyes were compassionate. "You don't know what God has in store for you. He might bring you back together or have something even better in store for you. We don't know, but I can tell you this. Let God tell you what to do. Let Him give you peace."

"Take him to my car, Ray," Steven said.

"I'm to going pay our bill."

"Hold up, let me give you some money," Ray said, reaching into his pocket.

"No man, I got it. Just get him to my car."

Ray walked an exhausted Malcolm over to Steven's vehicle and talked to him, brother to brother. He surprised himself with the words that were coming out of his mouth. He'd come a long way from finding salvation in his office that night. He had grown in faith to the point where he could quote the Word of God to Malcolm.

"Trust in the Lord with all your heart and lean not on your own understanding. In all your ways submit to Him, and He will make your paths straight."

"Ray, man, no disrespect, but stop quoting those Scriptures to me. I don't want to hear shit about God. Where is God now? My wife is having an affair with someone that used to be my best friend. I have no money, no job and am minutes away from being homeless, and you're telling me to trust God? I did...now look!"

Steven rushed back to the car and unlocked the doors. "It's a trick of the enemy, Malcolm. You're on the verge of walking in destiny. The devil's mad."

"Well, damn-it, I'm mad too."

"Get in the car!" Steven yelled.

"Now!" he added with authority.

Malcolm and Ray looked at each other in amazement, not used to hearing Steven shout. Malcolm got in the passenger's seat, still heated. Steven walked over to Ray.

"I'll take it from here. Just keep him in prayer. You and I know the power of God. This one is hard-headed," Steven said, and they chuckled in a low voice.

"Malcolm is as strong as an ox. I couldn't get him off of that boy. He's another Samson," Ray smiled.

"You're sure you want me to give him a job? You might want to talk to your boss about hiring him for security." Ray joked under his breath.

"Just make sure he fills out the application," Ray said warmly.

"I will, thanks, brother. Let me know when you move back in. I can help if you need me," Steven offered.

"It probably won't be necessary, but thanks man."

The two men gave each other a manly hug and went to their vehicles. Steven didn't say a word to Malcolm, who was sitting back in the passenger's seat with his eyes shut. He prayed inwardly for his dear brother, unable to imagine what he was going through. He did know one thing the devil didn't have any new tricks, only new faces. Steven had been saved long enough to recognize how the enemy worked. Not only had Malcolm heard an awesome prophecy from the Lord regarding his life, but the enemy had heard it too. He would do anything he could to block Malcolm from receiving what the Lord had for him. Steven was determined. No matter how much Malcolm fought, he was going to walk in the blessings that God had in store for him. A few minutes later, Steven pulled up to an old dingy building in a small alleyway.

"Where are you taking me, Steven? I just want to go home," Malcolm said, feeling sorry for himself.

"Just get out of the car," Steven said sternly.

"You're not my daddy," Malcolm growled.

"You're right. I'm not your daddy; God is. I'm your brother, and our Daddy wants me to make sure you get where He wants you to go."

Malcolm sighed.

Both men got out of the car and headed into the building. Right away, an old gentleman walked up to them.

"Hey, Steven, I haven't seen you in a while."

The man's beard stubble was gray and his cheeks were drawn. Malcolm noticed how lively and sharp the fellow's eyes were. Steven reached for the man's hand and shook it.

"I know, Mackie, how have you been?"

"What can I do for you?" Mackie asked with a grin.

"Mackie this is one of my good friends, Malcolm."

"Nice to meet you sir," Mackie smiled, revealing his missing tooth.

"How are you doing?" Malcolm seemed to have calmed down some.

"Can we get some gloves and get in the ring?"

Mackie gestured behind him.

"Sure, y'all go on in the back and get suited up."

Malcolm stared at Steven.

"You're kidding right?"

"No, I'm not kidding. Let's see what you got," Steven said.

"This is the perfect place to work out your frustrations and energy."

Malcolm laughed, "Man, I'll hurt you in there. Trust me, you don't want none of this."

"It's cool," Steven said.

"I'm not scared."

"Okay," Malcolm stretched his arms.

"I need a workout."

Both men walked to the back and changed into some clean sweat suits, and then met in the ring. Steven prayed, as he was changing, that the Lord would not allow Malcolm to beat him up too badly. Mackie's errand boy dinged the bell, and they both came out swinging. Steven got in a few hits, but Malcolm had him on the ropes repeatedly. Steven let Malcolm punch his body all over to work out the long held tension in his shoulders, back, and arms. He made hardly any defense but jabbed him when he could. When Malcolm was finally exhausted, he fell into Steven's arms, eyes spilling tears. His heart was heavy and the pain was harsh.

"It's okay Malcolm let it go, let it all out," Steven said holding his brother in Christ tightly.

"We're in this together."

Malcolm didn't reply. His heart was hurting bad. He couldn't speak. Steven's compassion for Malcolm ran deep. He too, knew what it felt like to lose his family. He'd never see his again until he got to Heaven. Steven walked Malcolm over to a punching bag.

"I want you to hit this. Whenever you get frustrated or mad, come in here and hit this bag. Your hands aren't to be used for violence towards others. That's not what God wants, but you can take out all your anger and frustration on this," Steven said, holding the punching bag steady.

Steven left Malcolm alone with the punching bag and walked over to Mackie, who was sweeping the concrete floor and pretending not to have noticed the impressive display of power in the ring.

"Mackie, whenever he comes in, you tell him everything is on the house." Steven handed Mackie some money.

"If you need more, just put it on my tab."

"Okay, Steven," Mackie answered, pushing the bills into his jeans pocket.

"That boy's got some power. I was worried about you."

"I was too," Steven said ruefully, holding his sore arm.

Malcolm hit the punching bag for several minutes straight. He had to admit he did feel better. Once he and Steven were back at Moe's to pick up Malcolm's car, Malcolm apologized for acting the way he had and thanked his friend for not giving up on him so easily.

"I'm going to see Moe to apologize to her, too, and then I'm heading home for some rest."

Steven gave his frequent sunny smile, "That sounds good. I want you to go to the company that Ray was talking about in the morning and fill out that application."

Malcolm sighed.

"Okay," he said.

"But I'm just telling you they aren't going to hire me."

Steven looked him in the eye.

"Let me tell you something. I rebuke what you just said. Life and death are in the power of your tongue. If you want the job, speak it and believe it. Do you know who your Daddy is?"

Malcolm smiled, "Every man should have someone like you in his life."

"Get you some rest," Steven said, and the two parted.

Malcolm got ready to turn the ignition. He glanced over in his passenger seat and noticed a white envelope, addressed to him. The letter heading had a Zanderbilt Logo on it. He opened the envelope to find $500 cash enclosed with a note:

"Malcolm, hold your head up, man, and don't give up. This is a gift to help you get on your feet. I know you'd do the same for me. I'm just helping you pick up the pieces until you can pick them up for yourself man. You be encouraged and always know I'm here if you need a friend... Ray"

Malcolm's heart danced, not because of the money, but because of the love. Ray didn't really know him from Adam, but his compassion for his brother in Christ was a treasure. He had hoped that one day he'd be in a position to bless someone like him. Malcolm sat back in the driver's seat and deeply sighed. He figured he'd take the long way home so he could just think. He decided he would call his sister Lauren in the morning and ask her if he could stay with them until he got himself straightened out. He loved his mother Louise, but he couldn't stand to be there too long, for it wreaked with the odor of Bengay.

The whole ride home, Malcolm kept seeing snapshots of Telese and Morris together. The more he thought about it, the madder he got. He couldn't understand how Telese could be so low. How could she treat him like that, knowing how much he loved her. What would the kids think? Every ounce of him wanted to go find Morris and rip him to pieces. That would only make matters worse. So, he would do the right thing and trust God. Malcolm looked up in his rearview mirror at the blue lights behind him. He knew he wasn't speeding. Maybe Morris had called the police on him, that no good punk. Malcolm gritted his teeth and pulled over to wait for the clean-cut young officer to get to his car.

"How are you doing tonight, sir?" the officer's tone was polite.

"I've had better days," Malcolm replied, trying to be cooperative.

"Did you know your left tail light was out?"

"No sir I sure didn't," Malcolm answered respectfully.

"Well, it is. Let me see your license and registration, and we'll let you be on your way."

Malcolm handed him the forms and waited for the officer to return. He thought about calling Steven so they could laugh at the trap the enemy was trying to set, but he decided to wait for morning. Minutes later, the officer walked back to the car, handing Malcolm his license and registration.

"Sir, did you know your license was suspended?"

"Suspended – for what?" Malcolm asked.

"You don't have any insurance, and you owe child support," he said in a different tone.

"Would you step out of your vehicle, please?"

Dazed, Malcolm pushed open the door and got out, wanting badly to punch the young officer in the jaw. "Put your hands behind your back sir," the officer ordered.

Malcolm sat in the back of the patrol car and watched the tow truck take his vehicle. He wanted to break down and cry about today's events, but what was the use? Tears wouldn't give him back his family.

Chapter 12　　　　　*Raymond*

Ray's private line rang. He set the production cost reports that he was reviewing to the side of his desk and answered. "This is Raymond," he said.

"Ray, what's up man? It's Steven."

Ray noticed Steven's voice sounded different and he became immediately concerned. "Hey man, you okay? You don't sound like yourself."

"Yeah man, I'm fine," Steven said, breathing heavily.

"It's Malcolm," he exhaled sharply.

"Oh, crap! What happened? I know he didn't go see that guy!"

"Nah man, he got pulled over by the highway patrol the other night, and now he's in jail."

"For what?" Ray sat straight up in his desk chair, fearing the worst.

"I don't have all the details of why they pulled him over. I just know the information they gave me at the detention center was that his license was suspended for driving without insurance and a bench warrant had been issued for failure to pay child support."

"Wow," Ray sighed.

"When it rains, it pours."

He rubbed his head with his free hand.

"It's okay. We just have to trust this is all part of God's divine plan," Steven replied.

"So how much is his bond?"

"I think they said $45,000." Steven's voice was low.

"How much does he have to pay to get out?"

"Around $4,500...I'm telling you, his wife, Telese...man she almost made me lose it." Steven groaned heavily.

"No, Steven, not you!"

"Yes, me," Steven said.

"Don't try to put me in this holier-than-thou box. I've told you guys I'm a man just like you."

"You do keep telling us that," Raymond agreed.

"I talked to Telese shortly after church service. She didn't know he was in jail, but she was sure to add her two cents about his being lucky Morris didn't press assault charges on him. Then she had the audacity to say he needs to sit in there and rot."

"No, did she?" Ray asked in surprise.

"Yeah," Steven confirmed.

"That's why I almost lost my cool."

"I can see why you'd be upset. First she cheats on the man, and then she flips on him. Did she know he wasn't working?" Ray asked.

"Malcolm said she did. He said she told him she would drop everything if he granted her a quick divorce," Steven said, disgusted.

"Wow!" Raymond shook his head.

"Do you need me to post his bail?" he offered.

"No, that won't be necessary. I'll post his bail, but if you could check in on him for the next few days, that would help. I'm going out of town for two days. I've got some personal business to see about."

"Sure, I can do that, but are you positive you don't need help with his bail? That's a lot of money Steven, and no disrespect, but security can't pay that much."

"No, buddy I can handle it. I've got some bail bonding connections," Steven laughed.

Suddenly Ray's office door flung open, and Amanda stormed in, face livid, fists clenched.

"We need to talk," she rudely demanded, breathing down his neck.

"Hey, Steven, let me put you on hold for one sec."

Ray pressed hold before Steven had a chance to reply.

"What's your problem?" Ray replied in a tight voice.

"I'm on a call. We can talk when I'm done," he said, getting up to escort her to the door.

He stood there without saying a word, waiting for her to move from the spot she was standing in. Amanda moved forward, close to his face.

"I'll expect you in my office within the next thirty minutes, or else."

Her perfume smelled strong and distasteful. "Or else what?" Ray asked.

"Just be there!"

She marched down the carpeted corridor, shoulders back, head held high as if to remind him that she was the commander-in-chief. Ray's secretary, a competent but meek middle aged woman shrugged to let Ray know she had had no way of stopping Amanda. Ray closed the door and locked it. He picked up the receiver.

"Sounds like you might need a prayer too," Steven said in a thoughtful tone.

"Yeah buddy, send one up for me if you have time," Ray chuckled.

"...now where were we?"

"I was about to tell you I'd call after I've picked him up, and will forward you Malcolm's address," Steven said.

"Okay, that sounds like a plan, and don't worry, he'll be all right," Raymond said.

"And oh, make sure to have him fill out that application." he remembered quickly.

"I sure will," Steven said.

"Thanks, man. God bless you."

Ray hung up the phone feeling bad for Malcolm. The guy had really caught a bad break. He was determined to do everything in his power to help Malcolm get back on his feet. Thirty minutes later Ray's secretary buzzed his line.

"Mr. Durrant, Ms. Sheridan is on line one."

Ray picked up the phone with a loud sigh.

"I'm on my way," he said, slamming the phone down in its cradle. Ray headed toward her office, trying to adjust the chip on his shoulder. He knocked on Amanda's office door and she slung it open. Her eyes were red as if she'd been crying. Ray sat down in the European chair in front of her desk.

"What's wrong with you, Ray?" she blurted, as she returned to her desk chair.

"Or better yet, what's wrong with me? I know you're attracted to me. Why can't we be together?" Amanda began to cry.

"I love you."

Ray shifted in his seat, not knowing what to say.

"I've given you everything: my love, my body, company power. What else do you want?"

She wiped her eyes with the balled-up tissue.

"Amanda, I don't know what to tell you," he sympathized.

"I never lead you to believe I was going to leave my wife. I've fought like hell trying to get my marriage back on track. I can't risk losing her because of an affair. Look at you. You're a gorgeous, woman. You can have any man you want. Don't waste your time on me."

"I don't want any other man," she gritted her teeth.

"I want you."

Ray looked the other way, not wanting to see her cry, embarrassed for her to see the black eyeliner running down her cheeks and her lipstick smeared as though she were a circus clown. They sat in the well lit room in total silence for several seconds. Finally Amanda stood to her feet and began to walk around Ray. His heart started thumping as he quickly prayed and asked God for a way out of this uncomfortable situation. He knew in his heart if he didn't deal with it, it would never go away.

"Amanda…"

Ray cleared his throat as she stood in front of him. Amanda's eyes were soft and loving. Ray could tell by the sincerity in her expression that she truly was in love with him, and that made him feel badly. He had honestly felt like Amanda knew that the little fling they had before wasn't going anywhere.

"You don't need or want me. You're missing something in your life, but baby, it's not me," he said shaking his head.

Returning to her comfortable chair, Amanda looked up from the paper she was drawing circles on, delighted that Ray would call her "baby."

Ray continued gently, "Sometimes in life we search for things that we think we want, but at times during the process we find something else, something better than we could ever imagine."

She looked at him with a baffled expression. "In my search for power and prestige, I found something even greater, and what I found has turned my life around. It's helped me to be a better father, a better husband, a better colleague and a better friend. What used to drive me still does, but it doesn't have dominion over me anymore."

"Ray, what you talking about?"

Amanda frowned, wiping her smeared makeup with the rumpled tissue as her aggravation grew.

"I found God."

Amanda laughed as if Ray had just said something hilarious. Pulling out her lipstick, she flipped it open and applied color to her lips, then checked the effect in the small mirror.

"That's fine. I go to church sometimes, too."

Wiping her stained eyes, she got up again from her seat to walk toward him again, pausing to rub his forehead. Ray jerked away.

"I don't think you understand, Amanda. I've changed. I'm not the same man I was months ago. I'm sorry if I hurt you. I never meant to, but I pray God will mend your hurt and give you peace."

She stepped back from him, arms folded across the front of her expensive suit.

"Okay, Ray, this is ridiculous. Did God give you the promotion years ago to become the Director of Operations? No," she answered her own question.

"I did."

Ray kept a steady, but low key gaze as she continued speaking, her voice escalating in volume and pitch. "You were a flunky, wet-behind-the-ears, green engineer when you started here. Did God promote you the position of plant manager? No!" she shouted.

"I did. God didn't answer your prayers...I did! Your so called God is...."

Ray stopped Amanda by holding up his index finger. "Please don't disrespect my faith, Amanda," Ray said calmly.

"If you don't choose to listen, that's up to you, but I believe it and that's all that matters."

"Raymond Durrant, I'm surprised at you. I thought you had more sense than that. What preacher has been filling your head with these pipe dreams of religion and faith?"

Ray grinned to himself, remembering the night Steven had led him to Christ.

"Actually, it wasn't a preacher. It was a regular guy that enlightened me," Ray smiled.

"Who, some stupid bum off the corner?" Amanda laughed.

"Nope, no bum," Ray smiled.

"It was Steven."

Amanda raised her eyebrows.

"Steven... the security guard?"

Ray nodded.

Amanda broke into peals of laughter until tears filled her eyes and she gasped for breath. "Raymond, you're a ridiculous fool. I'm disappointed in you. You're not the man I thought you were. I will tell you what," she continued to laugh.

"I'm going to pretend that this conversation never took place. In three weeks we're scheduled for a two day meeting in New York. By then, you need to have this ridiculous phase you're going through out of your system, or else."

"Or else what?" Ray questioned a second time.

"You don't want to know," Amanda said in a hushed voice.

She reached for her office phone and buzzed her secretary. "Eva," Amanda spoke firmly.

"Tell Zerrico, I said to report to my office immediately. I'm suddenly in the mood to axe some employees," she smiled devilishly.

"Raymond, we're done!" She waved her hand to shoo him out of her office.

Lord, what have I gotten myself into, Ray thought once he got to his office. He reached for his phone to call Donae. At least if he heard her voice, he might feel a little better.

"Hi, baby," Donae answered energetically.

"How's your day going?" he could hear her smiling through the receiver.

"It's better now."

Ray smiled as he sat back in his chair, feeling his blood pressure drop in hearing his wife's reassuring voice. "What's wrong?" her energy faded.

"Nothing, sweetheart, everything is A-okay," Ray said jokingly.

"You're such a liar," Donae giggled.

"How was work today?" Ray changed the subject.

"It's a wonderful day, baby, just selling these drugs."

He could hear the laughter bubbling in her voice, and could almost see her sparkling eyes. More than ever he wished he could hug her right now.

"Good thing they're in a prescription bottle," Ray added.

"Actually, I'm training a new pharmacist," Donae giggled.

"That's great," Ray said.

"Maybe we can start making that baby after I move in. I got my U-haul rented, and I'm ready to go. Next week can't get here soon enough for me."

"I'm ready for you, Ray," Donae felt her cheeks grown warm with a blush.

"I've missed you."

"I'm glad, baby, but you didn't comment on the baby part."

Donae giggled a girlish laugh, "We'll start practicing; how about that?"

Ray smiled a big smile, glad that he had called her, as he lifted his favorite framed photo of her from his desk. "So what are you doing right now?" Donae asked, concerned in remembering he had sounded stressed at the beginning of the conversation.

"I'm looking at your afro," he chuckled.

Donae sighed. "I hate that picture. You need a new one," she demanded.

"Oh, Ray, I saw your friend in the store this morning, or should I say our friend."

"Who?" Ray asked casually.

"Steven," she said.

"He was surprised to see me. I guess he didn't know I was the pharmacist here. He came to pick up his prescription."

"Oh, he's going out of town for a few days. I talked to him a while ago, but he didn't mention seeing you. Do you remember me telling you about the guy I met at the men's conference, a guy named Malcolm?"

"Yes," Donae answered.

"How could I ever forget him?"

"He's in jail," Ray said, still dumbfounded.

"What! Why?" Donae demanded in a shocked voice.

"It's a long story, baby. I'll tell you later, just keep him in your prayers, but that's what Steven and I were discussing."

"Oh, Okay," Donae got quiet.

"What's wrong? Why the sudden deflate?"

Donae fidgeted with her name tag on her lab coat.

"Honey, Steven is taking a high dosage of Paxil," she said feeling embarrassed.

"Paxil? What's that?" Ray asked, now curious.

"Paxil is a medication prescribed for depression."

"Depression?" Ray felt confused.

"Are you sure?" He didn't want to believe it was true.

"Yes," Donae answered.

"I'm certain. I've been doing this a long time."

"Wow!" Ray mumbled.

"Maybe I shouldn't have told you," she said. "I could lose my job."

"Don't be silly," Ray insisted.

"I guess I'm just shocked."

"I was too," she admitted.

"We'll have to keep him in our prayers."

"Yes, baby, we will. Thank you for telling me," Ray said appreciatively.

"Don't cook tonight. I'm taking you and the kids out for dinner."

Donae perked up, "You don't have to tell me twice!"

"I'll see you tonight," Ray said.

"I love you."

"I love you too," she answered warmly.

Raymond thanked God for finally being able to hear those precious three words from her lips addressed to him again. He had never thought it possible. He was anxious to slip her wedding ring back on her pretty, slender finger. He hung up the phone, heavy-hearted. He wondered what in Steven's life could cause him to suffer from depression. It didn't add up. Raymond locked his office door and fell down on his knees at the leather sofa, lifting a heartfelt prayer for his brothers in Christ.

Ivy continued to think about Apostle Reed's prophetic words weeks after the men's conference was over. Never in a million years would he expect God to do what He had done. Ivy had no clue that Apostle had a prophetic gift, but he was certain that God was using that man in a mighty way. Deeply moved by the spirit, Yolanda remained in steadfast worship after receiving the word, and prayerfully decided to go on a seven day fast. Ivy couldn't get into his prayer room because his wife wouldn't leave it. She had even fallen asleep there some nights.

Ivy was happy that Yolanda had deepened her relationship with the Lord, and he was determined that he would not be the cause of her pain. If God had set her free, he was not going to return her to bondage. It wasn't until Apostle spoke to her that he realized how much stress his sex addiction had contributed to his wife's misery. God was about to do reconstructive surgery on the men of His congregation, and it was starting with the pastor.

Sunday was an awesome, unbelievable spiritual beginning, but the whole week touched countless lives, and would live on in memory for many years to come. Hundreds of men were led to Christ each night, going home with changed hearts. They were in turn, strengthening their marriages and becoming strong, loving parents who instilled and modeled spiritual values for their families. No one could remember a time like this before when the Holy Spirit was doing such great work in so many lives.

Now Ivy understood why Apostle had brought so many men with him. Every man seeking salvation, deliverance, or to be set free from any stronghold was assigned a Gate Keeper: Someone they were accountable to. This Keeper would stay in contact with the man assigned to him, and walk with the growing believer in word, faith and prayer. The Keepers were available day or night for consultation and inspiration. Apostle called them street ministers. Men of faith, they had been trained to walk alongside those who were struggling and give a hand to help them reach their next goal. These Gate Keepers were from all over the world. Surprisingly, his very own Armor bearers, Kevin and Steven, had been Gate Keepers for quite some time now: Steven for nearly seven years and Kevin three years.

As the men's conference continued that week, each Keeper gave a powerful testimony about how God had delivered him out of the pits of hell. It was incredible how these men, full of the spirit of

God, took everything the devil had used to destroy them and allowed God to transform their lives in a mighty way. Ivy had never seen anything like it in all his life. My Brother's Keeper was a much needed ministry. It was changing the lives of men all over the world. The mission was to produce men of God who bore fruit and were not content to be just good looking trees. Each Keeper was assigned two to three men. There were eighteen to twenty year old keepers to minister to the teenagers. These Godly men knew the Word of God inside and out, and their enthusiasm was contagious. Ivy was excited about the effect this ministry was having on the men of his congregation, and he was certain that what Apostle said was true - change had indeed come.

"Hello," the female voice hummed into the receiver, sounding in an upbeat mood.

"Hi, Mel, it's me, Ivy. How are you?"

The short silence was an indication to Ivy that this conversation might not go in his favor.

"Hello?" Ivy tried to remain optimistic.

"That's Meloney, to you. I was doing fine until I picked up the phone. What do you want?"

Ivy chose his words carefully.

"I would love to get the twins this weekend, if that's okay with you."

"They're busy," she blurted.

"Meloney, please, you're not being fair. What about Jessica and Jordan?" Ivy pleaded.

"Don't you think they would like to spend some time with their father?"

Their mother sucked her teeth, "You've got a lot of nerve to talk to me about being fair after all the havoc you've caused in my life. Was it fair to me when I was two months pregnant to find out you've got another woman across town pregnant too; only to find out I'm having twins with a two timer?

"You go off to Maryland, get married, and father another child. Now you want to call yourself a man of God? Please, give me a freaking break!"

He sighed. "People change, Meloney. I'm not that same immature boy anymore."

"Tell that to someone who doesn't know all about you. Personally, I think Mr. Bailey should have done us all a favor and put a cap in your behind when you got Alicia pregnant. Now tell me this, 'Pastor...'" Meloney said sarcastically.

"Your son by Alicia Nicholas, he's 14 right?"

She didn't give Ivy a chance to answer.

"Then there are Ebony and Dominic, the two across town. They are around thirteen-ish? Then we have my dumb butt with the twelve-year-old twins, Jessica and Jordan. Last but not least, Bryson, the son with your precious wife, who is now what, about seven? Did I get them all?" She paused.

Ivy was tempted to be devilish and tell her a little white lie by suggesting that Yolanda might be expecting again, but he knew better.

"Yes, Mel, you've about covered it."

Ivy flipped it on her, trying a much different approach.

"You know, my mother was diagnosed with Alzheimer's. She's been asking to spend time with her grandchildren while she can remember things. Looks like Courtney won't ever have any kids, so my basketball team is all she has." He tried to joke about it.

"I'm rounding everybody up to head over to her house. I've been trying to reach you for the last two days and didn't get an answer."

Meloney changed her tone, "Jessica called her about three weeks ago. I'm really sorry to hear that. You know I love Ms. Jo."

"Look, Mel," Ivy blurted out.

"I agree I've hurt you. I hurt you bad. I was a young, dumb kid who didn't care about anything or anyone but himself. You didn't deserve to be treated like that, and as for ruining your life..."

Mel stopped him mid-sentence, "Don't, Ivy...don't even bring it up."

"But," Ivy tried to reason.

"I need you to know I'm sorry. I'm truly sorry, Mel, for what it's worth. I've moved here for good and would love to have a positive relationship with all my kids, not just some of them. I wouldn't try so hard if I didn't love them. Will you please work with me, Mel?"

Ivy felt a sense of relief and thought he might be getting through to her. That is, until he heard the dial tone. Ivy was disappointed, because he'd been looking forward to spending more quality time with all his children this weekend. Although, he had been back home nearly two months, he had only seen the twins when, he caught them getting off the school bus. Despite his many efforts to see his five illegitimate children, when it came to Dominic, Jessica and Jordan, the "baby momma drama" always interfered. Even his attempts to send extra child support didn't work. Meloney blamed every wrong thing in her life on him.

Yes, it was true she was raising his twins as a single mother, but he did send child support payments as well as birthday and Christmas gifts. He tried to see the kids every time he came to town.

Her bitterness alienated him from his kids, causing him resentment toward her, but he suppressed his hurt for the sake of his children, and continued to try. She had poisoned the twins' minds with lies about Ivy because of her misery, causing his relationship, or lack thereof, to become a wedge between them. It appeared to the twins and Dominic that he favored the three children he could see over the three he couldn't not see, which wasn't true. In his absence JoAnn stepped in and helped raise the twins until they started first grade. She babysat so that Mel could work a full-time job and wouldn't have to pay daycare expenses, hoping that one day Mel would not be so harsh when it came time for Ivy to spend time with his children

After they started school, the bus would drop them off at JoAnn's house, and she would feed them, help with homework, and give them baths until Mel picked them up. This routine had lasted until five years ago when Mel got a big promotion, which moved her across town. Of course, Ivy was grateful to his mother for helping with the twins. He even sent her $500 a month to help with expenses. Most of the time she chose not to accept it, so he got her banking account number from Courtney and started depositing money directly into her account each week.

Even after the twins stopped coming to JoAnn's house, he still deposited funds to help out. He didn't want his precious mother to want for anything. The house and cars were paid off. All she had was utility bills. It seemed like once the twins stopped coming over to be watched, JoAnn's health started to decline. She said looking after the kids kept her youthful. The loving grandmother adored every single one of her grandchildren and had a special relationship with all six of them. They all loved Grandma Jo just as much. They didn't visit as often as she would have liked, but she hoped since Ivy had moved back in town, she would get to see them more. Her relationship with their mothers, unlike Ivy's, was good. She and Ivy both thanked God for that.

"Daddy!" Ebony raced into Ivy's arms for a hug.

"Hey you," Ivy swooped her up in his arms.

"You need to lay off those candy bars girl, you're getting heavy."

"Momma said that's thirteen years of love," she snapped her fingers.

"I guess you told me," Ivy grinned.

"Where's everybody else? I thought all the kids were coming to Grandma Jo's house."

Ivy sighed, "Well Jessica and Jordan can't make it this time, but we're going to pick up Dominic when we leave here. Nicholas' mom will bring him to Grandma Jo's, and Yolanda and Bryson will meet us over there."

"Aw," Ebony frowned.

"Why can't the twins come? I wanted to show Jessica my new game."

"I'm sorry, sweetheart. I know you're disappointed, but at least you'll get to see three of your brothers."

"But I'll be the only girl," she whined.

"Stop pouting. You're too big to be acting like this."

The voice came from inside the house.

"Good afternoon, Ivy."

Ebony's mother, Lynn, came smiling through the door.

"This child has worried me all night about what time her daddy was coming. She hasn't been able to get enough of you since you've moved back in town."

Ivy laughed at her still pouting face.

"Where is Thomas?" he asked.

"Somewhere on that doggone motorcycle. You know how y'all are about your silly toys," she smiled.

Ivy chuckled, "Come on, now. Yolanda won't let me have one."

"I don't blame her. Those things are just too dangerous. People don't respect them like they do cars," she replied.

"Thomas doesn't need his."

"Lynn motioned at the girl. Go in the house, Ebony, and grab your overnight bag."

Ebony pulled her daddy's hand to follow her toward the door.

"Ebony!" Lynn hissed.

"Your daddy ain't going nowhere. You have him all weekend, girl. Go get that bag!"

Ebony hurried into the house.

"So how is married life?" Ivy asked, making small talk.

Lynn smiled widely, "It's good," she said pleasantly.

"Thomas is a wonderful man, and he loves me and Ebony."

"That's great," Ivy said.

"Marriage is a beautiful thing. I'm glad you found someone who treats you like you deserve to be treated. It's wonderful to hear that you and my baby are happy."

Lynn's eyes smiled as her lips parted. "I hear you're turning Mt. Emanuel upside down. My neighbors have been visiting and said service was out of this world."

Ivy couldn't help but smile. "I can't take the credit from God. He is stirring up the hearts of His people. I'm just the man He's using to do it through."

"Thomas and I may visit one Sunday," Lynn added.

"My neighbor's husband got saved at the men's conference, him and his brother."

"Praise God," Ivy said.

"Trust me, we did," she said as if it were a miracle.

"We have been praying for him a long time. He's still talking about that conference. He said it changed his life. He also said something interesting about you."

"Really?"

"Yes, really," she said.

"He felt your worship was genuine. He said he watched you weep and admit your struggles before hundreds of men you didn't know. It made him want to know your God."

Ivy started to tear up at the mention of someone being delivered. "It does my heart good to hear that. I admit it changed my life."

"Let's go, Daddy." Ebony ran out the door, opening a bag of ranch flavored chips.

"I guess that's my cue," he said, watching Ebony put her bicycle in the garage.

Ivy hugged Lynn and tried to pull away, but she squeezed him tighter. He felt a bit uncomfortable. The sound of Thomas's Harley from a distance broke her embrace. As he soared into view, Ivy stepped a few feet backwards, not knowing if Thomas had witnessed anything as he drove up. Ivy grabbed Ebony's hand and started making his way to the car. Thomas jumped off his bike, lifting his black and silver helmet from his head.

"Hey Thomas," Ivy called, extending his hand in greeting.

"Hey there to you," Thomas shook his hand.

"Congratulations, man. I hear you took over the ministry at Mt. Emanuel. I'm hearing about good things over there."

Ivy smiled, relieved at his friendliness.

"Bye, baby," Thomas waved at Ebony who was already sitting in the car.

"Bye," she smiled.

"See you Sunday."

"Okay, squirt."

Thomas walked over to Lynn, planting a soft one on her lips. Ivy got into his car. "We'll see you good people later. Enjoy your weekend," he said, starting the ignition.

133

Moments later, Ivy pulled up into the parking space facing apartment 12B. The two men standing outside the building quickly rushed from eyesight when he turned off the ignition.

"Daddy, you want me to stay in the car while you get Dominic?" Ebony asked.

"No, sweetie, you come with me. I don't feel comfortable with you out here by yourself," he said.

And grab your game; don't leave it on the seat. Someone might try to steal it."

Ivy and Ebony walked up to the concrete slab entrance and rang the doorbell.

"Ivan Jessie James!" the voice echoed in Ivy's ear.

"Look at you! The picture of your father, God rest his soul."

"Hi, Ms. Irma," Ivy gave the short, heavyset woman a heartfelt embrace.

"You are as handsome as I remember, and smelling good, too. Lord, if my daughter would have acted right, you'd be my son-in-law," she pinched Ivy's cheek, much to Ebony's delight.

"You want something to eat? I'm frying some pork chops with seasoned pinto beans."

She led the way into the house, followed by Ivy and Ebony.

Ivy grinned, "Goodness, some pintos would be nice, but I'll have to pass this time," he said, putting an emphasis on *this time*.

"My mom is expecting us shortly. She has this big spread prepared, like she always does. Where's that knuckle head son of mine?" he asked.

"I told him last night you'd be here to pick him up at 3:00. He's got his bag packed, He's probably down the street somewhere with those hoodlums he can't seem to stay away from. Let me try his cell phone."

Ms. Irma grabbed a phone off the foyer table and hit the speed dial number for her grandson.

"I want a cell phone, Daddy," Ebony interrupted.

"Dominic says you're a pastor now," Ms. Irma said, waiting for the call to ring through.

"Yes, ma'am. When I talked to him last week, I told him I wanted him to come to church with me. Thank you for helping me to finally be able to see him."

"Oh, you're welcome, baby. He needs his father in his life. I don't know what's wrong with these silly girls and women keeping these kids from their fathers. It's just selfish. But Ivy, he doesn't have any church clothes to wear."

"That's okay," Ivy answered.

"We don't dress up at our church. It's 'come as you are'."

A voice answered on the other end of the line.

Dominic!" his grandmother shouted into the receiver.

"Where are you?" she paused.

"Your daddy's here waiting for you with your little sister, Ebony."

She clicked off the call and sighed.

"That boy gets on my last nerve, but he's on the way."

"Where is Kandice?" Ivy asked.

Ms. Irma dropped her head in silence as Ivy looked at her with concern.

"Pray for her, Ivy. She's not good at all."

"What do you mean, not good? Everytime I call for Dominic, she's quick to let me know she's great and how much they don't need me. She tells me just to make sure the checks keep coming." He shook his head.

Ms. Irma didn't say anything, but her eyes were sad.

"Ms. Irma, please tell me what's going on." Ivy pleaded with concern.

Irma exhaled loudly, "Kandice has been on that crack stuff for about four years now."

Ivy's heart sank. "Ebony, baby, can you go sit in the other room over there and play your game?"

Ivy stepped closer to Ms. Irma. "How in the world did this happen? I had no earthly clue," he looked sad.

Ms. Irma's mouth tightened. "I'm going to tell you the truth. I don't care if she does get mad. Those checks you send every week, she not taking care of Dominic with that money. I had to buy him a few pairs of pants for school because he's gotten so doggone tall. He needs a pair of shoes, some underwear and other stuff."

"I'm on a fixed income, but I'm doing the best I can. She's smoking up that check every week. That's part of the reason why she hasn't let you see him all these years; that and the fact that she has no idea that a real mother who loves there child encourages a relationship with the father whether they are together or not." Ms. Irma shook her head.

"She ought to be ashamed of herself for keeping Dominic away from you. He's already a teenager. She's just selfish. She didn't want you to find out she was a crack head."

The hurting mother started to cry. "She got kicked out of her place because she was letting some drug dealer sell cocaine and pills out of her apartment so she could get free crack. Dominic has been here with me for almost three months. We haven't seen Kandice going on four weeks now."

"Lord, have mercy."

Ivy sat down in the oversized chair, feeling disgusted. He had had no idea Kandice was on drugs. He thought she was being foolish and spiteful like Meloney.

"Ms. Irma, I am so sorry. I didn't know. Is Dominic okay?" he asked.

Ms. Irma shook her head.

"He's just mad at the world, and I can't teach a boy how to be a man. Dominic is getting out of hand, hanging out with these little thugs around here, thinking he's grown, and getting more and more unruly. One of those no-good friends of his, gave him a cell phone and I'm trying to figure out where the money is coming from to keep minutes on it. I don't even have a cell phone. Dang on things cost too much. I'm scared these streets have replaced you Ivy. He needs his father," she cried harder.

"I just don't want him to end up making dumb mistakes."

Ivy dropped his head, ashamed that he hadn't known anything that was going on in his son's life. Although he tried Kandice and Mel had the upper hand. Despite his efforts of going through the courts, the two ex-girlfriends chose to not comply with court orders. Ivy had the option to go back to court, but how would it look to his children to have their mothers thrown in jail. It would only make matters worse. Ivy prayed that once they got older his children would one day know the truth.

"Ms. Irma, don't worry. It's going to be okay. Let me pray for you," he said, taking her shaking hands.

With a heavy heart Ivy prayed down heaven from the depths of his soul. By the end of the prayer Ms. Irma was praising and thanking God. She couldn't help but smile as she stared at Ivan, all grown up.

"I'm glad you're back in town." She kissed his cheek.

"Me too…Ms. Irma, me too."

The slamming door caused Ivy to glance in the other direction.

"What's up, Ebony," Dominic nodded at his sister.

"Hey," Ebony answered, barely looking up from her game.

"Hello son," Ivy said as he got up to embrace the boy, but Dominic turned away.

"What's up," Dominic nodded curtly.

"You ready to go see your Grandma Jo? She's looking forward to seeing you guys."

"Do I have a choice?" He looked at Ivy pointedly.

Ivy frowned.

"Get your bags, son," Ivy said sternly.

"Sure, Daddy!" Dominic said with a mountain of sarcasm.

"Ms. Irma, we will talk later."

Ivy gave her a much needed bear hug. He put few hundred dollars in her hand and said, "God bless you. I'll make sure he has some shoes and clothes when we come back on Sunday."

Ivy left the apartment with racing thoughts. He had let his son down by not being there, but what can a man do when he wants a relationship with his children, and a spiteful woman stands in the way? Feeling discouraged by the truth, he and so many other men like him were victims to women who didn't love their children enough to put aside their selfishness for the sake of their children. His heart was heavy, and all he wanted to do was be alone with God to ask for some direction. He had to stay calm for the kids' sake as they drove over to his mother's home.

Alicia Bailey was already at JoAnn's house with Nicholas by the time they got there.

"Hello, y'all," JoAnn's voice resounded in the room when Ivy walked in behind two of her grandchildren.

"Where's the twins?" she asked in her soft, rich voice.

Ivy hugged Nicholas, who stood head to head with him. "I couldn't get them, Momma," Ivy said, dreading the disappointment in her deep brown eyes.

"You're getting short, Dad," Nicholas laughed, showing a handsome grin and white teeth.

"You're shorter than you were at church Sunday."

"Yeah, right," Ivy laughed with him.

"I can still whoop your butt! Remember that."

He turned to the woman nearby.

"Hi, Alicia." Ivy hugged her lightly.

"Hi, Pastor, how are you?" she smiled.

"I'm okay," he answered, not really feeling it as much as he wanted her to believe.

"And you?"

The woman with coffee colored skin and loose, dark waves that flowed to her shoulders gave a brief smile.

"I'm great," she replied.

"Just taking it one day at a time."

"You're looking well," Ivy commented.

"You don't look too bad yourself, in your old age." She adjusted one of her dangling silver earrings that had come loose.

"If I recall correctly, you've got me beat by two months, old lady," Ivy teased gently.

"I hear you and Spencer Gillespie are engaged."

"About time I tied the knot, don't you think?"

Earring adjusted, her hands were tucked into the pockets of her designer jeans. Ivy wouldn't touch that with a ten foot pole. Hearing a car door slam, JoAnn slowly made her way to the window.

"That must be Yolanda and Bryson, Mom," Ivy said, stepping into the kitchen and taking the lid off the crock pot to smell those delicious pinto beans.

"I guess I'll be going," Alicia said as she took her purse from the sofa and moved toward the door.

"Don't rush off," Ivy said sincerely.

"No, really, I have to. Spencer and I are going cake tasting today."

"Yes," JoAnn yelled from the window.

"It's Yolanda and my handsome little Bryson," she giggled.

"Oh, look," she paused.

"Someone is pulling up behind them."

"Oh, my goodness!" JoAnn seemed very excited.

Ivy assumed it was Courtney coming in a day early. She lived in Atlanta after graduating with honors from Spellman College.

"Ivy, it's the twins! Meloney brought them."

"Really?" Ivy grinned with joy. He wanted to do a two-step. It had been years since all his children had been together in the same room. JoAnn hurried out the door and hugged Yolanda on her way to meet the twins. Alicia walked past Yolanda on her way out, and the two women smiled respectfully at one another.

"Hey, Ms. JoAnn," Meloney yelled from her car.

"I miss you."

"I miss you too, baby. Thank you for letting the kids come," JoAnn grinned, so she could see her appreciation.

"It's because of you, Ms. JoAnn," Meloney shouted.

"Only because of you. Tell Ivy to have them home by eight Sunday evening."

"Okay," JoAnn answered.

Ivy walked out the door to talk with Meloney, but once she saw him, she quickly sped off, leaving him to look like a fool in the middle of the driveway.

Alicia rolled down her window as she backed out of the driveway. "I see you still got baby momma drama,'" she laughed.

"Pray for me." Ivy looked pitiful.

"I will," Alicia smiled.

"I will."

"And, oh, by the way," Alicia added.

"My father says hello."

"Deacon Bailey? Yeah right," Ivy grinned.

"I see you're full of jokes today."

He headed toward the house to enjoy this priceless moment with his wife, mother, and all of his six children.

Chapter 14 *Malcolm*

Malcolm had only been released from custody nearly two weeks, but who'd have thought he'd have such a smile on his face when he stepped out of the jail cell? Three weeks ago he'd spent three days in jail because of a bunch of bull crap. He was thankful that Moe saw the officer handcuffing him on her way home that night, but it took her nearly a day to catch up with Steven to let him know. Thank goodness Steven was a regular customer at the diner. Malcolm had sat in that cell block mad at the world and mad at Telese, along with Mr. Riley, Morris, David Lee, himself and even God. He felt like the more he tried, the more he failed. Why did he even bother to try when he kept getting knocked down?

Staring at the gray walls around that narrow cell, he held his face in his hands or lay on the small, hard cot, wondering whether he had any kind of future beyond that place. The couple of days he sat there waddling in his grief his thoughts of suicide offered him a temporary peace. However, sensing the look of fear and terror in his 17 year old roommate's eyes, he felt the need to encourage him. The poor kid had just been sentenced to life in prison. Malcolm's heart went out to the skimpy boy. He'd been hanging around the wrong crowd and got caught up in their influence.

Taking pity out of his own party Malcolm prayed for the kid. It was just that quick God reminded him he had a purpose and something to live for. Before being released Malcolm wanted to give the boy his address to keep in touch but the truth was he had no clue of where that address would now be. When Malcolm was changing from the jumpsuit into his regular clothes Ray's business card fell out of his pocket. Malcolm was blown away by the title beneath Ray's name. Now he understood why Steven and Ray had been so persuasive in getting him to apply for the job. Why didn't those two jesters just say that Ray was the man? When Steven got Malcolm out on bail, Malcolm didn't know what to say. He was severely broken. His Spirit, his mind and his soul were shattered. He didn't know how he was going to pick himself up, but he did know he had to. Steven had paid a large sum of money to get Malcolm released, which included catching up his child support payments that were in the rears. He promised Steven somehow he'd pay him back every cent. All Malcolm had to give was a heartfelt thank you.

Shortly after his release, Malcolm moved his things into his sister's house, and had to calm Lauren down from wanting to beat the stuffing out of Telese and Sydney for what they'd done. Since his child support was caught up and he was starting his new position at Zanderbilt on Monday. He'd decided to opt for child support to be payroll deducted from his paycheck. The next thing he did was called Telese and agreed to the quick divorce as she had requested.

"Great, but it's going to take more like ninety days than forty-five," she cautioned him.

"That's fine."

After a pause she said in a low voice, "You don't need to pay child support."

"That's what you said the first time, but it's cool. I want to take care of my kids. I've already made arrangements."

"Thank you. I appreciate it," Telese said warmly, with a bit of guilt from her broken promise.

A few days later, Mackie from the ring offered Malcolm a part-time job in the evenings as a sparring partner for $150 a week. As an incentive he also gave him free ring time anytime he wanted, so Malcolm was on his way up. Now with two jobs he could get on his feet and pay Steven back for bailing him out.

Malcolm sold his SUV and bought a smaller sedan so he could afford the insurance and get better gas mileage. Life was finally starting to improve, and he felt more in control than he had in years. Steven was good at car repairs and mechanical things. He'd helped a lot of single women at church with free alignments and tire rotations, as well as oil changes and tune-ups, so he checked out the new car for Malcolm to make sure it wasn't a lemon. Although Malcolm only had $36 in his pocket to his name, in spite of everything he'd been through he found hope. Ray had been calling and checking on him faithfully.

"You okay, man?"

Malcolm sensed the concern in his new friend's tone. "I'm fine, better than I ever expected," Malcolm chuckled, giving Ray a big sense of relief.

Their friendship had blossomed greatly over lunches, occasional jogs in the park and brief phone conversations. Ray was going to be leaving for a business trip in a few days, and he wanted to make sure Malcolm was okay. Malcolm walked into Moe's and sat in the last booth. The place was extra crowded, and no wonder, with the delicious home cooked food at reasonable prices. He waited nearly fifteen to twenty minutes when finally Steven called and said he wouldn't be able to make it.

Steven told him that one of the ladies at church had a blow-out and was stranded on the highway. So Malcolm, realizing he would be dining alone, began looking over the menu. Ms. Moe strolled over to the table and sat iced tea before him.

"You ready to order, baby?" she said in an agreeable tone of voice.

Malcolm looked up with a grin, "Ms. Moe, I just want to thank you for telling Steven about what happened."

She flashed a grin right back.

"You're welcome, baby. God is going to see about you," she assured him.

"Looks like you need some help in here," Malcolm smiled, glancing around.

"I know, baby. My son got in some trouble, and they sentenced him to ten years the other day."

Moe's eyes began to water. "It's just broken my heart into tiny little pieces. He's an 18-year-old foolish kid."

"Oh Ms. Moe, I'm sorry, don't cry," Malcolm looked over at her tenderly, remembering his youthful roommate at the jail weeks ago. "God will watch over him. You have to hand him over to the Lord. Trust me...I served eight years in prison."

She shook her head sadly. "I would ask you about your experience, but I'm afraid of the truth. I know it's all about survival in there, and it scares me to death to think about all the horrible things that could happen."

"Some days are just unbearable. I wouldn't wish this heartache on my worst enemy. My baby was on house arrest for nearly a year before they sentenced him. The anxiety of his court date sent me to the hospital four times, but it damn near killed me to watch them take my son away in shackles. There was nothing I could do about it. These foolish kids have no idea what they put their parents through."

Moe wiped her wet eyes. "I'm sorry, Malcolm," she smoothed out her black apron.

"I shouldn't have dropped all my problems on you," she attempted an artificial smile.

"No, Moe," Malcolm nearly jumped over the table assuring her it was okay.

"If you ever, and I do mean ever, need to talk, Moe, please give me a call," he begged.

He scribbled his number on the back of a napkin from the napkin dispenser.

"You're not in this alone. You've got plenty of people around here who love you, Moe," he said, touching her shaking hand.

"Thank you, baby, please pray for him and me," she said, eyes moist with tears.

"You keep looking at the menu. I've got to make some room for all these customers," she hurried away.

Malcolm looked up and saw a dozen people waiting at the door to be seated. He spotted one of his church members and motioned for her to come over.

"Hi, I'm Malcolm. I recognize you from church. Don't you attend Mt. Emanuel?"

"Yes, nice to meet you. I'm Vanessa Reardon."

"You're welcome to join me, I'm dining alone," Malcolm said with a smile, admiring her beautiful almond eyes and coffee colored complexion.

Her short tapered hair gave him an eyeful of her natural radiant beauty.

"Oh no, I couldn't impose," she smiled shyly.

"Impose?" Malcolm frowned.

"I'd enjoy some company for a change," he said as his frown arched into a smile.

"Please," he pressed both his hands together as if praying.

"Are you sure?" Vanessa searched his face for any hint of uncertainty.

"I can't insist enough," he said sincerely, motioning to the seat across from him.

"Bless you," she said.

"I'm hungry as an ox," she smiled politely back, peeking at the muscles rippling under his shirt.

"Could you order me water?" Vanessa asked.

"I'll be right back," she raced to the restroom.

Malcolm's mind started racing, and he felt bad. He wanted to buy her dinner, but was worried he didn't have enough to pay for both of them. At first he thought he had $36, but he forgot he had bought a cheeseburger, fries, and drink for lunch, so now he only had $29.63 left.

Vanessa came back to the table after what seemed like five seconds, and took her seat.

"That was quick," Malcolm smiled.

Vanessa laughed.

"What's so funny?" Malcolm asked.

"I don't mean to be rude, but I got the worst case of gas ever. The beans I had for lunch are holding me captive."

Malcolm laughed until his eyes watered. He could hardly believe this lovely woman could make such an earthy statement.

"I know I should be more lady-like and hold it for your sake, but bump that," she giggled.

"I ain't trying to be all up in here with my stomach in knots to be cute."

Malcolm shook his head at the beautiful woman across from him. He'd noticed her several times at church, but of course he'd been in a different position then and would've been a fool to attempt to talk to a woman as broke as he was she'd probably laugh in his face. Truth was she still might laugh. He was a long, long way from having his life together. He was lonely. The thought of having a beautiful friend to talk to now and then sounded good. Besides, she made him laugh, something he hadn't done in a long time.

Moe came back to the table holding a glass of water with clinking ice cubes. "Well, well, well," Moe smiled.

"What do we have here?" she eyed Vanessa pleasantly.

Vanessa smiled her girlish grin, "The place is so crowded, Moe!"

"Malcolm was a gentleman and offered to share his booth with me."

"Aw…and I thought chivalry was dead. Now Malcolm, you be a gentleman. This here is my angel in disguise. She's prayed me through many rough nights."

"I promise to be good company, Moe," he said after tasting his perfectly sweetened ice tea.

"Okay," Moe grinned at the pair.

Malcolm was glad to see the older woman's smile after the earlier tears for her son.

"Y'all ready to order?" she asked.

Malcolm let Vanessa order first, hoping she'd go light on the pocket. He wanted to get the pot roast, which was $12.99, but he had to see what Vanessa wanted, and he might have to settle for a kid's meal.

"I'd like the pot roast and potatoes," Vanessa said.

"What about you Malcolm? I know you want the pot roast too, don't you?"

Malcolm tried to add up in his head how much two pot roast dinners, drinks, and tax would be. Then quickly realized he wouldn't be eating pot roast today.

"Nah, not today," he answered.

"I think I'll have the soup and salad special."

"You sure, baby? The pot roast is on special, two for $22.00 while quantities last."

Malcolm smiled, thanking God for a hookup. "Then…pot roast it is."

Malcolm and Vanessa took their time enjoying the meal. The crowd had died down, and they ate at their leisure. They sat in the booth nearly forty-five minutes after their meal was over, talking and laughing like there was no tomorrow. He had to admit, Vanessa's conversation soothed his soul. She had a way with words that no matter what the topic, she exhorted and edified a person, turning the bad into something good.

When Moe came over and asked if either wanted dessert, Malcolm started panicking. He was already on pins and needles waiting on the check. If Vanessa ordered dessert, he'd be in trouble. He couldn't help but be relieved when Vanessa politely said. "No thank you."

He breathed a sigh of relief. This had been one of the most joyous times he'd had in a while, and he didn't want it to end. The remainder of his night would be at Lauren's house watching game shows, and he wasn't looking forward to it. For now, his little sister's house was home.

Moe brought the check over, and Malcolm praised God in secret. The bill was $25.44. *It's a good thing Vanessa ordered water*, he thought or Moe wouldn't be getting a tip. Malcolm reached for his wallet and Vanessa reached for her purse at the same time.

"I got you, girl," Malcolm smiled proudly.

"Oh, you're so sweet, but I got this today. That's the least I can do since you let me join you, and I won't take no for an answer," she said firmly.

"You're going to have to take no for an answer this time, pretty lady," Malcolm said with joy.

"This one is on me." He laughed to himself.

Saying those words made him feel like a man again. It didn't matter if he would have less than a couple of dollars in his pockets when he left. Vanessa smiled at his choice of words.

"Pretty lady, huh?"

She couldn't help but admire his smooth cocoa skin.

"Moe didn't tell you I have a black belt in karate?"

She sliced the air with her hand, "Don't make me hurt you. I'd be offended if you wouldn't allow me to pay."

Vanessa shoved her debit card along with the tab into Moe's hand as she walked by. Then she stuck her tongue out at Malcolm as she threw her hands in the air as though she was about to do a victory dance.

"Damn girl, you're quick. I'll get you back, though.

"Oh, Vanessa, I'm sorry, I didn't mean to curse. I'm still working on that," he said, disappointed with himself.

Vanessa giggled, "Don't apologize," she said.

"Be yourself. You don't have to put up a front for my sake. We're saved, but we're still living in this human flesh. You never know what might come out of my mouth sometimes, too. Nevertheless, I still love Him."

"Well," he laughed.

"I guess I heard that." Malcolm cleared his throat.

"Can I get the next dinner?" he smiled a devilish grin.

"Hum…" Vanessa pretended to think. " I might like that," she smiled back.

"Just don't eat any beans before you come."

Malcolm loved laughing at this woman. Her sense of humor was a breath of fresh air.

"Can I get your number?" he asked.

"I guess you would need that, huh?"

Vanessa tore off a piece of paper from her purse to write her number down. Moe walked up smiling with the receipt in her hand requiring her signature. Malcolm felt good walking Vanessa to her car. He wanted to hold her hand, that's how comfortable he felt with her, but he didn't want to risk his chances by moving too fast. Vanessa leaned over and gave Malcolm a friendly hug. Her feminine perfume lingered in his nostrils, bringing him great delight. He hadn't been this close to a beautiful woman in months, and Lord forgive the fantasies that were running through his head. She got in her cute little sports car and tooted the horn before driving off.

Malcolm watched her drive away until she was no longer in sight. Then he walked to his car, smiling and singing.

"God is great," Steven called as soon as Malcolm pulled out of Moe's parking lot.

"Hey, man," Steven bellowed into the receiver.

"Hey to you too," Malcolm said, full of life.

"I just want to apologize for not being able to make dinner. I'm sure you have a lot that you want to get off your chest."

"Nah, man, actually I'm good. I realize, more than you think, this is all part of God's plan."

Steven held the receiver away from his face and stared at it, not believing this was Malcolm he was talking to.

"Alright, Alright, Alright!" Steven shouted.

"You'll never guess what happened" Malcolm sounded excited.

"What!" Steven asked, curious.

"You not showing up turned out to be a blessing in disguise," Malcolm said.

He began to explain how he shared dinner with Vanessa, and how she had ministered to his soul without even knowing it. The two men laughed at how Malcolm was sweating bullets before ordering his food, and how he had just enough money to cover the check, even though he didn't have to.

"Man, you are too funny," Steven chuckled.

"I'm just keeping it real," Malcolm laughed with him.

"But if you needed more money you could have called," Steven said.

"No, Steven, you've already done too much. Besides, I'm picking up my check from Mackie in the morning, and you know I start my new job at Zanderbilt on Monday."

"Man, Steven, Ray hooked a brother up. I'll be making more money than I've ever made in my life. Check this out, they hired my homeboy, too."

"Wow, that's awesome," Steven said, delighted by his friend's good fortune.

"I'm even getting the kids," Malcolm said with a grateful spirit.

"I guess once Telese got what she wanted, she stopped pushing so hard."

"How do you feel about that?" Steven asked.

"I'm still hurt about how it went down, but if that's what she wants, it's her loss. Trust me, when God gets finished with me, I'll be turning movie stars away," he laughed.

"I hear you, boy," Steven giggled at his chipper spirited friend.

"After talking to her, I feel like a million bucks," Malcolm said, feeling great to be happy for a change.

"So are you going to ask Vanessa out?" Steven asked.

"Is Hell hot?" Malcolm asked.

"Yeah, boy got them digits. Malcolm about to start mack'n again," he said referring to himself.

Both men roared over that. Steven didn't mention a word to reveal the fact that First Lady Yolanda had been trying to hook him up with Vanessa. He had planned on asking her out, but she was off-limits now, and Steven was cool with it.

"Well, make sure when you take her out, you got enough money for the evening. If not, you can always order her something from the value menu." he laughed.

"Oh, you got jokes," Malcolm chuckled again.

"You just wait until I get you in the ring next time, you'll pay for that comment."

"Oh believe you me that will never happen again," Steven chuckled, "I'm still sore from the last time."

Donae laid back in the bathtub filled with bubbles and enjoyed the fragrance of the apple a la mode-scented candles as they brightened the cozy dark space. She sang her heart out to the soothing melody as the song ministered to her soul so intimately. Tears began to fall from her eyes as she thought about the Word of God that had been sent from Heaven through Apostle. Although she was concerned about her husband, she made a conscious decision to trust God. If God asked her for one more chance, how could she tell Him no? Her soft sobs echoed through to Ray's heart. He loved that woman with all his might. He'd never do anything to hurt her again. Ray stood at the bathroom door quietly and listened as Donae cried to the lyrical words and moving melody, and then he heard her praying.

'Lord, I'm scared. I trust that You won't let him hurt me again. I love the man You are making of him, and I've fallen in love all over again. Please anoint him to know how to love me, show him what I need, and teach me, God, how to minister to him as he learns how to minister to me. Please don't let him let us down. Amen.'

Ray said, *'Amen'* in his heart. He waited patiently a few minutes before knocking on the door to make sure her intimate moment with God had concluded.

"Come in."

Donae sat up in the soapy water as Ray opened the door and stepped into the room.

"Hey, baby, the kids have already eaten dinner and are taking showers. I'm just waiting on the cab to get here to take me to the airport."

"Okay," she said reaching for her towel on the nearby rack.

Ray slipped it off the bar and opened it wide, waiting as she stepped out of the tub. "I love you," he said as he dried her body.

"I know you do," she said.

Ray saw a tear fall from her eye. "Baby, what's wrong?"

He embraced her, feeling the warm fluffy fabric of the towel draped around her form. "I'm scared," she whispered.

"Look at me," Ray insisted, turning her face toward him.

"I will never let anything or anyone come between us, ever again," he stressed.

"I'm grateful for and cherish everything that God has given me, especially this second chance."

Ray turned her around to face the bathroom mirror. He stood behind and wrapped his long arms around her, looking up at both of them standing in the mirror. "This is where I want to be," he said staring at their merged image in the mirror.

"No Devil in Hell is going to separate what God joined together, not even me!"

As those words echoed in her heart, a smile came across Donae's face. There was no question in her mind that Ray was committed to making this marriage work. Her concern wasn't so much with him, but with Amanda. The taxi driver outside was laying hard on the horn. Ray kissed his beautiful wife on the cheek, and then brushed her lips. He wished he had a little more time, but didn't want to miss his flight to New York. He had a lot riding on this trip.

Ray would be meeting with all the head honchos from around the world, and he had to make Zanderbilt Virginia look good. He was proposing his Code Red expansion, opening a new line of products and high tech machinery that could earn Zanderbilt billions in profits if things went right. Amanda had bought into the idea, and she was on board one hundred percent. Ray was still heated about Amanda. She had fired Luke Zerricho and contracted another security company to take over when the contract with Steven's employer ended. Ray called her, furious about what she had done. Her nonchalant attitude infuriated him even more. He would never hit a woman, but she came close to being one he'd definitely choke.

When Ray called Steven to apologize for Amanda's actions, Steven wasn't nearly as concerned as Ray thought he might be.

"Don't sweat the small stuff, my friend, Steven seemed humored. Other companies have contracted us. Her getting let us go wasn't a big deal. Besides, I have a few other irons in the fire."

Ray was relieved to know that Steven had himself together, and it encouraged Ray greatly that Steven didn't put all his faith in a job, for his faith was in God. Ray learned a lot from this man, and even when he was down his friendship with Steven ensured he was still lifted up.

Ray boarded the 7:30 flight and sat comfortably in his first class seat. Surprisingly, Amanda hadn't booked a seat close to his. She had brought along her secretary, Eva, which was unusual for a business trip. Maybe she needed the assistant to run errands around the city before the big meeting in the morning. Ray made small talk with a few colleagues who were flying with him, but the main conversation for the majority of the plane ride was why Luke Zerrico had gotten axed. Word had quickly spread that he wasn't out of work a month before his young wife had left him. It made Ray nauseous every time he thought about how ruthless Amanda was.

She didn't care about anything but herself. She really disgusted him. He called Luke three times, but each time got no answer. He left messages, but never got a return phone call. Ray hoped Luke would be able to land another job soon.

An hour later the pilot announced they were nearing their destination. As the plane rolled to a stop and passengers poured into the terminal to get their baggage, Ray made a quick phone call to Donae to let her know the plane had landed safely, and he'd be calling her shortly with his hotel room number.

"Call me anytime you feel like it, baby, no matter what time it is."

"I will, Ray. Do your best," she smiled into the phone.

After checking in, Ray decided to relax in his suite and mentally prepare for the next morning's meeting, but his colleagues kept banging on his door every five minutes to urge him to join them for a drink. He didn't drink anymore, but just to get them out of his hair, he agreed to have one glass of wine and then return to his room. This project was his baby, he had a lot riding on this, and it could be the biggest break of his career. The idea of going even higher in the company would be wonderful, but getting out of the clutches of Amanda would be even better. It would open the door to a peaceful career.

The music at the hotel bar was lively. His male traveling companions were in good spirits within the hour of settling onto their stools for a few drinks. When Amanda walked in with Eva, Raymond decided he'd finish up his glass of wine and leave. Amanda stared at him from across the bar, with a devilish look on her face. She sashayed toward him with a smile that read trouble. Reaching his side, she turned his face toward her to be heard above the music and noise.

"Can I get a dance with a friend?" she asked politely.

"I don't think so, Amanda," Ray said sipping his second glass of red wine.

"I'm here for business, not pleasure."

"We're all here for business, but a little fun in between never hurt anyone. Loosen up and stop acting so holier-than-thou."

Eva startled Ray when she snuck up behind him to order two Grey Goose and Sprites at the bar.

"I think I like New York," she giggled as she waved to one of her co-workers.

"Don't get too happy," Amanda smiled.

"You're working too young lady."

"So I guess no dance, huh?" Amanda shrugged.

"Come on, Ray," she urged, pulling him toward the dance floor.

"I promise to be a good girl."

"Nope," Ray said.

"I'm sure you'll find someone to enjoy your evening with."

He reached behind him to grab his wine and finish it off. "You know, Ray," she winked.

"I might have to agree with you on that one, I think I will be enjoying my evening. This is New York City, the land of opportunity," she smiled, holding up her apple martini in celebration.

Amanda watched from the corner of her eye as Ray walked over and sat down at a table with some of his cheerful male employees and colleagues.

"You guys don't know how to act when you get away from your wives," Ray laughed at his clearly drunken friends.

"We don't?" One of the guys, Travis, bellowed from his drink.

"From what I hear, you're the one who doesn't know how to control yourself when your better half is out of the picture." He chucked down the rest of his drink.

"Hey, little lady," he signaled for the cocktail waitress.

"Another drink please, and how about a lap dance for some extra cash?" he said waving a twenty dollar bill in the air.

"Travis, dude, I think you've had enough," another of the men kicked him underneath the table.

"Man, do you know who the hell you're talking to? You need to sober up," the gentleman said politely, trying to save him from Ray's wrath.

"What?" Travis asked, still motioning for another drink.

"Everyone knows he's Amanda's boy toy. How do you think he got his job?" Ray's stern look sobered some of his employees instantly and caused his colleagues to chuckle.

"Let's see," Ray spoke clearly.

"It could be my master's degree in business management or my bachelor's in mass communication. Maybe it was the many long hours I spent working night and day getting this company on top, but I'm sure all that doesn't matter when it comes to gossip.

"I think he needs to sober up, too, before he finds himself in the unemployment line. You fellas enjoy the rest of your evening. I will see you all in the morning bright and early."

"As for you..." he said firmly to Travis.

"I'd like to see you in my office the day after we land in Virginia. Oh, and just a head's up, you may want to update your 'resume'."

152

Ray strolled away grinning inside. Although Travis' little comment ticked him off, he thought he had handled it well. He had no intentions of firing the man, but he would enjoy making him sweat. Taking the elevator up to his floor, Ray stood in front of his room door with a terrible headache. *Something on the plane must have made me sick*, he said to himself. Maybe he shouldn't have drank that second glass of wine. It had been nearly a year since he'd taken a sip of anything. Maybe his tolerance level wasn't the same as before. He rumbled through his pockets for his hotel card key, but he couldn't find it. Feeling sicker by the minute, he just wanted to lie down.

"Maybe I shouldn't have had any wine," he thought.

Maybe he had allowed Travis's comment to get under his skin. Catching sight of the housekeeper waiting at the elevator, he motioned for her as the doors flew open and asked if she would let him into his room. Inside, Ray flopped on his bed, suit and all. The room was spinning, and his heart was pounding a thousand beats a minute. Donae sent him a text message saying she loved him, but Ray could hardly see the keys to respond, though he tried. He felt himself drifting off to sleep, hoping he would feel better in the morning.

Hours later as sunlight peered around the edges of his the drapes of his room Ray woke up, feeling terrible. He still wasn't able to focus. Vomit threatened to erupt from the pit of his stomach, and he stumbled out of bed to race to the bathroom. At the first step he tripped over a high heel shoe. Dismissing it as he made it to the bathroom in seconds, but missed the commode, landing vomit all over the floor. Finally the retching stopped and he grabbed a white washcloth, running it under cold water, wiping his face of perspiration and spit. Then he noticed a white dress lying near the bathroom door and next to it was a pair of lacy underwear.

What the heck? Ray lifted himself fully upright to stare into his room, not believing his eyes.

"Baby, are you okay?" Amanda stepped into the bathroom wearing Ray's heavily starched shirt.

"What are you doing here?" Ray demanded. Suddenly he heaved again and this time got it into the toilet.

"Honey, are you okay?" She knelt down beside him, offering comfort.

"Get away from me!" Ray yelled.

"What did you do to me?"

"What do you mean?" she yelled back.

"I brought your hotel key that you left at the bar last night, and you invited me in. You attacked me like a wild animal. You've never made love to me like that, and I loved it," she smiled impishly, turning his queasy stomach even more.

"You're a liar!" he yelled, trying to rise up to a standing position.

Ray's legs were weak, his head was spinning, and now it was about to come out the other end. He shoved Amanda out of the bathroom and slammed the door, locking it, before settling on the toilet. When he was done, he staggered to his bed. Amanda had ordered some orange juice and Pepto Bismol.

"Ray, I don't know what's wrong with you, but there is no way you'll be ready to give a presentation like this," Amanda shook her head.

"I'll have to cover for you."

Ray tried to sit up, but all he could do was fall back like a limp rag doll. He stared at the ceiling, wondering why God had allowed this to happen. Amanda was right. There was no way he could give his presentation. Ray rolled over on the bed and wanted to cry. Not only had he defiled his marriage again, but he was disappointed in himself for giving Satan a crack in the doorway.

"Don't worry, Ray," Amanda blurted.

"I'll take care of everything. I'll do the presentation. I know all the details, and we'll close this deal. I promise. I'll call room service to get this place cleaned up, and you'll feel much better in a few hours. Don't worry," she knelt down by the side of the bed, trying to look into Ray's eyes.

Ray turned his head away. Shame wouldn't let him lift his head. How could he have let this happen? What, in fact, had happened? He closed his eyes, wishing this had just been a nightmare, but Amanda's soft touch reminded him that she had somehow become part of his reality. After the orange juice and stomach medicine arrived, Amanda made sure Ray was comfortable in bed after doctoring him up. He looked awful, and she hated leaving him in such bad condition. It was obvious he needed care.

"Ray, I will be back in a few hours to take care of you. Don't you worry, everything will be fine. It's probably just a bug."

"Stop calling me 'honey!'" Ray yelled at the top of his lungs as he held his hands tightly over his ears, shaking.

Ray's hotel room phone rang loudly, increasing his throbbing headache.

"Do you want me to answer that?" Amanda asked, reaching for the phone.

"No!" Ray growled, knowing it had to be Donae. She was the only one who knew his room number.

It might be someone about the meeting, Ray," Amanda insisted, hoping to goodness it was really Donae. She picked up the receiver so that the caller heard her last few words.

"Amanda?" The voice echoed through the line.

Amanda handed Ray the phone without saying a word. Ray's heart sank, he was afraid to even touch it, not knowing who was on the other end.

"Ray, I'm sorry to bother you, but I just need to apologize about last night." Travis tried to plead his case.

"I was drunk and out of line. Please forgive me, sir."

"Not now."

Ray hung up the receiver and chastised Amanda with a look that could kill. He fell back on the bed, feeling worse than he'd ever felt in his life. Amanda walked toward the door still wearing Ray's dress shirt.

"I'll see you in a few hours," she said as she grabbed her dress, underwear, and shoes off the floor.

"Don't worry about the deal. I'm going to seal it for you. I won't let you down, baby." Amanda slipped out the door in only Ray's dress shirt and her underwear. Travis opened his hotel door and quickly closed it back once he spotted Amanda tip-toeing down the hall to her own room.

Three hours later Ray started feeling well enough to take a shower and get dressed. He dialed Donae, but she didn't answer, so he left a message just to say he loved her. Thank goodness his "I love you 2" text message had gone through last night. After showering, he walked downstairs to the hotel dining room to put some food in his stomach. The orange juice and Pepto Bismol seemed to have settled the nausea.

After ordering a light brunch, he put his menu to the side and got a quick glimpse of Eva as she approached in his direction, carrying a zillion bags. He tried to make eye contact with her, but she flew past quickly, practically running to the elevator. The voices of his colleagues filled the room as he looked toward the front door entrance. Three or four of the guys were laughing and joking as they entered the foyer.

"Ray!" One of his colleagues cheered.

"Amanda closed the deal! We got approved for a $13.6 million expansion. They loved Code Red, man, and said it was the brainstorm of the century."

Ray couldn't help but smile. In spite of everything that was going on, it was still his project, his idea and his baby. Then Amanda appeared and flitted to Ray's side, even more confident than usual.

"It's true, baby," she grinned.

"We did it, Ray, we did it! You're a genius, honey."

She tried to kiss Ray's lips, but Ray turned his head squeezing his eyes shut in anger.

"Sit down, Amanda," Ray demanded.

Travis walked by the table and never looked in Ray's direction. His pace quickened, and he flew past quicker than Eva had. Amanda sat down like a school girl waiting for her scolding.

"I don't know what the hell you did to me last night, but I'm telling you right now, I plan to get to the bottom of it. Just so you know whatever happened in my room, it means nothing. I love my wife, and I'm never leaving her. As long as there is breath in my body I'll be by her side. So...," he cleared his throat.

"Whatever you think you may have accomplished with your little trick, it didn't work."

Amanda stared at him. "I don't know what you're talking about, Raymond. I was just returning your hotel key," she twirled her finger around in his beverage.

"You were the one all over me."

Ray looked at her intently. "I had two glasses of wine. I'm not stupid. I would never come on to you in that way and you know it. Stop with your games and get on with your life. You need to go fishing in another pond."

"I'll take this to go," Ray told the server as she set his meal down on the table.

"Better yet, could you please send it to room 2210?" He walked away in disgust.

Amanda sat down at the table with a smirk on her face. "That's what you think. I own this pond," she said aloud

The server came to the table holding a rolling cart for Ray's food. Amanda took a big bite of Ray's corned beef sandwich from the plate that the server was now holding in her hand and set it back on the shiny silver plate.

"Damn, I love corned beef," she smiled before getting up to leave.

Ivy allowed Dominic to pick out his new bedroom suit. The furniture company was scheduled to deliver at noon, but they were already twenty-five minutes late. Glancing at his watch, Ivy was disappointed because they were taking up too much of his Saturday. His flight was scheduled to leave for Detroit that evening, and he'd like to have studied his sermon a little while longer.

Dominic had already plastered posters of his favorite rappers all over the wall and a huge "Keep Out" sign in blood-red letters on his bedroom door. Against his better judgment, Ivy compromised on the posters, but he refused to budge when it came to the half naked women in string bikinis, who unfortunately made Ivy's mouth, start to water. The transition of Dominic moving in with him, Yolanda and Bryson was already a difficult one.

Ivy expected that it would take a lot of work on his behalf to mend the fragments of a relationship. Dominic made it crystal clear that he despised his father for being absent in his life, and he didn't hold back in letting Ivy know that he had no intentions of leaving his grandmother's house. Once Ivy and Miss Irma sat down and discussed the situation, they agreed it would be best for Dominic to come and live with his father immediately. Dominic hadn't been living with the family a week yet, and Ivy was ready to pull his hair out. It was obvious to everyone that Dominic was on a brutal mission to do everything in his power to make Ivy so frustrated that he would send the boy back to his grandmother. Yet, Ivy was determined that things were going to work out. He prayed that God would give him strength.

On top of the transition with Dominic, Yolanda decided that they would only be intimate three times a week. Not three days, but three times. So that meant if he got it twice in one day, he only had one more for the whole week. He'd already had his three for the week, and it was only Wednesday, so now he really felt like hassling somebody. Thank goodness he was going to Detroit to preach for a few days. He prayed the distance might cool him off, but who was he fooling, he thought. He was worse than a dog in heat. Yolanda had made quite a few friends since the move to Virginia, but she and Evangelist Vanessa Reardon seemed tighter than peas in a pod these days. Ivy had no issues with that. Yolanda was always good at discernment, and Vanessa was an awesome woman of faith. She had a gift to minister the Word of God in a mighty way. She walked in the fullness and the power of the Holy Spirit.

At times when Ivy went away to preach, he'd allow Vanessa to minister on Sunday mornings, and she never disappointed him. He had several ministers at the church who could preach the house down, but there was just something about her that drew people to God. This was probably why she and Yolanda had such a connection. Yolanda had a contrite and humble spirit as well. Ivy knew the moment the two ladies started getting to know each other better that it was just a matter of time before Yolanda would start poking her nose into Vanessa's business.

Yolanda was bound and determined to hook Vanessa up with Steven, but Ivy warned her right away to stay clear of match-making. Ivy had to admit that Steven would be a good catch for any woman. Many ladies in the church were batting their eyelashes and smiling like there was no tomorrow. There were rumors floating around the congregation that Steven might be gay, but that was only because he wasn't taking the bait that the women were throwing at him. He just wasn't interested in any of them.

Ivy had secretly hoped that when his sister, Courtney came to town last month from Atlanta she might go out with Steven, but he too had learned his lesson from trying to introduce her to men. She came home, stayed a week, and was gone. She said she hated coming home because the whole time she was there, JoAnn wanted to cast out her lesbian spirit. Ivy didn't condone her lifestyle, but he knew she had been taught the Word of God at a young age just as he was, so he prayed that God would deliver her from that spirit that she was struggling with. One thing was for sure, he wasn't in any position to judge or condemn her, as he too had his own issues to bear. So until he pulled the "log from his own eye," he wasn't about to pick at the speck in hers. She was his baby sister, and he loved her, whatever her sexual preference was.

"Ivy," Yolanda yelled from the kitchen.

"You and the boys come down. Lunch is ready."

"Okay, honey," Ivy confirmed.

"We're almost done putting everything together. We just have to put the dresser and chest of drawers in place."

"Okay," Yolanda yelled back.

Bryson got downstairs first. Mom, can I hang some posters on my wall and get a rap CD?"

He sat down at the kitchen table, waiting on a reply.

Here we go! Yolanda sighed loudly.

"You'll have to talk that over with your father, Bryson."

"Dominic listens to rap, and he's got posters on his wall, so I should be able to do it too," he frowned.

"Dominic is a teenager. You've got a little ways to go before you're a teen," she said calmly, stirring the spaghetti sauce before turning to drain the pasta.

"So does that mean 'no'?" he said with a hint of contempt.

"It means ask your father, Bryson."

She looked at him firmly.

"Why can't you make some choices around here sometimes? It's just like Dominic said, you can't make nobody do nothing," he folded his boney arms defiantly.

"What did you say?" Yolanda frowned as she walked toward him.

"You better slow your roll, little boy, before I show you exactly how much authority I have! I don't know who you think you're talking to in that tone."

"For the last week your mouth has gotten downright disrespectful, and I won't stand for it another day. I said ask your father," she said affirming her tone.

"Better yet, since I can't make anybody do anything around here, I'll just start now. Your answer is NO. You can't get a rap CD or posters!" Yolanda said sternly.

Bryson pouted almost in tears as Ivy and Dominic came downstairs and washed their hands before sitting at the table.

"What's wrong, Bryson?" Ivy asked with a concerned glance.

Yolanda answered for him. "Nothing," she said.

"He just needed a reality check."

She glanced at Bryson who was now laying his sad face on thick big time.

"So how does the bedroom look?" she asked, looking toward Dominic for an answer as she set the plates of spaghetti before each of them.

Dominic didn't mumble a word.

"It looks great," Ivy answered after the long silence, putting a napkin on his lap.

"That's good." Yolanda gave a partial smile.

No matter how hard she tried, Dominic always seemed to make her feel like she meant nothing.

"I'll put the sheets and comforter on later, and I'm sure it will look even better," Yolanda added in her normal cheery tone, refusing to allow a child to break her Spirits.

Yolanda tried to make small talk as she sat down to join the others while they ate. "So honey, I was thinking about having a dinner here at the house. Do you think you can invite Steven?"

"Sure," Ivy answered, swirling spaghetti around his fork, and then stabbing a plump meatball.

"As long as you don't invite Vanessa," he grinned and chewed at the same time.

"You're so funny," Yolanda smiled dryly.

"Is Steven going with you and Kevin to Detroit?"

"No, it's just Kevin and I," Ivy said.

"Steven's not in town for a few days."

Steven sure does go out of town a lot. I wonder what's up with that, she thought.

"How's your lunch, Dominic?" Yolanda was determined to make an effort.

"It's not my Grandma's," he said snobbishly.

"I'm sure it's not," Yolanda replied.

"Would you like another helping since you've already devoured that one so quickly?"

Dominic's fork hit the empty plate hard.

"Can I ask a question, Dad?" he asked with his usual sarcasm, as he purposely ignored Yolanda's question.

"What makes this Bitch so special that you married her instead of my momma?" he looked directly into Ivy's face.

Bryson's eyes got as big as half dollars. He watched in anticipation because he knew Dominic was about to hit the floor hard. Ivy jumped up from the table so quickly that he spilled lemonade all over the floor.

"Let's go!" he pointed Dominic toward the door.

Dominic smiled as he headed toward the stairs to start packing his clothes.

"Oh, no, son," Ivy insisted.

"This way." He pointed to the door leading to the garage. Ivy led the way to the garage and sat him down on a plastic crate. In a calm voice Ivy started talking as he walked over to unlock his gun case.

"Now look, son. I know your mother told you a lot of bad things about me, but the truth is I love you. I always have and I always will. I've been trying to have a relationship with you, but she made it difficult for that to happen,"

Ivy sighed as he pulled the 38 special out of the cabinet, along with a cleaning brush. "So here is the deal," Ivy took the safety off the gun.

"I'm planning on getting custody of you. You and I are going to make this work. I can only imagine what your mother has put in your head about me."

"The truth is that some of it may very well be true. I admit I've done some things in my past that I'm not proud of. I've hurt people, but I'm not that man anymore."

He lifted his gun and looked through the chamber. Dominic's eyes widened. "The bottom line is this. I want us to be a family. I want you and your mother and your stepmother to have a healthy relationship. I insist that you and I are going to have a loving father-and-son relationship. One that's filled with love, and I want to get your mom help to conquer her addiction," he said still looking through the chamber.

"I've already been in contact with a rehab facility, if she would be willing to go through the program. But son…," Ivy paused an extended minute before blowing his breath into the chamber and grabbing the silver bullets from another locked compartment in the wooden gun cabinet.

"Going back to your Grandma Irma's house for anything other than a visit is not an option."

"Bryson!" Ivy bellowed through the garage door.

"Sir?" Bryson stuck his head through the door leading to the garage.

"Come here, son," Ivy said, sitting another crate near Dominic.

Bryson sat down on the crate, not knowing what to expect. The look on Dominic's face was confusing. He looked angry, scared and sad all at the same time.

"Now, when you boys grow up and get wives and start having children, you're going to do everything in your power to protect what belongs to you." He smiled as he loaded up the gun.

"And if someone tries to hurt what's yours, you're going to do everything in your power to protect it, right?"

Both boys nodded as they carefully watched the black piece of steel. "Now I want both of you to listen, and I want you to listen well, because I'm only going to say this once."

He finished loading up the gun and laid it on the table. "That woman in there loves both you boys very much. There isn't anything she wouldn't do for either of you," he pulled another gun out of the case and loaded it.

"Not only does she love the both of you, but she wants what's best for you, and so do I. If either of you ever does anything to purposely hurt her or disrespect her while I'm alive, trust me, you will not like the consequences. Believe me when I say that you will feel the same way about protecting and honoring your wives one day when you have them," he said aiming the gun toward the bulls-eye hanging on the wall in between the two of them.

The loud sound of rushing air from the pellet gun made both boys jump as Ivy fired it into the cushioned bulls-eyes on the wall. After firing, he laid the pellet gun beside the 38 special for both boys to see.

"Now if either of you want to continue to challenge me because you don't believe me to be the protector and provider of what God has required me to cover, you're more than welcome to."

Everyone, including Ivy, was now staring at the black iron lying on the wooden table. "I'm a man who loves the Lord."

Ivy looked at both boys without blinking. "And I strive to walk in his will. God called me to protect my family, and that's just what I intend to do until the day God calls me to heaven. Do I make myself clear, sons?"

Both Dominic and Bryson said a soft spoken "yes, sir."

"Now Bryson, you go apologize to your mother for your sassy mouth lately, and Dominic, you go apologize for temporarily losing your mind. Do either of you have a problem with that?" He walked over and picked up the 38 to take the bullets out.

"No, sir," Bryson said fearfully.

"No, sir," Dominic echoed, feeling the need to give Ivy respect.

Bryson walked back into the house first, thinking to himself that he'd never talk back to his mother again for the rest of his life. Dominic stood at the bedroom door, a bit shaken, as he patiently waited on Bryson to finish with his apology to Yolanda. He felt the need to go check his pants. He couldn't help but think to himself how Ivy was one crazy Motha.

****

Ivy and Kevin checked in at the Hyatt Regency Hotel around 10:00 p.m.

"Do you want to grab something to eat, or would you rather order room service?" Kevin asked Ivy as they got their room keys.

"I'm thinking room service," Ivy answered, which was right up Kevin's alley since he was exhausted from the plane ride.

Ivy called home once the plane landed, wanting to make sure things were okay on the home front. He wasn't one hundred percent sure about leaving Dominic at the house with Yolanda without him being there, but she assured him that everything would be fine. She could tell by the look in Dominic's eyes when he apologized that Ivy had literally scared the hell out of him. Yolanda confirmed to Ivy that things at home were fine. Bryson was asleep, and Dominic was in his room listening to his headphones, the last time she had checked, and she was preparing to take a shower.

"Can I take one with you when I get home?" Ivy asked.

"You've already had your medicine this week, Pastor," she replied.

"Yolanda, baby, please, can we reconsider this silly three times a week thing?"

"It's not silly, Ivy, its fair," Yolanda answered.

"And, no, we can't reconsider."

"But Yolanda, you know I can't survive off three measly times a week."

"And just what does that mean, Ivan?" Yolanda asked.

"What will happen when I don't budge?"

"Yolanda, why are you doing this? You know I need my wife more than three times a week."

"Ivy…what about me? Do you think I want to screw 24/7? I'm tired. You've turned making love into a chore that I just downright dread!" Yolanda said honestly.

"What!" Ivy raised his eyebrows.

"Are you telling me you don't enjoy it anymore?" he sounded surprised.

"Ivy, it feels like a job and no, I don't enjoy it so often."

She hated to admit it, but if she didn't, the burden would continue. "You've taken the intimacy out of it by doing it so much. How about allowing me some time to want it? Instead of it being…."

"Being what?" Ivy asked, as he tried his best not to let his temperature rise.

"Instead of it being what it is," she exhaled, "a constant duty."

The silence through the phone line was uncomfortable for them both.

"Goodnight, Yolanda." Ivy hung up the phone without waiting for a response. He knew if he continued the conversation he might say something he'd surely regret.

The first night of Revival was out of this world. Ivy couldn't put into words how the Holy Spirit used him. He gave God all the glory for the many lives that were saved. The songs reached into the rafters, and people's faces were alive with joy. You couldn't be in that room and not be touched by the Spirit. After service Ivy and Kevin had dinner at a popular restaurant near downtown Detroit. Women diners were eyeing both men when they took their seats. One even had the guts to send her phone number to the table, addressed to the guy in the grey suit, who was Ivy. When the woman saw Kevin discreetly ball up the small piece of paper, she got up from her table where her girlfriends still sat and seductively made her way to their table.

"Hi, Pastor James," she smiled innocently.

"I'm Cindy Williams. You sure did preach a word tonight. You are awesome," she said, as she looked down at the diamond and gold band on Ivy's finger.

"Thank you, dear," Ivy replied, recognizing the familiar flirtatious spirit.

"Where are you gentlemen staying? I'd love to send over some pastries from my bakery."

"Oh," Ivy smiled.

"I love sweets. That's so kind of you. We're staying at the Hyatt."

Kevin interrupted Cindy's deceptive ploy. "If you want sweets, Pastor, we'll order you some dessert," he said, annoyed that Ivy had broken Rule 102: *never let a woman know where you are staying.*

"Thank you for your kind offer, but I'm sorry, that won't be necessary. Pastor James' wife is really funny about who she allows to cook for her husband," Kevin gave a partial smile.

"I see." She rolled her eyes at Kevin, ticked at his sidekick's block.

"Well, do you have any CDs, tapes, or books with you? I wasn't able to purchase anything after service, as the lines were extremely long."

"I'm sorry. I don't have anything with me right now. Everything is all packed up." Ivy wiped his mouth with the napkin, and smiled apologetically.

"If I swing by your hotel, do you think it might be possible for me to get some of your promotional items?"

She pressed him as one of the other ladies sitting at her table walked over to make small talk with Kevin as a distraction. Unfortunately for her, Kevin was on top of his game.

"If you'd like some of Pastor James' teachings, you can stop by the table in the next two days since we will be here for two more nights of Revival. Also, you're welcome to log on to the church's website and order anything you like," Kevin smiled again handing her a card with the church's website information

"Please excuse us," he added.

He watched their server heading in the direction of their table with steaming platters on a large round tray. When he stopped at their table, Kevin felt relieved.

"Our food has arrived, ladies, and we need to eat and get our rest. It's been nice meeting you."

Cindy and her girlfriend walked away like sad, hungry puppies.

"It's going to be a long two days," Kevin said, spreading honey butter on his lightly browned yeast roll.

Ivy laughed. "Can't get nothing by you, soldier, that's for sure. Maybe I should have brought Steven," he joked.

Kevin laughed. "It wouldn't have made a difference. Steven's on his 'A' game too."

The last night of Revival, Cindy showed up at the Hyatt and got a room three doors down from Ivy. When Kevin and Ivy entered the hotel doors like clockwork, she watched patiently as Kevin strolled into the dining area to order their dinner. Cindy pranced her way toward the elevator, wearing a skimpy bikini, to where Ivy was standing, waiting for the elevator to reach the lobby floor.

"Hello, Pastor James."

Her voice startled him, as she had snuck up behind him. Ivy smiled once he realized who she was. The pair eagerly conversed about the previous day's service. She conveniently mentioned that she'd been stressed since her divorce was finalized nearly six months earlier. She had decided to treat herself to some much needed rest and relaxation.

"I understand," Ivy agreed.

Ivy was telling the Devil in the back of his mind to back away. He struggled not to stare at Cindy's perfectly shaped hips or berry red lips.

"Sometimes when I've got something heavy on my mind, I like to go someplace and unwind too. There isn't anything wrong with that," he said as they both stepped into the elevator.

Ivy pressed the number six and waited for Cindy to tell him her floor number.

"I'm on the sixth floor too," she smiled suggestively.

"I bet after preaching like you do, night after night, you could probably use a deep massage to help you unwind and sleep better. I could help relieve some of that tension," she said, not giving him a chance to answer.

"I'm a licensed massage therapist, and I'm good with my hands, Pastor."

Ivy pondered her proposition. What could it hurt? He did have some tension built up. Only it wasn't tension, he was horny. On the other hand, it was only a massage.

"I might just take you up on that offer," he said.

"Let me get out of this suit," he cringed the moment those words parted from his lips.

He knew he was walking down a path of destruction. Kevin caught up with the two of them, rolling a small tray of food. He shook his head at Cindy as he couldn't help but notice her sexy white bikini.

"Pastor, take this tray to your room. I will see you shortly."

Kevin didn't ask. He pretty much insisted with a hint of force behind his voice. Ivy didn't dispute Kevin's demand. He inwardly felt relieved by God's provision of escape.

"What about your massage, Pastor? The offer still stands."

Cindy gave Ivy a pleading look of disappointment as he grabbed the tray.

"Massage!" Kevin rebuked Ivy with his eyes.

"No ma'am," he looked directly into Cindy's gorgeous face.

"Thank you, but no way in the world is that happening, not now, not ever."

Kevin watched Ivy swipe his card key and walk into the room before he decided to give Cindy a few choice words.

"Look, lady," he pushed up close to her, almost smelling her breath.

"Don't you know how many times I've seen this?"

"Seen what?" Cindy said, playing dumb.

"Women like you throwing themselves at men of God. Not only is his wife his First Lady, she's his *only* lady. Maybe if you acted more like one, you'd have a man of your own. Now stay away from his room before I call security and tell them you are harassing him."

"I'm not harassing him!" she exploded.

"He was more than willing until you came along with your self-righteous attitude," she rolled her eyes.

Kevin stared at her frankly.

"It's my job, Jezebel, to make sure no Devil in hell or on earth,"

He looked at her perfectly shaped curves up and down, and continued..." is going to contaminate his anointing. So, Devil, move on."

Kevin never cracked a smile. She glared at him so furious that she wanted to smack his handsome face. Unloosening her bikini top, she let it fall to the floor. She grabbed his hands and cupped her full breasts in his palms.

"Feels good, doesn't it, man of God?"

Cindy leaned in and pressed her soft lips against Kevin's and smiled as he battled within his flesh and pushed her away.

"You might want to get some ice for that." She looked down at the hard rock between his legs.

"I'd have shown you both a good time." She picked up her bikini top from the carpet and left Kevin standing there in embarrassment and disbelief.

Ivy walked out of the bathroom after showering and shaving. Kevin was already sitting at the table eating his food.

"I guess no massage, huh?" Ivy laughed.

Twenty minutes later there was a soft knock on the door. Kevin got up to answer it.

"Who is it?" Ivy asked, a little nervous.

"Oh, it's your massage, Pastor." Kevin opened the door wide.

Ivy wore a confused smile that only lasted a second once he saw the obese woman lumbering into the room in her print uniform.

"Mr. James, are you ready for your massage?" she asked.

Kevin grinned as he stood near the door, about to go to his own room.

"Hey, hey, where are you going?" Ivy asked.

"To my room, enjoy your one-hour massage Pastor" Kevin said wanting to burst out in laughter.

"Nah man, I'm cool," Ivy said, trying to usher the masseuse from the room.

Malcolm was delighted to see Vanessa standing in the pulpit Sunday morning to preach. She had never mentioned that she would be ministering this morning. All he knew was that he couldn't wipe the smile off his face. She looked determined to get the message across by touching the hearts of the congregation. A light seemed to shine from her eyes as she spoke. Pastor Ivy was there, but he had been preaching revivals for the last three weeks, and his voice was nearly gone. Sitting in the front row off to one side, he seemed weary but content, nodding occasionally as Vanessa made her point.

Malcolm stood holding his Bible. Steven stood beside him as they both turned to the scripture in Genesis to which Vanessa was referring. She explained how God had made woman to be a helpmate to man, and she defined and dissected the concept of marriage while explaining God's purpose for marriage. She educated many people sitting in the pews that morning about things they didn't know and maybe didn't even want to know. Malcolm was on his feet praising God with the rest of the congregation as Vanessa harshly chastised women who tried to keep good men down, rebuking those who refused to let their children have a healthy relationship with their fathers, whether these men paid child support or not. She adamantly stressed that a mother had no right to decide whether a father could spend time with his child.

"Who are you to make yourself God, to judge another human being?" she called out.

Even Pastor Ivy was finally on his feet, yelling for her to preach it. Brothers all over the sanctuary were sending waves of high-fives and 'hallelujah's 'in almost every pew. People who normally sat back and said nothing during service were now shouting, "You better tell the truth!"

By the church members' reactions, you could tell Vanessa knocked her sermon out of the ball park, and Malcolm couldn't be more proud. Although they'd been dating for only a few months, he had to admit he wouldn't mind her being, 'bone of his bone and flesh of his flesh.'

The anointing that rested on her spirit made the woman even more attractive, and as much as Malcolm hated to admit it, he was quickly falling in love. Everywhere he went he wanted her with him. He couldn't fall asleep without saying good-night to her. Malcolm smiled when he reminisced about the comment Ray had said that day in Moe's parking lot when he had beat Morris.

"Maybe God has something better in store for you," he had said earnestly. Who would have thought how right he would be.

Even Steven had to acknowledge that he had let a good one slip away, but he was rejoicing to see his friend so happy and full of joy. Malcolm was feeling grateful for his life at this time. His mom Louise and sister Lauren were tickled pink with Vanessa. They thought she was a breath of fresh air for Malcolm, as did everyone else. The relationship with his kids was shaping up in encouraging ways. KJ was starting to come around. They had been to a few baseball games, and KJ really enjoyed the boxing ring.

Malcolm saw potential in him, so he promised his son he could come down to the gym on the days he was working out and dance around the ring a little. Sydney, on the other hand, wouldn't be satisfied even if she had a million dollars. The more Malcolm gave her for Crystal's support, the more she wanted. Her child support checks were coming in every week like clockwork, but she made sure to have Crystal call him for extra money for any number of things. Malcolm knew Sydney was using his child to lie on her behalf to extort more funds, but he never told his daughter "no" if he had it to give. Sydney played Malcolm for stupid.

Crystal let it slip one day that her mother and her live-in boyfriend Tony had gone to the courthouse and gotten married. Sydney thought Malcolm wouldn't remember, but this Tony guy was the same dude that she had been with when he was released from prison. Crystal made Malcolm promise not to tell her mother that she had let it slip, afraid she would get in trouble.

Malcolm was patiently waiting on his divorce papers to come through. Telese had mentioned months ago that it would take ninety days, but ninety days had come and gone. Believe it or not, he now couldn't wait to sign on the dotted line. He kept asking Telese what the hold-up was, but she said she didn't know and she was still working on it. Malcolm was ready to make it official and move on with his life. From what he knew, Telese and Morris were still seeing one another, but that no longer bothered him. They could get married for all Malcolm cared. Heck, he would even give her away.

After church service ended, Malcolm couldn't get a foot next to Vanessa. She was bombarded by every member in the congregation. Malcolm stood to the side making small talk with a few brothers in Christ, waiting to see an opening to get to his woman. Vanessa was eyeing him as well, hoping for a hug. Finally after a few minutes, the crowd started thinning out. Suddenly, when Malcolm looked up, Telese was standing in front of Vanessa, smiling, and Pastor Ivy and First Lady Yolanda was heading in their direction.

"That was an awesome message." Telese gave Vanessa a warm hug.

"I have to say, I felt convicted. You were telling the truth," Telese shook her head.

"Thank you so much, but the glory belongs to God," Vanessa said meekly.

"I just love your humble spirit," Telese added.

"Thank you I appreciate that. What's your name, by the way?" Vanessa asked.

Pastor Ivy stepped forward, giving Vanessa a huge bear hug.

"Girl, you and the Holy Spirit are a force to be reckoned with," he chuckled.

"I second that motion," Yolanda smiled at her beautiful best friend.

"Vanessa, that was a word," Pastor Ivy said proudly.

"I know that's right, Pastor," Telese chimed in.

"Hi there." Pastor gave Telese a hug.

He recognized her as attending the church, but for the life of him he couldn't remember her name.

"Where in the world have you been? I haven't seen you here in ages."

"Oh Pastor," Telese grinned.

"I've been in and out of town," she lied, not wanting to tell him the truth about her going to worship at Morris' church.

Since Malcolm had started attending church there, she decided it best to worship in two different places. She knew if she wanted to invite Morris with her, it would incite another world war.

"Well, it's nice of you to visit with us," Ivy grinned.

"Please come back and worship with us again."

Turning to the other woman, he asked happily, "so, Vanessa, where's this 'friend' of yours that my wife won't shut up about? I need to check him out."

Vanessa blushed, bringing more color to her rosy cheeks. Malcolm was standing close, talking to his kids. Vanessa motioned for him to come over, so he and the kids joined the small group standing there.

"Pastor," Vanessa paused shyly.

"I'd like you to meet Malcolm Stuart, and these are his beautiful children, Layla and KJ"

Both kids waved at Pastor and First Lady Yolanda.

"Nice to meet you Malcolm, I know you've been at Mt. Emanuel a while now. I recognize you from the men's conference. Who could forget the prophetic word Apostle gave you?"

"Yeah, Pastor, I know. I've been living off that word ever since. That men's conference changed my life. It made a new man out of me."

"My armor bearer Steven is pretty fond of you. He says you've been helping in the ministry, and we're grateful," Ivy beamed at Malcolm.

"I appreciate that, Pastor," Malcolm smiled.

"I'll gladly serve. God has done too much for me not to give back."

Telese stood frozen in place not wanting to believe what she was seeing or hearing. She felt faint and light-headed. Over the past few months she had noticed a change in Malcolm but just couldn't put her finger on it. Now it all made sense.

"Are you okay?" Ivy asked. "You look faint sweetheart."

Ivy was totally unaware that Malcolm was her husband. Malcolm looked at his wife too, a little concerned.

"Are you okay, Telese?"

"Yes, I'm fine." Telese snapped from her daze.

"We'll see you guys later." She turned to walk away.

"Layla, KJ, you all let's go. I've got to get dinner started."

"Mom, we want to talk to Dad," Layla begged.

"Layla, let's go."

Telese tried her best not to lose her temper in the church, but her patience was slipping.

"Is Mr. Morris coming over again?" the girl pouted.

"You guys better go with your mom," Malcolm insisted, aware that Layla's comment made Telese cringe.

"I will get with you soon." Malcolm kissed them both.

Vanessa was in shock. She tried to hide the surprised look on her face when Malcolm said the name Telese and Layla addressed Telese as "Mommy."

When Telese had hugged her earlier, she had no idea that the attractively dressed, full-figured woman standing before her was Malcolm's wife. Nor did Telese have any inkling that Vanessa was Malcolm's new boo. Malcolm had been honest and told Vanessa about his anger issues, the fighting, and how Telese was seeing his ex-best friend. He also told her that Telese had insisted on a quick divorce, and they were waiting for it to be finalized. Vanessa couldn't get upset with Malcolm, especially since he had already told her about Telese, even mentioning that she used to attend Mt. Emanuel.

Malcolm watched Telese snatch Layla's arm as they headed out the double doors. Everything in him wanted to go confront her about jerking his baby like that, but he knew it was best to leave it alone. He stood next to Vanessa, holding her from behind, everybody now trying to ignore and forget the tense mini-scene that had just taken place.

"So Malcolm, was that your ex-wife?" First Lady Yolanda asked.

Ivy poked Yolanda in the arm, eyeing her, for she knew better.

"Yes," Malcolm answered, lying.

He didn't have the guts to explain the complicated situation, but it didn't matter, as Yolanda already knew he was still married. Vanessa had told her all the details since they were now best friends. She had met Malcolm already, but wasn't sure if he was the right one for Vanessa. This little scene had waved another big red flag in her face. KJ and Layla sat in the car, pouting.

"But Daddy said earlier we could go with him if it was all right with you!"

"No!" Telese stormed at them.

"Close the door right now."

The awesome sermon Vanessa had just preached moments ago faded into obscurity, with no chance of working a positive effect on Telese.

"How dare he have a girlfriend when we're not even divorced yet," she mumbled under her breath.

"Just because he's got a decent job now he thinks he's all that," she whispered, losing her little bit of religion.

"I'll be damned" she cried aloud.

"So tell me, you two," Telese turned to look at them in the back seat.

"How long have you known about Ms. Vanessa?"

Both Layla and KJ shrugged.

"We went to the zoo and to the movies, and skating too," Layla smiled.

"Oh, really?" Telese frowned, unable to believe Layla kept it a secret.

"When was this, KJ?" She looked directly at her son for answers.

"Mom, I don't know, a while back," he said,

"And you didn't tell me?" she glanced at them both.

"Mom, do you think she was preaching about you?" KJ asked innocently.

"Are you mad, Momma?" Layla asked, upset because she couldn't go with her father.

"No, I'm not mad." Telese turned the wheel abruptly.

"Then why are you driving like that?" KJ asked.

"Are you made because Dad has a girlfriend?"

"No, son," Telese said calmly.

"I guess I'm just surprised, but no, I'm not angry," she lied through her pearly white teeth.

"I'm happy for your father. He has really changed this time."

"He sure has," KJ answered.

"We went to his graduation ceremony and everything."

"What graduation ceremony?" Telese asked, glancing at them with a curious expression in the rearview mirror.

"You didn't know about him graduating from anger management class? He was the speaker," KJ grinned happily.

"The speaker?" Telese answered surprised.

"Wow! What did he speak about?"

"He talked about how he used to hit you, and how he would hate himself afterwards. He told everybody what happened the day he actually decided to change. He said that day was when I came in your room with a BB gun. He said once he found God, that God helped him to change."

"Daddy thanked Ms. Vanessa a lot for supporting him through everything. Grandma Louise and Aunt Lauren were there, Mr. Ray and Mr. Steven, and some of Dad's friends from the ring came. I'm proud of him," KJ continued.

"That's great," Telese replied.

"Looks like he has a whole new circle of friends, huh?"

"Ms. Vanessa had him a graduation cookout afterwards. All her family was there."

"Mom, she has this uncle named Rufus. Man, he is so funny," KJ laughed just thinking about him.

"Momma, since you're not mad can we go chill with Daddy today?" Layla asked.

"Please, Mom!" KJ piggybacked on Layla's question.

Telese laughed at her daughter's choice of words.

"You've been hanging around your brother too long," Telese smiled. She paused a moment.

"Yes, I guess you rug rats can spend the rest of the day with your father."

"Yes!" KJ fist pumped the air.

"Yay," Layla shouted.

"I hope Ms. Vanessa comes with us."

"Shh!" KJ nudged Layla in the leg.

"Ouch!" Layla whined.

"KJ, it's okay," Telese said, a bit embarrassed.

"Ms. Vanessa is a very nice woman. Maybe she's just what your father needs."

"And she's so pretty too, Momma, ain't she?"

"Isn't she," Telese corrected Layla.

"Yes, sweetie, she's a beautiful little thing," Telese added, a tad bit jealous of Vanessa's perfect shape.

"I'll give your father a call once we get home. That way you two can change into something more comfortable."

Telese detoured to the convenience store to grab some snacks, the kids picked up a couple of items but Telese had a basket half full of junk food just for her. Her diet was officially out the window and her new plan was to eat herself out of her on coming depression. The rest of the ride home was quiet. Telese had mixed emotions concerning Malcolm. She started mentally getting down on herself about her weight. Seeing Vanessa's beauty and figure made her feel fat and ugly. She was partly happy for him, but she kind of wished she would have gotten to see the Godly Malcolm in their marriage. Had she given up on him too soon? Seeing the sparkle in Malcolm's eyes when he stood at the church holding Vanessa from behind, made Telese feel sad. She knew for certain he was in love, but today she would make a vow that she wouldn't stand in the way of his happiness. Besides, once her divorce to Malcolm and Morris's divorce to his wife were final, Morris had hinted around at eloping.

Malcolm stopped by the convenience store to grab a bottle of Tylenol. He could feel a headache coming on. He and Vanessa grabbed a quick bite to eat at a local hot dog shop and changed clothes at Vanessa's house before heading for the ring. In the car they discussed the uncomfortable scenario at church. Vanessa couldn't be upset with Malcolm, as he had been honest about everything. Vanessa had to be honest too, and let him know that the little scene had made her think twice about some issues.

"How long do you think it will be before your paperwork is finalized?" she asked.

"It shouldn't be much longer," Malcolm said, a little fidgety.

"I think maybe we should cool off from seeing each other until all that is over with. You are still married, even if it is just a technicality."

"No, Vanessa, I don't want to do that!" he insisted.

"No, way!" he gave her a pleading glance.

Patiently, Vanessa said, "Malcolm, think about how this looks. I'm an Evangelist in the church dating a married man, for goodness sake."

"I don't care what anybody thinks," Malcolm said, his heart starting to flutter.

"This is our lives, not theirs. We haven't been doing anything wrong. For all anyone knows, we're just friends."

After a pause she said, "You're right. We are just friends."

"I don't want to be your friend, Vanessa. We're more than just friends, or at least I thought we were," Malcolm said sadly. "Why would you say that?"

"I think Telese is still in love with you." Vanessa avoided Malcolm's questioning glance.

Malcolm started laughing.

"You're crazy!" he laughed again.

"I'm telling you the truth," Vanessa said, glancing out the passenger side window.

"I could tell by the way she looked when Pastor alluded to us seeing one another."

Malcolm laughed again as he stared at the road. "She's seeing Morris, Vanessa," he said.

When she didn't answer, Malcolm looked over at her. Once he got a clear look at her glossy eyes, he immediately pulled the car over into an abandoned grocery store parking lot. Turning off the ignition, he turned to face her.

"Listen, Vanessa." Malcolm grabbed both her hands.

"I know this situation is a little complicated, but I'm telling you the truth. Telese isn't in love with me, and even if she was, which she isn't, it doesn't matter, because I'm in love with you."

After a slight pause, Vanessa broke free from his hands and pushed open her door, jumping out.

"Vanessa, what's wrong, baby?"

He pushed his door open, a bit confused and got out to catch up with her. She turned her back, trying not to expose her tears, a manifestation of her overflowing heart.

"Baby, what's wrong?" Malcolm tried to pull at her arm and turn her towards him.

"I love you, too," she shouted over her shoulder as she continued to walk away, unable to look him in the face.

"Look at me, Vanessa," he called.

"Vanessa please, I don't understand."

She paused. "Malcolm, I'm scared. I didn't want to fall in love with you. I didn't want to fall in love with anybody," she said.

"You know about my past. I've been hurt too many times, and I don't want to be hurt again."

"Vanessa, I'm not going to hurt you, baby."

Hearing the peaceful tone in his voice, she slowly turned to face him.

Malcolm continued. "I love you. I know you have this issue trusting men. I'm not like them. I want to be like the man you preached about today in your sermon. I want to be your Adam, your protector and your provider. I want to be all you ever want and need. Please just give me a chance," Malcolm begged.

"Don't let go before we even get started."

"If you won't trust Malcolm, the fleshly man, at least trust the God in Malcolm, the spiritual man. That Man won't disappoint you."

Vanessa smiled. She'd never heard anything so beautiful. He embraced her, and it felt good. He kissed her strawberry-flavored lips and melted.

"You feel wonderful," Malcolm murmured.

"Strawberries have never tasted this good."

"We better stop this," Vanessa said, "or we might end up in trouble."

"You're right," Malcolm agreed.

He thanked God in his heart that he finally had told Vanessa how he felt, and he was so glad she felt the same way.

As Malcolm drove to the ring, the two of them kept looking over at one another, giggling. It was official. They were now a couple. Malcolm felt like he was on top of the world. This woman brought out the best in him. He was grateful that they weren't back at Vanessa's house because as the good Lord was his witness he was ready to know Vanessa like Adam knew Eve. From the way Vanessa was eyeing him as they rounded the street near the ring; she wanted him to know her too.

Malcolm looked down at his ringing phone. When he saw Telese's name pop up on the caller ID, a part of him didn't want to answer, but he knew if he didn't, that might look suspicious. He always answered his phone in front of Vanessa to show her he had nothing to hide.

"Hello," Malcolm answered and then paused.

"Hey Telese, what's going on?" he said, grabbing Vanessa's hand and squeezing tightly.

After a moment he said, "Hold on."

"Hey baby," he said to Vanessa.

"The kids want to hang out with us. Is that cool with you?"

"You know it is," Vanessa smiled.

"Sure, Telese, that will work. I'll give you the address to the ring. Do you mind bringing them up here? And grab them something light to eat on the way 'cause we'll be here a while. I'm sparring today. We'll go out to eat afterwards." Telese fire re-sparked when she heard Malcolm asking Vanessa for permission for the kids to come along.

"We got snacks a little while ago. They should be fine until then." She played her anger off.

"O.K. Cool." Malcolm clicked to end the call.

"Telese is dropping them off shortly," he said to Vanessa.

"That's wonderful," she said, turning to smile at him.

"I love spending time with your babies, especially since I have none of my own."

Malcolm smiled. He couldn't have a better woman. God had sent him an angel. At the gym, Malcolm suited up and was taking playful mini jabs at Vanessa in the ring while waiting for whoever he was supposed to be sparring against. Mackie kept smiling at the two love birds. He figured he was delighted to see his fighter finally happy for a change. He'd seen Malcolm show up at the ring plenty of days frustrated and beat down because life just wouldn't give him a break. He'd watched that boy punch the boxing bag so hard, he joked that it was going to fly out the door.

"What are you smiling at, ole man?" Malcolm asked jokingly.

"Nothing, youngster," Mackie grinned.

"You look like you're up to something." Malcolm eyed him suspiciously.

"Finish letting your lady beat you up," Mackie teased.

Just then Steven entered the front steel door and came over to the ring, grinning like a Cheshire cat.

"Hey, Steven, what's up, man?" Steven tilted his chin up.

"Hey, Steven," Vanessa smiled.

"Hi, Ms. Vanessa, good word today. I was truly blessed."

"Thank you," she replied appreciatively.

Malcolm watched Steven, who had now made his way to the other side of the room, with Mackie. Both men were leaning over at the counter laughing about something.

"Hey," Mackie yelled.

"Get back in the ring; your sparring partner just pulled in."

Someone walked into the building wearing a black hoodie. He headed straight to the back dressing room to change, never saying a word to anyone. Everyone there looked at each other in total disbelief, with the exception of Mackie and Steven, when the

177

lightweight champion of the world, Shabazz Duke, walked in behind him with a dozen guys.

"Can you believe that? It's Shabazz Duke!" Malcolm jumped out of the ring.

"I know that's not!"

Vanessa stood up from the ringside folding chair to get a better look. Mackie walked over to embrace the champ.

"Man, I hope you got your wife to make us some of her famous fried sweet potato pies," Shabazz rubbed his belly with a smile.

"I traveled a long way to get me some. I could smell them from the airport."

"You know she sent you a dozen," Mackie joked with him and his crew.

Malcolm didn't know it, but his friend Mackie was acquainted with many famous fighters, several of which periodically visited the gym. Malcolm raced over to Shabazz, almost tripping over a table to reach the champ. The four strongly-muscled men with Shabazz jumped in front of the icon to protect him.

"He's okay," Mackie advised them.

"That's Malcolm; he's with me."

The oversized men backed away, leaving a smiling champ within reach. He seemed surprisingly human and friendly looking despite his superstar status. When Malcolm got to him, he almost felt like bowing before the man. This was one of his favorite lightweight fighters of all time. Malcolm was speechless. For the first few moments, all he could do was stare. Steven came over and punched Malcolm in the back with an open hand.

"Say something, boy." Everyone laughed.

Malcolm laughed too. After pulling himself together, he started to speak, but as soon as he opened his mouth, the kids barreled through the entrance racing toward him with hugs and kisses. The champ's bodyguards again jumped into action surrounding Shabazz until Mackie gave the signal. Mackie walked over to lock the gym doors so no one else could come in.

"Malcolm, do you know this woman?" Mackie called.

Telese stood at the door wondering why she couldn't enter.

"Yeah, Mack, she's cool," Malcolm said.

Malcolm wondered why she just hadn't dropped the kids off like she said she would, but he figured she had seen the limo outside and came in to be nosey. KJ was the first to notice Shabazz, and then Telese stared in disbelief from the entrance. Malcolm knew he and Telese shared a love for the title fighter that was beyond belief. He knew how much it would mean to Telese if she could meet him in person. Shabazz was one of her all-time idols. She had collected all kinds of memorabilia and replicas of his likeness.

"Oh, my goodness! Malcolm, it's really Shabazz Duke!" she screamed, running in place as Mackie stepped aside to let her come in.

Dashing toward him, she grabbed the champ's hand and almost shook it off. "You are one of the greatest fighters of all times, Mr. Duke, and I am one of your biggest fans," Telese gushed.

"Thank you, ma'am," Shabazz smiled a kindly grin. Turning to Malcolm he said.

"We've heard some good things about you, Malcolm." The boxer's voice was soft.

"We're hearing you've got some power behind those punches."

"You have?" Malcolm questioned.

"Who is 'we'?"

"Man! Malcolm, stop all that jibber jabber and get in the ring," Steven yelled.

"Are you crazy? I'm not about to fight Shabazz Duke!" Malcolm yelled back.

"Not him, you idiot...him!" Steven pointed toward the ring.

Telese, Vanessa and the kids stood back in the corner still in awe and a loss for words. All of them questioned if they were dreaming.

Malcolm looked up toward the ring and saw someone suited up wearing a sparring helmet. All anyone could see was his eyes. You couldn't get a clear view of his facial features. Malcolm's opponent started dancing and swinging in the air.

"I need some sugar for good luck." He stepped over toward Vanessa and planted a quick peck on her lips as Telese watched.

"Go Daddy...get him!" Layla screamed as Malcolm stepped through the ropes.

"Yeah, knock his lights out, Daddy," KJ added with a joyful grin.

Telese backed further into a corner to watch as Vanessa and the kids drew closer to the ring. There was no doubt that she was struggling to suppress her jealousy. Malcolm had moved on and was now happy.

The bell rang and both men came out swinging. Malcolm's sparring partner got in a number of hard hits even putting Malcolm on his butt a few times, but Malcolm quickly had him on the mat twice before the bell rang at the end of the fourth round. Malcolm couldn't believe that his favorite fighter in the world was watching him fight. This was a dream come true. He had to make a good impression and give the champ something that was worth the trip.

Mackie and Steven stood near Telese, chatting with two of the guys who had come with the champ. Shabazz stood near the ring, arms folded across his chest, occasionally rubbing his chin with one hand as he studied the strategies unfolding before his eyes. Malcolm gave it all he had, but his sparring partner was getting the best of him. Whoever this dude was, he definitely wasn't playing around. When the bell rang at the end of the seventh round, Malcolm was breathing heavily, landing on his behind again. The two guys had been tagging each other hard, giving the onlookers a good fight.

Telese smiled inside. She was really proud of Malcolm. Vanessa had what she herself had always wanted: a changed Malcolm.

"Okay guys, that's it," Mackie shouted.

"Good job, youngster! We've got to think of a name for you,"

Mackie smiled at Malcolm as he approached to hand him a towel.

"You did better than I thought you would. I figured he'd murder you in there, but youngster, you went toe to toe."

Malcolm's competitor climbed out of the ring and headed back to change just as quietly as he had come in. Steven and Malcolm caught up with him and walked alongside the pro athlete as he took off his headpiece. Malcolm, Vanessa and the kids sat at a small table, talking with the champ. Vanessa took a few photos of Malcolm, the champ, and the kids together, and then asked someone to get a few shots of them all together. Malcolm thought KJ would never wipe the smile off his face.

"Mom, come here," KJ motioned with his hands.

Malcolm watched as she approached. He whispered to Vanessa for her to snap a picture of Telese and Shabazz, knowing it would mean the world to the mother of his children.

"Telese, stand beside the champ and I'll take your picture," Vanessa said politely.

"Okay," Telese smiled, grateful to stand beside the boxer she adored.

"I'll make sure you get a copy," Vanessa said after snapping the shot while Shabazz patted Telese's back and offered a cheek for her to peck.

"You were a beast in there, Daddy," KJ said, showing his jabbing technique.

"You're pretty fast there, son," Malcolm said.

"If we keep working on your skills, you might do well in the ring someday."

KJ kept sticking and moving quickly, showing off in front of the champ. The world renowned boxer smiled and nodded, offering an occasional point for improvement. Then a couple of security team members accompanied him from the gym as everyone waved and called out good-byes.

Vanessa walked over to offer Telese a friendly hug. "I'm sorry for what happened earlier at the church. I had no idea you were Malcolm's ex-wife."

"I'm still his wife," Telese said warmly.

"That's just a technicality," Malcolm interrupted.

"By the way, have they sent those papers yet?"

"No, I'm still waiting," she said with a hint of contempt.

"What's your rush?" A few months ago you wanted..."

She stopped, knowing her comment would only make her appear to be jealous. "Well, you wanted it so quickly, I figured you were preparing for something," he said.

"Something like what?" Telese asked.

"I don't know, Telese," Malcolm said.

"I heard Morris was divorcing his wife quickly too, so I just put two and two together and figured you all were...you know."

Telese didn't respond, she knew she had it coming.

"What time are you bringing the kids home?" she asked, defeated, but elated from her encounter with The Great.

"Later on, after we have dinner. It won't be too late. I know they have school in the morning."

"Okay," she answered.

"Bye, kids." She waved as she stood at the door for the huge man to unlock it.

"Yo, Malcolm," Steven motioned for him to come over.

"Let's talk business, fellas."

Mackie came over to the table. "Hey, man," Mackie addressed Malcolm.

"You're going to be sparring with "Bone Crusher" four days a week, starting Monday through Thursday from 4-7, and you'll get paid $2,500 weekly. You cool with that?"

"T.C. 'Bone Crusher' Evans?"

"Man, stop joking around with me. He's one of the heavyweight champions of the world, y'all full of it." Malcolm looked over at Steven.

"Do we look like we're joking?" Mackie said with a straight face, but couldn't help cracking a smile.

181

"Yeah, you do," Malcolm answered, not knowing what to think.

"Man, have I ever lied to you?" Steven asked with a straight face.

Malcolm looked anxious for the first time in his life. He wanted to believe it, but something just wouldn't let him. All his unanswered questions came to an end when Bone Crusher walked out from the dressing room, carrying a duffle bag.

"All right, fellas, see you on Monday." Bone Crusher gave both men a handshake.

"I'll see you too." He shook Malcolm's hand.

"I got to give it to you, man. You bring it hard. That's what I need for my comeback. I thank God Shabazz gave Mackie a call and found you. I need a man with your strength to challenge me and get me back on my toes. The fact you hung in there with me so long shows I've got a lot of work to do."

Malcolm stared at the man in disbelief. He had to be dreaming, he thought. KJ looked like he was about to pass out. He was snapping pictures with his camera phone until finally he just recorded the conversation on video. As Bone Crusher exited the building to join Shabazz and the bodyguards in a large black car at the curb, Malcolm sat down beside Vanessa to take a deep breath.

Steven came over and shook Malcolm by the shoulders as he stood over him. "If I'm right, I think I heard a man of God prophecy that God said he'd put you among kings," Steven smiled.

Malcolm looked at Vanessa, remembering those words from Apostle Reed. They burst into joyful laughter at realizing the word was becoming manifest.

Yolanda and Vanessa sat across from each other in a cozy booth at Moe's diner and ordered the lunch special. It was turkey and cheese salad, with a special raspberry vinaigrette dressing and fresh corn muffin, hot from the oven. Vanessa was concerned because, she hadn't seen Moe at the diner the last couple days. When the young college student, who was Moe's niece, brought their food, Vanessa discreetly asked if everything was okay with the diner's owner.

"She's been under the weather lately," the young lady replied softly.

"Please keep her in your prayers," she said, glossy eyed.

"What is it? You're scaring me," Vanessa's concern grew deeper.

The girl sighed. "This thing with her son getting ten years in prison has really kept her down. She's on all kind of anti-depressants. She's been losing weight and sleeps all the time."

"It's consuming her life and she worries about him non-stop."

"Aunt Moe just can't get over it. Her life has stopped and now her other son got kicked out of school. He's completely out of control.'

"Moe is the best person in the world, she doesn't deserve this." The college student closed her eyes.

"I hate to even let these words come out of my mouth, but I think she's suicidal."

"The devil is a liar," both Yolanda and Vanessa exclaimed in unison.

"So who's running the diner in her absence?" Yolanda asked buttering the muffin as Vanessa sipped her ice tea.

"Me, my Aunt Carol, and Gloria, we've been trying to keep the diner afloat, but none of us know anything about running a business. All we know is how to cook good food, but none of us can cook anything like Moe."

"Do you mind if I go to the back and talk to your aunts?" Vanessa asked politely.

"That's fine," she said, glancing toward the cook's window to see if her next order was up yet.

Yolanda worked on her salad while Vanessa stepped to the rear of the diner to speak with Moe's sisters. Her heart was already heavy with the weight of her and Ivy's relationship starting to crumble. They had sex three times a week, but it still wasn't enough. She was miserable, and Ivy felt like he had been issued a death sentence not being able to get some two times a day. She even purchased a padlock for the bathroom door.

Yolanda couldn't help but notice a strange man sitting at the counter staring at her. The more she tried to glance in another direction, the more uncomfortable she became. She grabbed her lemonade with her ring finger aimed his way, just so he could get a clear view of her freshly sparkled diamond. She hoped Vanessa would soon get back to the table before she had to give this creep a piece of her mind. When Yolanda saw him approaching, she shifted in her seat.

"Hi beautiful," he said, exposing gleaming white teeth.

"Hi," Yolanda slurped her lemonade rudely.

"Are you the wife of Ivy James, Pastor of Mt. Emanuel?"

"Oh, yes." Yolanda straightened her posture, feeling a bit embarrassed, yet relieved.

"Yes, I'm Yolanda James."

"You sure are a pretty thing," he said sizing her up from the parts of her he could see.

Yolanda frowned, totally confused. "Is Ivy taking good care of all that?" he grinned.

"I beg your pardon!" Yolanda looked angry.

"If he ain't handling his business you be sure and give a real man a call," he said setting his business card on the table.

"But if I know Ivy like I think I do, he has totally worn you down, and you need some rest from him pounding all over you."

Almost losing her religion, Yolanda cleared her throat. "I don't know who you are Mister, but I won't sit here while you purposely insult my husband. You need to leave!"

"I will," he smiled politely.

"But please, let Ivan know his old friend Perry Ellison inquired about him."

"Don't be offended if I forget," Yolanda said looking the other way, annoyed, not believing this stranger just read her mail.

Mr. Ellison left the diner, with his exquisite-smelling cologne lingering in the air. Vanessa returned and slipped into the booth, holding a folded piece of paper.

"Who was that? Dang, he's fine."

"Nobody," Yolanda said quickly.

"This is Moe's address," she said.

"I figured maybe we could pay her a visit to see if she needs anything. I've called her a few times, but she hasn't answered."

"That's a good idea," Yolanda said.

"Who's Perry Ellison?" Vanessa asked, holding up the business card in front of her.

"Some clown that Ivy used to know," she shrugged it off.

"And why are you looking at him anyway? I thought you were so head-over-heels in love with Malcolm," Yolanda retorted semi-jokingly.

"Why are you looking like that?" Vanessa frowned.

"He has a wife, Vanessa, that's why. What's up with her anyway? She looked like she saw a ghost last Sunday after service."

"I know," Vanessa agreed, quietly eating her salad greens and turkey strips.

"I think she still wants him."

Yolanda dropped her head.

"I was hoping you wouldn't say that. We both know the signs of jealousy. So what are you going to do?"

"Trust my man," Vanessa said.

"That's all I can do. He keeps asking her about the divorce, so I'm patiently waiting."

"Doesn't he have a record?" Yolanda inquired.

"Yolanda," Vanessa whined.

"That doesn't have anything to do with it. I don't judge people by their past. He's told me all about his shortcomings, and none of them matter. Malcolm is good to me and he's getting himself together. Besides, we both know if he knew all the ugly details of my past, he'd probably run for the border," Vanessa laughed.

"But you were young then," Yolanda tried to smooth it over.

"So now you're holding him to a double standard?"

"Stop being so defensive, I'm only looking out for your best interest. Does he have a nice house?" Yolanda asked, finishing her salad neatly.

"You sure are being superficial today. He's between blessings right now. He's living with his sister, Lauren, and her husband for the moment. He's working on getting a place."

"Vanessa," Yolanda frowned before sipping her tea.

"What is wrong with you? You can do better than that. What about Steven? Now he's got himself together, he's a great catch."

Vanessa shook her head nibbling the last of the corn muffin. "So is Malcolm; I love him."

"Well, Miss 'I-love-him', he's still married so the two of you should cool off, until his divorce is final. The last thing the church needs is a scandal involving a minister."

Vanessa kept quiet. She knew Yolanda was right, but she had to follow her heart. It was true that Malcolm didn't look good on paper. However, she dated ones who did look good on paper, but who turned out to be animals.

"Well," Yolanda's nostrils flared.

"Just keep your options open," she said, digging her fork into a juicy tomato slice glittering with sweet dressing.

Vanessa didn't fret over Yolanda's opinion of Malcolm. She saw the real man, despite his ugly past. They'd been together non-stop since the day they met. She adored his three children, and they seemed quite fond of her as well. Malcolm called her, or texted her everyday- all day. Whenever his name popped up on the caller ID, her heart would flutter. The only problem she foresaw was Telese, so she prayed the divorce would be final soon.

****

Ivy pulled up to Dominic's school and parked. He was really angry that this was the fifth time in a month that he had to come up there because of foolishness. The boy had gotten into three fights and had been suspended, but this time the school wanted a conference between the principal and one or both parents for a much needed intervention. Ivy walked into the principal's office in his tailor-made suit and took a seat in a cushioned chair. Dominic arrived with the principal and two teachers, head held low. The middle-aged administrator shook Ivy's hand.

"Hello, Mr. James. My name is Mark Pennington, and I'm the Principal here at Riverbend Middle School."

"It's a pleasure to meet you, sir," Ivy replied.

"It's been a rough transition for Dominic," the principal smiled.

Dominic has only been a student here a little over a month, and has been suspended twice already. Today he got into an altercation with another student and threw a desk at him, nearly injuring four students. The young man he was fighting injured his hand and the authorities had to get involved, Mr. James," Mr. Pennington said firmly.

"The authorities?" Ivy questioned.

"Yes sir. Mr. James, the students' parents are filing criminal charges against your son: assault with a deadly weapon."

Ivy shook his head with a glance at Dominic.

"You're joking, right?" he posed his question to Mr. Pennington.

"Unfortunately a child was severely injured, and we have to take matters like this very, very seriously."

A tall, slender police officer walked into the office, holding papers for Ivy to sign. "Mr. James, I'm Officer Trenton."

He held out his hand to shake Ivy's, and Ivy stood up to grasp the officer's hand firmly.

"We're going to release Dominic into your custody since he is a minor, but he has a court date in a month. So please, make sure he's there. If you need information on obtaining an attorney, you can call the court house, and someone will be able to assist you."

"Good heavens," Ivy said, feeling sick to his stomach.

"Mr. James, I'm sorry to add more grief to this situation, but we're going to expel Dominic for the rest of the year if he gets into any more trouble.

"At this time he's suspended for ten days. He will be allowed to make up his work when he returns."

Ivy agreed to everything he was told. Within twenty minutes he and Dominic walked out of the building, but neither mumbled a word to the other. Ivy knew if he said anything right now while he was angry, and Dominic mouthed off, he'd probably choke the boy. So, he waited until he calmed down. The next few minutes passed in tense silence until Ivy's cell phone rang.

"Ivy," Yolanda breathed heavily, clearly in a panic.

"Baby, what's wrong?" Ivy pulled the car into a McDonald's parking lot.

"There's been a fire at your mom's house and they're transporting her to the hospital by ambulance. I don't know how serious it is, but I'm on my way. I've been trying to call you for the last twenty minutes but your voicemail kept picking up."

Ivy felt fear clench his stomach. *Lord, please let my momma be all right*, he prayed.

"I'm sorry, baby. I had my phone turned on silent. Dominic got suspended, and I had to go up to the school for a conference with the principal."

"Oh, no," Yolanda said, "not again. Well baby, hurry. I'm pulling up at the hospital now," Yolanda's voice lowered as she tried to calm herself.

"Okay," Ivy whipped his car out of the parking lot and headed back in the other direction.

"I'm on my way. Don't worry, everything will be okay."

Ivy dialed Courtney's number and left a message. He turned on his vehicle emergency flashers and drove as fast as he safely could. He ran through every yellow light he came to with no intention of stopping. Fifteen minutes later, Ivy and Dominic raced through the automatic doors at Chesterfield Memorial Hospital. Ivy told the receptionist his mother's name and waited for floor information. As soon as he stepped off the elevator, he spotted Yolanda talking to the doctor. Ivy ran up behind them and asked what was going on. The doctor turned in surprise but quickly explained that JoAnn was going to be fine, although she'd suffered second-degree burns on her arm and hand.

"Oh, my goodness," Yolanda cried.

"Thank you, Lord, because it could have been worse!" she praised God in a low voice.

"Thank you, doctor," Ivy exhaled deeply.

"Can we go back and see her?"

"Yes, in a short while. They're still doing a few treatments right now, and she'll be ready for visitors. However Mr. James, we're going to have to address her Alzheimer's disease," the doctor said firmly but kindly.

"I knew this day was coming," Ivy said sadly.

"She was fine the other day when I stopped to check on her. I mean, she forgot where she had put some things, but she wasn't that bad."

"I understand," the doctor agreed.

"This disease usually increases gradually. On the other hand, there are a few rare cases where it grows rapidly, and unfortunately, that is where we are right now."

"Oh no!" Ivy felt a lump in his throat as he teared up. "Will she know who we are?"

The doctor shook his head. "That's hard to say. She may recognize you today and not tomorrow, or she may stop knowing you at all. One thing is for sure: she can no longer continue living at home alone. She'll need 24-hour care."

Ivy nodded, "That's fine, doctor. We understand. That won't be a problem."

"She'll be staying with us," Yolanda added quickly.

Ivy squeezed his wife's waist for comfort. His heart ached terribly to see his loving mother's health decline. The doctor walked away after another handshake, leaving Ivy and Yolanda in the waiting area. Dominic and Bryson had gone down to the cafeteria for something to eat.

"What happened?" Ivy asked Yolanda.

"The neighbors said she was frying pork chops and forgot she was cooking, so the kitchen caught fire. Mr. Harper, the guy across the street, broke in through the front door to get to her when he saw smoke coming from the open kitchen window. If he hadn't gotten there in time, it would have been bad," Yolanda cried, clutching his hand at her waist.

Ivy squeezed her for comfort, feeling her solid curves. He held on tightly, embracing the moment. Although the situation wasn't a happy one, he enjoyed the closeness between him and his wife.

"Is the house burned badly?" he asked.

"Yeah, the kitchen is totally wiped out," Yolanda said, still upset. "But thank God she's still alive."

"I do, baby, I do." Ivy hugged Yolanda tight. He couldn't imagine going through this without her love and support.

"Did you call Courtney?" Yolanda asked.

"Yes, she called back and said she'd catch the earliest flight. I'll call her again in a few minutes to give her Mom's status."

"Okay, I'll head downstairs to check on the boys," Yolanda said, wiping her eyes with a tissue.

She broke from his hug and spotted Vanessa racing through the doors, not seeing Yolanda.

"Vanessa!" Yolanda yelled.

The rushing woman glanced their way as a look of relief passed over her features. She hurried toward them.

"Yolanda, Pastor, thank God you're here."

"Of course we are, Vanessa," Ivy said reassuringly.

Yolanda and Ivy assumed Vanessa was there to comfort them concerning JoAnn, but that wasn't the case.

"I went to check on Moe after you left to pick up Bryson from school, and no one answered the door. I left, but something told me to go back, so I turned around. I broke in through Moe's bedroom window and found her slumped over in a chair in her living room with an empty bottle of pills on the floor beside her. She was non-responsive. I called 911 and followed them here.

"I tried everything to revive her! Lord please don't let her be dead." Vanessa cried.

"Dear God." Ivy felt so defeated. He didn't understand what would make Moe do something like that.

"Why would Moe do such a thing?" Ivy said in disbelief.

Yolanda and Vanessa both looked at one another with tears in their eyes

"She's going through a lot," Yolanda said sadly.

He sighed. "Let's try to calm down and believe God that she's going to be alright. We need to pull together as a body of believers."

"Yes," both women nodded.

An hour later Ivy and Yolanda, with Vanessa beside them, were still waiting to see JoAnn and hear something concerning Moe's status.

"Hi, are you related to Moeisha Dillard?"

The tall woman came toward them in her lab coat.

"No, we aren't relatives, but I'm the one who found her." Vanessa jumped from her seat.

"We've stabilized Mrs. Dillard and pumped her stomach, so hopefully she'll be fine in that aspect of treatment."

"What do you mean 'that aspect of treatment'?" Yolanda asked.

The doctor gave her a sympathetic look.

"Mrs. Dillard's brain tumor is spreading rapidly. She is going to need chemotherapy immediately."

Vanessa fell to her knees and started praying as though she were confronting Satan face-to-face. She prayed aloud with so much force that Ivy and Yolanda got goose bumps. Yolanda turned to Ivy and dissolved into tears in his arms. Moe had become a good friend since she had moved to Virginia, and now she felt helpless. Ivy was right, the children of God needed to be on their faces praying against sickness and disease.

JoAnn's nurse returned to the waiting area with orders from the doctor to let Ivy and Yolanda come back and see JoAnn. As Yolanda grabbed her purse, a few things, including the card on which she had written the hospital address fell from a side pocket. Ivy picked it up to hand her and noticed the name as he flipped it over.

"Where did you get this?"

She looked annoyed as she stuffed items back into her purse.

"Some clown at Moe's diner today named Perry Ellison said he knows you, and left it on the table."

"Did he say anything else?" Ivy asked.

"Just a bunch of gibberish." Yolanda clicked her purse shut and turned to head toward the cafeteria.

"Forget that clown." Ivy raised his eyebrows and made a mental note to give his old friend a visit. Moe's sister's Carol and Gloria raced through the double doors and followed everyone inside.

Chapter 19   *Raymond*

Ray took an earlier flight from New York. He didn't want to ride on the same plane as Amanda. She would stop at nothing to control or destroy him. All kinds of thoughts were running through his mind. She and Eva had to have slipped something into his drink, but how? His glass had been sitting in front of him the entire time. *What should I do?* Ray thought. *Should I tell Donae the truth? If I do, I'll risk losing her again.* Ray dropped his head in his hands, feeling disgusted.

How could he have let this happen? He was certain that Amanda had something else up her sleeve, and this wasn't the last of her. Ray reached for his cell phone, and then remembered that he was thousands of feet in the sky. He'd have to wait until the plane landed. An hour later Ray called Steven in the cab on the way home and explained the whole ugly nightmare.

Steven held the phone speechless for a few seconds, before speaking. "I know man," Ray interrupted the silence.

"You just don't know what to say."

"Tell her the truth," Steven blurted.

"Steven, I can't do that. She'll leave me again man. I just moved back home. Do you realize what you're asking me to do?"

"Ray, you and I both know Amanda has something evil up her sleeve. If you don't tell Donae the truth, it's going to hurt you in the long run. When she finds out and you're not the one who told her, she never will believe the truth. Look at it this way," Steven paused.

"The Devil can't hold anything over your head if you've already exposed it. Don't give him any power over you. If you don't tell the truth, you're giving him power to make you do what he wants."

Ray paused to mull this over. "Steven, I know you're right, but I don't know if I can. I'm going to have to really think about this," he said, knowing in his heart he had no intention of considering such a risky thing.

"And while I have you on the phone, be in prayer for Moe. She got hurt a few days ago, and they diagnosed her with cancer."

"Lord have mercy!" Ray didn't want to believe his ears.

"Is it true she tried to commit suicide?"

"She did," Steven said, feeling Moe's heartache.

"She took an overdose of pills."

"Poor Moe." Ray felt sad and mad at the same time.

"I've been to the hospital to see her twice. She's in good spirits now. I learned something else about Moe, too," Steven said.

"What?" Ray asked.

"How old do you think Moe is?" Steven asked.

"I don't know, early fifties," Ray guessed.

"Man, she isn't even forty," Steven said.

"You're kidding," Ray said, surprised.

"She looks older."

"Her previous marriage dragged her through the ringer, trying to take care of her kids alone with crappy jobs here and there."

"Then her boys staying in trouble all the time just took the life out of her. She mentioned her only fulfillment came from opening the diner four years ago. I feel bad for her," Steven said, sighing in his spirit.

"She said that she may not be able to keep the restaurant open because of all the medical bills piling up. I heard she spent over $40,000 in legal fees for her son, and the crook didn't even try to defend the boy."

"What can we do to help?" Raymond asked with deep compassion.

"I don't know," Steven said.

"She's so stubborn, and won't take help from anybody."

"Have they already started her cancer treatments?" Ray asked.

"Yeah, she's had a few."

"What kind of cancer is it anyway?" Ray asked.

"Brain tumor," Steven answered.

"But God is going to heal her."

"I'm in agreement with that," Raymond said without a doubt.

"And what's this about Malcolm and Bone Crusher Evans?" Raymond asked, trying not to be envious.

Steven perked up. "His prophetic word is coming to pass." he explained to Ray what had happened at the ring that day.

"Bone Crusher is trying to make a comeback in the boxing world. Word got out that Malcolm had some power behind those punches."

"I wonder how that got out," Ray chuckled at Steven with mounds of suspicion.

"Mackie and I may have made some phone calls to a few buddies we know."

"Man, do you have wings or a halo somewhere?" Ray teased.

"No wings or halo," Steven answered.

"I wrestle with the same issues any other man does, my issues just have a different name."

Ray was ashamed for feeling comfort in knowing that Steven struggled, too. He couldn't help but wonder what his issues were.

"I heard Bone Crusher came down with a posse of guys, including the lightweight champ, Shabazz Duke."

"Yes, sir. It's true, man. Apparently Shabazz and Bone Crusher are good friends. Shabazz is helping Bone Crusher with training for his comeback. Bone Crusher and the heavyweight champ, Kenny "Hammer Hand" Hopkins, are scheduled to fight an exhibition match in a few months.

"The trainers traveled down to see what Malcolm was working with and hired him on the spot. This is a great chance for Malcolm to make some extra cash, and of course, keep himself out of trouble. If he keeps his nose clean and head straight, he might be all right," Steven laughed, remembering his hot headed friend.

"Yes, Lord," Ray agreed.

"Hammer Hand Hopkins, boy, I'd love to see that fight."

"Nine times out of ten, you will. I'm sure Malcolm will make sure his boys are hooked up," Steven laughed.

"We're hoping this opens up an opportunity for Malcolm to spar with more heavyweights later."

"Wow!" Ray said.

"Go ahead, Malcolm, do your thing." Ray smiled, feeling proud of his buddy.

"Sitting among kings," Ray shouted, remembering Apostle Reed's prophetic word.

"My God is all right!"

"Ain't he, though?" Steven gladly joined in his friend's praise.

"Man, I always miss the good stuff," Ray pretended to pout.

"Don't worry! You'll have plenty of time to meet some of Malcolm's new friends," Steven's heart danced.

"I love the way God's kingdom operates, don't you?" Ray said.

"The ones people count out are the ones God anoints for his purpose."

"I couldn't have said that any better," Steven exclaimed.

"Well, I'm pulling up at home," Ray said.

"I'll call you later, but keep me lifted up man."

"I will, but I hope you heed my advice. It's the only thing that will make you free. If not, you'll be in bondage," Steven stressed.

"I hear you man, and I know you're right, but…" Ray paused, not knowing what to say.

"Thanks, Stephen. I'll get back with you. I promise," Ray ended the call.

Ray strolled through his home, appreciating its decor and its natural beauty. It had been so long since he'd been there that he had forgotten how elegant it really was. Donae planted a small garden in the backyard with peppers, cucumbers and tomatoes. He smiled with pride, knowing she had talked about doing that for years. He was tickled that she finally had fulfilled her plan. Making his way to the bedroom, he ran his fingers through Donae's clothes that were hanging in the closet. Some still had her perfume lingering on them. He picked up a silky blouse to inhale the sweet fragrance that he loved so much. His suits and clothes hung neatly on his side of the closet, and he was so delighted to see that vacancy now filled.

Oh, how good it felt to be back at home. He wouldn't trade it for anything. The thought of Amanda walking around the hotel room with his shirt on crept into his mind. Now he couldn't enjoy this victory for worrying about the possible drama to come. Maybe Steven was right. Maybe he should just tell the truth. Maybe Donae would understand. Perhaps he wasn't giving his wife enough credit for her spiritual growth. The truth was Ray was scared to chance it.

"Ray," Donae's voice echoed through the house as the sound of her jingling keys hit the table.

"Hey, honey, I'm here," Ray walked out into the foyer.

"Hi," Donae smiled, giving him a big hug.

"Hey Dad!" both kids said as they walked through the door.

"Why are you guys home so early? School isn't out yet."

"I had to leave work, because I wasn't feeling well, and on my way, the school called saying both of them were at the nurses' office with stomach aches."

"I think we may have food poison or something," Donae suggested.

"Well, let's go to the doctor," Ray grabbed his keys.

"I think that might be a good idea," Donae said, feeling nauseous.

"Let's grab a barf bag in case someone has to throw up," Ray urged.

At the doctor's office, both kids had already thrown up, and Donae was keeling over, holding her stomach. Ray was getting impatient. They had been nearly an hour in the waiting room. Walking up to the receptionist's desk he inquired how much longer it would be.

"Sir, you didn't have an appointment, so we have to work you all in."

Ray was on the verge of using a few choice words until finally, after fifteen more minutes of waiting, a nurse called them back to an examination room. The doctor confirmed that Donae and the kids in fact had food poisoning. He said the best thing was to let it run its course. Ray thought about asking the doctor if he could check his blood to see if something was in his system, but he couldn't with Donae right there.

The doctor wrote the kid's doctor's notes for school and gave them prescriptions for nausea. He also suggested something over the counter to coat their stomachs. They walked toward the door to check out, but Donae quickly rushed to the trash receptacle to unload her lunch.

"Here you go," the doctor said once Donae seemed to have settled her stomach.

"I need to give you this." He scribbled another prescription on his little white pad and handed it to Donae.

"Make sure you start taking these immediately."

"Okay," Donae answered as she looked down at the prescription. Her knowledge as a pharmacist instantly kicked in.

"Wow!" she said, amazed.

"What?" Ray looked confused.

Donae handed him the prescription. Ray looked at it.

"What? I can't understand his handwriting."

Both Donae and the doctor giggled.

"It's a prescription for vitamins," Donae chuckled.

"And?" Ray was aggravated that the two of them were keeping him in the dark.

"Prenatal vitamins," Donae looked at him sideways.

Still seeing that it didn't compute with Ray, the doctor decided it best to put him out of his misery.

"That's what women take when they're having a baby," the doctor smiled.

"Hot diggity dog!" Ray twirled Donae around.

"We're having a baby?"

"Yes, silly, I guess that means we are."

Donae pinched his smiling cheeks while he lifted her in the air. Ray pointed his hands up toward Heaven, and all he could say was. "Thank you, Lord."

Once Ray made sure his lovely pregnant wife was now comfortable in the car, he called everybody to share the good news. This was what he'd been wanting for years, and finally it was about to happen. He was thrilled! Ray set his phone down on the console, and it slid to the floor next to Donae's feet. It rang as she was picking it up.

"Hello," Donae spoke into the receiver.

Her smile faded as she handed Ray the phone. Ray knew instantly that it could only mean one thing – Amanda.

"This is Raymond," he said, still living in the clouds.

"Ray, why didn't you tell me you were catching an earlier flight?"

"I can't talk about business right now. I'll see you at the office in the morning," he ended the call.

"So, I wonder how far along you are," he said with glee.

"I don't know, baby," she smiled.

"It can't be too far though."

"I hope it's another boy," Ray said.

"No," the kids interrupted.

"We want twins."

"Twins," Donae turned up her nose.

"No way," she said.

"Yeah," Ray agreed.

"I think I could go for twins."

Amanda was fuming with anger. Ray didn't end the call properly, and she heard every disgusting word.

"That hussy!" she screamed.

"I'm going to kill her! She can't have him. He's mine. I'm tired of playing with her. She doesn't know that what I want, I get!"

Amanda paced the hotel room floor. Then she raced down the hall to Eva's room and banged on her door.

"Are you finished packing?" Amanda breathed heavily.

"Yes, Amanda, what's the matter? Why are you so upset?" Eva opened the door and looked perplexed.

"I need you to hurry and get these negatives developed," she said, handing her the digital camera.

"And bring them back ASAP."

"But Amanda, we don't have time. We'll miss our flight," Eva pleaded. "And where can I go to get negatives like these developed anyway? I can't just walk up and expect them to print X-rated photos. Can't this wait until we get home?"

"No, absolutely not," Amanda insisted.

"I want them now. I don't care where you have to go to get them printed. We're in New York City, find someplace, now! We can catch a later flight if we miss this one. I don't care!" she demanded furiously.

"Here," she said shoving cash into the other woman's hands.

"Go now," Amanda banged her balled up fist against Eva's hotel door.

"Amanda, calm down." Eva looked concerned.

"I'm fine."

Then she flipped like Dr. Jekyll and Mr. Hyde, seeming to calm down a bit.

It's okay, she told herself. *If that doesn't work, I'll figure out a backup plan.* She patted her smooth belly. *The doctor said I should be ovulating. He better be right.*

"Malcolm, hey, are you busy?" Telese asked.

"No," Malcolm paused.

"Not really. I'm about to leave the ring."

"All right, good job in there. See you later, man."

"You too, Bone Crusher; have a good one."

"Sorry, Telese, what's up?" Malcolm asked, turning patiently to her voice with a towel draped around his neck.

"Layla has a fever. I really don't want to leave the house. Can you swing by with some children's Tylenol ? You don't have to stay. I know you've been busy."

"Of course I'll bring it over," Malcolm answered.

"I'll make time for my baby, but it might be about thirty minutes before I can head over. Is that okay?"

"Sure, that's fine," Telese said, glad that he agreed to come.

"Great, I'll see you then," Malcolm said.

"Oh, by the way," Malcolm tried to catch her before she hung up.

"Don't tell Layla I'm coming, okay? I want to surprise her."

"Okay," she smiled.

"I'm sure it will perk her up to see her precious daddy." She wanted to remind Malcolm how much Layla adored him.

"By the way, did you get any news yet?"

"The last I heard, it could be any day now," she sucked her teeth.

"It shouldn't be much longer."

"That's great," Malcolm smiled.

"Let me know when they come. Is signing the only thing I need to do?"

"I believe so," she said.

"Okay. Well, if they don't come this week, give me the number and I will call and try to get information as to what the holdup is."

"I'll see you when you get here, Malcolm." Telese hung up, greatly annoyed.

She called Malcolm right back. "Yeah?" he answered.

"Are you going to be by yourself?" Telese asked.

"Yeah, unfortunately, I know Vanessa would want to see the kids, but she had to preach tonight. I was going to try to catch the end of her sermon, but I guess I won't since my baby isn't feeling well."

"Oh, okay, "Telese smiled.

"I made some fried chicken, rice and gravy, and spinach for dinner, so don't worry about stopping to grab yourself anything."

"That sounds great, but Vanessa and I are going out after she finishes preaching tonight. Thanks anyway."

"Okay," Telese said.

"I just thought I'd offer. I know how much you love spinach and fried chicken."

"I do," Malcolm smiled.

"I haven't had any spinach in a long time. What was it that you used to put in yours to make it so good?"

Telese grinned. "It's mozzarella cheese, onions, and a little bit of butter, but it has to be fresh spinach, not from a can."

Malcolm laughed. "I remember Morris and I use to go to Applebee's and eat spinach dip and tortilla chips until we literally got sick. Those were the good old days."

Telese was quiet.

Malcolm realized what he'd just said. "Vanessa is going to make it for me, but she asked me to get the recipe."

"Okay, that's cool. Let me check on Layla. I will see you when you get here," Telese said, pretending to sound chipper.

Malcolm's new job at Zanderbilt was working out great, and sparring with Bone Crusher was a personal and professional triumph. Bone Crusher seemed to be a real good guy. He was known to love the Lord, and working with him in the ring was a dream come true. Malcolm made a promise that he would do everything in his power to help the champ prepare for his comeback. His trainers made it clear to Malcolm not to hold anything back in the ring.

They asked him to bring it and bring it hard, and that's exactly what Malcolm did four days a week. He gratefully earned his $10,000 a month, giving it all of his heart and soul not already devoted to God. He didn't know how long this opportunity of a lifetime would last, so he had to make the best of it. This was by far the best job he'd ever had. If he had his wish, he'd do it full-time.

Who knows, he thought, *if word got out that he was a good sparring partner, maybe other fighters would hire him to help out during training.*

Malcolm prayed for the opportunity, and free ringside seats. Over the last two months, Malcolm had saved up enough money for a nice down payment on a house. Vanessa had been helping him look for a place. He was ready to get out of his sister's home. Her hospitality was great, but it was time for him to feather his own nest. He looked forward to having a place that his kids could come home to. Bringing them to Lauren's house for a visit was starting to get crowded. She had three kids, and it felt like the Brady Bunch.

Vanessa had a small condo just big enough for her and her pet Doberman, Bubbles. Malcolm was starting to feel agitated. Vanessa urged him to look at smaller houses, but he wanted something bigger. She kept on and on and on about how Malcolm didn't need anything too big for just him and the children. She insisted that a cozy three-bedroom ranch would be sufficient for him, Crystal, Layla and KJ.

Malcolm didn't want a large house just for the kids' sake. He had bigger plans in mind. He had already decided that once his divorce was final, he was going to ask Vanessa to be his wife. He didn't care if they had a ten-year engagement. If that's what she wanted, it was fine with him. He was determined she was not going to get away. He wanted to put a ring on her finger. Malcolm's impatience grew. Telese's ninety-day divorce was more than sixty days overdue. He was ready to put the past behind him as soon as possible, so he could expedite his plan for the future.

Hearing Telese tell him it could be any day now was like hearing an orchestra concerto. Malcolm pulled into Telese's driveway twenty-five minutes later. The grass looked like it hadn't been cut in months, and the outside of the house needed a little work. The door leading from the house to the garage was broken and hanging on the hinges. When KJ spotted his dad's car, his eyes lit up.

"Dad," KJ ran toward him.

"What's going on?" He gave his dad a cool boy handshake, one Malcolm wasn't familiar with.

"Did you see Shabazz Duke today?" he asked excitedly.

"No son, not today. I haven't seen him since that day we were at the gym," Malcolm answered with a smile.

"What about T.C. 'Bone Crusher' Evans?" K.J asked.

"Umm, hey, I think I did see him today," Malcolm joked.

"Not only did I see him, but I kicked his butt."

"That's my daddy, that's my daddy!" KJ danced in the humid heat.

Malcolm was delighted to see the way his son now loved having him around. It was a day he longed to see and was determined to make sure their relationship continued that way.

"When can I go to the gym with you, Dad? I got some new moves," KJ said, showing off his same old moves. "Or I could be the water boy," he grinned eagerly.

"I'm trying to work something out so you and some of your buddies can come to the ring and play around a little bit, when Bone Crusher's there, of course."

KJ started jumping up and down like a million-dollar lottery winner.

"Yes!" He cheered with glee.

"I can't wait."

"I know you can't, son, just give me a few days. Where is Layla and your mom?"

"Oh, they're in Layla's room," KJ answered.

"By the way, dad," he whispered, "Layla's faking, she probably doesn't want to go to school tomorrow." K.J winked.

Malcolm laughed at his son's comedy before walking through the door quietly. He tried to sneak up on Layla, tiptoeing down the hall and stood at the door to overhear a conversation that definitely wasn't intended for his ears.

"Now Layla, you have to remember everything Momma told you, okay?"

The little girl nodded solemnly, sitting in her bed under the covers and wearing her princess nightgown.

"Yes, Momma, I remember. When Daddy comes, I'm supposed to act like I'm sick and tell him I want him to stay."

Telese nodded, "…and what are you going to say if he says he can't spend the night?"

"I should start crying and say he doesn't love us no more," the child said innocently.

Kissing her daughter's head, Telese added, "That's my girl, now give Momma a high-five." Telese raised her hand halfway so Layla could smack it.

Malcolm waited a few seconds before softly knocking on Layla's bedroom door. "I hear I've got a sick baby girl in here," he opened the door.

Layla jumped behind the covers. "Hey, Daddy," she smiled wide, forgetting she was supposed to be acting.

"Dr. Stuart's in the building." Malcolm held up the children's Tylenol medicine.

"You don't feel too warm," Malcolm said, placing his palm on her forehead. Did you take her temperature, Telese?" Malcolm asked.

"Yes, I did earlier. It's been slowly creeping up."

"I'll give her the medicine." Telese started to open the bottle.

"Can you go to the kitchen and fix her a glass of orange juice?"

Malcolm answered, "Daddy will be right back, little princess."

"Okay, Daddy." Layla tried her best to sound pitiful, pinching her eyelids together to look sick.

Malcolm didn't know what Telese had promised her for the performance, but she was sure earning her reward. He laughed at his little faker as he walked down the hall. If Malcolm hadn't overheard their little ploy, he would have fallen for it like a novice. He quickly poured the juice and returned to the bedroom.

"Here you go, sweetie." Malcolm sat at the edge of the bed to hand Layla the cup.

Layla pretended to be weak. "Thank you, Daddy," she said taking a big sip from her cup.

She gave him a sideways glance as she handed the cup back to him.

"Daddy, can you spend the night with me? Please!" The little girl played her role to the hilt.

"There's been a monster in my closet ever since you moved out, Daddy."

"Layla," Telese said firmly.

"I told you honey, there is no such thing as monsters. I'm sure your daddy is pretty busy these days."

"Ah, please, I want you to....can he, Momma, please?" she looked at Telese for a favorable answer.

"That's up to your father. It's all right with me," Telese shrugged.

Malcolm, wanting to burst out in laughter, held it in. "Sit tight, squirt, let me talk it over with your mom, okay?"

"Okay, Daddy. Don't worry, Mr. Morris isn't spending the night, so you can stay," she smiled brightly.

Telese's smile was instantly deflated. "Layla, you lay down, we'll be right back. Telese followed Malcolm down the hallway.

"I don't think spending the night will be a good idea, so here's what I suggest." He paused.

"I'll tell her I'm staying the night, and then after she falls asleep, I'll take off."

"But she'll be disappointed if you're not here in the morning," Telese said.

Telese didn't know why she was playing this game. She didn't think she wanted Malcolm anymore, but she wasn't sure. The changed Malcolm was very appealing.

"By morning, she won't even remember I was here," Malcolm said.

"I guess you're right." Telese sounded disappointed.

"Let me make a phone call," Malcolm said.

"Sure." Telese walked back into Layla's room.

"Vanessa, hey baby, it's Malcolm. Give me a call when service is over. I'm at Telese's house. Layla isn't feeling well, so

I'll be here until she falls asleep. We may have to get some late-night food, if that's okay, but call me when you're done."

Telese stopped eavesdropping when she heard Malcolm's footsteps headed toward them. Malcolm walked into Layla's bedroom, smiling.

"Okay, squirt, you win. Daddy's staying."

"Yay!" Layla jumped up and down on the bed.

"Daddy's spending the night, Daddy's spending the night," she sang.

"Mom, when can we get my new baby doll?" Layla asked, still jumping on her bed expecting a reward for her starring role.

"Wait a minute." Malcolm tried to appear confused.

"Are you tricking me? I thought you were sick."

Layla quickly jumped under the covers. "I'm feeling a little better now, not a whole, whole lot, but a little bit. Daddy, let's go watch cartoons." Layla looked around the floor for her slippers.

"Okay," Malcolm agreed, picking her up from the bed.

"I'm going to take a shower while you two watch TV," Telese said, heading for her bedroom.

"Cool," Malcolm said.

By the time Telese was finished showering and threw on her heavy cotton robe, Malcolm and Layla were sound asleep on the sofa. Telese eased Malcolm's phone sitting neatly beside his car keys from the end table. She looked quickly at Malcolm and Vanessa's picture on the screen saver of his phone. She roamed through his settings and put his phone on silent mode. She watched Malcolm sound asleep as Layla lay cuddled to his side. She couldn't help but miss seeing the two of them together like old times.

Telese nudged Malcolm. "She's asleep already. You can go lay her down."

Malcolm lifted Layla from the sofa and kissed her rosy cheeks softly as he headed down the hallway. He had never realized how much he missed living in the same home with his children. He had to admit sometimes he wished he had them to come home to. Seeing Layla's face light up when he walked into the room made his heart smile. He laid her gently in her bed, pulled the quilt up around her shoulders, and kissed the top of her head before closing the door behind him and returning to the living room.

"I guess I'd better get out of here." Malcolm said walking down the hall rubbing the crook out of his neck.

His heart dropped, along with his mouth, when he saw the candles flickering lights as they hit the beige walls leading to the living room. Telese was standing there, no longer in her heavy cotton robe but in sexy lingerie. She smiled when she saw the reaction on Malcolm's face. She had been fearful that he no longer felt anything for her, although she still had feelings for him. She hadn't left him because she didn't love him. It was because she couldn't stand the fighting. But now that he'd changed, she didn't know what she wanted. Her relationship with Morris was great, but now she felt confused.

Malcolm closed his eyes tight, hoping this was all dream. He opened them slowly, but this time Telese was standing in front of him. Malcolm was nervous, because he hadn't seen bare curves on a woman's body in a long time. Telese grabbed his hands and placed them on her breasts. She kissed his lips tenderly, trying to savor the moment. Malcolm stood frozen without saying a word. His mind was telling his feet to move, but his flesh kept saying, *"Boy! You better get you some."*

Telese's body felt and smelled like a ripe melon and before he knew it, Malcolm was kissing the nape of her neck.

"Let's take this to the bedroom," Telese smiled, pulling him down the hallway.

Everything on Malcolm's body was rock hard. Telese whispered softly, "I still love you, Malcolm. I see the man you've become, and I love it. God has changed you for the better. I know you'll never hurt me again," she whispered.

"We want Daddy back."

Malcolm knew what Telese said was true. He was no longer that violent man he used to be. He had completed his 12-week anger management class and knew how to channel his rage in a healthy way. For him the ring was a place to let go of frustrations. He held a lot of anger in his heart, but the ring allowed him the opportunity to get it out of his system. It ministered to him and freed his emotions as nothing else could.

Telese pulled Malcolm onto the bed, allowing his body to rest on top of her. The look in her eyes was soft, and her touch was soothing. She really wanted him. She might be confused about what she wanted long-term, but she was very sure about what she wanted tonight. Malcolm couldn't believe this was happening. A few days ago he was waiting anxiously for divorce papers. Now look at him.

"What am I doing? This is crazy." A vision of Vanessa's face flashed across his mind. He had many people to thank for his journey, and one of them was Vanessa. She was the one who had stood by him. When the chips were down, she had encouraged and lifted him up, and ministered to his soul. The three times he asked Telese to attend his classes with him to help with anger management, she was always too busy; but once he met Vanessa, she never hesitated when he asked.

"I'm sorry, Telese. This isn't what I want. I can't do this."

He jumped to his feet and tried to walk away, adjusting his shirt.

Telese panicked. "Malcolm please."

She pulled the back of his shirt. "Let's just have sex, with no strings attached. I know you want it too. I'm not saying we have to get back together right now. I know you're in love with Vanessa, but Malcolm, I'm still in love with you too. Can we please just satisfy this craving tonight?"

Malcolm was silent.

"Malcolm you have nothing to feel guilty about. I'm still your wife. You're not committing a sin. I still belong to you."

"Telese, you're sleeping with Morris," Malcolm said, remembering that dreadful day in the parking lot as he turned to look at her.

She got up from the bed to face him. "Malcolm, you hurt me. I needed someone to talk to. Morris was there. I know that it wasn't right because you two were friends, but I swear we weren't intimate until after you and I separated."

"You're sleeping with him, Telese. It doesn't matter if it was before, during or after we called it quits. He was still my best friend."

Telese dropped her head. She couldn't blame Malcolm for his feelings. She dropped the skimpy nighty.

"Malcolm, I'm sorry. Let me make it up to you."

Malcolm stared at Telese for what seemed like an eternity. She had to seize the moment. If she didn't make a move now, she didn't know what might happen. She darted toward him and pressed her naked body against his. She pulled his large hands onto the cheeks of her behind and kissed his lips again almost desperately. Once she noticed that Malcolm didn't resist, she had to go in for the kill. She started unzipping his pants, never taking her eyes off of him.

"I'm sorry." he hurried to the living room and grabbed his phone and keys.

Telese rushed after him. Crocodile tears flowed from her eyes swiftly.

"Can you at least think about our family? Maybe I don't want to let you go. Can you answer a question?" she dried her tears as she slipped the nighty back on.

"How do you feel about me?" she embraced him snugly. "Please tell me the truth," she whispered.

"I don't know," Malcolm said, looking at the six missed calls, two from Vanessa.

"I've got to go."

Malcolm headed quickly for the door, ignoring Telese's soft cries as she pleaded for him to come back. He kept walking, locking the door when he got safely to his car. Telese stood at the door half naked in tears as she watched Malcolm speed off. She headed to the refrigerator and grabbed the gallon of ice cream from the freezer. She cut half the apple pie and slammed it on a plate. Heading to the bedroom, she sat on her bed still crying and ate her aching heart away. Once Malcolm was out of the subdivision, he pulled the car over to get to get his thoughts together.

What just happened? He shook his head in disbelief. Why didn't he hear his phone ring? Vanessa was going to kill him if he didn't have a good excuse. She knew he was at Telese's house. Malcolm's heart began to flutter. He was ashamed of what had almost happened. He knew he didn't love Telese anymore, but something was still there. He just didn't know what. One thing she said definitely rang true. The kids really did want Daddy home.

The thought of being back together as a family made Malcolm think, but his love for Vanessa was strong. He believed they could have a beautiful life together. Malcolm called Vanessa, afraid of what she might say. He wondered how upset she would be that he hadn't answered his phone. She'd probably not believe that his phone was on silent, and if she did, it didn't take a rocket scientist to know how it got in that mode.

Surprisingly, Vanessa wasn't upset at all. She was more concerned about Layla. Malcolm told her Layla wanted him to stay until she fell asleep. He lied and told her he left his cell phone in his car, and of course he left out a lot of incriminating details. Vanessa didn't show a hint of uncertainty, but she did make a mental bookmark to protect her heart. She knew Telese might have a change of heart, so she made sure to save room for disappointment. But nothing could have possibly ruined her mood. She had received a letter from Apostle Reed's Ministry inviting her to be the keynote speaker at their women's conference. Vanessa was delighted for the opportunity to speak at such a huge church and even more excited about a free trip to Florida. Relieved that Vanessa wasn't upset about him not answering the phone, Malcolm felt much better. He felt sick at the thought of what almost happened. His ringing phone interrupted this train of thought.

"Hello," he answered without checking the ID, hoping it wasn't Telese.

"Hi, is this Malcolm?" the brisk female voice asked politely.

"Yes, who is this?"

"You don't know me. The woman got directly to the point. My name is Stephanie Newman. I need to meet with you as soon as you're available. I have some information that I think you need to know."

"What information? About what or who?"

"I'd rather not discuss it over the phone. Can we meet somewhere and talk soon?"

"I guess, but I need to know what this is about," Malcolm insisted.

"I can't go into the details right now, but I promise this is something you really need to know. You're being played. I can tell you that much."

Malcolm answered, "I don't have time for games," he said ransacking his glove compartment with the other hand for aspirin.

"Trust me, Malcolm, this is not a game."

"Okay," Malcolm said, brushing her off.

"Call me later and we'll set up something." He ended the call.

He had no time for nonsense. Something about this had "Telese" written all over it. He made a mental note of the phone number so he'd remember not to answer it the next time she called.

"Mr. Durrant, Luke Zerrico is on line one," Ray's secretary buzzed in.

"Luke, man, how's it going? I'm glad you finally returned my phone call," Ray said happily.

"Ray, I'm sorry, man, but I had to regroup. I just wasn't in the mood to talk at the time," Luke said.

"I understand," Ray said affably.

"I just wanted to let you know that I am here and will make myself available if there is anything you need."

"Thanks, Ray," Luke said appreciatively.

"That means a lot."

"So, what's been going on?" Ray asked.

"Have you found anything yet?" he said adjusted the phone in his hand to hear more comfortably.

Ray raised his eyebrows when Luke informed him that he was working for Zanderbilt's top competitor, Drexelle. "Get out of here," Ray said, surprised.

"It's true, Ray."

"I'm making more money, with less stress."

"That's great," Ray answered.

"I know you're the man out there at Zanderbilt, but we all know that Amanda pulls the strings. You're all just paid doughboys." Ray laughed, knowing it was the truth.

"I'm telling you, man, she's the devil with curves," Luke laughed.

"I know," Ray joined in.

"Don't trust her for a minute. She's an undercover rat, a manipulative, scheming wicked witch." The man was getting heated.

"But I'll tell you what," Luke calmed himself.

"I've thrown your name around here to several of my colleagues. I've let them know that you're the real brains behind that operation. So if you ever get tired of having your strings pulled, give me a call. We both know they'd welcome you here with no questions asked."

"All right, Luke, you take care." Ray hung up.

Ray checked on Donae at home. She had called in sick the last few days. Her morning sickness had kicked in, and Ray loved it. He had been waiting on her hand and foot, and enjoying every minute of it. They had narrowed the baby names to Stephen or Joshua for a boy and Elizabeth or Danyelle for a girl. It would be a few months before they found out the sex of the baby, but Ray didn't care if it was a boy or a girl. He knew the pitter-patter of little feet would bring his family even closer. It already had.

The last couple of times Ray, Steven and Malcolm had hung out, they went to see Moe. She seemed to be doing better these days. She'd come back to work, which made a lot of customers happy. The food had still been good while Moe was away, but it just seemed like Moe brought the place to life. Her spirit was one you'd notice, especially if it wasn't there. Moe's boys were still giving her a fit. She constantly worried about the one in prison, and the other one was headed in that direction. Her life was consumed by worries over them. It seemed as if taking care of her health issues wasn't a priority. A part of her just wanted the stress to be over and done with. She knew it was the prayers of Pastor Ivy and the church members that had kept her alive. Yolanda maintained close tabs on her dear friend, but she didn't have as much free time now as she used to. Between having a man and caring for Ms. JoAnn, her days were pretty busy.

Malcolm introduced Raymond and Donae to Yolanda after church one Sunday, and they both agreed that she was the best thing that could've happened to Malcolm. He even shared with Ray his little mishap with Telese. Raymond politely informed Malcolm that his almost little slip-up could have cost him a year's wait for the divorce to be finalized.

The office was tense. Ray knew it was just a matter of time before Amanda found out that Ray and Donae were expecting, and he knew she'd be upset about it. He was surprised she hadn't been by his office, hounding him about this or that, but for the time being he appreciated the peace. Today he decided to eat lunch in his office so he could finish up work early and get home to cater to his wife. He enjoyed being her manservant. It made him feel protective.

Taking a bite of his pecan chicken salad sandwich, he savored the delicious spicy dressing as he began reading his forty-two new emails. He was delighted to see how well the plant was doing under his leadership. But once he read the memo from CEO Blake Sheridan, his chicken salad almost came up. The memo discussed details of the Code Red expansion and what it could mean for Zanderbilt. Mr. Sheridan praised Amanda for her great business sense in coming up with and executing the idea behind the project. He also congratulated the Virginia plant on a job well done on record breaking numbers of safe man hours, cost efficiency, and profit that year.

Ray felt uneasy. From the sound of the memo, Amanda had presented the project as her idea, taking all the credit for Ray's hard work. He was livid. How could she be so cut-throat? Ray banged his fist on his desk, "That conniving witch! Luke Zerrico was right. Amanda was a lowdown snake in the grass."

Ray tossed the rest of his lunch in the trash and immediately buzzed Amanda to let her know he was headed to her office.

"What is this about?" he said, striding into her office with the memo he had just printed from the computer.

Irately, he took a seat before her desk and placed the memo in front of her. "Oh, that." Her eyes met his with a smile.

"That's nothing for you to worry about." She got up and walked around her desk and sat down beside him in the matching chair, patting his knee. Then she got up quickly and cracked open the office door to tell Eva that she was expecting a very important phone call, and to buzz it through.

"What do you mean nothing for me to worry about?" Ray jumped to his feet.

"I've been developing this project for over a year now, and you think I'm going to let you take credit for something so huge that you didn't even have a part in?"

"You have no details other than what I've told you, and what do you know about implementing and troubleshooting? Amanda, you are in over your head. Without me, you won't be able to see this through."

"What do you mean without you?" She smiled.

"Who cares whose idea it was? We're in this thing together, honey." She sounded excited.

"When I look good, you look good," she gleamed.

"Amanda, you stole my idea, and you sold it to the shareholders as your own, and from the sound of the memo, this is the project of the century for Zanderbilt, but it's my idea!"

"Why are you making such a big deal about this?" she appeared unfazed.

"After all I've done for you, you should be grateful. I needed to show my ability, Ray, so I used your idea. You'll still reap the benefits," she leaned toward him, almost gloating.

Ray was furious but forced himself to take a deep breath.

"Have you picked out baby names yet?" she winked.

Ray hadn't seen that coming. He wiped his forehead, wondering how in the world she had found out.

"So aren't you going to answer my question?" she looked serious, but her smile never faded.

"We've thrown some names around," Ray answered honestly, taken off-guard.

"I like Taylor. What do you think about that? Or, better yet, Hailey, that's nice don't you think?"

"What do you think of those names, that is, if it's a girl of course.

"What are you hoping for?" she asked smugly.

"Amanda," Ray was tired of her game.

"I didn't come here to discuss baby names. I came here to discuss how you drugged me on a business trip, raped me and stole the biggest project of my career."

"Wow," Amanda raised her eyebrows.

"I don't recall it like that," she mumbled under her breath.

Ray followed up his accusation. "How can you be so cruel and cut-throat? I've seen you do a lot of things I wouldn't agree with, but this has got to take the cake."

He paused before adding, "I'm setting up a meeting with Blake Sheridan immediately and shedding some light on this little fiasco."

"You'll do no such thing," Amanda demanded.

"Calm down. We all can benefit from this project, Ray."

"No, Amanda," Ray shouted.

"I've already sent out an email requesting a meeting ASAP."

"Why did you do that?" Amanda glanced away to steady her thoughts.

"I'm not going to sit back and let you treat me like some trained dog on a leash. I've worked my butt off for this company. I've proven by my accomplishments that I'm more than able to run this business. Hell, the record-breaking profits speak for themselves. I refuse to allow you to make me believe that my talent or opportunity came from you. They came from God."

"There you go on that kick again. I thought we were past this stage, Raymond." She clenched her hands in her lap.

"You cancel that meeting immediately," she demanded.

"You go back to your office and keep running this place like you've been doing like a good little boy, and then after work you come by my place and relax," she said without the smile.

Ray laughed. "Amanda," he spoke clearly.

"I think you need medication. You really are delirious."

"No, Mr. Durrant," she smiled again.

"I just love you, and what I want, I want."

Ray sneered. "Well Amanda, we can't always have what we want."

"And why not," she said, handing him the vanilla envelope.

Ray opened the flap and pulled out a photo, letting the rest drop to the floor. Looking at Amanda's nude body on top of his disgusted him to the core. The picture of his eyes half open appeared that he was enjoying every minute during the snapshot. Ray couldn't stand to look any longer. He walked out of Amanda's office, wanting to choke her.

"I'll see you at my house around 8:00 p.m., honey," she yelled as he walked away.

"Dinner will be waiting, Ray, with all your favorites."

Ray walked by Eva's desk with smoke coming from his ears. He stopped halfway through the hall and headed back in the opposite direction. He stood in front of Eva and looked her square in the eyes as he leaned over her desk.

"You helped her do this, didn't you?" Ray breathed slowly.

Eva couldn't even look Ray in the eyes.

"Answer me!" he yelled, as he watched her face go pale.

"Ray!" Amanda raced out of her office to Eva's rescue.

"What are you doing? Get a grip," she pleaded.

Ray snatched the phone from Eva's hand and jerked the cord from the jack before throwing it against the wall, smashing it to pieces. He walked toward his office, got his briefcase, suit jacket and car keys and left the building with everyone staring in his direction, including Amanda.

"Ignore that," Amanda called out to the bystanders as she tried to justify his actions.

"He's just having a bad day."

Eva sat at her desk, shocked and crying. Guilt was written all over her face, and she was ashamed of what she had allowed Amanda to con her into doing. She was destroying a man's life and hurting his family. How could she have been so low? Eva looked into Amanda's eyes to see a lack of remorse and downright evil. It was at that moment that Eva wished she'd never spent a dime of the $5,000 Amanda had given her for slipping that powder and ecstasy into Ray's drink or for playing the photographer in the X-rated photo shoot. She had sunk to her lowest of lows and didn't know how in the world she could return to work in the morning.

Courtney came into the bedroom that Ivy and Yolanda had set up for JoAnn. Her mother had made it crystal clear that she was fine and capable of staying at her own house, but this was far from the truth. Her memory was fading quickly. Some days she couldn't remember who anyone was. She started swearing, which she had never done before. Many nights she'd call out for Jessie, her late husband. Seeing his mother like this was tearing Ivy apart. He asked God to heal her, and he believed that it would happen. JoAnn recognized her daughter Courtney the moment she walked into the neatly kept bedroom.

"Lawd have mercy, there goes my baby," JoAnn smiled, reaching for Courtney's hand to pull her to the bedside.

"Hey, Momma." Courtney began to cry.

"What in the world are you crying for child? There is nothing for you to fret about." JoAnn patted her hand.

"God is a good God. Goodness child, I had the most awful dream about you." JoAnn held her chest.

"Thank you, Jesus, it was just a dream."

"Oh no, Momma," Courtney tried to comfort her.

"What was your dream about?"

JoAnn laughed, knowing it had been just a silly nightmare.

"Baby, JoAnn seemed a bit embarrassed, "I dreamed you liked coochie-cats. Lord aint that crazy? You liking women instead of men," she giggled.

"The devil is a liar. Ain't that right baby?"

Courtney had to laugh. "Yeah, Momma," Courtney agreed, "That was a crazy dream."

"Baby, can you please get me out of here? I know Jessie is at home right now waiting on his dinner, and if it ain't ready he'll be mad as fire." JoAnn expressed with a stern face.

"And baby, you know I can't leave him alone by himself too long cause them cravings of his will get the best of him. I've got to watch over your daddy until the good Lord sets him free."

"Momma, it's okay." Courtney held back tears as she patted her mother's hand.

"Yolanda and Ivy are seeing about him. They took him something to eat," she lied.

"Oh Lord," JoAnn began to panic.

"That wife of his can't cook a lick. The green beans she made tasted like burned rubber, and the meatloaf is like dog food. Lord, poor Jessie gon', wonder where I am," she tried to get up.

"No, Momma." Courtney tried to lean JoAnn back onto the mattress.

"No!" JoAnn yelled.

"I got to get out of here. You need to pray for your brother," JoAnn exhaled.

"He done inherited part of your daddy's demon. Him and that wife of his arguing every night about 'doin it' every…single…night, seems like."

"Ivy storms out the house, mad as hell. It's driving me crazy. Then when he do get some, the headboard keep knocking the wall, and they making all these awful noises. I had to yell for them to stop all that screw'n so I could go to sleep."

"Momma!" Courtney laughed at her childlike parent.

"That wasn't nice. They are married, Momma," Courtney laughed again.

The disease had caused her mother to be bold and candid, which she never was before. There was no way JoAnn would talk about sex so candidly in the past.

"Momma, you sit tight, I'll be right back." Courtney walked toward the door to go speak with Ivy and Yolanda.

"Okay, my sweet Courtney. You gone take me home when you come back?" JoAnn asked with a whisper. "I can be packing my stuff up until you get back."

"We will see, Momma. We might have to wait until everybody is sleep and then sneak out, okay?"

"Okay." JoAnn smiled at the thought of leaving

"You just sit back and watch your favorite show. I know Nelly Olson is going to do something to get Laura Ingalls in trouble."

"I know," JoAnn agreed.

"She just makes me sick."

Courtney closed the door and headed down the hallway to Ivy's living room where the rest of the family was. She couldn't believe how tall Dominic had gotten, and he was the spitting image of his daddy. She'd seen all her nieces and nephews except for the twins. As usual, their momma, Mel, wouldn't let go of the baby momma drama. Courtney decided she would drive by her house one evening before she left to at least see them for a few minutes.

Ivy noticed the tears as Courtney stepped into the living room. "Are you okay?" he asked with concern.

"No," she nearly screamed.

"This is harder than I thought it would be. I'm sorry, Ivy. I can't stand to see Momma like that. Can't they give her some medicine to bring her memory back?"

"I wish it were that simple," Ivy answered gently as Yolanda came to stand beside Courtney and placed her arm around her shoulders.

"We just have to keep praying."

Courtney's heart ached for her mother. "She doesn't want to be here. She wants to go home, and she thinks Dad is there waiting for her."

"Is that what she is saying now?" Ivy asked.

"Yeah, and that you and Yolanda need to get a hotel room," Courtney smiled.

Yolanda dropped her head and smiled. Ivy ignored the comment.

"Ivy, you and Yolanda can't continue to handle all this by yourselves, you need help."

"Yolanda has a full-time job, and with your full-time ministry with the church, how can you all take care of Momma?"

"We're okay," Yolanda said.

"My friend Vanessa is a licensed home-health nurse, so we've hired her to stay with Momma until we get home from work."

"Well, that's good, and it makes me feel a little bit better to know you have someone with her who is qualified. I'll be sure to come home more so I can do my part. I'm ashamed that I've stayed away so long."

"I'm glad to hear that," Ivy smiled.

"I miss having my baby sister around."

"I know you do," Courtney laughed.

"I see you still need me to get Mel straightened out."

"Good luck with that one." Yolanda chuckled along with Ivy.

"I'll go check on her," Yolanda said.

"Hopefully *Little House on the Prairie* has put her to sleep."

Yolanda grabbed the rail to head up the stairs. Ivy watched her every move as she started up the stairs. He licked his lips just thinking about her curvy hips between the sheets. His fantasy was rudely interrupted when they heard a car door slam, and then a woman racing toward the house cursing at the top of her lungs.

"Who the heck is that?" Yolanda hurried toward the door behind Ivy and Courtney.

"Where the hell is my son? You low down dirty dog!" Dominic's mother, Kandice yelled.

215

Dominic looked through the window and saw his mother, and raced down the stairs.

"Ma!" he said, excited to finally see her.

"Hey baby," she wrapped her arms around Dominic.

Her matted hair smelled like it had been on fire. Her clothes were filthy, and she looked like she had been in a fight. Ivy told Yolanda and Courtney to go back inside the house and that he'd handle everything.

"You think you're slick, kidnapping my son. I'm his mother! You're just a sperm donor. Go pack your stuff, Dominic, you're coming with me," she demanded in a hoarse voice.

"No, you're not, Dominic," Ivy looked at his son sternly.

"Dominic is not going anywhere. This is where he lives, and this is where he stays until you get yourself together."

"I'll be damned!" she screamed.

"Where have you been for the last three to four months? The only reason you're here is because I stopped the child support checks," Ivy couldn't hold back.

"You're a liar!" she said, rebuking the truth.

"Dominic, go inside," Ivy said.

"I promise you can visit with your mother before she leaves."

Dominic reluctantly walked into the house. After getting suspended from school, he expected Ivy to go off and call him everything but a child of God, but Ivy did the contrary. He embraced his son and told him how much he loved him. Ivy stressed that he wanted him to be successful in life, and he wanted to show him the way. Ivy let Dominic know through love that he didn't want to ever give up on him. In spite of Ivy pouring out his heart, Dominic still harbored a lot of anger toward his father.

"He's going back with me," the disheveled woman yelled.

"Over my dead body," Ivy replied.

"We can make that happen," she said, approaching Ivy in a menacing manner.

"Look, I've got temporary custody of Dominic, and I've got the papers to prove it. You abandoned him. You have nowhere to live and no way to provide for him. When you get yourself together, then we can talk about other arrangements," Ivy insisted.

"I'll even pay for you to go to rehab."

"Rehab! I don't need no damn rehab," Kandice got feisty.

"I ain't on no drugs."

Dominic ran to his room and began to quickly pack. Ivy looked at Kandice, not believing that she could let herself go like that. He felt sorry for her, and he was moved with compassion to help her get her life back on track.

"Kandice," Ivy pleaded.

"The first step in deliverance is admitting you've got a problem."

"I ain't got no problem," she ranted frantically, shaking her finger in his face.

"You've turned my son against me. I can't stand you, Ivy, you make me sick. I hope you die and go straight to hell." Her face was livid, her features contorted.

"You need to lower your voice." Ivy's tone came with force.

"I didn't turn our son against you. You turned him against me with all your lies. You know I tried to be part of my son's life, but I couldn't because of you. You wouldn't let me see him."

Ivy's heart began to spill over into his eyes. "It's not fair what you did by keeping me away from my son. Now he hates me because of the lies you told. I'm going through hell trying to prove to him that I've always wanted to be in his life. Why didn't you tell him the truth?"

Kandice dropped her eyes. She wanted to continue cursing him, but guilt had a hold on her.

"I wanted to be with you, but you chose to be with someone else. You didn't tell him that, did you?" Ivy blurted in anger.

Hearing Ivy remind her of the bad choice she had made fueled Kandice's anger even more.

"So, what? Yeah, I lied to him. You shouldn't have moved away," she yelled.

"Kandice, I asked you to marry me before I left, and your answer was no. So I went off to college to do something with my life. I'd made enough mistakes and wanted to change. Since things hadn't work out with your boyfriend, you tried to come crawling back to me, but it was too late by then. I had moved on, but that was no reason for you to keep me away from my son."

Kandice turned her back to Ivy. She couldn't look at his face any longer.

"No! Look at me." Ivy turned her around to face him.

"You kept my son away from me for a mistake you made, not me." Ivy quickly dried his tears with his hand.

Staring at the sadness in Ivy's eyes moved Kandice. Deep down in her heart she knew Ivy was telling the truth, and even if Ivy hadn't wanted to be with her so many years ago, it still gave her no right to keep Dominic away from him. Who knows what Dominic's life could have been like if it hadn't been for Kandice being so self-centered?

217

"Now, you are welcome to visit with Dominic anytime you like, but only if you promise to be respectful of my home. I won't stand in the way of you seeing your son like you did to me....Deal?" Ivy extended his hand, implying that they should shake on it.

"Ok, for now..." Kandice rolled her bright eyes.

"Until I get myself straightened out," she refused to shake his hand so instead she folded her arms.

"But I'm telling you, I want my baby back with me."

Kandice adjusted her clothes and tried to smooth down her hair, but it was useless. She looked a mess. Walking over to the car, she told the woman who had brought her to Ivy's house that she would be right back. Kandice walked into the foyer behind Ivy and was blown away by his beautiful home. Ivy introduced her to Yolanda and reacquainted her with Courtney.

Courtney couldn't believe what she was seeing. Kandice used to be the most beautiful girl in high school. She had been the captain of the cheerleading squad and had been very popular. After she broke up with Ivy, she started seeing a big-time dope dealer who promised her, after she had this baby he would make her into a model. He had made her a model alright, but not modeling anything she could be proud of.

Ivy lightly knocked on Dominic's door. "Hey, son, you okay?"

He knew the whole drama scene had to have taken something out of him. The door opened slightly, and Dominic nodded.

"Your mother wants to talk to you, son. I'll leave the two of you alone so you can have some privacy. I'll be down the hall when you guys are finished."

"Wow!"

Kandice poked through the bedroom door and looked around Dominic's room.

"This looks great. It's sure different from the projects."

"Why did you lie to me?" Dominic charged right in.

"Why did you tell me my daddy was no good and didn't want to take care of me or have nothing to do with me?"

"That was a lie! He does care about me and wanted me in his life. I heard everything through the window."

Kandice sat down on the edge of Dominic's bed and didn't mumble a word, allowing Dominic to have his say.

"That wasn't fair," Dominic teared up.

"I missed out on a lot of things because you only cared about you."

"Dominic, that's not true," she interrupted.

"I love you with all my heart. I'd die for you," she began to cry, realizing her son's deeply rooted pain.

"I wish you would have died," Dominic said, wiping his eyes.

"Dominic!"

Kandice looked like her heart was about to break, not remembering she had said the same thing to Ivy moments before.

"I don't mean die and go to the grave." Dominic tried to clear up what he meant.

"Sometimes in my dad's sermons he talks about a person dying to their flesh. Maybe if you would have died to your flesh, the spirit of God could have flowed into your heart to let the past go and to forgive Dad, and even to forgive yourself. I could have had a much better life if your flesh would have died."

"I would have given anything, growing up, to have had a relationship with my dad and do all the father-and-son things I missed out on. All the other kids had fathers who loved them, but I had no one but you're in-and-out no good boyfriends who wouldn't even acknowledge I was in the house, let alone spend time with me. The truth was I had a dad who tried to be there. Why would you do that to me? Mom, that's not love, that's control."

Kandice's heart ached so bad, she wanted to flee and never come back. Seeing the hurt of her heart, Dominic spoke powerful words to soothe her broken soul.

"But I forgive you, Mom. I have to and I still love you, no matter what you do," he said remembering what Ivy had said to him when he got suspended from school.

Kandice sat on his bed and cried until her nose started running. Dominic embraced her frail body as if she were a child, and he the parent. Between tears and hiccups, she told her son how sorry she was, and gladly enough, she really meant it.

"What can I do to make things right?" she continued to wipe away tears with her shirt sleeve.

"I don't know, Ma, but I think saying 'I'm sorry' is a start, and trying to get off drugs is the next step."

Kandice paused a few moments and thought. Something in her wanted to tell her son 'yes,' she'd stop smoking crack, but she had two more rocks in her pocket that she really craved. A moment passed.

"You're right, I've got to start somewhere," she said, removing the hard rocks from her pocket and holding them tightly in her hand.

"Maybe you can come to our church sometime," Dominic said.

"My daddy is awesome. I want to be like him when I grow up."

"I think that's a good idea," she said.

"Your dad is a great man. I can see how much he's changed by listening to you. I guess I really do need Jesus in my life," she smiled, feeling proud of her son.

"Do you really mean that?" Dominic asked.

"Yes, son, I do. I'm tired of living like this." Kandice felt better as the words rolled off her tongue.

Dominic smiled. "I learned in church how to lead someone to Christ. We can do it together," he said.

"That's the best thing I've heard in years," she said, smiling at her son.

Kandice was a bit nervous and even downright scared, realizing this was the most important moment in her life.

Dominic took his mother's hands and prayed: "Father, we ask You to forgive us of our sins. We ask Jesus to come into our hearts and lives. Lord, please guide us to be better people, because we need You. We want to live a life that is pleasing to You and one that gives you glory. Lord, I pray that You give my mother the strength and the courage to get off drugs. I believe that You can deliver her and set her free. I thank You, God that You will do these things, in Jesus' name we pray. Amen"

Ivy had just seconds before walked to the door, not believing what he was hearing. If he hadn't known any better, he'd have thought that was himself leading Kandice to Christ. Dominic had used the same words Ivy used in his salvation prayer. Ivy struggled hard to suppress his emotions. He wanted to glorify God with the fruit of his lips, but all he could do was ponder it in his heart. His son was leading his own mother to salvation. This was a moment he'd never forget. An hour later, Dominic's bedroom door opened. Kandice raced down the stairway to embrace Ivy as if her life depended on it.

"Can you please find it in your heart to forgive me, Ivy?" Kandice said lovingly.

"I was selfish and wrong. I've been holding a grudge against you for years, for no reason. If I had to do it all over again, I never would have kept you from your son."

Ivy rejoiced. "Of course I forgive you," he said warmly, and the two embraced once more.

"Dominic coming here was a blessing in disguise. He's turning out to be a fine young man," Kandice smiled at her handsome son.

"Never in a million years would I have expected the day to end like this."

Ivy smiled. "I've got some people I'd like you to meet."

"Okay," she said, with a look of confusion.

Dominic flew down the stairs when he saw his grandma, Irma, smiling up at him.

"Grandma!" Dominic rushed into her arms, nearly knocking the older woman off her feet. Yolanda and two uniformed women stepped in from another room holding vanilla folders. Ms. Irma made her way toward them.

"What's going on?" Dominic asked.

Kandice looked around the room and quickly realized that this was her intervention. One of the official looking women introduced herself as Shelby Richards, a counselor at Wyatt Hill Rehab Center. She began her speech regarding the intervention services available. Kandice tried to interrupt her, but never got a chance to say a word before Ms. Irma chimed in.

"Kandice," Ms. Irma cried.

"Baby, you need some help. Ivy went through a lot of trouble setting this here up for your benefit. He's been working on it for months." Dominic smiled proudly at his father.

"You got all these people here who love you and want to see you get better."

"Momma, I know." Kandice interrupted her.

"I'm ready to go," she said, putting the two sweaty crack rocks on the polished oak coffee table.

"Jesus is in my heart now, and I'm ready to make a change. I can't say I'll be all holy and all that stuff. All I know right now is I need Him in my life."

Ms. Irma fell to her knees, thanking the Lord. Kandice grabbed her mother and held her tightly. Ms. Irma kissed her only child as if it was the last time she'd ever see her.

"Thank you, Jesus," she kept saying over and over.

"How long will my mom have to live there?" Dominic asked Ivy.

"At least six months to a year," Ivy answered.

"…but she'll be fine."

"I know she will," Dominic smiled.

"I'm happy for her."

Kandice's friend who still sat in the car cried when Kandice told her what had just happened, but she inquired about the two crack rocks she knew Kandice was carrying. Kandice didn't reply. She gave her friend a long hug along with everyone else and made her way with Mrs. Richards. Ivy and the family waved good-bye to Kandice as she rode away with Shelby Richards and her assistant to Wyatt Hill. Dominic ran to his room faster than the speed of lightening. Yolanda, Ivy, and Courtney looked at one another, concerned.

"Maybe you need to go talk to him, Ivy," Courtney said.

"It's been a heck of a day."

A few minutes later Ivy walked upstairs and knocked lightly on Dominic's door. When he opened it, Dominic was pulling himself up from a kneeling position beside his bed.

"Are you okay, son?" Ivy asked.

"Yes sir," Dominic said.

"I was just telling God 'thank you' for answering my prayer."

Ivy stood at the door, not knowing what to do. Everything inside him wanted to embrace his son, but he wasn't sure if it would be welcomed or not. Dominic looked into his father's eyes from across the room and watched the love twinkling there. Racing into his father's arms, Dominic exclaimed,

"I'm saved!"

He started to cry as he murmured the words he'd wanted to say his entire life, "I love you, Dad."

Vanessa's Uncle Rufus invited her and Malcolm over to his house to celebrate his fifty-third birthday. Malcolm had already met several of her family members, all of which were pretty fond of him. Uncle Rufus and Aunt Johnnie Mae were a lively couple, very much in love after twenty-eight years of marriage. They often invited people over for food and fellowship. They had loving spirits, and they would give the shirts off their backs to anyone in need.

Rufus was a nut. Anybody who knew him would tell you he had missed his calling. He could have easily made a living as a standup comedian, since everything that came out of his mouth was funny. He was humorous even when he was serious, and after a few drinks, he was downright hilarious.

"Malcolm!"

Johnnie Mae's face lit up when she saw Malcolm and Vanessa standing at her side door holding two grocery bags of beverages.

"Lord, we sure do need these. Thank y'all for bringing them at the last minute," Johnnie Mae smiled.

"You're welcome, Aunt Mae," Vanessa embraced her petite aunt and showered her with kisses.

"Drinks!" Rufus yelled from the backyard grill.

"As much as she and that new boyfriend of hers can eat, those knuckle heads should have brought some ground round," he joked.

"Slow your roll, Uncle Rufus." Malcolm peeped through the sliding glass door that led to the backyard deck.

Rufus jabbed the air, weaving and bobbing with his grill spatula as Malcolm approached.

"Watch out now," Rufus grinned, embracing Malcolm with a firm, manly hug.

"Where's my sweetie?" Rufus face lit up, resembling a half-moon.

"It's not 'Sweetie,' Rufus," Johnnie Mae corrected him.

"It's Evangelist Vanessa Reardon."

"Well, excuse me," Rufus bellowed.

"You all high and mighty now," he winked at Vanessa as she shook her head at him.

"Oh, hush your mouth, Uncle Rufus, and give me a hug. You're always starting trouble." Vanessa gave him a playful scolding look.

Rufus gave his favorite niece a big bear hug. So, how are things going with you, Sweetie?" Rufus tried to be serious.

"Everything is fine," Vanessa answered happily.

"I've been sitting with my pastor's mom Monday through Friday, and boy, is she a piece of work. She has Alzheimer's disease. It's sad to see someone go down so quickly like that. It just breaks my heart."

"I'm sure it does," Rufus said.

"I know JoAnn James, she's a sweet woman, always has been. I need to get on over there and lay holy hands on her," he smiled.

"I know your pastor too. I use to coach his softball team when he was a youngster, pretty nice fella," Rufus smiled.

"They say he's doing great things down there at the church. I need to make my way on over there and teach him what the Word really says," Rufus chuckled.

"Uncle Rufus, stop it. You're a mess!" Vanessa chuckled.

"Everybody keeps telling me that," he said jokingly.

"Tell me this?" he changed the subject.

"Is Malcolm treating you right?" he asked, never mentioning the rumors he'd heard of Malcolm's hot temper or past abusiveness.

"Yes, Uncle Rufus, I couldn't ask for a better man," she smiled with a sparkle in her eyes.

"Aw, my little sweetheart is in love," Rufus teased Vanessa, and she blushed.

"I already warned that fella, if he ever hurts you; it's going to be me and him, toe to toe, blow to blow."

"Sorry, Uncle Rufus. You won't get that chance."

Malcolm interrupted the conversation by sneaking up behind Vanessa, planting a sweet kiss on the nape of her neck. "This here is my queen-to-be." he sang.

"I hear you," Rufus sang along with him.

"But look, boy," he flipped over the hamburgers one at a time.

"That there queen gon' be wanting some kids after a while."

"Uncle Rufus, don't you start that now," Vanessa glared at him nervously.

"What?" Rufus looked innocent.

"Ever since your momma made you give up your baby for adoption, that's all you ever talked about is having kids."

"Okay, Rufus, you need to hush up," Johnnie Mae popped Rufus in the arm.

"You're talking too much."

Rufus looked over at Vanessa and could tell he had put his foot in his mouth. "I'm sorry. I am talking too much. Blame it on the alcohol," he raised his red cup filled with beer.

Malcolm tried not to show his surprise. He and Vanessa had spent countless hours on the phone talking about everything under the sun, and she had never mentioned that she'd given up a child for adoption. Why wouldn't she tell him something that important? As much as Malcolm had struggled to pay child support, he thought he was done having kids. The thought of having another one made him uneasy and almost ready to panic.

"Come on, my Queen," Malcolm teased Vanessa, trying to take her mind off her uncle's comment.

"Let's eat, baby. I'm hungry as an ox."

"Me too, baby," Vanessa forced a half smile.

"We will talk about that later," she whispered to Malcolm.

"Okay, baby," Malcolm answered.

"Whenever you're ready, I want you to be comfortable."

Vanessa gave Malcolm a hug around his neck and whispered a soft "I love you" in his ear. He always knew the right things to say to soothe her soul. Malcolm followed his beautiful woman to the laid out buffet table. They grabbed paper plates and dug in. Rufus and Johnnie Mae had enough food to feed an army of folks. Roughly close to fifty people came rushing in to join in the food and fun, mingling and making small talk.

"So, Malcolm, what's the new Pastor like down there at Mt. Emanuel?" one of the visitors asked.

"Oh, he's awesome," Malcolm replied.

" Ivy James is a great Pastor. I've learned so much under his leadership."

"That's good to hear." The guest shook his head, "Maybe I'll make my way back down there for a visit."

"Where do you attend now?" Vanessa asked the guest.

"Nowhere at the moment," he replied.

"Churches these days have just turned me off. They judge you for this and that, and seem like ain't nobody getting blessed but the pastor. I got tired of giving my tithe and offering and watching a man get rich.

Rufus chuckled as he looked over at his friend. "I should have just put two bags of groceries in the collection plate," the guest said jokingly.

Everyone in the room burst out in laughter. "Don't get me wrong," the guest added. "I really don't mind giving to the church but, my goodness, it seems like everybody and their momma wants to pastor a church. Is it for the love of God or is it the money?"

"You know what I'm saying?" The guest looked at Rufus for his opinion.

Rufus smiled, "There are some good churches out there that really want God and nothing else, but I understand what you mean, buddy. You're not the only person who has that opinion. If you really feel that way I think you should have just given the groceries. That would have been alright with God."

Malcolm, laughed again at the thought of putting groceries in the collection plate.

Rufus bumped one of his buddies on the arm and said, "Watch this...So, Young Buck, which was the nickname he had for Malcolm when he was drinking. What is so funny?" Rufus asked. "Do I need to take you to bible school?"

"Oh Lord, here we go," several relatives shouted in unison.

"He's about to start preaching again."

"Rufus, don't you get everybody stirred up now," Johnnie Mae called from the kitchen.

"I got to take them to church," Rufus grinned cockily.

"How much money you paying that church every week?"

"I give my tithe and offering," Malcolm said proudly.

"Malcolm, baby, he's setting you up," Vanessa warned her handsome boyfriend. "You know he is."

"It's okay, baby," Malcolm said.

"I'm ready for him this time, Malcolm recalled their last get together and how Rufus enlightened him. I've been studying my Word." Malcolm finished his BBQ ribs and set his plate to the side.

"What's the purpose of the tithe, Young Bucks?" he asked, now speaking to the whole room of people.

"Y'all can answer, don't be scared." Rufus burped loudly.

"To give back to the community," Cousin John blurted.

"Wrong." Rufus shook his head.

"To pay the churches expenses," another yelled

"The purpose of the tithe was to teach the people to fear the Lord," Malcolm called out with confidence above the whispering chatter.

"Okay, Young Buck, you seem to have read a verse or two," he chuckled. " God wanted you to fear him. He was the one who made your crops grow and your cattle to be born. Fearing him proved that you acknowledged your increase came from nobody but God and he could stop it from producing if he wanted to."

"What was the tithe supposed to be?" Rufus asked.

Everyone looked around, a bit confused.

"The tithe was weekly earnings," someone yelled. "The first fruits." Rufus nudged his old buddy again.

"The tithe was 10% of your income," another blurted. Rufus shook his head and smiled a wide smile.

"The tithe was supposed to be crops, grain, oxen and sheep…It was food!" Malcolm called again.

"You think you're smart, don't you, Young Buck?" Rufus smiled, taking a swig from his cup.

"You're right again," he raised up his beer as if toasting.

"Now let me ask you this, Young Buck," he continued.

"If you're so smart in knowing that the tithe was supposed to be food, why is your dumb ass giving the church a tenth of your money?"

"Uncle Rufus!" Everyone in the room burst out laughing, including Malcolm. "Stop cussing," Vanessa chastised as she got up to throw away her and Malcolm's finished plates.

"What?" Rufus glanced around the room. "I didn't cuss. Ain't Hell, Damn, and Ass in the bible? If Jesus can say it then, hell, so can I. Johnnie Mae looked over at her husband and shook her head.

"Wait a minute, wait a minute." Malcolm waved his hand to quiet the crowd, wanting to continue on the subject.

"We have to give money now. The church has to pay the light bills and maintain running water. We can't give sheep and oxen anymore. They didn't have money back then."

"Wrong!" Rufus burped again, this time even louder.

"They had money in those days. Deuteronomy 14:25-26 says in reference to the tithe, if the place where God told them to go to honor him was too far, they should take the tithe and exchange it for MONEY, and then when they got to the place that God told them to go, to buy back crops, grain, oxen, sheep, wine and whatever they wanted, and to eat it there with their families in the presence of the Lord. They stored it in the temple." This was followed by an admiring whisper around the table.

"Listen," Rufus stood to his feet.

"Do you really think God needs your money? He wants your heart. Jesus said render unto Caesar what belongs to Caesar, and render unto God what belongs to God. Jesus didn't want your money, Caesar did and who was Caesar? A man."

There was an appreciative buzz from the others, with a few "Amen's!" and "preach it, Brother Rufus."

"You got all these pastors out here building buildings to house more people. Didn't God say your body was the temple of the Holy Spirit? He's not dwelling in a building. He's dwelling in you. Check out Acts 7:48. God wants you to take care of his people: the poor, the widows, the orphans, those single mothers struggling and that man who can't seem to get on his feet. He wants you to make sure your neighbor isn't living in lack; that's what the tithe is for."

That comment hit home for Malcolm. Wishing someone would have helped him when he needed it. The church had him fill out a five page questionnaire on why his finances were so jacked up.

"I understand what you're saying," Malcolm said, now not joking but really listening closely to Rufus.

"Isn't that what the church does? It helps the poor, the widows and those in need."

"Some do, and I dare say some don't." Rufus agreed in part.

"You got more than a few greedy preachers taking money so they can live in mansions and giving God's people in need the leftovers, the devil is a liar. The world is making money off the church. Deceivers are putting up huge buildings, putting burdens on God's people that they weren't intended to bear, read it! It's right there in Matthew 23:4. Stop letting a man get rich off your ignorance because you believe what he says and won't study the Word for yourself."

"Come on, Rufus," Malcolm said.

"We can't perform animal sacrifices anymore. That was Old Testament."

Rufus nodded, setting down his beer. "You're right, Young Buck. That's why Jesus came. He was the sacrifice. After his death and resurrection, the sacrifices ended, along with the Old Testament law. Jesus came to set you free. Don't let man keep you in bondage to a law from which Jesus freed you. Once Jesus left you were free from the law and should be lead by the Spirit. Laws keep people in bondage. He freed us from the law because He wants his children to have a close enough relationship with Him to where the Holy Spirit will convict you, not a law. When you are lead by the Spirit you are no longer under the law. You're either under the law or you're free; one or the other."

Rufus was starting to get feisty. He was passionate about seeing God's people set free. "It ain't but a few places in the New Testament where Jesus ever mentioned tithing, and that was in Matthew 23 and Luke. Each times he was rebuking church folk."

"Now I'm paraphrasing this He said: 'YOU even tithe not only on the food, but down to the freak'n spices, mint, anise and cumin and have neglected the weightier matters of the law: Justice, mercy and faith'."

"I say it again: God does not need your money! He wants your heart; because when he has your heart, he knows you will freely give to your brother, but who can give to their brother or sister when they are in debt and in need themselves?"

Malcolm sat in his chair, baffled. His mind was telling him one thing, and his heart was saying another.

"Malcolm, Matthew 7:6 says don't give pearls to the swine, son. Don't give your hard earned money to a man so he can get rich off of it. If they don't have jobs, you tell me how they get rich?" Rufus asked.

"What they will tell you is, we take our money and invest it."

"No, they take *your* money and invest it. They ride around in luxury cars, live in huge houses and eat at the best restaurants. They want you to call them spiritual fathers. I rebuke that bull." Rufus started getting worked up.

"Read it, that's what it says in Mathew 23:6-12."

"Tell me this, if Jesus himself rebuked them, why would you follow a man who's doing the same thing? Jesus said don't follow their example. Paul did full-time ministry, but he worked at a job, too. He said, 'I'm worthy of my wages.' Peter said 'We worked so we wouldn't be a burden to you,' that's in Thessalonians 2:9. If Jesus didn't make money off his ministry, why should they? There are single mothers with kids without transportation, but they're riding in Bentleys. The devil is a liar. The purpose of the tithe was to teach us to fear the Lord so his people wouldn't be in lack. If she's walking and he's riding, that's 'lack' where I come from."

Rufus sat back in his chair to let the others contemplate this.

"So, Rufus, are you telling me that I shouldn't pay a tithe?" Malcolm was confused.

"No, son I'm not. You don't pay a tithe. When you pay something, you pay out of obligation or 'LAW', but when you give, that's freedom because you do so from your heart. Study the Word for yourself and show yourself approved. God has hidden mysteries in his Word that he wants you to dig for. The truth is in this Word."

Rufus walked over to his old, worn out Bible on the aged credenza and lifted it up. "This empowers you to get whatever you need. I am not telling you not to give. I REPEAT... I AM NOT TELLING YOU NOT TO GIVE YOUR TITHE. You should give your tithe, he repeated but son, the tithe was food. When did Jesus ever say it changed to money? If you choose to give money it's okay. There's nothing wrong with that, absolutely nothing. As a matter of fact I'm in agreement with giving money to the church. I always have, and I always will. I give it as an offering, and to tell you the truth, at times my offering may be more than my tithe. That's based on the need. When I give I don't put my name on an envelope. What I give is between me and God, but the church wants to keep a record of your giving. Why? Cause they tell you to write it off as a tax deduction." Rufus shook his head.

"Wait a minute Rufus," Malcolm squinted his eyes. Let's go back to what you said about based on the need. What do you mean based on the need?" he questioned.

"The needs of the church or the people. If the church says they have a need I don't mind meeting the need with my offering, but hear me... if the tithe was food then, the tithe is food now. A greedy Pastor might get fat off the tithe, but he damn sure won't get rich. If food was stored in the storehouse, nobody in the community would go hungry. God meant for the tithe to be food. Food would spoil if you had too much, so you shared it with your neighbor. "

Malcolm grabbed the Bible and started flipping through the pages. He turned to Matthew 23 and read the whole chapter. Every single word Rufus had said was in there. Malcolm shook his head in disbelief.

Rufus exhaled, "I'm not saying don't give, but I give what He asked for. The tithe is, was, and always will be food. God never intended for it to be money. God knew how greedy people would be. He didn't want them to center the church around money. He wants the church to be centered on nothing but Jesus. 1Timothy 6:10 says: 'for the love of money is the root of all kinds of evil. Some people craving money have wandered from the true faith and pierced themselves with many sorrows'.

"Because the love of money is the root of all evil, that's why he doesn't want your money, he wants your heart. I want you to be honest. The first thing they look at when they choose a Deacon is the tithe record. The people giving the most money get reserved parking spots close to the Pastor and seated on the front row, daring someone else to sit there. Come on now, if you can't buy your way into Heaven, then you shouldn't be able to buy your way into God's house. God don't work like that. In His kingdom, the servant is first. What some of these high and mighty pastors, bishops and apostles need to realize is, one day the people are going to get fed up with this nonsense and get free."

"What's wrong, Young Buck?" Rufus chuckled.

"Look at it like this: Jesus taught his disciples for three years. The Holy Spirit taught Paul for three years, and he was released to do ministry. Pastors nowadays should equip the people as they grow, study, and learn by the Holy Spirit on their own. Take John the Baptist, his job was to get people to Jesus. That's the pastor's job, to get you to Jesus."

"Once John the Baptist got them ready to know Jesus, he said, 'I must decrease so that he can increase.' He knew that as long as he was in the picture, people would keep following him, but then they should look at Jesus. Jesus told the disciples, 'Okay, you've rolled with me for the past three years. Everything I've shown you, teach to others: cast out demons, lay hands on the sick, feed the poor, love your neighbor, empower people and teach them truth'."

"Then he said, 'Now look, I've got to leave here, but I'm sending you a Comforter to teach you all truths. From now on He is going to be your guide. You won't need a BODY,' he emphasized the word, 'to follow; you listen to Him.' So in other words, John the Baptist said, 'Follow Jesus,' and he left. Jesus said, 'I'm going to the Father and now you must follow the Holy Spirit.' So why are you following a man when you got the Holy Spirit to teach you? He isn't supposed to teach you and keep you, he's supposed to teach you and release you when you read the Bible….You've got to really read the Bible, son, but again I say, don't believe me. Read it for yourself."

Aunt Earlene clapped while Cousin Jerome nodded. Johnnie Mae stood in the living room entrance smiling at her husband. Although he was in a drunken state, she didn't stop him from doing what he did best, his way of ministering.

"Are churches still trying to build a bigger building to house more folks? When will some of the people ever graduate? Biblically, when the church grew it wasn't necessarily the building that grew. It was the people that grew spiritually and scattered all over ministering the good news. They need to branch out and start ministering. It's a messed-up world out there, looking for something. They need Jesus, but y'all too busy sitting in the church, shouting and praising 'Hallelujah,' when his people out there are dying and going to Hell!"

"Man, can't you see that? The church and it's people are so far in debt. They need to get out of debt. If they were don't you think they could build a building and be debt-free? That's how God's kingdom operates, not this foolish borrowing. Jesus didn't owe anybody."

Malcolm's head was spinning in circles. Rufus was not going to let it go. Some of the family members were getting up to help with the dishes or gather the children and leave, but Malcolm was stuck to Rufus's every word, like a child waiting for candy.

Rufus paused to think about his next words. "Let your house be God's house, and then your house can be the storehouse, and whoever is in need, can come to you, son. That's where they can find Jesus, in you."

Someone knocked on the door. As the ladies were busy in the kitchen, Rufus got up to answer it. Malcolm was still in his chair, flipping through the Bible.

"Hey, Mr. Rufus, how you doing?"

"I'm good, Angel." Rufus burped lightly.

"What can I do for you, baby?"

The young woman smiled and said, "My car won't start, and I've got to take my son to my cousin's house to watch him before I go to work. Could you give me a boost?"

"Sure, baby, what's wrong with the battery? Did you leave the lights on?" Rufus asked, following the girl out the door.

"No sir. I just need a new battery, but money's been extremely tight lately." She said, embarrassed about her misfortune.

"Hopefully, I can get a new one next week when I get paid. It's been doing this for about a month. I have to get a boost every morning when I get off third shift, but I gotta do what I gotta do," she smiled.

"I'm grateful to even have a car."

Malcolm got up and walked outside with Rufus to help. Once they boosted the battery, Rufus looked around in the engine and asked if he could drive it around the block. Once he got back, Malcolm, Angel, Vanessa and Johnnie Mae stood outside, making small talk.

"Here, Angel, you take this," Rufus handed her three-one hundred dollar bills.

"You buy yourself a battery, go get you some brake pads and some gas, and come back by on your day off so Johnnie Mae and I can talk to you."

Angel started to cry. "Thank you, Mr. Rufus. You and Ms. Johnnie Mae are such good people. I promise I will pay back every cent," she said, still teary-eyed.

"You'll do no such a thing." Johnnie Mae chimed in as she grabbed the girl's hand and placed another balled-up fifty dollar bill in it. You come in here and get you some food out of this deep freezer, and you grab anything else you need out of the pantry too." Minutes later Angel drove away with cash in her pockets and a two weeks supply of groceries.

Rufus headed back to his dining room chair and plopped into the seat, glancing at Malcolm.

"That's the tithe and offering, huh, Rufus?" Malcolm asked softly.

Rufus smiled a wide eyed smile. "Yes it is, son, yes it is. When she comes back over here, me and my wife are going to minister Jesus to her and show her how to live in the fullness of God."

Malcolm felt almost excited.

"She had a need," Rufus said.

"After I met the need, then I can minister Jesus. If someone is hungry and you try to tell them about Jesus, can they really hear you when they need food in their stomach? You feed them first, and then what you say can fall on fertile ground and be effective. Jesus always met the need, he always met the need."

"Come on, Malcolm," Vanessa smiled at her man from the doorway.

"You ready to go?"

"Just a second, baby a few more minutes."

"You need to stop listening to my Uncle Rufus. You can see he's drunk." Vanessa giggled.

Rufus spoke up. "Nah, see that's the problem, y'all won't listen to the truth, especially if it is coming from a drunk, but you'll listen to a lie coming from a sober man. The Word says man looks at the outward appearance, but God looks at the heart."

"You are so right, Rufus." Malcolm had to agree.

"You are so deep, man." Malcolm now looked at Rufus in a different light.

"Malcolm," Vanessa whined.

"I don't know why you letting Uncle Rufus get you all wound up."

Rufus didn't give Malcolm a chance to answer. "When Jesus came, what did he do? He broke every religious law they threw at him. The Pharisees wanted to follow the law, but Paul said what Jesus did: if you are lead by the Spirit of God, *you are no longer bound by the law* - Galatians 5:8. Jesus came to set you free."

Malcolm jumped up and started pacing the floor. "Oh my God," was all he could say. Scriptures were coming to mind, and he was in awe.

"Malcolm, let's go! Don't you let Uncle Rufus put a curse on your finances."

"One more question, Uncle Rufus." Malcolm looked over at an annoyed Vanessa.

"I promise, baby, we will go after this."

Turning to Rufus he asked, "What about in Malachi where it asks will a man rob God?"

"I'm so glad you asked me this, Young Buck, so glad," Rufus smiled.

"That's the one scripture every Pastor and they momma use to trick you and keep you in bondage."

Malcolm nodded, and Vanessa was listening with interest as she took a seat at the table.

"Now you listen, and you listen good." Rufus cleared his throat. "God wasn't talking to the people, they were bringing it to the storehouse, he was talking to greedy, stealing priests who were taking all the good animals and keeping them for themselves, and giving God the crippled, blind, and lame animals."

"Bottom line: the church says for you to trust God, when they don't, they trust your money. The truth is man has taught you wrong for so long that you reject and rebuke the truth. I'll tell you what; don't believe me, read it for yourself. What these pastors, teachers, and ministers don't realize is, you are accountable for what you teach, and if your teaching and preaching people wrong, keeping them in bondage while you know the truth, that guilt is on your hands. God wants his people free, but again, don't believe me, read it for yourself, son. Read it for yourself. Bottom line is this, son... there's nothing wrong with giving tithe as money if that's what you choose to do. I'm just shining some light on darkness is all."

"There are some good churches out there who love God and don't want anything other than to worship him in Spirit and truth. If those churches would just trust God, I guarantee you it's those churches that will SEE God. There are millions and millions of people who unfortunately want no part of the church because of either the church people (and that's another sermon) or they see a pastor getting rich from other people's money. God doesn't want that to stop them from coming to the church and learning about him. If you know someone in a situation like that, encourage them to still come and just bring some food! I know your head is spinning Young Buck. I dropped a lot on you at one time, and I know that many might say, 'Oh that Rufus ain't nothing but an old washed up drunk'. Just let me tell you something, son, me and God have been talking for years. Maybe I can't teach in a church because of this," Rufus held up his almost empty beer cup.

"God's not finished with this ole man yet. We've just got some things we need to get straightened out."

Malcolm was speechless.

"Now, I know you're going to call up the Pastor and want to have a little discussion about this, and if you do, it'll just prove my point, that you don't study the word for yourself. You need someone else to lead and guide you, but don't rely on a person to do the job of the Holy Spirit. The Spirit is supposed to guide you in all truth. Now, if I told you everything I said to this entire conversation was jibber jabber, you'd go right back to your pew and keep doing what you've been doing; trusting in man."

"Rufus! Man are you for real?"

Rufus smiled a wide smile, "I just want you to study, Young Buck. I'm just an ole drunk, don't believe me." Malcolm's phone rang three times while he was going back and forth with Rufus, but he ignored it. Finally, he clicked to answer.

"Crystal, hey baby. I'm sorry I didn't pick up; I was in the middle of something. You okay?" Malcolm asked.

"Yeah, Daddy, I made the cheerleading team. I need $400 for a uniform and cheerleading camp."

"How much of that is for your mother?" Malcolm asked.

Crystal was silent.

"It's okay, baby. I will bring it to you tomorrow."

"Thanks, Daddy," Crystal said dryly.

"What's wrong, baby, you don't seem like yourself." Malcolm said, concerned.

"I'm okay. It's just that time of the month," she said.

"Oh, Lord," Malcolm smiled at the reminder of how his big baby was growing up.

"I'll stay out of that one. I hope you feel better."

"I will, Daddy, I just have real bad cramps."

"Where is your mom?" Malcolm asked.

"She and Tony went out of town for two days. I'm at my friend's house."

"Do you want me to bring you something for your stomach?" Malcolm asked.

"No, Dad, I've got some Motrin. I'll be fine."

"Where did your mom and Tony go?" Malcolm asked.

"I think to Las Vegas," Crystal answered.

"Las Vegas?" Malcolm sounded surprised. Sydney had just begged for $300 to get her car fixed.

"Tell me the truth, Crystal," Malcolm said.

"How much of this $400 is for cheerleading?"

Crystal paused.

"Daddy, please don't say nothing. I don't want to get in trouble."

"I'm not going to say anything. I just want to know."

"My cheerleading stuff is only $150."

"Okay," Malcolm replied, trying to control his temper.

"They want me to wire the rest of the money to them in Las Vegas."

Malcolm shook his head. "Baby, while I've got you on the phone, tell me what's up with this step-father of yours."

There was a sigh on the other end of the line.

"I don't like him, Daddy. He's mean and likes to fuss all the time about nothing. He bosses my momma around like a dog, and makes us go outside when his friends come over, smoking, drinking,

235

and gambling. He curses at me all the time and stuff." She sounded emotionally exhausted.

Malcolm wanted to explode. He was about ready to revert to some of his old ways. He made a mental note to have a conversation with Tony.

"Daddy, I'm going to lie down. I'm tired."

"Okay, baby. I'll see you tomorrow."

Malcolm drove down the highway, pissed. What Crystal said had him fuming. He tried to calm himself so Vanessa wouldn't see that side of him. He counted from ten backwards slowly under his breath.

"You upset with me?" Malcolm asked Vanessa.

"No," Vanessa answered.

"I just don't want you listening to my foolish uncle's nonsense. Ever since I was a little girl, my mom always said my Uncle Rufus was full of it. My momma and him were brother and sister, but they didn't get along. She went to her grave still hating him for what he did."

"What did he do?"

She laid her head back against the seat rest.

"I really don't know the whole story. I know Uncle Rufus did something that she hated him for. She said whenever she died for him not to come to the funeral. She died doing time in prison. Uncle Rufus used to come to the prison and try to make things right. He used to tell her about the Lord and all that, since Uncle Rufus used to be a preacher."

Malcolm gave her a quick look. "Are you serious? No wonder...."

"Yes, it's true. He stopped preaching after his little girl got sick with leukemia and died. He got mad at God and quit preaching and, instead, started heavily drinking"

"Wow," Malcolm was in total shock.

"Man, that's deep. I'm going to be honest, Vanessa. Maybe you shouldn't judge him from what other people say, and just listen to him. Some of the things he was saying could actually be from God."

"I don't judge my Uncle Rufus. I love him to death. I wouldn't be the woman I am if it wasn't for him. I just know sometimes it's the alcohol talking."

"You're a minister, you know the word. Everything that came out of his drunk mouth was the truth." Vanessa was quiet.

Malcolm laughed, "Baby, whose idea was it to build the new Life Center, Pastor Ivy's or the former pastor's?"

"The former pastor always had that vision. Malcolm, please don't tell me you're influenced by my drunk Uncle Rufus's ghetto Bible study."

Malcolm smiled at her. "Let's put it this way. I listened enough to want to go study the Word for myself. I know God will lead me in all truth."

"Amen," Vanessa laughed.

"Speak to him, Lord." She patted his hand and then dozed off after the heavy meal, leaning against the head rest.

Chapter 24   *Raymond*

Ray worked from home the remainder of the week. After that week passed, he decided to take another week's vacation to clear his head. He left one of the department heads in charge of running the plant, knowing how gung- ho he'd be for the opportunity to show strength and leadership in a top notch position. Ray loved the fact that he could promote deserving employees based on skill, drive, and faithfulness, and not be like other dream killers who only choose their picks based on race or the brownest nose. Ray thought that perhaps in his two-week absence Amanda might realize he wasn't going to continue to let her push him around, but from the looks of things, his absence only enraged her even more. She'd called him a thousand times, but he didn't answer. She sent him numerous emails with exclamation marks in the subject line. He felt good deleting them without reading a single word. He wasn't going to listen to her threats and tirades.

Ray didn't realize the extent of his stress until the migraines started. His blood pressure continued to soar, so his doctor prescribed blood pressure pills. Donae, was concerned with his health and insisted that he make an appointment for a complete physical right away, so Ray complied, not having the heart to tell her that Amanda was the one making him sick. He seriously contemplated resigning and threw around the idea in his head to possibly take Luke Zerrico's advice and apply with Drexelle, but the thought of starting over again so late in his career was not appealing at all. He had invested too many years and too much sweat in the company to just throw it all away, so he decided to put in for a transfer and see what happened. Donae, being a pharmacist, could get a job anywhere.

Ray was stuck between a rock and a hard place. If he told Donae the truth, he was at risk of losing her, or he could continue to keep the secret and deal with the stress and anxiety from being, as Travis so aptly put it, Amanda's boy toy. Either way he was screwed. Ray had no clue how he was going to get out of this mess, but he prayed it would be soon. He walked around the house in his boxers and t-shirt, checking out talk shows on the TV from time to time. In spite of his gloomy situation, the sanctity of home soothed his spirit. Donae had decorated the rooms beautifully, the lovely and creative décor a tribute to her homemaking talent. Ray could feel the love from her hands and heart each time he looked around. He was truly blessed to have a wife like her.

"Can you connect me to the pharmacy, please?" Ray asked the woman who answered the phone at the drugstore.

"Pharmacy, This is Donae speaking, how may I assist you today?" Donae sang in lifted spirits.

"Hey, Big Momma," Ray laughed.

"I'm not big yet," she smiled into the receiver.

"I'm not even showing, silly."

"I know, but I can't wait until you do," Ray sounded jolly.

"What are you doing?" Donae asked.

"Walking around in your drawers, I bet."

"You're just jealous because you had to go to work," he joked.

"I admit it," Donae agreed.

"I wanted to lay under you for a while longer."

"You can come home for lunch. I'll make it worth your while," Ray tried to entice her.

"That sounds good, but your son or daughter would really love some Japanese food. That's going to be what this one craves. I can see that now."

"Is that right?" Ray asked his heart filling with love.

He laughed, remembering how during her first pregnancy she had craved hot dogs, crushed ice, and Frosted Flakes. In the second one, she couldn't get enough crab legs and corn starch.

"Yes, indeed," Donae swayed back and forth as her co-worker chuckled.

"Some Hibachi rice and shrimp sounds heavenly."

"Hold on, baby," Ray said.

"I'm getting another call."

"Hello," Ray answered the call waiting line.

"Is this Ray?"

"Yes it is. How can I help you?

"Ray, hi, It's Pastor Ivy James. How are you, brother?"

"Pastor!" Ray's voice perked up two notches.

"How are you doing, man?"

"I'm blessed," Ivy answered.

"Did I catch you at a bad time?"

"Shoot, no," Ray said, honored that the Pastor would call him for any reason.

"How's First Lady doing?

"She's doing well. Putting up with me is a great task in itself," Ivy added a touch of humor.

"Trust me, Pastor, I know the feeling. I could say the same thing for my wife and I could even go so far as to say she loves me far more than I deserve."

Ivy chuckled in agreement. "It looks like we took the same boat ride. I hope you don't mind that I got your number from Brother Steven Hill."

"No, Pastor Ivy, of course I don't mind. You can call me anytime."

"Oh crap!" Ray remembered Donae was on the other line.

"Hold on one second, Pastor. I forgot I was talking to my wife on the other line."

"Sure, take your time. Tell her Pastor says hello."

"Okay, hold one sec."

"Donae…my bad, baby," Ray apologized.

"That's Pastor Ivy on the other line."

"Really? What does he want?"

"I don't know, but I'll be there to pick you up for lunch around noon, okay? And Pastor said 'hi.'"

"Yay!" Donae expressed her gladness and repented silently from being mad that Ray had left her on hold so long.

"Tell him I said 'hi' too, baby. I love you."

"Love you too, Big Momma," he chuckled.

He ended the call and returned to Ivy.

"I'm so sorry, Pastor. My wife loves to talk."

"How's the pregnancy coming along? First Lady said you guys were expecting. Are you excited?"

"Yes and yes. Everything is going great. I've been wanting another child for a while now, so I'm super excited to have little footsteps on the way."

"Goodness," Ivy said.

"I remember those days, but if you wanted another, you could have adopted one of mine. I've got plenty," Ivy joked.

Ray laughed, "I've seen Dominic, Bryson, Ebony, and Nicholas, but they say you have a basketball team with subs."

"And the baby momma drama to go with it," Ivy chuckled.

"I have a set of twins too, Jessica and Justin."

"Man, Pastor, at least you keep it real," Ray said appreciating the man's transparency.

"Hey, being real is all I can be. I've got to be me. I'm no good at being anybody else."

"Amen… Pastor Ivy… Amen."

"The reason for my call, Brother Ray, is I talked with Malcolm a few weeks ago, and he shared with me that you are a plant manager at a local manufacturing company. He mentioned that you helped him get a job."

"Yes, Pastor, I'm the plant manager for Zanderbilt Industries. Do you know someone looking for employment?"

"Brother Steven and I have some gentlemen that we've been mentoring through the Gate Keepers Ministry. A few of them have blemished backgrounds, but they're great men of God. I can vouch for them. I was wondering if you could take a look at their resumes if possible the next time your company is hiring. Perhaps you could contract them out through the temporary services. I know sometimes big companies like yours use that option before they hire permanently to see how the person will work out. In any event, if you can't, I totally understand…no pressure."

"Pastor, please," Ray acted offended.

"I'd love to help out any way I can. I'm My Brother's Keeper. How about emailing me their names and resumes, and I'll see what we can do." Ivy gave Ray his email immediately.

"I would be eternally grateful, Ray. These men are similar to Malcolm with child support issues, and suspended licenses because of it. They just need someone to give them a second chance."

"I understand. We all need a break sometimes."

"Amen," Ivy answered.

"If there is ever anything I can do for you, just let me know. I'd like to return the blessing."

"Okay, Pastor," Ray said.

"Just keep me in your prayers. I'm going through a few personal obstacles that I need God to move out of my way."

"You got it, brother. Let's pray now," Ivy said.

Ivy prayed for Ray over the phone and invited him to lunch one day when he was available. Ray looked forward to that. After talking to Pastor Ivy, Ray felt lighter. He didn't know why, because nothing had changed, but he danced around as though life were suddenly bright and sunny. He believed God was going to move on his behalf. Ray sang around the house as he got dressed, thanking God in advance for better days to come.

"Excuse me, Miss," the lady called out to Donae as she finished filling a cough syrup prescription.

"Yes, ma'am," Donae smiled widely as she walked over to the edge of the counter.

"How can I help you?"

Donae's smile somewhat faded as a perky Amanda showed her pearly whites from ear to ear.

"I know you."

Amanda turned her head sideways, pretending to wonder where she knew Donae from.

"Donae exhaled and adopted a polite tone. "What can I do for you?"

"I know you from somewhere. I can't for the life of me figure out where I know you from. Do I look familiar to you?" Amanda kept playing her childish game.

"Oh, I know," she added quickly.

"You're Raymond Durrant's wife, aren't you? I had no idea you worked here," she lied though her veneers.

"Yes, I'm Mrs. Durrant. What can I do for you?"

Amanda cringed at the proud announcement that she was Mrs. Durrant.

"I guess I didn't recognize you right away. The last time I saw you, you looked much thinner." Amanda threw her rock.

"I'm expecting." Donae was happy to burst the woman's bubble.

"Aw, that's so precious." Amanda pressed a fake smile on her lips.

"Do you have nausea all day?" she asked.

"My doctor prescribed me this prescription for it." She handed Donae the prescription with glee.

"Silly me, I thought it was just supposed to be morning sickness, but it seems like it's all day sickness." She parted her lips with a real smile.

"When are you due? My bundle of joy is scheduled to arrive in September," Amanda rubbed her tummy as if a big bump were there.

"The end of August," Donae answered.

"I can't wait to find out the sex of the baby," Amanda sounded excited.

"Do you want to pick this prescription up later, or would you prefer to wait?" Donae stopped the charade.

"How long do you think it will take?" Amanda asked.

"About fifteen to twenty minutes, tops," Donae answered.

"I'll wait on it," Amanda smiled her girlish grin.

"I really need to take one now," she added.

"I'm feeling kind of ill." Amanda sat down in the chair, truly feeling nauseous.

Donae handed Amanda a barf bag and started working on her prescription. Fifteen minutes later, Amanda felt a tad better. She set the opened vanilla envelope she was carrying on the pharmacy counter before she walked away. She slowly glided through the baby aisle, shopping for little doo-dads as she patiently waited for Donae to get done. Amanda's head looked up over the aisle the moment she heard Raymond's voice saying "hello" to the clerk up front. Her timing couldn't have been more perfect.

"Hi, gorgeous," Ray smiled at Donae as she quickly worked to finish for their lunch date.

"Hi, handsome," Donae answered.

"I'll be right with you. Let me finish these last two orders."

"Okay honey, take your time," Ray said.

"I've got all day."

"Your friend is out there somewhere," Donae smirked, looking up from the pills she was counting.

"My friend...who?" he asked.

"Hi, Ray." Amanda stepped out of the aisle so he could see her, enjoying the surprised look on his face.

Ray jumped almost out of his skin. "Hi, Amanda, what on earth are you doing here?"

"Here you are," Donae handed Amanda her medicine and prescription card, and started to ring up the purchase.

"Just picking up some meds," she handed Donae a $20 bill.

"Thank you so much," she smiled at Donae.

"I hope to see you soon."

"Baby, give me two minutes," Donae said softly.

"I need to go tinkle, and then we can go to lunch."

Donae looked down at the yellow envelope that Amanda had purposely left on the counter.

"Does this belong to you?" Donae picked up the envelope as Amanda walked away.

Ray stared at the envelope fearfully, hoping it wasn't what he thought it was because it sure did look familiar.

"Yes," Amanda grinned.

"It sure is. I definitely don't want to forget that."

Donae handed the envelope to Amanda. Once Amanda got it in her hand, she shook it, allowing the photos of her and Ray naked to fall to the floor. The snapshots, including the one exposing room number 2210, jarred Ray's memory of that awful morning. The old woman who had just walked in to drop off her prescription got an X-rated visual that she wasn't expecting.

"Oh my goodness," the elderly woman looked disgusted as she quickly turned away.

"What's wrong with people nowadays?" the elderly woman sneered her nose up at a smiling Amanda.

Seeing the elderly woman's reaction, Donae tried leaning over the counter to see what had been so offensive. Ray bent down quicker than lightening to scoop up the photos. He shoved them in the envelope, practically balling them up before Donae could get a peek. Thank God she was behind the counter. His heart started to race. If he didn't know it before, he definitely knew it now.

243

Amanda was crazy with a capital "C". At that moment he could have literally told her off in the vilest language.

"What are you doing?" he mumbled under his breath.

"I guess I will see you at the office bright and early in the morning, right?" Amanda looked confident as she smiled back at Donae.

"I thought you weren't going back until Monday, honey," Donae questioned.

"I was, but they seem to be having problems getting the Code Red Project off the ground," Ray said, unaware that it really was true.

Ray was nearly shaking when he went back to his car. He sat in the driver's seat, waiting on Donae to finish up. He thought he was about to have a panic attack. A moment later Donae was opening the passenger side door and sliding into the seat.

"Boy is she a piece of work," Donae said, fastening her seatbelt.

"What did she say, baby?" Ray was almost afraid to ask.

"First she sashays into the place and acts like she doesn't know I'm your wife. Then she babbles on about morning sickness and baby names. I think the heifer is just psycho."

"Yeah," Ray agreed.

"That among other things, I hope she was filling a prescription from her shrink."

Donae laughed, leaning over to kiss his sweaty cheek.

"I'm starving." She rubbed her tiny bump.

"What about you?"

"I was earlier, but not now," he said. He had lost his appetite.

"I know you're glad she has a new boyfriend. Now she can leave you alone," Donae giggled.

"Is it someone at the plant?" she asked, looking at Ray.

"I don't know, honey." Ray pretended not to be surprised.

"Well, whoever it is, I'm sorry for him. He has to be a fool to have a child with that nut. She says she's due in September."

Ivy was scheduled to minister at a local church not far from home. He accidentally left his briefcase holding the sermon he was going to preach at the church office. Kevin had to race back to the church at the last minute to get it, but when Kevin called to say he was stuck in traffic because of a bad car wreck, Ivy knew he wouldn't make it back in time. Kevin had been put on the program to introduce Ivy, but now they'd have to find someone else.

Steven asked for the night off. Rumors were floating around that he had a love interest from out of town, but no one knew who it was. Ivy would believe that when he saw it. He assumed Steven had taken a vow of celibacy because he'd heard him mention the word a few times, although he had never really just come out and said it. One thing was for sure, he'd turned down some pretty good-looking women who were saved and had themselves together.

"Pastor Ivy, we asked someone from your church to do the introduction. Is that okay?" the Pastor from the church where he was ministering asked.

"Sure, Brother, that will be just fine," Ivy said, adjusting his cuff links.

"I'll be right out."

For some reason he kept feeling a tugging away. He didn't know if God wanted him to preach another message. All he did know was that he wanted to be obedient. Ivy came out to join the praise and worship segment before it ended. Praise and worship was one of his favorite elements. The music and voices always lifted him to a higher place. He took his seat and leaned back, enjoying the joyful noise unto the Lord. When the music stopped and he opened his eyes, the look of terror on his face was obvious. Deacon Bailey was approaching the podium, and someone had just handed him the microphone.

God, you must be joking right? This is about to become a train wreck. Ivy didn't know whether to run and grab the mic out of the man's hand or sit there and take the embarrassment. All he knew was when his eyes locked with Deacon Bailey's, the smile on his face read, "Gotcha." Ivy dropped his head and prayed for mercy, because the Lord knew he was going to need it. Kevin walked in to take a seat in the back row. When he saw Deacon Bailey holding the microphone, he continued to stand, anxiety preventing him from sitting down. He tried to ease forward toward the pulpit and slide the mic from Deacon Bailey after handing Ivy his sermon, but swiftly the older man made his way to the other side of the podium, somewhat close to Ivy.

Deacon Bailey cleared his throat before speaking. "Good evening, saints," he smiled at the congregation respectfully.

"I'm here today to introduce a young man I've known for quite some time now. I've probably hated him for most of his adult life.

"I've had an opportunity to observe for many years a selfish, knuckle-head boy."

The congregation laughed.

Ivy started coughing and asked one of the ushers for a bottle of water. He was coughing so bad that several members of the congregation stared in his direction.

"Is he okay?" Deacon Bailey asked the ushers.

The man closest to Ivy nodded.

"Okay," Deacon Bailey continued.

"Where was I? Oh, I watched him grow from a knuckled-headed snake in the grass to an anointed, appointed and powerful man of God. I haven't always felt the way I feel right now about him, but the more you see God working in your own life, the more your heart begins to change toward others.

"His teaching has taught me a lot of things, but through him God showed me I needed to change. So with that, it gives me great, great pleasure to introduce to you, MY PASTOR, the Pastor of Mt. Emanuel Baptist church, Mr. Ivan Jessie James."

Ivy couldn't believe his ears. He stood up with a loss for words, and then walked over to Deacon Bailey.

"You're a fine man, son. I'm proud of what you've become." Deacon Bailey handed him the microphone. I hope Nicholas grows up to be just like his father." The two gentlemen embraced.

"Glory!" Kevin shouted as he began to pace the room.

"Hallelujah!" Another said from the pew.

"Thank you, Jesus," someone shouted loudly.

Ivy set the microphone on the podium and took a much needed praise break. Members of Mt. Emanuel were shouting and dancing like there was no tomorrow. The others had no clue what had just transpired, but the praise became contagious, and no one was able to stay seated. The entire church began praising God in a mighty way. The spirit of love enhanced the atmosphere. Ivy changed the text of his sermon and preached on the fly.

He titled his message "The Power of Forgiveness," and the Spirit of God preached the Word in a mighty way. Several people made their way to the altar. Deacon Bailey sat in the pew and wept the entire service. It was obvious he had a heavy heart. Then, when Pastor Ivy paused in his sermon, Deacon Bailey asked if it was okay for him to give a short testimony. Ivy gladly passed him the mic.

With tears in his eyes, Deacon Bailey testified, "I hated a man for years for something he did to one of my family members. I made a vow to make this man's life miserable every chance I got. It didn't matter that I was a deacon in the church, but one Sunday morning at a men's conference, an apostle came and preached a powerful illustration, and I went down to the altar. I clearly heard the Lord say, 'If you'll forgive a man, I'll heal one.'"

A woman in the church screamed, "My God, my God!"

"Amen, sister," Deacon Bailey agreed.

"Instantly, after God said that, I dropped my pride and was able to release the anger I had built up over the years."

Suddenly Deacon Bailey started to weep.

"I felt this burning feeling in the pit of my stomach that traveled down my legs and into my toes. I stayed at the altar as this burning feeling kept jolting through my body like flames. It didn't hurt, but it was warm inside of me. Even the people who touched me could feel the heat. I stood up to walk and I couldn't. Someone had to carry me to my seat."

"For three days I couldn't walk. Finally my wife and daughter took me to the doctor in a wheelchair. A few days later my legs gained strength. My doctor called a week later to confirm that my prostate cancer had dried up. They couldn't find it at all. I was completely healed, but before I hung up the phone and I told my doctor I needed to correct him on something. That cancer didn't dry up. It burned up! Hallelujah!"

The man shouted as he cried even harder.

"I'm telling you, church, God is real. When I left un-forgiveness at the altar, God left that cancer at the altar too, but I had to believe to make the exchange."

Deacon Bailey gave the mic back to Ivy. Now Ivy understood why he had left his briefcase and why Kevin was stuck in traffic. God tugged on his heart because God wanted him to minister the power of forgiveness, and that's exactly what he did. The altar was now flooded with people. Ivy didn't want to interfere with the anointing of God that now flowed so freely, so he asked Deacon Bailey to come and pray, and lay hands on God's people. Ivy understood the power in the pews. He understood you don't need a title to walk in the power of the Holy Spirit. All you need is to be willing to let God use you, love people and accept the anointing of the Holy Spirit. To let the truth be told, Ivy's anointing at that moment went no further than the pulpit, but Deacon Bailey's anointing went throughout the church, because Deacon Bailey still had the fire, and it was now in his hands.

****

Yolanda pulled the covers up snugly to her neck. Today had been one exhausting day. JoAnn had been fussier than usual. She insisted that she had promised her late cousin she'd bake a sweet potato pie for her birthday. Yolanda tried to explain that her Cousin Bessie had been dead for eleven years now, but JoAnn repeatedly called her a liar.

Vanessa and JoAnn had grown pretty close. Vanessa seemed to be the only person who could calm JoAnn down when she got into one of her fits. It was now the weekend, Vanessa's two days off. It took everything in Yolanda not to call Vanessa and beg her to stop by just to calm JoAnn down. JoAnn was downright irate, but Yolanda didn't want to ruin Vanessa's day with Malcolm and his children at the amusement park. Yolanda never would have imagined it could be such a difficult challenge to care for her mother-in-law.

Between working a full-time job, taking care of the house, the children, JoAnn, her responsibilities at the church and Ivy constantly hounding her for sex, she was about to have a breakdown. All she wanted to do now was dream about a much needed vacation, and she smiled as she drifted off to sleep. Her head hadn't hit the pillow twenty seconds, and she was already calling the hogs.

Ivy's heart danced with exceeding great joy the whole ride home. He couldn't help but be thankful at how good and awesome God is. If God could turn the situation around with Deacon Bailey and Dominic, he had faith that he would work out his other issues. He hadn't seen the twins, Jessica and Justin, in months, and every time he called Mel to talk, she hung up on him. Ivy didn't know what else to do, but in any event he had no other option but to trust God.

Things were going well with Kandice at rehab, and his relationship with Dominic had blossomed beyond his wildest dreams. He and his boys, Nicholas, Dominic and Bryson, were spending quality time together on a regular basis. They went fishing, bowling and even hiking whenever Ivy didn't have to travel. He felt bad that Justin couldn't join them, but all he could do was pray and hope Mel would come around sooner rather than later. He and Steven were scheduled to fly out to Cincinnati, Ohio, at 10:00 a.m. the next morning for a three day revival. Ivy put the petal to the

248

metal once he realized it was Thursday, his night for intimacy at home. He didn't want to go out of town in a weak state of mind or flesh.

The Word says "come together, lest ye be tempted," he repeated to himself. Yolanda had reneged a couple of times this week, so he was literally about to explode. He hoped she was still up so he could share the awesome experience he had witnessed tonight. She would be thrilled that he and Deacon Bailey had buried their differences. Unfortunately, when he pulled up to the house, all the lights were off, indicating that everyone was already in bed, asleep. Ivy showered and shaved, and made sure his luggage was already packed and ready to go for his trip in the morning. Minutes later he was in his king-size bed, pulling his wife close to him.

"It's Thursday, baby," Ivy said, tugging at Yolanda's pajama pants.

You know I have to leave early for Ohio in the morning," he whispered as he softly nibbled her perfumed earlobe.

Yolanda sleepily tried to evade his grasp.

"Ivy, I know baby, but I'm beat. JoAnn was fussy all day. She and I were practically fighting over a sweet potato pie."

"Huh?" Ivy frowned, confused.

"Nothing, Ivy, go to sleep."

"Yolanda, please," Ivy begged.

"We haven't made love in almost a week. What's the deal?" he asked, trying to be sweet about it.

"The deal is you need to practice some self-control, PASTOR!" she blurted, as she pushed his hand away from her.

"What's wrong with you?" Ivy lowered his voice.

"This is ridiculous."

"I'm tired of having sex all the time. I need a freakin' break. I can't even go to the toilet without you knocking on the door."

"Every day you look at me like I'm prime rib. Can you hold my hand and say you love me without always expecting something in return?" she slung back the covers and grabbed a pillow.

Ivy rolled on his back. "That's not fair, Yolanda. I tell you I love you all the time...you know I do. It's not always about sex."

Yolanda looked back at him as if he'd said something untrue.

"I'm going to sleep in Ebony and Jessica's room. At least I know I'll get some rest," she stomped away.

"Fine!" Ivy, sat up and threw himself back on the mattress.

"Take your stingy tail in there then."

Yolanda quietly entered the kid's room and pulled back the pink comforter on Ebony's twin bed. She wanted to cry. Her day had been awful, and now here was Ivy with his issues.

"Lord, help me!" she wanted to scream at the top of her lungs.

Yolanda closed her eyes, thinking she could finally get some rest. But sensing motion, she opened them to find Ivy standing over her, staring down.

"What are you going to do, rape me?" her tone was angry.

"Are you kidding me?" Ivy looked down at her, not believing what had just come out of her mouth.

"Well, you're standing there like you're about to attack me," Yolanda glared at him.

"All I want is to make love to my wife. Is that such a crime?" he said, trying to be tender.

"Huh!" Yolanda breathed heavily.

"I just want to rest. Can I please get some sleep?"

"Yeah, you can rest. Come back to bed. I'll leave you alone," he whispered as if defeated.

"No! You know good and well you'll keep bothering me until I give in."

"So you'll just send me to Ohio horny as hell?"

"Can you please just screw the man?" JoAnn yelled from Nicholas's room.

"So we all can get some sleep."

"I'm sick of this!" Yolanda yelled, embarrassed as all get out. That was the last straw for her.

Yolanda jumped up and walked to their bedroom. Ivy thought she had given up, but Yolanda grabbed her duffle bag from the closet and started shoving clothes into it.

"Where do you think you're going?" he demanded, following her into the bedroom.

"To a freaking hotel where I won't be disturbed," she blurted, racing downstairs to grab her keys.

Ivy quickly tried to find some sweatpants to throw on, but by the time he got into a decent pair, Yolanda was already backing out of the garage full force.

"Yolanda!" Ivy yelled from the porch door in anger.

"Yolanda!" he yelled again, louder, pounding his fist inside the palm of his hand.

"For goodness sake, Ivy," JoAnn stepped out the bedroom door and called downstairs to him in a soft, hushed voice.

"Just go buy you some coochie, son. It don't cost that much. Your Uncle Russell used to do it all the time.'

"Here," she said, taking a five dollar bill from her bossom and tossing it down the stairs.

"Momma, go back to bed. I'm sorry I woke you up."

Ivy picked up the money from the middle stair and laid it on the coffee table, and then headed to the bedroom to find a quick shirt and shoes to throw on. He drove around in the middle of the night, looking for his wife. He had searched three hotel parking lots before finally spotting her car at the upscale hotel downtown.

Sitting in the parking lot, staring at Yolanda's car, he wondered how he could be such a heel. It was time he finally sought out help for his sex addiction. If he didn't, he would surely lose his wife. How could he let the enemy come in so quickly after that powerful church service? He was angry at himself for becoming a satanic tool.

"Can you tell me what room number Yolanda James is in?" Ivy asked the clerk at the front desk, showing his pastoral I.D. as her husband.

"Yes sir," the clerk answered.

"Mrs. James is in room 302."

"Thank you," Ivy said. He realized maybe he shouldn't try to persuade her to come back tonight. He honestly just wanted her home, he didn't intend to bother her, but if he went up to her room, he knew she wouldn't believe it. Ivy turned to walk away, feeling ashamed for putting Yolanda through hell. Yes, she was his wife, but he was her protector and provider. Who was going to protect her from him? She shouldn't have to run away from her husband, but rather feel free to run to him.

"Well, well, well," the familiar voice echoed from behind.

"If it isn't Mr. Ivan James…what's up, ole friend?" Perry Ellison smiled as he walked away from the bar.

"I see you're up to your old tricks again, skirt chasing."

Standing there in sweats, a cut-off t-shirt, showing his tight abs, and flip flops, Ivy shook his head, embarrassed, knowing he surely appeared a mess.

"Hello, Perry, what are you doing here? I thought you moved to D.C."

"I did. I'm here for a few months on business. My construction company is heading up the expansion over at Zanderbilt Industries. Call me if you need a job." Perry tried to slide Ivy a business card.

Ivy glanced at it. "No thanks, you already gave my wife one," he snarled.

"Oh that…she sure is a pretty little thing, just like we used to like em back in the day. What's the problem, can't keep your woman under control?" he laughed.

"I saw your sweet thang check in a little while ago. It looked like she was still in her pajamas. I see some things never change; you're still a hound dog."

"I'm warning you, Perry, stay away from my wife." Ivy got up in his face.

"It don't feel good, does it, PASTOR," he stressed.

"When another man is messing with your wife?"

"Perry, that was a long ways in the past. Let it go, man. We were young." Ivy tried to be respectful, aware that Perry still felt hatred towards him.

"I think I'll pay Ms. James a little visit. I understand what she really needs. I know you. Remember the games we use to play to get in them panties?" Perry smiled devilishly.

"One warning is all you get." Ivy sized him up.

"If you go anywhere near my wife, they'll be picking you up in a body bag."

"Oh my, I'm shaking in my boots," Perry laughed.

"You don't scare me, PASTOR," Perry stressed.

"Don't let my title fool you, Perry. I love the Lord, but I'll knock you on your butt and pray for you and forgiveness later." Ivy glared at him, letting him know he meant business.

Perry laughed almost hysterically. "Don't get it twisted, Mr. Pastor."

Perry pressed the arrow for "Up" on the elevator.

"If you think you want to try me, PLEASE, bring it on. I'm not that same skinny, timid dude that I used to be." Perry winked at Ivy and pushed "6" on the elevator to go to his luxury suite.

"Yolanda, Yolanda, what a beautiful name," Perry smiled as the elevator doors closed.

Ivy hit the "Up" button quickly and once inside, hit the button for the right floor. He stood at the door of room 302 for twenty minutes or longer until he felt safe that Perry was bluffing, at least for now. He could hear Yolanda sound asleep in her room

He sat near her hotel door ashamed of himself. Minutes later he picked himself up and headed home to try to get a few hours of rest before his flight in the morning.

Chapter 26 _Malcolm_

Malcolm had been feeling a little bummed the last few weeks. Bone Crusher had fallen down a flight of stairs at the airport and sprained his leg, ending up on a crutch. So the fight was pushed back, giving Bone Crusher time to heal. In light of this occurrence, Malcolm's quick cash was about to quickly dry up. He still had his local sparring at the ring, so he wasn't completely dry. He'd been able to save some, so he had a little safety net. He was more disappointed that he wouldn't get to see Bone Crusher make his comeback anytime soon. The two men had become good friends over the last several months. Malcolm had been praying that Bone Crusher would have another opportunity to relive his dream, and he wanted to be part of making that dream come true. Bone Crusher, being a man of God, offered to buy Malcolm, and a guest front row seats to the next championship fight, just because his injury had caused Malcolm financial discomfort.

Kenny "Hammer Hand" Hopkins had been talking so much smack to Bone Crusher that Malcolm believed it had gotten to the champion. He had started getting slower in the ring, which was a serious concern. Malcolm had knocked him on his butt far more often than he should have. He didn't want to discourage the pro, but he felt if he didn't snap out of it quick, serious damage could occur at the next match. Even though this was supposed to be an exhibition fight, Bone Crusher looked at it as a real fight. If he went into a match and knocked Hammer Hand down a few times, people would realize his talent was still there. Malcolm was furious when he heard Hammer Hand on the news saying Bone Crusher was claiming he had gotten hurt because he was afraid to fight him. Malcolm knew that was ridiculous. In any event, Malcolm was more determined than ever to make sure Bone Crusher would be ready on fight day.

Vanessa volunteered to cook Malcolm a home cooked meal to cheer him up. She knew how much going down to the ring and sparring with the champ meant to Malcolm. Being in the ring brought him joy. He had already talked with Mackie about the possibilities of sparring permanently, and Mackie said he was working on it. He added that if Bone Crusher won the exhibition fight, it would open up opportunities for Malcolm. This was another reason that he wanted Bone Crusher to rip Hammer Hand's reputation to shreds.

Malcolm had to admit when he stepped out of the shower and grabbed his beige monogrammed towel trimmed in chocolate that it really did make him smile. He'd only been in his four-bedroom, 2 1/2 bath home for almost three weeks, but it felt like he'd lived there forever. He had fully furnished every room, and Vanessa was a talented decorator. Malcolm insisted on the life sized portrait of the two of them that hung elegantly above the gas log fireplace, adding a cozy element to his simple abode.

The tasty aroma of cooking in the kitchen caused him to reminisce about his journey to get where he was, so he took a moment to give God the glory for the many blessings he and his family had received. Pulling his t-shirt over his head, he heard the phone beep, indicating he had received a text message.

"Baby?" Vanessa lightly knocked on the door to make sure he was decent.

Her beautiful smile illuminated Malcolm's heart. "Dinner's almost ready," she said, sticking her head in the door.

"Okay sweetie, I'll be right out," he smiled before glancing at his phone.

"She's a nut," he said to himself. Sydney had been texting him for weeks nonstop, begging him for money. He would have loved to see the look on her face when Crystal called her and her husband in Las Vegas a while back to tell them Malcolm didn't leave any cash. He had left a check for $200 written out to the high school cheerleading camp. Malcolm had heard through the grapevine that Tony had a bad gambling problem. This explained why he couldn't take care of his household. He made sure Crystal had cash stashed in a safe place for anything she needed.

Now his phone was ringing. "Hello." Malcolm answered reluctantly.

"Malcolm, I need $300," Sydney blurted.

"For what Sydney?" Malcolm breathed heavily.

"I've got to get Crystal some new clothes and stuff. She's outgrown just about everything."

"Okay," Malcolm answered, sending a radiant smile across Sydney's face.

"Vanessa and I will pick her up this weekend and take her shopping."

Sydney's smile deflated quickly. "I don't need that heifer to pick out my daughter's clothes. I'm the mother, not her. Tell her to have her own kids."

"Excuse me?" Malcolm rose from tying his shoe.

"You heard me," Sydney said nastily.

"I'll take Crystal shopping."

"Fine, you take her shopping with your money, and I'll take her shopping with mine."

Sydney inhaled sharply, realizing if she wanted to get some cash she'd better calm down. "Will you just please give me the money? I know what I want my daughter to have."

"What else do you need the money for, Sydney?" Malcolm asked her straight up.

"I already told you," she insisted.

"Well, I don't have it," Malcolm said.

"Okay, okay," she admitted.

"I need a little extra to pay our cable bill."

"Look, Sydney, I give you more than enough to take care of Crystal. You need to talk to your husband about taking care of his household," Malcolm said firmly.

Sidney didn't seem surprised that Malcolm knew she and Tony had tied the knot.

"You have a daughter here, remember?" Sydney's voice raised a notch.

"And I take good care of her, too," he added.

"It's your husband's job to take care of you, not mine."

"You make me sick!" Sydney screamed through the receiver when she realized he wasn't going to surrender any funds for her personal use.

"I hate you."

"Here we go with that again." Malcolm brushed his waves.

"I'll pick Crystal up to take her shopping Saturday, and if you and Tony can't get it together, then Crystal can come and stay with me. That might be better anyway cause she doesn't care for him too much, from what I hear."

"That's a lie!" Sydney was well heated now.

"Whatever, Sydney, good-bye," Malcolm said.

"I'm not about to let you ruin my night." Malcolm pressed 'end' and turned his phone on silent.

Moments later he saw numbers shoot across his cell phone screen, and his breathing deepened.

"Hello," he answered.

"Hey Malcolm," Telese sang.

"Oh, hey, girl, what's going on?" Malcolm was relieved to hear her voice instead of Sydney's.

"KJ is the most popular boy in school now, ever since you let him and his buddies meet Bone Crusher. Little girls are calling here all hours of the night wanting to be his girlfriend."

Malcolm smiled, "It feels good to finally make my son smile."

"Guess what I'm holding in my hands," she said.

"The divorce papers," Malcolm smiled.

"Yep," Telese said.

"Can you come over and sign them?"

"I can't tonight, but I will tomorrow," he said, fist pumping the air.

"I thought you were in such a freaking hurry," she said.

"You've been sweating me for months."

Malcolm laughed, "I know," he said.

"But tonight my girl cooked me a romantic dinner, so I'm...." He stopped in mid-sentence, remembering who he was talking to.

"I'll be there tomorrow, okay?"

"Okay," Telese said wanting to throw a glass bottle against the wall. Immediately she headed to the refrigerator.

"See you then." Malcolm danced around the room.

He wanted to scream "Yes!" at the top of his lungs but he contained his joy. Finishing brushing his hair, he reached in the top of his closet for the gift and 'just because' card he'd bought for Vanessa.

Flickering candles filled the dark room as jazz music played. Malcolm smiled at Vanessa frequently during dinner. Her spinach dip tasted better than Telese's, and Malcolm gladly told her so.

"I love you," Malcolm whispered before stuffing his mouth with the dip.

"I love you, too." Vanessa blushed across the shiny cherry tabletop.

She paused before continuing. "I forgot to tell you that Moe had to shave off all her hair. She's completely bald now. It is so sad. She said she feels ugly and doesn't want to go out of the house."

"Oh, no!" Malcolm felt sorry for Moe.

"How are the treatments going?"

"Not well. The cancer is growing rapidly, and her body is not responding to the medicine," Vanessa wanted to cry.

"It's going to be okay," Malcolm said.

"The Lord is going to heal her completely."

"Please, Lord," Vanessa replied.

"Her spirit is so exhausted. She can't focus on herself due to constantly worrying about those boys of hers. I feel so bad. Sometimes I think she's mad at me for finding her and not letting her die."

"Baby, that's crazy." Malcolm stretched his hand past the shining candles to comfort Vanessa.

"I'm sure she's grateful."

"She tried to kill herself," Vanessa didn't smile.

"I know how it feels not to want to live," she dropped her head.

"Baby, it's okay." Malcolm got up and went over to give her a hug.

"I'm just glad you turned back around and went back over there to see about her."

Vanessa got up from the table to grab a tissue. Malcolm embraced her tightly, and they walked over to the oversized chaise lounge.

"I know how she feels," Vanessa said it again, leaning back in Malcolm's arms as they lay back in the soft leather chair.

Malcolm hugged her tighter. "Talk to me, baby."

He kissed the side of her forehead. "I want to know what makes you hurt so I can make it better. You can tell me anything."

"I've told you a lot about my past, Malcolm," Vanessa said.

"A lot of which, I'm not proud."

"I know that, Vanessa, and I've never judged you for it, just like you've never judged me. I love you for the woman you are now."

"My mom made me give my daughter up for adoption when I was twelve," she finally said it.

"Is that why your relationship with her was estranged before she died?"

"Yes, and many other issues including beating the living daylights out of me and all my siblings," she said honestly.

"Baby, you've got to let that go. I know she hurt you. Maybe she knew y'all couldn't afford another mouth to feed, and wanted to do what was best."

"No, she was just evil and abusive. Anything that made me happy she wanted to tear it down."

"My father was the only one who really loved me, and when he died, my life became a living hell. I used to lay in bed wishing someone would come to say she had left us for good."

"Vanessa, don't say that." Malcolm felt sympathetic.

"I'm serious. My sisters and I couldn't go outside and play, we couldn't go to dances and school plays, because we had to stay at home and clean house. She's the reason why I made some of the horrible choices I made," Vanessa sniffed.

"No, baby, you can't blame her for choices you made. You just got to let the past be the past."

"You're one to talk," Vanessa said.

"Don't you hate your father?"

Malcolm was quiet.

"See," Vanessa answered.

"Well, have you ever tried to find your daughter?" Malcolm asked.

"I have, but my mom sealed the papers on the adoption, which has made it difficult to locate her."

"What's her name?" Malcolm asked.

"Anjoelina' with a 'J,' she answered.

"How old would she be now?" Malcolm asked.

"She turned twenty in November."

"Wow," Malcolm said, hugging Vanessa tightly as he witnessed her heartache.

"I tried to kill myself the day my mom took her from me," Vanessa softly wept.

"I keep wondering how she looks, and if she's trying to find me."

"We'll find her," Malcolm kissed Vanessa's forehead.

"I promise you'll be reunited, and we'll be a big happy family." Malcolm turned her face to his.

"It's not for you to worry about," Vanessa insisted.

"Maybe its God will, that she stays hidden from me."

Vanessa turned to the side and snuggled against his cologne-scented chest. "I'm content right here with you," she said, though still full of hurt.

Malcolm hugged her tightly, placing his hands over her belly. "We'll find Anjoelina, and then we'll have our own bundle of joy."

He set a small red box on the arm of the chair facing Vanessa, and opened it, exposing the bright, shiny, princess cut diamond. Vanessa's tears flowed harder.

"Malcolm, you're not even divorced yet," she giggled between sobs.

"I will be tomorrow. The papers came today."

Vanessa jumped to her feet, almost letting the ring drop to the floor.

"Malcolm... what! Are you serious? But we've dated only six months and ten days," she said.

"And?" Malcolm laughed as he realized Vanessa was keeping count of how long they'd been dating.

"I want you to be my wife. I'm sure of that. I realize everything has happened so fast but I know I don't want to be without you. We can have a long engagement if you want, but I know what I want," he said bending down on one knee.

"Vanessa Reardon, will you be my wife?"

Vanessa paused as she stared into Malcolm's warm amber eyes. The long silence had Malcolm thinking maybe he should have waited a bit longer, but then Vanessa nodded yes, and Malcolm smiled as he gracefully slipped the engagement ring on her finger. The newly engaged couple swayed from side to side as jazz music played intimately in the background. Flickering lights from the candles made Vanessa's eyes look even more beautiful. Malcolm knew he was taking a risk, but she had to know now how much he was in love with her. He grabbed Vanessa's hand to lead her back toward the bedroom. Although her heart raced, she didn't resist. She hadn't been with a man in a long time, and everything in her was calling his name. He would soon be her husband. The Lord knew they both wanted to do right, but neither could resist the passion that burned within them.

Chapter 27   *Malcolm*

An hour later, Malcolm lay beside Vanessa's caramel colored body, feeling like he needed to smoke a cigarette. He watched Vanessa as she slept quietly. Her two-karat diamond sparkled in the softly lit room, filling Malcolm's heart with joy. She was going to be his wife, and soon they would start their family. He hadn't wanted any more children before, but once Vanessa shared her painful experience with him, he wanted nothing more than to be the father of her child.

Vanessa turned sideways to get more comfortable and noticed Malcolm staring at her. She smiled at the thought of what had just happened, and thanked God in her heart for giving her such a great man who loved her. She repented for not being able to contain her lust for Malcolm, and hoped that God would not look on it as sin, for in their hearts they had made a covenant with God that they were already married, and God himself was their witness. Vanessa's sweet smile was instantly interrupted by the loud banging on the door.

"Who is it?" Malcolm jumped up in aggravation that someone was interrupting one of the best moments of his life. The more the intruder pounded on the door, the angrier he became. If that was Sydney, it would not be good. Malcolm quickly slipped on the pair of basketball shorts lying on the oversized chair in his bedroom, and raced to the door. Vanessa picked up his bathrobe from the hook on the back of the bathroom door.

"Telese, what are you doing here?" Malcolm looked surprised to see her standing there.

"What's wrong?" Instant fear gripped him.

"Are the kids okay?" he asked in panic.

"KJ and Layla are fine," she said, seeing the relief in Malcolm's face.

"It's Crystal. She called the house looking for you and said you wouldn't answer the phone," Telese hinted with a bit of attitude.

Shoot! Malcolm thought remembering he put his phone on silent after hanging up with Sydney.

Vanessa walked up behind Malcolm, tying his black terrycloth robe tightly. "What's wrong, honey?" Vanessa looked concerned.

"Good evening, Evangelist Reardon." Telese reminded her of her title.

"Hi." Vanessa glanced down, embarrassed.

"What's wrong?" Malcolm wanted answers immediately.

"I don't know," Telese said, unable to take her eyes off Vanessa or, more specifically, the shining ring that nearly blinded her, sitting high on her finger.

"Something is going on over there. Crystal was crying, and I heard Sydney in the background yelling at a man to stop. I told her I'd try to find you. I've called a dozen times until finally I just came over."

"Oh, my goodness," Vanessa said to Malcolm.

"Baby, let's go." She ran to the bedroom to get dressed.

Malcolm raced behind her, grabbing a t-shirt and tennis shoes. Telese stood in the living room, admiring Malcolm's beautiful home. The picture of him and Vanessa above the fireplace caught her immediate attention. The empty plates on the table, the soft jazz music and the candle-lit room did more than make her angry. She became furious when she saw a photo of Malcolm, Vanessa, Crystal, Layla, and KJ sitting on an end table nicely framed, as though they were one big happy family.

Although Telese had feelings for Morris, their relationship had been more physical than meaningful. They went out to dinner and on weekend trips here and there. The sex was good, but it lacked intimacy. Her jealousy surfaced once she witnessed that Malcolm and Vanessa had something far more precious than what she had with Morris. They were deeply in love.

"Let's go, Telese," Malcolm yelled to snap Telese out of her trance.

"You can ride with us." Malcolm snatched his keys from the key rack.

The three of them headed to the garage to get inside Malcolm's car. Telese purposely jumped in the front seat, leaving Vanessa no choice but to climb quickly into the back. She didn't feel the need to pull rank. She knew her place in Malcolm's life. Unfortunately for Telese, she didn't know hers.

Twenty minutes later they pulled up to Sydney's house. All the lights were on in the house, and Malcolm could hear the yelling long before he got to the entrance. He banged on the door with heavy force, calling Crystal's name. The yelling stopped, but no one answered.

"Sydney, open the door!" Malcolm shouted.

"Hey, man, you need to get away from my house," Tony yelled from the other side of the door.

"Open this door, man! I'm here to get my daughter. Don't make me break this door down!"

"You have it twisted, Bro." Tony swung open the door.

"This is my damn house. That's my wife," he pointed to Sydney who was walking from the bedroom crying.

"And these are my kids," he pointed to his two sons and Crystal, who were sitting on the living room sofa, wide-eyed and scared.

"Step daughter," Malcolm rudely corrected him.

"Daddy! Crystal yelled as she ran into Malcolm's arms.

"Can I please come live with you?"

"Tony, calm down." Sydney tried to pull him back toward the bedroom.

"Everybody just needs to cool off," she said.

"What in the hell is going on here?" Malcolm demanded.

"You shouldn't have come here, Malcolm. This is just a misunderstanding," Sydney said, trying to defuse the tension as she looked nervously at Tony.

Telese stood near the door with her arms folded, staring Vanessa down, as Vanessa held onto Malcolm, sensing that he would soon explode.

"It looks like more than a misunderstanding to me." Malcolm looked around at the sofa pushed to the wall and a chair lying on its side.

"It looks like someone's been fighting."

"Crystal ain't going nowhere," Tony yelled.

"I run this house. You better get him out of here, Sydney, 'cause I'm about to go off." He picked up a glass vase and threw it against the wall, shattering it to pieces.

"He don't want me to burst his little bubble." Tony walked into the bedroom to cool down as Sydney raced behind him, begging him to be quiet.

"What the hell is going on?" Malcolm was about to lose his cool.

"Calm down, baby," Vanessa tried to keep him level headed.

"Let's find out what's going on before you start to tip over." She looked at Crystal for answers.

"What happened, Crystal?" Vanessa asked calmly.

"I was on the phone talking to my friend, and I told her I had money, a lot of money, stashed in my room that my daddy gave me if I needed it."

"Mr. Tony overheard me talking and came into my room, tearing it up, opening drawers and turning over stuff, trying to find it. He found $200 in my tennis shoes and got $40 out of my purse. He wouldn't give it back, Daddy," she cried.

"It's mine. When I tried to get it from him, he pushed me into the dresser, and I cut my head on the corner." She showed Malcolm and Vanessa a huge knot that was slightly bleeding.

"Mr. Tony said I was being disrespectful and needed my A.S.S., beat," she spelled the word.

Malcolm punched his hand through the wall, leaving a big hole near the picture of Sydney's nightclub photo. Vanessa's eyes grew wide as she stared at the huge hole in the wall unable to believe the strength Malcolm possessed.

Crystal continued. "He took off his belt and started beating me."

"What!" Malcolm looked at Sydney as she came back into the living room.

"You let this clown put his hands on my child? Are you crazy?" he yelled.

"Go pack your stuff, Crystal, you're going with me." Malcolm started pacing the floor.

"This dude must think I'm a punk," Malcolm barged through the living room, out of control. Vanessa looked toward Telese to help calm him down.

"Malcolm, let's think about this now. You have too much to lose, honey. Let's just get Crystal and go."

Malcolm didn't hear a word Vanessa was saying. All he saw was red as he rushed towards Sydney's bedroom door while Sydney, Vanessa and Telese screamed for him to stop.

"Malcolm, please!" Sydney began to cry.

"Just let it go. I can handle this." All three ladies tugged at his t-shirt.

Malcolm burst through the bedroom door and charged Tony as he was rising from the bed.

"Don't you ever put your hands on my daughter again, man. I'll kill you!"

Tony tried to punch him back, but Malcolm's blows were like iron. Tony struggled to recover.

"Malcolm, no!" Vanessa yelled, trying to pull Malcolm off Tony, along with Sydney and Telese.

All three women were begging him to stop. Malcolm came to himself once he realized he had completely zoned out. He thought that madman in him had died. He got up off Tony, who was trying to breathe.

"Malcolm, let's go," Vanessa said, feeling afraid. She had never seen him so angry and violent.

"I'm sorry you had to see that, baby," Malcolm apologized. "Crystal, let's go."

"You're a stupid punk! A real dummy!" Tony yelled.

"You just keep them checks coming."

Malcolm ignored Tony. The beaten man knew there was no way to win against Malcolm with his fists, so he tried to hurt him with words.

"Tony, shut up!" Sydney yelled.

"No, you shut up," he yelled back at Sydney.

"You need to tell the fool what time it really is."

Vanessa grabbed Crystal's suitcase in one hand and the girl's hand with the other.

"You okay, baby?" he looked at Crystal's bruises as they all headed toward the door.

In a violent burst of temper, Tony pushed Malcolm away from Crystal.

"Tell him the truth, Sydney," he demanded.

"...or I will."

"Tony, shut up!" Sydney pushed him toward the bedroom.

"No, you tell me man, since you want me to know," Malcolm shouted back.

"You ain't her father; I am."

"Man, please go somewhere else with that bull," Malcolm started to laugh.

"I've been her daddy since she came home from the hospital. You're just a poor excuse for a fill-in." Malcolm started walking out.

"I'll say it again," Tony snarled.

"I'm her biological father. She came from my loins." Tony grabbed his private parts.

"You've been paying child support all these years for my child, sucka. You got played, homie," Tony winked.

"Sounds to me like, you're the fool."

Malcolm looked at Sydney. "You better tell your husband he needs to stop doing drugs or whatever he's on."

"You see that butterfly birthmark in the palm of her hand? That's me, homie."

Tony opened the palm of his hand, exposing the same birthmark that Crystal had. All my kids have it." He called both his sons over. One had the birthmark on his arm, and the other had the same mark on his chest.

Telese and Vanessa's eyes grew as big as quarters once they saw the birthmarks and the resemblance of all three children.

"So we appreciate those checks for the last fifteen years, bro," Tony smiled, feeling good about the bomb he had just dropped.

Malcolm stared at Sydney, confused, as she shook her head in shame. Hurt, anxiety and sadness all swept over Malcolm's face.

"You make me sick, Tony," Sydney yelled.

"Why did you do that?" She punched him with all her strength.

Tony smirked, finding comfort in the hurt look in Malcolm's face. Crystal stood in the living room in shock, and then the tears flowed from her eyes like a summer shower. She looked at Sydney, then at Tony, then at Malcolm and finally her two half-brothers, and then raced out the door. Malcolm followed her, running down the street, calling her name.

"Crystal!" he yelled, but she wouldn't stop.

Malcolm ran faster. He finally caught up with her, and she collapsed in his arms, out of breath.

"Please, Daddy, say it's not so. I don't want him to be my daddy," she cried.

"You're my daddy. Please, Dad," Crystal begged.

"I know you adopted me, but he can't be my real father, he just can't. I don't want him to be. Daddy...please!"

"He's not." Malcolm held her tightly, rocking her in his arms.

"I'm your father, and I always will be, no matter what he or anybody else says. Nothing in this world is going to change that. I promise you."

Malcolm picked Crystal up and carried her to the car. He looked up at Sydney with tears in his eyes, wondering how she could have played such a dirty game. Vanessa got in the driver's seat and let Malcolm sit in the back, still holding Crystal like she was a baby. Telese jumped into the passenger seat, unable to take her attention off the diamond ring on Vanessa's finger.

"Make sure you put that check in the mail, bro," Tony yelled as he waved from the front porch.

"Y'all have a good night," he smiled, as Sydney walked in the house and slammed the front door.

Ray hadn't been able to rest all week. He called Amanda several times, but she wouldn't answer. Her secretary Eva resigned, and her replacement, Missy, didn't know if she was coming or going. The only information she could give him was that Amanda was out of town on business, and she'd be back any day. All her appointments for the week had been cancelled, so Ray didn't know what to think. Her disappearing act infuriated him. All he wanted was for this to go away. He didn't wish any ill will toward Amanda, but if something happened to her he probably wouldn't feel bad. He had met with Pastor Ivy several times concerning the men who needed employment, and then he hired all seven of them. Ray shared with Ivy the truth, the whole truth, the ugly, ugly truth.

Ivy shook his head sadly. "If Amanda is really pregnant and you're the father, you need to come clean."

Years ago he had been in a similar predicament with two women pregnant at the same time, so he understood what was at stake.

"You're right," Ray agreed.

It was obvious to everyone that Amanda would do anything to have a relationship with Ray.

"Don't give her anything to hold over your head. At least if you tell Donae the truth, you'll be free from the lie. I can counsel you two if you want me to." Ray really appreciated that.

In an effort to let Ray know he wasn't the only one being attacked by the enemy, Ivy shared with Ray some of what was going on with him and Yolanda. Lately these days Ray felt like a failure, but Ivy assured him that according to Scripture, a just man falls down seven times, but he always gets back up. Ray found much comfort in that verse. He felt the Lord was giving it directly to him, especially since Steven had given him the same Scripture.

Ray didn't know how to feel once he discovered that the Code Red project wasn't going as smoothly as Amanda had led him to believe. They were far behind schedule, parts hadn't come in and progress promised to the shareholders wasn't panning out. A part of Ray was glad that Amanda's scheme was backfiring in her face, but on the other hand, he was the plant manager, and if the project didn't go as predicted, he'd be held accountable for its shortcomings. So whether he wanted to or not, he was forced to bite the bullet and call an emergency meeting so the team could regroup and get this project to running efficiently.

"So does everyone understand their new assignment?" he asked the men and women sitting around the mahogany conference table.

Everyone nodded and murmured assent. He had spelled out the situation very clearly. Many of the staff seemed relieved and encouraged by Ray's straightforward leadership rather than Amanda's playing favorites or changing her mind so frequently. He made it clear that Amanda was no longer supervising the project.

"All changes need to be approved by me to keep the project running smoothly. Any infractions of my guidelines will be dealt with harshly. We can't afford to lose any further time on the project."

After the meeting was concluded, Ray seemed confident that progress would soon follow. Although he wouldn't get the credit for this money making project, he still felt a sense of pride for his leadership abilities. He knew in his heart that he was the man, and that was good enough for him. He laughed at the thought that maybe the Lord was showing him that sometimes leaders lead more effectively from the background and don't necessarily need recognition for a job well done.

Back in his office, Ray had a hard time concentrating. Every few minutes his mind would drift back to Amanda being pregnant. He decided to take a break from the four walls to get his mind off his problems. Heading down to the production floor he searched for Malcolm. Maybe hearing more of Malcolm's good fortune could possibly give him some encouragement. Unfortunately, what Malcolm shared with Ray over chips and salsa at the Mexican restaurant they went to for lunch, was an atomic bomb. Ray sat in the booth, sweeping crumbled chips off the red checkered table cloth with his mouth wide open.

"Let me get this straight," Ray said, hoping he'd heard wrong.

"Did you say Tony, Sydney's husband, is Crystal's biological father?"

"Yep," Malcolm answered, dipping his tortilla chip into the extra hot salsa.

"How can this be true?" Ray searched Malcolm's face for answers to the twisted puzzle.

"It's true," Malcolm answered.

"When I saw the birthmark in the palm of his hand, I knew he wasn't lying."

Ray took a big bite of his steak fajita. "Did Sydney confirm it?" he asked, trying to find a glimmer of hope.

"She didn't have to," Malcolm said, sipping water to cool his burning tongue.

"She couldn't even look me in my face, that lying...."

Malcolm stopped himself before calling her something besides her name.

"You remember when I told you about the mysterious phone call I got the night Telese tried to seduce me?" Malcolm asked.

Ray's eyes squinted as he tried to recall.

"You remember, man," Malcolm tried to jog his memory.

"I told you I thought Telese was behind it, remember? The woman's name was Stephanie."

"Oh, yeah," Ray said, as the name jogged his memory.

"It turns out that Stephanie was Tony's ex-wife. Years ago she found out he was cheating on her with Sydney. Once Sydney realized that he wasn't going to leave his wife of ten years for her, she showed up on his doorstep claiming to be pregnant, demanding money for an abortion. Stephanie said when she found out a child had been conceived, she wanted a divorce."

Ray adjusted his position in the booth as he listened carefully. This story showed similarities to his own drama. Malcolm shook his head before continuing.

"Tony decided instead of paying $500 for an abortion, he would give fifty bucks to some hood rat friends of his to 'gang' Sydney so she would lose her baby. At least that was the word on the street, but of course she didn't lose Crystal. That's when I met Sydney. She told me she was raped, but she was lying." His voice took on an edgy tone.

Ray looked startled and laid his fork down to fully absorb Malcolm's story.

"Then Tony ended up going to jail for kidnapping his wife, because she wanted to leave him after finding out that Sydney was pregnant. He was sentenced to fifteen years, and Sydney coerced me into adopting Crystal."

"Now mind you, the two of them were still having this long-distance relationship, making all kinds of plans on being a family once he got out of prison. Stephanie showed me the letters and everything, and stupid Sydney, she still had no idea Tony had paid somebody to beat her up."

Ray couldn't believe what he was hearing.

"After Sydney and I got married, she hired an attorney to reopen Tony's case and got his charges dropped to 'assault', reducing his fifteen year sentence to six years. That's why she never came to visit me in prison."

"She was too busy going to see him and she divorced me after they reduced his time, thinking that I would be in for a while. But, I got out early too. So, it threw her for a loop when I showed up."

Malcolm's story almost made Ray's troubles seem trivial.

"The two of them conjured up a plan to let me continue paying child support until Crystal turns eighteen."

"Stephanie told me that one of Tony's friends let her know that I had adopted the baby, and that Sydney and Tony were back together. She was curious whether I knew the truth, so she started looking for me."

"Man, this sounds like something out of a movie." Ray had to sit back and take it all in.

"How are you holding up?" Ray saw that Malcolm was clearly struggling.

"I'm not going to lie," Malcolm said.

"I want to see both of them in jail for what they did to Crystal and to me, but I'm cool. I know the truth, but I just don't know what to do."

"Legally, is there anything you can do to reverse this?" Ray was sympathetic.

"I don't know, man. I'm looking into it now. I went to see an attorney yesterday, so he's working on some things for me. Even if he's able to get the child support payments stopped, I still have to consider Crystal. She didn't do anything to deserve all this. She's the one most affected by this terrible mess."

"I love her, man. She'll always be my daughter. This is tearing me up." Malcolm turned his face away from Ray.

"How is she?" Ray wished he could offer some comfort.

"Not good. She stayed with me nearly three weeks after it all went down, but Sydney made her come back home to try and salvage what she could. Crystal and I are close. She loves her daddy. I don't think she will ever forgive Sydney for what she's done. Crystal was home with her two days and called me wanting me to pick her up."

"This is crazy." Ray's heart sank.

He thought about how an innocent child could be affected by grown people's mistakes, and he wondered if one day his and Amanda's child might hate him because he didn't want a relationship with her. Malcolm's ordeal really hit home. Ray had a lot of thinking to do.

"Malcolm, I don't know what to say. I'm so sorry," Ray said honestly.

"Trust God, man."

269

"I'm trying, but I'll tell you this. If he puts his hands on her again, it will not end up good, and that, my friend, is a promise."

"I've been down at Mackie's gym so much lately, he gave me a key," Malcolm laughed.

"I damn near punched a hole in one of his sparring bags."

Ray leaned back in the booth, wanting to help his friend.

"Have you talked to Steven or Pastor?" Ray asked.

"Yes, I talked to them both. They stopped by the house and prayed with me," Malcolm smiled.

"The three of you guys are some mighty good dudes."

"The Lord is going to work it out, Malcolm, don't worry," Ray said, trusting in God to come through for his friend.

"The same thing for you too, Ray," Malcolm replied.

"Don't let that woman get to you. The Lord will work it out and take care of you."

"I hope so," Ray smiled.

"If not, do you think I can get those hoodlums' number from Tony and have them scare Amanda?" he joked.

Malcolm laughed at Ray's twisted humor.

"I can tell you this much," Malcolm said.

"All jokes aside, if you don't face your giants, they will always be there."

"Speak of the devil."

Ray looked at the text from Amanda asking him to stop by her house promptly at 6:00 p.m. As much as he knew it probably wasn't a good idea, he had to go see where her head was at. So he texted her that he would be there.

"You need me to tag along? Maybe I can talk some sense into her," Malcolm joked.

Ray grinned, "Nah, I think I better do this alone. By the way, Malcolm," he said, remembering the good news he had heard.

"Congratulations on your engagement to Vanessa. I see you finally signed those papers, huh?" he scooped the last of the salsa onto a crispy chip and popped it in his mouth.

"No, actually I haven't yet. After everything went down at Sydney's house, it just kind of slipped my mind. I've been so focused on my options where Crystal is concerned."

"I understand," Ray slid out of the booth.

"You should head on back to work. You've gone over your lunch hour by eight minutes." Ray glanced down at his watch.

"I'm not worried as long as I don't make it a habit." Malcolm leaned back against the leather booth.

"I'm good friends with the boss," both men laughed.

Ray nodded, "I guess it's good to know people in high places, huh?" The two friends shared another chuckle.

"I'd better go prepare for this meeting. If you don't hear from me, call down to the detention center to make sure I'm not in jail for choking her," Raymond joked.

"You got me covered if I need bail money, right?"

"That's the best one I've heard all day," Malcolm grinned, leading the way to the cashier's counter to pay his check.

"You know I've got you covered, bro. It goes without saying."

Ray left the Mexican restaurant with a full belly and a warm heart. He was relieved that Amanda had finally come back to town. He was curious to know exactly what she had up her sleeve. Her disappearing act had him puzzled.

Returning to his office, Ray sat down and began scrolling through email messages while getting his thoughts together. The things that Malcolm had shared with him lay heavily on his heart. If Amanda was really expecting, and if he was the father, he had to take full responsibility, no matter how the child was conceived. If in fact it was his seed, he'd never want his child to feel the way Crystal felt about her biological father. Ray was going to be part of his child's life whether he loved Amanda or not. His fear, of course, was losing the love of his life as a consequence.

Ray leaned back in his chair, closed his eyes, and thought about his beautiful relationship with Donae. The two of them had never been so close. The idea of her leaving him again, this time with a newborn would be heartbreaking. He didn't want to hurt her, but he knew the only way out of this predicament was to tell her the truth. All he could do was pray for God's mercy. He searched the Internet for a nice bed and breakfast to visit, because he knew Donae loved those. Perhaps he'd take her to one and break the news to her there.

As he sat in his office and began to sulk about his heavy burden, the Holy Spirit reminded him of something. He remembered when Apostle Reed had given Donae the prophetic word nearly a year ago that changed the face of their relationship. God told Donae, not Ray, to give him one more chance to save the relationship. Whew! Ray wiped the sweat from his shiny forehead. *Surely God didn't have that much faith in me*, he thought, feeling disappointed in himself again. *I'm a flawed man. I couldn't please Him even if I tried. God, you knew I'd mess this up. Why did You tell her that?*

Ray felt even worse than before. Not only had he disappointed Donae, but he had let God down. Mysteriously, the more Ray thought about it, the more he supernaturally became encouraged. He had to believe that if God had given Donae that specific prompting. God would work things out for everyone's good. It was at that moment that Ray knew it was time for him to move.

Although being plant manager for Zanderbilt was a dream come true, it came with a hefty price tag. He realized that when God really blesses you, there won't be any burdens attached. Coming to work stressed out every day was not the will of God. It was time for him to trust the Heavenly Father and walk in His will. Who knew, maybe God had something better in store for Ray, as He did for Malcolm. Ray decided to stop putting limits on God. He thanked the Heavenly Father for using Malcolm's situation to show him that all he needed was to trust and believe, and that no weapon formed against him would be able to prosper. Instead of seeking gain through success, he'd seek first the Kingdom and God's righteousness, and all those other things would be added.

Ray called Steven and asked for prayer.

"Hey, bro, can you lift up some special words to God for me?"

"Sure, man. How can I help?"

As Ray briefly explained the circumstances, Steven felt moved in his spirit. What Ray didn't realize was that he was strengthening Steven too. Ray could hear in Steven's voice that his heart was heavy, so instead of Steven praying for Ray. Ray prayed for Steven. Before the call ended, both men were in tears. *'Thank You, Holy Spirit, for taking over my mouth to minister restoration and forgiveness to my brother.'*

Even though Ray didn't understand why he had spoken the words he did, God knew, and more importantly, Steven did, too. Ray hung up with Steven needing time to get himself together, for the Spirit of the Lord had taken him to another place of worship. After composing himself, Ray made a phone call to Luke Zerrico, letting him know that his 'resume' would soon arrive via email. Ray left work shortly after lunch. He had a lot to consider before six o'clock. Several hours later Ray rang the doorbell to Amanda's house. He looked down at his favorite photo of Donae on his cell phone and exhaled deeply. Somehow, her beautiful face gave him strength. As the door opened, Amanda's Hispanic cleaning lady smiled once she saw Ray, and she escorted him in.

"Hi, Ray." Amanda's eyes grew wide as she saw him standing in the foyer.

"You're twenty minutes early." She smiled like a school girl who had just seen her first love.

"I'm glad you could make it." She came whisking down the spiral stairway, dressed in a flattering sundress that exposed her white shoulders and still slender form.

"I thought you were just telling me a line to get me off the phone like you usually do."

"Amanda, we need to talk," Ray said calmly.

"Can we sit down?"

"Yes," she answered lightly.

"Just a second," she smiled.

"I must show you something." She grabbed his hand to lead him upstairs.

"Amanda, no!" Ray jerked his hand away.

"Just tell me. Are you pregnant with my child?" Ray blurted out.

"I'm not trying to seduce you, silly. I just want to show you something."

She motioned for Ray to follow her upstairs. He walked behind so he could quickly get down to the business at hand. Amanda slung open the bedroom door, and Ray was blown away.

"Look at your son or daughter's nursery," she smiled with joy.

"I had the crib imported from Italy, and the curtains and comforter are custom-made." She couldn't contain her elation.

"Look at the handcrafted animals on Noah's ark."

She took Ray's hand and glided it across the rough carved drawing embedded into the wall. Ray could still smell the fresh paint as he looked around the room.

"I can't wait," Amanda's cheeks glittered with tears.

"I'm really going to be a mother. I've picked out names; Jennifer if it's a girl or Taylor for a boy. How do you like those?"

Ray slowly walked around the nursery. He had to admit it was the most beautiful infant's room he'd ever seen. Amanda had a set of hand carved rocking chairs imported from France. One was painted green, and the other yellow, flanking each side of the crib. Finally he sat down in the yellow rocking chair and took a long, deep breath. He glanced at Donae's picture once more on the cell phone in his hand to remind him what was at stake. Amanda pulled the green rocking chair close to Ray and dried her tears with a tissue from the box on the designer changing table.

"So, it's true? You are carrying my child?" Ray sighed.

Amanda smiled softly, "I know you hate me, but I can't help that I'm in love with you, and now I have a part of you growing inside me."

273

She reached for his hands and placed them on her gently rounded abdomen. He quickly retracted them.

"Amanda," Ray was calm.

"You drugged me. That's how this child was conceived. I wasn't a willing participant. You know I want to be with my wife, and my wife only."

"I know that, silly," she sighed with a tremulous giggle.

"The reason I drugged you was because it was the only way. I knew there was only a slim chance you'd be with me again once you started believing in this silly God stuff."

"Don't say that! God is real," Ray said tenderly.

"How can you honestly live this lie or fantasy? You and Eva set me up. You drugged me, and now you're trying to destroy my life."

"Ray, don't be like that. I'm not trying to hurt you. I want to make things better. Once Donae finds out we're having a child, she won't be happy with you, but don't worry, honey. When the divorce is final, we can get married and put all this behind us. We'll make sure Donae gets a nice settlement, and I know you'll feel guilty because of the new baby, but you'll still be involved in the childrens lives, Ray."

"I've already been speaking to Uncle Blake about another promotion. Tell me what you want, and I'll make sure it happens. Uncle Blake plans to retire in two years, and we can arrange for you to take his place as CEO. Isn't that wonderful?" she smiled.

"That's where you're wrong," Ray explained.

"I no longer seek power from humans. It will come if it's God's will, but if not, I'm okay with that. Amanda, you're a beautiful woman, and one day you're going to make some lucky man a great wife, when you get your priorities in order. I'm sorry, I'm not that man," he stared straight ahead; feeling tired and yet determined to see this through.

"Ray, you're acting ridiculous." Amanda began to rock in the chair, moving faster by the minute.

"Why would you just take off, leaving the expansion in shambles?" he asked.

"You know how bad it will make me look if this project isn't successful?"

"I knew you'd get everything in order. I'm not worried at all. I had to fly around Europe to get things ordered for our baby." she looked very excited.

"Besides, once you're CEO of the company, you'll never have to work hard again. All the project deadlines and late nights will be over." Excitement spilled over in her voice as she recited her fantasy aloud.

"After the Code Red expansion is complete, I may consider resigning from my position with Zanderbilt," Ray said, looking directly into Amanda's ocean blue eyes.

Amanda laughed and slowed her rocking almost to a standstill. "Are you sick or something? You're acting crazy."

The rocking increased again. "I know you better than you know yourself." She rubbed the barely there baby bump.

"I know you're hungry for power. There is nothing in this world you want more."

Ray shook his head. "That's the Raymond you fell in love with, the one who wanted nothing more than power and prestige. That man would do anything to get ahead and stop at nothing to be on top, but I'm no longer that man.

"Although I'd love one day to be successful, I'd rather achieve my potential only through God's wills."

The other rocker stopped abruptly. "You're not going anywhere!" Amanda stood to her feet.

"Once your perfect little wife leaves you, power and success will drive you right back to me. You know as well as I do she will never forgive you for this. You knocked me up, remember?" She stepped over beside him and rubbed his head.

"I figured you'd play hard ball, so I'm sorry, Ray, but I had to take matters into my own hands. I've already sent the photos from our lusty night in New York to your home. They should be arriving any moment now." She looked at her Rolex watch.

"That's why I needed you here promptly. I didn't want you to interfere with the surprise for Donae. I also sent a copy of my positive blood test confirming the pregnancy. You're the only man I've been with in the last three years," she said proudly.

"Fed-Ex promised on-time delivery," she paused, expecting Ray to hit the roof, but his calm demeanor had her puzzled. This was easier than she had expected.

"Really?" Ray raised his eyebrows.

"None of that will matter, Amanda."

Stepping back to better see his face, Amanda tried to offer sympathy.

"It's going to be all right, Ray. I promise you, I will make you the happiest man alive," she approached him again for a hug.

Ray shook her off. "I already am the happiest man alive. I have a wife who loves me and a God who is with me every step of every day."

Amanda's features grew hard. "She loves you now, but I'm pretty sure any minute all that will change. She's going to leave you, Ray."

"Nah, she won't," Ray said, still calm.

Ray's tone as well as his confidence was starting to make Amanda angry. "You really think after she sees those photos of us naked in bed that Donae isn't going to leave you? Not to mention when she finds out about this little bundle of joy." She rubbed to her belly.

"This will be the third time you've been unfaithful, Ray. Come on, be realistic."

Ray sighed but said nothing, refusing to look at her.

"Your phone will be ringing any minute now." she looked at her watch again as though impatient.

"She won't call," Ray gave a half-smile.

"She already knows."

"What do you mean she already knows?" Amanda peered closely at Ray's face.

"I already told her." Ray stood to his feet, feeling God's love lift him, strong and sure.

"You're lying," Amanda shouted her face red.

"It's true. She knows, and you confirmed to her that everything I told her was true."

"What kind of game are you playing? I don't understand."

"Amanda...." Donae's voice echoed through Ray's speaker phone.

"You're a crafty, manipulative devil. What you did to my husband was cruel and illegal, but we plan to take care of our responsibilities. I stand by Ray. He loves me and always will, and no devil in hell is going to separate us, not even you. I'll make sure my step-child, Jennifer *or* Taylor, is well taken care of while in our home."

Amanda grew pale.

Donae continued sweetly. "By the way, from what I can see, the nursery is beautiful. If it's a girl would you consider naming her Donae? Its origin is American and means 'woman' or 'lady' for I'm sure the child will need the Spirit of a real woman in his or her life."

"For some reason I believe Ray and I are expecting another boy."

Amanda's eyes grew larger by the second. She couldn't believe what she was hearing.

Ray felt so proud of his wife. It was the hardest thing he'd ever had to do. Telling Donae the truth he knew somehow God had already prepared her heart. She was hurt by the painful ordeal, but when Amanda confirmed the truth about what really happened she couldn't be upset. She recognized it as a trick of the enemy, and she refused to let him win.

"Oh, Amanda, your pictures just arrived," Donae's voice grew louder as she ripped open the sealed package.

"My goodness," Donae giggled.

"I absolutely love your lingerie."

"Ray," Donae called for him to answer.

"Yes, honey, I'm here."

"Please hurry home sweetheart, these photos of you are making me hot!"

"I'll be right there, honey," Ray yelled

Ray ended the video call and looked at Amanda, who was enraged. He had never seen her so angry.

"Call us and let us know when your doctor visits are scheduled. I'm pretty sure Donae will be tagging along."

"I hate you!" Amanda threw the handcrafted lamp that sat next to the table by the crib.

"I hate you!" she screamed.

Ray made his way down the stairs quickly. Amanda was throwing things at him left and right, huge diaper boxes, blankets, baby bottles,anything she could get her hands on. Ray made his way to the door. Looking back once, he saw Amanda trip over the baby blanket and tumble down the steps until she hit the ceramic floor at the bottom.

"Oh my God," the housekeeper screamed as she came running.

"Ms. Sheridan, are you okay?" she knelt beside her employer.

Amanda clutched her belly in pain as Ray darted over to her from the front door.

"Call an ambulance," he yelled to the housekeeper as he began to pray.

"I can't lose my baby," Amanda cried.

"Please don't let me lose my baby."

The pain was excruciating. She grabbed Ray's arm.

"Please, Ray, ask your God to let our baby live. Please," she cried.

"Tell Him I will do anything!"

Chapter 29   *Ivy*

Courtney flew into town on a whim. Usually she'd arrive on the weekend, but this time she wanted to surprise her brother by appearing mid-week. He didn't know it, but she'd already made plans to move back to Richmond. The firm she'd interviewed for as an accountant had scheduled a second interview, and she was sure she was a shoe-in for the job. Courtney wanted to be closer to home now, and felt the need to help Ivy and Yolanda care for JoAnn, especially since the disease was getting worse. She called Ivy as soon as the plane landed at the airport, only to discover Bryson and Yolanda were visiting Yolanda's relatives in Maryland for a few days. Dominic was at his Grandmother Irma's house for a week. Ivy was grateful that Dominic had only had to pay a fine, take classes for anger management, and do forty hours of community service for the incident that happened at school. They'd been going to visit Kandice in rehab, which was going remarkably well.

Ivy wouldn't be home for a few hours yet. Mr. Bailey had asked him to officiate at the wedding of his daughter Alicia and her fiancé Spencer Gillespie. Today Pastor Ivy was hosting the couple's pre-marital counseling session. Twenty minutes into the cab ride on the way to Ivy's house, Courtney's cell phone vibrated in her baggy fitting jeans.

"Hello?"

"Hey, sis," Ivy shouted, exhausted.

"Hey," Courtney answered.

"What's up?"

"Mom's caregiver just called and said she was running to the store to pick up a prescription. Momma is taking a nap, so you may have to let yourself in. We keep a spare key under the flower pot by the rail because your knuckle-headed nephew Dominic seems to lose his key at least one a month."

"Okay," Courtney giggled, as she handed the flirty cab driver his fare. She didn't have the heart to tell him he was barking up the wrong tree.

"What's so funny?" Ivy asked.

Courtney giggled again as she rolled her luggage near the daisies. "I just find it a little humorous that you're going to, officiate at the wedding ceremony of your oldest baby's momma."

"Ha ha, very funny," Ivy answered, stepping into the hallway for a bit of privacy.

278

"You know all your babies' mommas still have googly eyes for you. Please make sure to persuade Alicia to send me an invite. That is one wedding I'd love to see."

"Oh, you've got jokes, huh?" Ivy chuckled a bit, not wanting to admit to the uncomfortable vibes he was getting from her fiancé Spencer.

Ivy was sure Alicia must have told him that Ivy had been her first love. This for him too, was a wedding to be observed on pins and needles, for Ivy knew all he had to do was say the word, and Spencer would be left on the front porch.

"Oh, by the way…" Ivy remembered.

"Kevin is coming by to drop off some papers. Just tell Vanessa to leave them in my office."

"Who's Vanessa?" Courtney asked, as she inhaled the piney scent while walking through Ivy's front door.

"She's the woman taking care of Momma," Ivy answered.

"Oh, okay," Courtney answered sweetly.

"Is she cute?"

"Courtney, don't go there," Ivy demanded.

"She is one of my church members, and her boyfriend is a sparring partner for Bone Crusher, so you better sit down somewhere."

"Calm your nerves, boy," Courtney laughed at Ivy's discomfort.

"I ain't trying to turn out none of your little church girls," she laughed.

"However, plenty of them are fairly good undercover freaks."

"I rebuke you, girl," Ivy said shaking his head.

"You can mess with Vanessa if you want to try. She'll have you saved and calling on the name of Jesus," Ivy chuckled, knowing the anointing that was on Vanessa's life.

Courtney joined Ivy's laughter. "We'll see who's calling on Jesus when I get through with her," she said with confidence.

"Girl, you need Jesus." Ivy started praying, knowing how much it annoyed her.

"Why is Yolanda's clothes scattered everywhere in the girls' room?" she asked, interrupting his casting out her demon.

"Long story," Ivy said, embarrassed.

"Are you two arguing again?" Courtney asked.

"Yes," Ivy shamefully admitted.

"She's been sleeping in the girls' room for a while now."

"Are you serious?" Courtney's smile faded.

"Yes," Ivy answered. He was ashamed of the situation, and it had been even harder some nights without Yolanda in bed. His nightmares seemed to have increased since she left the bedroom.

"Guess she and I will be roommates, huh?"

"Sorry," Ivy said. "Maybe she'll come to our bed now for appearance sake," Ivy joked.

"Mom took the spare room, so we don't have a guest room anymore, but don't worry, things will work out between Yolanda and I. Let me finish this session, and I'll see you after a while." He rushed off the phone to avoid Courtney prying into more of his business.

Courtney walked into Ivy's bedroom to be her usual nosey self. Picking up the prescription bottle, she shook her head when she read Ivy was taking a high dose of a sleep aid to help him sleep. She felt bad that her brother still suffered from those horrible dreams surrounding their father's death. The darkness, anxiety, and dying gasps she chose to block out of her consciousness. A spirit of sadness rushed over her as she thought about all that Ivy must have been going through. Witnessing JoAnn's health decline day by day, as well as his marriage falling apart, she knew things must be overwhelming for him. She quickly realized that her decision to move back home was right on time. At least being around to help might give Ivy a chance to get his marriage back on track.

Courtney picked up the phone and called Mel. She hadn't gotten to see the twins the last few times she'd visited. She figured it would be worth a try to ask if she and JoAnn could get the kids for a visit. With JoAnn going down so quickly, they'd be lucky if the formerly doting grandmother remembered any of them. Courtney was tickled pink when Mel offered to bring the twins over right away. She knew a surprise visit from them would surely lift Ivy's spirits.

"Hello!" Vanessa's voice echoed lightly in the foyer as she came rushing through the door.

"Hi," Courtney smiled from the top of the stairway, slowly making her way down.

When the women's eyes met, Courtney smiled brightly as she tried to give Vanessa a friendly embrace. Vanessa averted her gaze, racing to the kitchen to put up JoAnn's medicine in the cabinet.

"I haven't seen you in years." Courtney followed Vanessa into the kitchen.

"I didn't know you were my mother's caregiver. Ivy said your name, but I never would have thought it was you."

"I had no idea you were Pastor James's sister," Vanessa said timidly.

"Yep, he's my big-head bro," Courtney answered, trying to smooth the atmosphere.

"So what have you been up to?" Courtney asked.

"I haven't seen you since I came home for the summer after my sophomore year in college."

"I'm saved now," Vanessa blurted.

"I'm an evangelist in the church, and I'm getting married soon."

"Married? Wow!" Courtney looked confused.

"I guess I should say 'congratulations." She looked through Vanessa as if the woman was transparent.

"You're looking beautiful as always."

"I need to check on Ms. JoAnn," Vanessa said nervously.

"She's still resting peacefully." Courtney made her way to Vanessa, closing her into a corner.

"I love your hair short like this, but why did you cut it all off? I thought you liked it long?" she touched Vanessa's short, sleek style.

"I've been wearing it this way for years." Vanessa lightly moved away from Courtney's reach.

"It's been a long, long time since I've seen you."

"Where are you going, baby?" Courtney grabbed Vanessa's hand, pulling her close.

"Let me taste those beautiful lips again."

Vanessa broke free from Courtney's tight grip and was relieved that the Lord sent someone knocking just in the nick of time.

"Hi there!" Courtney's voice rang with happiness as Mel and the twins, Jessica and Jordan, came walking through the front door.

"Where's my dad?" Jordan chewed his colorful handful of Skittles.

"He'll be here shortly," Courtney answered, as she watched Jessica run up to her and her half-sister's bedroom.

"Whose clothes are all over my bed?" Jessica came to the upstairs rail and frowned.

"Why don't you go and see if your grandma is awake," Courtney said to avoid the question.

Mel, Courtney, and the kids walked into the bedroom and watched JoAnn as she sat up in bed with her arms folded; refusing to take the medication Vanessa was trying to give her.

"Ms. JoAnn, you need to take your medicine." Vanessa tried to reason with her.

Every now and then Ms. JoAnn would be stubborn. "It will make you feel better."

JoAnn slapped the pills out of Vanessa's hand as the bottled water Vanessa held went flying across the room.

"Ms. Jo, don't act ugly today now. You've got visitors," Vanessa tried to keep her calm.

"Look, your grandchildren are here."

"Is that you, Sweet Pea?" JoAnn motioned for Jessica to come near. Jessica walked up closer so her grandmother could get a better look at her.

"No, Ms. Jo, this is Jessica, your granddaughter," Vanessa tried to explain.

"I ain't got no grandkids!" JoAnn retorted rudely.

"Jessie, where's Jessie?" JoAnn tried to get up out of bed.

"You need to get that child out of here before Jessie comes home. We don't need nobody around her stirring up them awful taste buds of his. Get her out of here!" JoAnn yelled.

"She ain't safe. You hear me? Get her out!"

Courtney couldn't believe how much JoAnn had declined. Tears of hurt slid down her cheeks as she quickly whisked a crying Jessica from the room, with an alarmed Jordan following. Mel approached Ms. JoAnn's side with tears in her eyes.

"Ms. JoAnn, do you remember me?" Mel put her hand softly on JoAnn's shoulder.

"Who are you, child?" JoAnn sounded irritated as she got up from the bed and started looking for clothes to put on.

"Ms. JoAnn, you're already dressed," Vanessa said.

"Where are you going?"

JoAnn pushed Vanessa aside. "Get out of my face. You ain't trickin' me, girl. Get away from me right now," she exploded violently.

Mel stood by the door wiping away tears, ashamed for not letting the kids come by sooner. They loved their Grandma Jo with a passion. Seeing her like this broke Mel's heart into pieces.

"Momma," Ivy burst through the door, let's lay back down. *Little House on the Prairie* is about to come on," he said, as he smiled at Mel.

JoAnn looked up toward the television. "No!" she screamed as if someone was after her.

"I'm going to find Jessie." She knelt down in the closet in search of her shoes.

Ivy looked over at Vanessa, trying to figure out what to do.

"Ms. JoAnn." Vanessa grabbed her hand and held it tightly, looking deep into JoAnn's eyes.

JoAnn stared back into Vanessa's eyes, seeing something soothing, familiar, and peaceful behind them. JoAnn began to cry.

"You're such a sweet child. You've never left my side," she smiled, showing a few toothy gaps left vacant by the partial dental plate laying on the bedside stand.

"You take such good care of me, and I don't deserve it. Please don't leave me here. Take me with you, Jessie needs me."

"I know he needs you, Ms. JoAnn." Vanessa couldn't help but cry too.

JoAnn's hurt oozed from Vanessa's eyes. "But we need you more," Vanessa hugged her tightly.

"I need you," Vanessa whispered as if she were telling JoAnn a big secret.

"Let the God you love with all your heart take care of Jessie. He wants you to rest from this burden. Don't you trust him?" Vanessa looked behind the hurt in JoAnn's tender eyes.

"He is safe in God's arms. Nobody can care for him more than God. Remember, even when the weapon forms, it won't prosper."

JoAnn lowered her head in silence at hearing those familiar words. Her favorite Scripture in times of need always soothed her soul. Mel stared at Vanessa and JoAnn in disbelief. She'd never seen anything more touching. She had never seen ministry come so alive. Although she knew God was real, she had held so much anger in her heart for so long; pain had become a familiar companion.

JoAnn placed the shoes she held neatly in the closet. She grabbed Vanessa's hand and squeezed it tightly on her way back to the comfortable old green wingback chair next to the bay window.

"Thank you, baby," JoAnn smiled.

"God sure does answer prayer. I can see God all over you, and I can feel His presence working through your beautiful spirit." JoAnn sat back in the chair, staring out the window.

"Can y'all please leave?" JoAnn never took her gaze from beyond the glass pane.

"I need to give God praise."

Everyone quietly exited the room, and moments later Vanessa softly pulled the door closed behind her after JoAnn had cooperated and taken the medicine. Picking up her purse and car keys from the kitchen counter, Vanessa said a soft goodbye to all who heard her. Courtney stepped out of the room from talking to Jessica and Jordan to follow Vanessa as she stepped outside.

"Vanessa," Courtney spoke in a moderate tone as she caught up to the other woman.

"I never forgot about you," she said, trying to look into her face.

"Look, Courtney, I'm not that same confused person. I didn't know who I was at that point in my life, but now I do."

"So are you saying what we had was just a fling?" Courtney looked disappointed.

"I was in love with you, and you know it. How could you just leave without telling me anything? I at least deserved an explanation." Her features were quizzical and bore a trace of lingering hurt.

Vanessa sighed and looked across the street where a neighbor was watering his garden. "I'm sorry if I hurt you, Courtney, but that was a long time ago. Like I said, I was confused."

"My life has changed now I live to please God. I can't go back to living a lifestyle that's not in his will for me."

"So are you saying you are no longer attracted to women?" Courtney said, wanting the truth.

"I'm saying I love God more than I loved the desires of my flesh. Once I started feeding my spirit, my taste buds changed."

Courtney rolled her eyes at the words that were coming from Vanessa's mouth. Courtney's desire was to rekindle the flame that had never really died. Vanessa was a special and beautiful person that was easy for anyone to love.

"I have to go, Courtney." Vanessa started to walk away.

"My fiancé is waiting for me." She wanted to remind Courtney of her engagement.

"We have to finalize our wedding plans."

"Wait a minute." Courtney followed Vanessa to her car.

"If you're so confident of who you are, then why are you so nervous? You've been running from me ever since you got here. Maybe those desires of yours haven't completely died; you just haven't fed them."

"You're wrong, Courtney," Vanessa stated with force behind her words.

"I know without a shadow of a doubt that the old self has died, along with those desires," Vanessa now approached Courtney up close.

"And how do you know that?" Courtney asked

"Because, I starved them to death." Vanessa walked to her car slammed the door and drove away leaving Courtney standing there speechless.

Jessica and Jordan had headed down to the basement where Ivy had built a game room, complete with a big screen for the kids to watch movies. He'd warned the youngsters that he'd be down shortly to demolish them on a new video game which he had clobbered Dominic, Nicholas and Bryson already several times.

"Why didn't you tell me Ms. JoAnn's condition was so bad?" Mel sat on the faded soft leather sofa, drying her eyes.

"I tried to," Ivy said honestly.

"But everytime I called, you hung up on me."

Mel looked away, embarrassed and ashamed.

"That medicine won't bring her memory back?" Mel asked with hope.

"No, the medicine that Vanessa was trying to give her was for her blood pressure."

"Oh, no," Mel felt sad.

"They can't give her anything to help her remember the past or her family?"

Ivy shook his head in the negative.

"So she'll never remember us again?" Mel looked into Ivy's eyes for a glimmer of hope.

"Today she may not know you, but tomorrow she might. You just never know," Ivy said to lift Mel's spirits.

"You can start getting the kids whenever you'd like," Mel announced without a thought.

"I know how much she loves all her grandchildren."

"Thank you, Mel," Ivy said with gratitude.

"That means a lot to us all."

The thoughtful woman stood up from the sofa and straightened her tight fitting dress. Her curves made Ivy feel like he couldn't help but stare. Ivy embraced her slender frame tightly in his arms.

"I know how hard this is for you, and if it's worth anything, I'm sorry for everything I've ever done to hurt you."

Mel buried her face in Ivy's chest and began to weep. "I know Ms. JoAnn must hate me for keeping the kids away. She didn't deserve what I did, trying to punish you. She loves those twins so much. She always said Justin was the spitting image of your daddy."

Ivy smiled, "Yeah, everyone knows Justin is her favorite. She always gave him the biggest piece of chicken," Ivy laughed.

"I'm so sorry. I wish there was something I could do to change what I've caused her to lose," Mel said, regretful.

Ivy didn't mumble a word, he just held her tight to comfort her. Mel enjoyed the peaceful moment as she rested in Ivy's arms.

"It's okay Mel, we all make mistakes." Ivy lifted her chin to look into his face.

"Try not to beat yourself up. Take it from someone who has been doing that for a long time. You can't change what you've done in the past; you can only change the present and move forward."

Mel sensed that Ivy was not only talking about her, but himself as well. Her countenance began to glow once she looked deeper into his eyes. The scent of his clean smelling cologne sucked her in, and she couldn't move a muscle, reminding her of the night the twins were conceived. Ivy knew if he didn't get out of this situation right away, it would soon be sinful. Mel closed her eyes and moved in closer. Ivy anticipated tasting her soft, luscious lips. The sound of someone loudly clearing his throat quickly separated the two.

"Pastor, can I see you for a moment?" Kevin held up the envelope of the papers he was supposed to deliver. Ivy had forgotten he was dropping by.

"Sure." Ivy looked at Mel tenderly.

"Please don't leave," he said.

"I'll be right back."

"No," Mel said, picking up her Coach bag.

"I need to leave. I've already stayed way too long."

"Please, Mel," Ivy begged.

"No." Mel wouldn't budge an inch.

"See you when you bring the kids home?" Mel added a little smirk with an attached look that read 'danger zone'.

Ivy knew his returned smile was admission to march into the enemy's camp.

"Okay," he said, happily walking her to the door.

"Are you crazy?" Kevin pushed Ivy up against the wall as soon as Mel was outside the front door and it was closed.

"What are you thinking about? You need to practice some self-control."

"I know your problem with Yolanda is weighing heavily on your heart, but this is not how you get through it, Ivy, and you know it."

"Thanks for the papers." Ivy turned to walk away.

"Ivy, I'm not playing. You better start thinking with the right head and take heed of a way to escape."

"I'm a grown man," Ivy insisted.

"I can handle myself."

Kevin's anger flared. "I refuse to let you fall and be the trifling man you used to be. It's not going down on my watch. I promise you that. *I'll* take the kids back to Mel's when they are ready to go," he demanded.

"No you won't!"

"Yes, I will." Kevin refused to back down.

"What are you going to do, babysit me?" Ivy questioned, getting more heated by the second.

"If I have to," Kevin got into his face.

"Trust me Ivy; you'll thank me in the morning."

"I won't have to. I can handle this myself."

Kevin pushed Ivy backwards harshly, knocking him off his feet. He was startled once the nearby ceramic vase came crashing to the hardwood floor. Ivy rushed Kevin as he got up, and the two started to wrestle in the foyer. Courtney ran to see what the noise was.

"Stop it!" she yelled, not believing her eyes.

"What are you doing?" She tried to break them up.

"Ivy, you've got children downstairs."

The two men wouldn't stop.

"Ivy, stop it, right now!" Courtney demanded.

"Why are you two fighting like this? Stop it!" She started to cry, knowing once Ivy saw her tears he'd give in.

The two men broke apart, breathing heavily.

"Get out," Ivy yelled, still heated with fury.

"I'm going," Kevin punched the wall.

"And I won't be back. I quit."

Chapter 30   Malcolm

Malcolm wasn't surprised when the judge gave her ruling that he was still financially obligated to pay child support for Crystal until she reached the age of eighteen. He had chosen of his own free will to legally adopt the child, knowing her biological father was out there somewhere. Malcolm felt sick to his stomach every time he thought about how Sydney had him thrown in jail for non-payment, fully aware of his struggles. How dirty could she be to do something so deceitful? Malcolm found a little satisfaction when the judge scolded Sydney for having deceived him into thinking she didn't know who Crystal's real father was, but the real joy and praise came when the judge announced to them both that in the state of Virginia, once a child turns thirteen, he or she can decide which parent they want to live with.

When the judge announced after talking with Crystal that the young girl wanted to come and live with Malcolm, it was music to his ears. Malcolm praised God for his mighty power, for He had truly shown up and shone out. Not only would Malcolm have custody of Crystal, but, Sydney was also ordered to pay him child support. Malcolm rejoiced that her sinful plan had backfired. What she had intended for evil, God had turned around for his good. Things couldn't have turned out better if Malcolm had planned the situation.

On that glorious day, Sydney left the courtroom hysterical. Her tears were flowing so hard Malcolm thought he was going to swim out of the courtroom. He, Crystal and Vanessa left the building that day holding hands, one big happy family. For some reason he recalled the patriot, Patrick Henry, who had delivered his famous "Give me liberty" speech back in 1775 at Richmond's St. John's Church, not far from the courthouse. For once Malcolm could personally relate to a famous historical event.

The Hammer Hand and Bone Crusher fight was soon approaching. Bone Crusher was doing better, but Malcolm and the trainers were worried about him being too slow. His punches were powerful. Malcolm had the cuts and bruises to prove it, and he was determined that Bone Crusher would win this fight. Between working at the plant eight hours a day and sparring at the ring non-stop, he was worn down. He called Telese to let her know he'd be over to sign the divorce papers. Time had quickly gotten away from him. Those documents had been sitting at Telese's house for weeks.

Vanessa had already begun picking out household colors and making wedding plans. The thought made Malcolm's heart do a shuffle. She, Malcolm's mom, Louise, his sister Lauren and Vanessa's Aunt Johnnie Mae had been out shopping a few weekends, looking at wedding gowns. It didn't come as a surprise to Malcolm when Vanessa showed up at his house announcing a grand wedding . He knew once Lauren and Louise put their minds together, things would start rolling pretty quickly.

Although no date was set yet, Malcolm asked Pastor Ivy to marry them, and he chose Steven and Ray to be his best men. He called Steven weeks ago to ask him to stand with him at the altar whenever that day was determined but, Steven was missing in action. It seemed like everyone around him was in some sort of battle. Moe's oldest son had been injured in prison, and her younger son had joined a gang- roaming the streets like a fool. The heartache and stress must have been more than Moe could bear, as she ended up being hospitalized for weeks. Shortly after that, her illness was diagnosed as terminal, and they moved her into the Hospice.

Even Pastor Ivy hadn't been himself. He'd been on a spiritual fast for the past few weeks. He lost close to twenty pounds, and looked weak and feeble. Malcolm had also learned through Vanessa, that Pastor's marriage was on life support. Rumors were floating around the church that Kevin had moved out of state suddenly with no explanation. The church was in an uproar because Pastor stopped the building fund they had been raising money for these last three-and-a-half years. The few deacons and trustees who weren't in agreement with him had come to the conclusion that he had lost his mind or had started using drugs. He brought in a team of people to do a few seminars to the congregation on how to get debt free, and had suddenly made quite a few changes.

Ray had been paralyzed with guilt after Amanda lost her baby. He called everyone in the city to keep her in prayer, but the baby didn't survive the fall. Ray blamed himself for Amanda's accident, and so did Amanda. It was worrying Malcolm that he couldn't find Steven. Even Mackie had no clue where he was. This strange vibe he was getting was starting to alarm everyone. It was obvious the devil didn't take vacations. Malcolm just hoped maybe Steven was out of town on a short trip, which was something he did often. For someone in a security officer job, he sure did have a lot of free time.

Malcolm stood at the door, excited to see Layla. He'd been working so much lately, it seemed like he hadn't seen his baby girl much. Often he would laugh out of the blue, thinking about something funny Layla had said.

"Hi, Malcolm," Telese opened the door.

"What's going on?" Malcolm smiled.

"Where are the kids?" He looked around.

"KJ is at the skating rink, and Layla is spending the night with her dance instructor's daughter."

"Oh," Malcolm said, showing disappointment.

"You miss them that much?" Telese loved that.

"Is it that obvious?" Malcolm asked.

"They miss you, too. Have a seat," Telese said, holding the folded white papers in her hand.

Malcolm sat down and reached for the ink pen in his shirt pocket. Telese sat down beside him.

"Do you mind if we talk for a minute?" she asked.

"Sure." Malcolm started to feel a tad uneasy.

"I broke up with Morris yesterday," Telese lied.

"Morris decided to work things out with his wife once the courts told him how much he'd be paying in child support and alimony. So he went back to her begging for forgiveness."

"Shoot!" Malcolm thought before shutting his eyes.

"I'm really sorry to hear that," he said in all honesty, hoping her decision had no bearing on him.

There was a long pause of silence. "Don't you want to know why I wanted out of my relationship with Morris?" Telese asked.

A part of Malcolm was afraid to ask, but he did so as a courtesy.

"Why?"

"Because I want to stay married to my husband," she said, turning her body to him.

"No! Telese, please don't do this. Come on now, this is crazy. I think it's best if we just move on. I'm not in love with you anymore."

Malcolm's words stung her. The truth was she was relieved when Morris broke the news. She'd known months ago she wanted Malcolm back.

"I believe you do still love me, and if Vanessa wasn't in the picture, you wouldn't hesitate coming back home and giving our relationship another try."

Malcolm was devastated by this curve ball.

"Telese, why are you doing this now? It isn't fair. Please don't." Malcolm put his head in his hands.

"The kids want you to come home, and so do I. You just admitted how much you missed them. I still love you, I do, and I don't want to go another day without you. I miss your laughter, I miss your silly jokes and I miss your touch, your kiss. Malcolm, I miss everything about you."

Malcolm sat speechless. This couldn't be happening now.

Telese inched closer to him and hugged his shoulders. "Baby, I'm sorry," she said.

"I know I really messed up by turning to Morris for comfort, but I swear, Malcolm, that was not my intention. For what it's worth, he came on to me. I know that's no excuse. I made a horrible mistake. Tell me how I can make this right. I'll do anything."

"Telese." Malcolm sat back on the sofa and looked at the ceiling.

"I'm engaged. Vanessa bought a wedding dress, we're working on a date. We've made plans."

"I'll pay for the dress. Whatever she spent, I'll gladly give it back to her." Telese grabbed her purse and tore out a blank check.

"How much?"

She grabbed her pen. "How much, Malcolm?" she began to cry.

"Please, Malcolm, I love you. Please give me, give us, another chance," Telese pleaded.

With a sigh, Malcolm said, "Put that away. It's not about money," he said gently.

"I love her. I really love her. Just because you and Morris decided to call it quits doesn't mean I have to. I plan to move on with my life, and it only has room for one woman. That's Vanessa."

"Malcolm, you don't really know this woman," Telese said in an urgent tone.

"What do you think you know about her?"

Malcolm took a minute to breathe. "I know she was there when I needed someone the most, when everyone thought I was a worthless abuser, including you, she saw that I could be redeemed. She told me I could do all things through Christ who is my strength. She made me believe that I could turn my life around, and she made me want to be better."

Telese paused before answering. "Malcolm, I understand all that, and I appreciate her lifting you up when you were down, but we're a family. How could you just throw it all away?"

"I didn't throw it all away, you did. I went to the church that night looking for you, but you were in Atlanta living it up with Morris."

"I wanted to prove to you that I was going to change, but you weren't there. I'm grateful now that you weren't, because had you been there, I might not have found what I really needed."

Telese took a deep breath. "So are you saying that's where you found Vanessa?"

"No, that's where I found Jesus. He saved me from myself. So in a sense I guess I should say thank you because it was due to you that I went in the first place. Vanessa was a blessing God gave me after the fact, but Vanessa caused me to see one important truth. The enemy wanted me to believe that these hands were a curse to me." Malcolm held up his hands. "I used them in the wrong way, by abusing you, but I discovered that they were my gift once I used them in the right way. God made the man I am, and Vanessa ministered to the man I was becoming. I could never hurt that woman. "

Vanessa is not a blessing. You act like she is so grand. Telese wanted to scream. She buried her head in his chest. "I love you, Malcolm. Please give us one more chance. I can't. I won't let you go."

"I know you're hurting, Telese. I know how it feels to want someone who no longer wants you, but my mind is made up. I want to marry Vanessa."

"No you're not!" Telese started hitting Malcolm in his chest.

He grabbed her hands to stop the pounding. "Calm down, Telese, violence is not the answer," he said calmly.

"Hitting people is not going to make them have a change of heart. Trust me, baby, I used to feel it would too, but now I know better."

Telese shook the divorce papers at him. "Is this what you want?" she threw them at him.

Malcolm glanced down, noticing that she had already signed on the firm black line beside her printed name.

"Vanessa is a whore, Malcolm. She used to be a prostitute, a call girl. I had her investigated. Here look at this, it's all in there."

Telese handed him a file marked "V. Reardon." And to make matters worse, she slept with men *and* women, Malcolm, she's disgusting."

Malcolm threw the file on the coffee table. "I don't want to see that. Are you so desperate that you had to sink this low? I'm not going to listen to this nonsense." Malcolm stood up and headed toward the door.

"Why not?" Telese demanded.

"Your little Miss Perfect isn't so perfect now, is she?" Telese was proud to be so different from Vanessa with her reputation.

"Telese, you need to stop this. You should be ashamed of yourself." Malcolm paused with his hand on the doorknob.

"It's pathetic."

"Oh, I'm pathetic?" Telese said angrily.

"Did she tell you about the child she gave up for adoption? She probably didn't even know who the father was, the slut. Her name is Anjoelina. She was raised by some family two counties over."

Malcolm turned to walk back to Telese after hearing Anjoelina's name. He listened carefully; knowing there had to be some truth to what Telese was saying.

She smiled. "Where did you get this from?" Malcolm thumbed through the thick stack of papers in the file.

"I told you, I had a detective dig into her background. I can't let you make a horrible mistake like this," she said.

Malcolm looked through the mug shots of Vanessa arrested for petty theft, prostitution, and assault. There were photos of her in skimpy clothes standing on street corners, pictures of her and female companions coming out of gay bars, holding hands. Malcolm thought he was about to be sick.

"So what, Telese? I don't care. Is this supposed to stop me from loving her? She isn't that person anymore." He threw the envelope down, removing the information about Vanessa's daughter, Anjoelina.

"Malcolm!" Telese looked surprised.

"This woman sold her body for money, she could have AIDS."

"Stop being ridiculous and do you think I'm that stupid? We've both been tested, and she has a clean bill of health."

"I, on the other hand, had tested positive for Chlamydia, and you are the only woman I've been with."

Telese became irate at Malcolm's accusation. "That's impossible."

"It doesn't matter at this point. I used to be abusive, and I was no better than she was, even if she was a prostitute. I turned my life around, just like she did."

Telese stared at Malcolm, disappointed. "You mean to say you'd give up a life with me and your children for a whore? You've got to be kidding me."

"Stop calling her that," Malcolm said sternly.

Malcolm picked up the divorce papers that Telese had earlier thrown on the floor and pulled the pen out of his shirt pocket again to sign them. Telese raced to his side and snatched them away.

"You need to think about what you're doing. Let this information sink in, maybe you can think more clearly then," she folded the papers carefully, as if isolating a virus.

"I'll hold on to these. I'm sure by the time you come to your senses, we won't be needing them." she said, giving herself hope.

"And please, Malcolm," she stressed.

"While you are thinking things through, remember our children. They need and love you."

Malcolm's soul was vexed, and his head had been throbbing for the last three days. He'd wondered a few times if maybe he'd taken a few too many blows from sparring, for the aches had been coming off and on for a while now. He made a mental note to go to the doctor if they continued. Malcolm needed to vent, but everyone in his circle of friends was already going through hell. Steven was missing in action, and Ray was still grieving the guilt of Amanda losing their child. Malcolm had nowhere to turn. He refused to go to Vanessa with this, as she already struggled with her past. He didn't want her to know that he knew things she had never mentioned. He didn't blame her for not telling him. He was sure he wouldn't have breathed a word if the shoe were on the other foot.

Leaving Telese's house without another word, Malcolm surprised himself when he pulled up in Rufus's driveway. 'You must be crazy, man,' he thought to himself, 'this is Vanessa's uncle. He already said if you hurt her, he'll hurt you.' But something kept tugging at Malcolm to go talk to Rufus. Malcolm heard soft crying as Johnnie Mae quietly let Malcolm in the door. Angel, Rufus's neighbor from down the street, was weeping as she stood behind her son feeling his burning forehead. Rufus rebuked the fever from the boy with so much force and authority. It made Malcolm's skin crawl. He'd never seen or heard Rufus this angry, but he talked to the fever like it was an intruder and he was enraged that it was there.

After his words ceased, an undeniable spirit of peace filled the room. The child stopped crying. Johnnie Mae led the boy into the kitchen to feed him.

"Young Buck," Rufus smiled when he looked up to see Malcolm standing near.

"Hey, Rufus," Malcolm gave him a firm handshake.

Malcolm touched Angel on the back as she sat on the couch sobbing lightly, with her arms wrapped around herself, rocking back and forth.

"Is she okay?" Malcolm asked, concerned.

"Yes, son, she's fine, just giving God the glory."

"Can we talk in private?" Malcolm asked.

"Sure son, follow me." Rufus walked through the kitchen on his way to the deck and rubbed Angel's three year- old son on the head as he demolished a plate of chicken tenders and fries.

"What's up, Young Buck?" Rufus took a swig of his happy juice.

"I'm surprised to see you sober this late in the day. You're usually mellow right around this time," Malcolm laughed.

Rufus laughed along with him. "This is my first one today. It's starting not to taste the same anymore. I may need to try a new brand," he chuckled.

"I'm cutting back to a six-pack a day," he said proudly.

"That's good, Rufus," Malcolm said.

"Vanessa told me you started drinking after your little girl died."

"Yeah, that's true. Brew was my therapy," Rufus admitted.

"Well, I'm sure you didn't come here to hear my story. What's on your mind, Young Buck?"

Malcolm explained his complicated situation to Rufus as the other man listened thoughtfully, drinking from the can every now and then. Even though Rufus was his fiancée's uncle, Malcolm considered him a wise friend and most importantly, a great teacher. Uncle Rufus's advice was simple.

"Follow, follow, follow your heart. I know you love the kids, and you want to do the right thing, but you follow your heart. God won't lead you wrong, and whatever you decide, it's all right with me. I know you're a good man."

Malcolm was deeply comforted by Rufus's words. Although his world was upside down, he had peace in the midst of it. Malcolm smiled as he glanced up at Angel's little boy dancing to a popular music video.

"How is y'all's friend doing? I think Vanessa said her name was Moe?" Rufus asked.

"She's not good. She's in Hospice now," Malcolm answered.

"I told Vanessa to go over and have Holy Communion with her. Did she do it?" Rufus frowned after taking another swig.

"Yeah, she tried, but I think she said Moe refused to do it with her."

Rufus shook his head. "People just don't know."

"Know what, Rufus?" Malcolm asked.

"Why would you tell Vanessa to have Holy Communion with her?"

"Why?" Rufus smiled, as he poured out his beer onto the grass.

"You don't know why?"

Malcolm could feel a Bible lesson coming on.

"There is so much power in the healing virtue of Communion. People just don't understand. The Lord said to do this OFTEN 'in remembrance of me'. Often is "often," not once a month; try once a week or once or twice a day. The Word says if you do it unworthily it causes sickness, disease, and some to sleep. What he meant by unworthily had nothing to do with sin. He meant how you discern the body and his blood, remembering that it was sacrificed for you. If you don't take communion in remembrance of that, it's unworthily."

He paused to let this sink in, and then continued.

"So with that being said, if you do it worthily, remembering Jesus, his body being broken and his bloodshed, don't you think it would do just the opposite, cause you to walk in wellness, healing, and disease free? That's why there are so many sick among you."

"You don't do it often enough. Me and Johnnie Mae have Holy Communion every morning. How else do you think an old man like me can be so fine?" Rufus laughed heartily.

He chuckled once more before speaking. "But seriously, the blood was for forgiveness of sins, but the *body, the bread,* can heal her, son. Ain't Jesus the bread of life? Don't believe me. Read it for yourself."

Malcolm chuckled at the older man's amazing discernment. Before Malcolm left, he handed Rufus the papers he had gotten from Telese about Anjoelina. He hoped that perhaps he and Rufus could tie up some loose ends that might lead them to a trail to find Vanessa's long lost child. Malcolm drove away, shaking his head. Rufus had a powerful ministry inside of him, if only he'd walk in it. Malcolm had to pull over to the side of the road just to give God praise. Something in him wanted to leap for joy when the Holy Spirit whispered, "Where's your headache?"

296

Chapter 31   *Raymond*

Ray expected to be either demoted or terminated once Blake Sheridan found out the circumstances surrounding the miscarriage of Amanda's child he fathered, but months had already gone by, and surprisingly, Ray still had a job. He warned Donae one Saturday afternoon as they took a leisurely stroll along the Canal Walk that it was probably due to the Code Red project that he was still driving a company car. He figured after the project was complete, he'd surely get axed. Parts of the Code Red project were already in operation and doing well. The new machines he'd ordered to cut cycle times in half were causing production numbers to soar. Likewise, sending the machinists to school for maintenance operations turned out to be a big hit. Maintenance downtime was half of what it had once been because operators could now work on their own machines.

This idea saved the company substantial costs. Paying the operators $1.50 more an hour versus paying a maintenance worker an hourly salary eliminated the need for maintenance. However, one or two maintenance employees would be available on an on-call basis. Ray even offered a $25 gift certificate for gas to the employee if he had the machine back up and running within four hours.

"They can't afford to let you go," Donae breathed.

"You're the company's lifeblood."

The couple was enjoying the spring sunshine as Donae listened to Ray's update on the company's progress while tossing pebbles into the sparkling waters of the James River and Haxall Canal. Ray went on to explain that the best incentive he gave his employees was the "Abundance Bonus." It was given to every employee that exceeded production at the end of each calendar year. This incentive caused fewer machines to go down. Employees were doing more preventive maintenance, and if one employee's machine was running well, that person would offer to help a coworker with a machine that was not working properly.

Morale around the plant was awesome. Zanderbilt had boosted success rates tremendously by making on-time deliveries. Even employees from some of the competitors were beginning to apply there due to the fact that the staff was honored to work there. The new production methods eliminated the need for supervision, because Ray had empowered the employees. Employees would come in with the goal of getting work done. Ray assigned a team leader on every shift, and these hard workers ensured their areas met goals and objectives. People worked stress free without management breathing down their necks. There was just one supervisor for all three shifts, and he was on call for troubleshooting purposes only.

Strangely enough, perceiving he had one foot out the door, Ray was surprised when Blake Sheridan approved his request to hire contract employees for a weekend shift, through a new contract company called "The Second Chance Agency." This contract service found jobs for persons with blemishes on their backgrounds, who needed a second chance in life. Funded through the government, the work program helped to rehabilitate ex-criminals, giving them a fresh start to earn a decent income. Because Zanderbilt hired these reformed convicts, the company not only received sizable tax breaks, but they also got free advertising. The contract employees were trained to run high tech machinery and, at the end of the year if employees had a good production rating, track record and good attendance, they were hired by Zanderbilt without any need of a formal interview.

Although Ray felt his time at the company was winding down, he was proud of what he'd accomplished during his sojourn there. He had been on a few promising job interviews both in-state and out-of-state. Choosing to decline the offer of a lifetime to work with Mike Zerrico and his top competitor, Drexelle felt right. It just wouldn't have seemed like the Godly thing to do. He wouldn't make an unethical choice.

Amanda had been sending him emails and text messages, calling him a murderer. She made it very clear she had spoken with her Uncle Blake, making mention that he was not happy with some things that were going on at the plant. She'd asked Ray if he would like for her to draw up his resignation letter right away. She promised she'd stop at nothing until he got what he so rightfully deserved in her opinion. Aside from his pending issues with work, Raymond's relationship with Donae soared to higher heights.

What had happened in New York ended up being the biggest blessing that Ray could have ever imagined. In the end, Amanda's scheme backfired, pushing Ray and Donae even closer together. The trust they had toward one another was a thing of beauty: Amanda couldn't make either doubt the other. Nothing would ever again be able to threaten the love this devoted pair shared. Ray thanked God Almighty, for he knew God was the only one who could have brought him out on top of that perilous situation.

Weeks later, Ray finally got in contact with Steven, who said he had been out of town for a few weeks and then up to the Hospice home visiting with Moe. Steven didn't sound like his old chipper self. Something was definitely bothering him, but Ray had no clue as to what it could be, and Steven wasn't telling. When Steven quickly ended the call, it was the last straw for Ray. He was determined to find out what had his good friend so down in the dumps. Ray texted Malcolm and asked him to meet him at Steven's house as soon as he got off work. Then he called Pastor Ivy and asked him to meet him there in an hour. Ray tried calling Mackie, but he didn't answer, and his voicemail was full. An hour later, Ray heard a soft tap on his driver's side window as he lifted his head from a short prayer.

"Hi, Pastor, how are you?" Ray opened his car door. As the two men embraced, Malcolm pulled up, almost making skid marks in the concrete. Malcolm had been concerned about Steven for a while now, but no one had any idea where Steven lived. Luckily Donae had access to the database at the pharmacy and was able to look up Steven's address for them.

"Are you sure this is the right place?" Malcolm asked.

"I can't see Steven living here. This is a pretty rough neighborhood. It's crawling with pushers, prostitutes and drug addicts."

"I can't see that." Ray watched as a drug transaction was going down across the street with what looked like a clean-cut young man of college age and a street wise pusher.

"I hope this is the wrong address."

Ivy knocked on the scratched front door with a hint of force as Malcolm put his finger over the peephole. Looking around the porch, the friends noticed trash blowing across the neighbor's lawn and heard a barking dog in the distance. Steven opened the door and was startled to see three of his good friends standing in the doorway. He tried to wipe his bloodshot eyes as he tucked in his rumpled shirt and brushed a hand through his hair.

"Steven," Malcolm barged into the small apartment.

"What's going on, man? What's wrong?" he looked deep into his friend's eyes for answers.

"We've been worried. You haven't been yourself in months."

"Talk to us, man," Ray chimed in.

"Why are you living here in this dump?" Malcolm looked around the small two-bedroom apartment. Each room had a set of bunk beds with a small chest of drawers sitting between. A fresh, long stem rose caught the men's attention, as it stood alone and forlorn in a lovely glass vase.

"Did you get kicked out of your place or something?" Malcolm asked.

"Do you need money?" Malcolm pulled out his wallet.

"Steven, brother, tell us what's wrong. We're here for you. Don't shut us out," Ray added.

"You've been there for us, so let us help you now."

"I'm fine, guys," Steven pretended to perk up with a quick grin.

"Stop lying, man, we know something is wrong. Why won't you talk to us? We can't help if you won't share with us."

"I'm fine guys," Steven insisted.

"I just...."

"You just what?" Malcolm wanted answers.

"Be honest with us, Steven. Please, bro, we want to help." Ivy knelt on the worn gray carpet beside Steven as he sat on the soft cushioned faded chair.

"Steven, I know you're taking anti-depressants." Ray knelt on the other side of Steven.

"What has got you so depressed?"

Steven tried to hold back tears. "I'll be okay, guys. You don't have anything to worry about. I'm working through my issues," his face looked drained.

"What is it?" Malcolm's heart began to ache for his friend who was clearly struggling.

"We're not leaving until you tell us what's going on. I've got all night."

"I'm no angel," Steven dropped his head.

"I'm just paying what I owe."

"What does that mean?" Ray's face showed a look of confusion.

Steven exhaled loudly, and then took a moment to pause. Ivy placed his hands on the man's shoulders in comfort as Steven told them the story of the worst day of his life.

"Ray, do you remember when I told you my wife and son were killed in a car accident?"

"Yeah, you told me on the night you lead me to Christ." Ray's heart warmed at the memory.

Malcolm and Ivy sat intently listening as Steven began to pour out his heart.

"The car accident was my fault. My wife kept telling me for weeks she needed new tires and brake pads on the car. I kept putting it off because I was drunk." Steven tightened his grip on his late son's baby shoe he was holding.

"My wife begged me before she went to Bible study that night to change the brake pads. She stressed that she'd had to pump the brakes a long time before stopping. I was passed out drunk before she left, and hadn't done what she'd asked me to. She depended on me." Steven began to cry, tears sliding down his cheeks rapidly.

300

"It's okay, man," Ivy rubbed Steven's back.

"Let it out."

"The highway patrol officer woke me up the next day, pounding on the door to tell me my wife and son had been killed in a car accident. He said her tire burst, and the vehicle had veered into oncoming traffic. The brakes failed, and they hit a tractor trailer head on. They died instantly." Steven felt for the locket around his neck, holding the precious pictures of his wife and son.

"I killed them," he sobbed, unable to hold in his grief.

"If I hadn't been a sorry drunk, they'd still be alive today."

Ivy shut his eyes and felt the pain overflowing from Steven's heart. He sensed that the memory of Steven's wife and son's death was too heavy for him to bear.

"Oh man," Malcolm bent down in front of Steven.

"Let that go. You've got to forgive yourself."

"I can't, Malcolm," Steven wept.

"Don't you understand? My wife and son would be here with me right now if I hadn't been a stupid, selfish drunk."

"That's why you help all those ladies in the church with their cars?" Ray now saw how it all made sense.

Steven nodded.

Ray knew for certain he'd feel the same way if something that tragic happened to his wife and children. Ivy tried hard to comfort his dear friend, but Steven was inconsolable. The guilt he had built up over the years overwhelmed him. Malcolm stood back in the corner of the room, praying silently for his brother to regain strength. His heart ached tremendously for Steven. Malcolm could only imagine how deep his hurt had to be, carrying such a heavy burden of guilt for so long. Steven sat in the chair, wanting to die. Malcolm walked over and stood him up on his feet.

"Listen man, you ministered to me at one of the lowest points in my life. When I wanted to give up on everything and everybody, you wouldn't let me. God put you in my life for a reason. You are a powerful and mighty man of God. Your wife and your son are with Jesus, bro, you hear me?" Malcolm's voice was full of compassion.

"They are with the Lord. In what better place could they be? They are safe now; safe in His arms."

Steven almost fell to his knees. Malcolm's words rang true. The bereaved husband and father knew his wife and son were safe with God, but Steven missed them terribly. He hadn't dated since his wife died, because he didn't feel that he deserved to be happy anymore. That was the reason he hadn't asked Vanessa out before she and Malcolm started dating; he didn't feel he deserved happiness.

"You've got to live again. Don't erase what's in your future because of your past, man." Malcolm looked directly into his friend's haunted eyes. He wanted Steven to hear him.

Steven's tears stopped trickling as he returned Malcolm's intent stare.

"Why did you just say that?" Steven asked.

"Say what?"

"What you just said about my future," Steven replied.

"I don't know. I guess that's just what God wanted you to know."

Steven started to chuckle, shaking his head in disbelief. "The night of the men's conference I was helping Apostle Reed into the limousine when he touched my hand. He looked at me and said.

"Let it go, man of God."

Then he said, " The same word God had given the young lady in there. I hope you caught it, because the same word was for you too, son. He won't erase your future because of your past."

The change in Steven was amazing. Light shone from the man's eyes as he gained control over his grieving spirit. Malcolm was honored that God had used him to lift up his brother.

"Hallelujah!" Ivy shouted as a wide smile stretched across his face.

"God is so good," Ray breathed as he began to feel better.

"I remember Apostle saying that," Ray smiled.

"He set Vanessa free with that word. She was the one he spoke to."

Malcolm's face turned a shade of white. Ray's words echoed in his spirit. Malcolm turned his back to the fellows, looked up toward heaven, and pointed his index finger upward.

"I hear you, Lord," Malcolm whispered.

"I hear you loud and clear."

The smile that Steven wore comforted everyone in the room. Ray's phone vibrated on his hip. He stepped outside on the porch to answer her call.

"Ray," Donae breathed heavily.

"Baby, are you okay? You sound funny. Is it the baby?" Ray started to get nervous.

"No, it's Moe. Is Pastor with you?"

"Yes, he's here," Ray answered.

"Tell him to get over to the Hospice house. They're saying Moe won't make it through the night."

Ray walked back inside where three anointed men were now smiling in relief and joy. The spirit of heaviness had departed from the room, and Steven appeared to be himself.

"Guys, I have some bad news." Ray hated to break up the peaceful moment.

"Moe may not make it through the night."

Steven's heart pounded in his chest. "Oh no," he prayed.

"I just visited her the other day, and she was doing fine."

Ivy grabbed his keys. He searched his pocket for his cell phone, but figured he'd left it in the car.

"Pastor, Donae said they were trying to contact you."

Ivy nodded as he gave Steven a warm hug. All four men agreed to meet over at the hospice center immediately. Malcolm called Vanessa to tell her the news, but she was already pulling up at the facility as they spoke.

"I'll be there shortly," Malcolm said in a rush.

"Don't you let her go."

Ivy was the first of the four men to arrive at the Hospice house. Vanessa was sitting in the chair beside Moe's bed, holding her frail, small hand. Moe had lost a lot of weight, and the chemo had made her skin three shades darker than she normally was. Yolanda stood at Moe's bedside, holding the telephone to Moe's ear as the ailing woman talked to her son who was in prison. Yolanda could hear Moe's teary son in the background, begging God to please not take his mother. He promised God if she lived, he'd come out of prison a changed young man. Moe's other son stood near the window staring at his mother's weak form. Moe's hair had grown back to a good length, and one of the nurses had neatly braided it. Ivy walked over to Moe and kissed her forehead. Moe squeezed through a little smile.

"Ms. JoAnn is okay. I asked my sister to come and keep an eye on her for me," Vanessa whispered to Ivy.

"That's fine," Ivy said softly.

Ray walked into the quiet room with a sobbing Donae. Moe ended the call with her son and reached for Donae to give her a hug. Donae had ministered strength every time Moe had come into the pharmacy to get her prescriptions filled. Donae could hardly stand seeing her long-time friend in this failing condition. Steven rushed in like a whirlwind to Moe's bedside. Vanessa got up from the chair so he could sit beside her. He leaned in and placed his head on Moe's stomach, and began to weep.

Vanessa, Yolanda and Donae all shed tears as Moe weakly shifted her position. Moe patted Steven's head.

"It's okay, I'm ready to go."

Then she whispered softly, "You've been an awesome friend. You've stood by me every step of the way," she smiled.

"Everybody needs a friend like you."

"I couldn't get rid of him, Pastor." Moe pressed through another smile, as she continued to rub Steven's head softly.

The nurse came in to give Moe another shot of morphine. Vanessa stepped outside the room, wondering what was taking Malcolm so long.

"Does it hurt, Momma?" Moe's son came close to the bed, trying to hold back tears.

"I don't feel a thing, baby," she reassured him in her low voice.

Ivy held the son's hand, and the boy exploded with grief. "Momma, I'm so sorry for putting you through hell. Please don't die," he begged Moe, as if she had control over her sickness.

"Can't you do something?" he looked at Ivy.

"I thought you knew Jesus," he said loudly.

"Where is Jesus now? My momma is dying. I thought you so-called Christians were supposed to be able to heal people," the boy cried out in anger.

"All these years my momma raised me in church, every preacher, teacher, and Christian in the world telling us to believe in the power of God, and y'all don't believe. You're just a bunch of hypocrites!" The boy was clearly at his wit's end.

Ray and Ivy tried to calm him, each taking a hand to offer comfort.

"No!" the boy raised his voice a notch.

"What about the Scripture in Mark where it says 'these signs shall follow those who believe. They will lay hands on the sick and they shall recover.' Doesn't it say that?" He looked around the room for someone to answer.

"Aren't you all supposed to be believers? You mean to tell me not one of you can believe so my mother can be healed? What good is a church with an anointing to preach but has no power? You use this lame excuse that you're waiting on God to heal. You ever consider God is waiting on you to ACT on what you say you believe?"

Ivy tried pulling the child to the side, explaining that they all believed and were ready to surrender to the Lord's will.

"What do you mean the Lord's will? I was just reading Matthew 8:2 to my mother yesterday." He pulled the bible from the bedside table. "It clearly said that a man with Leprosy said to Jesus, Lord if you are willing you can heal me. It's evident that this man believed that Jesus could heal him but he didn't know if Jesus would. But look at Jesus' reply... He said, I am willing. So don't try to tell me that he's not willing because it says right here he is." The boy pointed out the scripture he had marked with a highlighter. It also said somewhere in there that Jesus' name was above every name.

Ivy shook his head in agreement for his spirit bore witness to the truth.

"Well if Jesus name is above all names then cancer is a name that has to bow down right?" The boy stood waiting on an answer. No one in the room had a response.

"You church folk don't do nothing but talk a good game. You talk about it, but won't be about it. You're the ones afraid to take God at his word and you wonder why people don't come to

305

church. Well I'll tell you why," he started to cry, "because you send them home with an encouraging word but they still leave sick and still bound," he pointed to Moe. Moe's expression looked like she was getting upset with his disrespectful tone. She weakly closed her eyes.

Malcolm rushed into the room. "Oh no, are we too late?" He looked fearful.

Everyone started to cry at the sight of Moe's face in respose. She made a moaning sound, and the entire room exhaled. Vanessa was shocked when she saw Rufus walk through the door, but her smile welcomed him.

"Moe," Malcolm whispered.

Moe gave a half smile when she looked up and saw him staring down at her.

"This is Rufus Reardon. He's a good friend of mine. He's also Vanessa's uncle. Rufus has the gift of healing. If you want to be healed today, you can." Malcolm didn't crack a smile.

"He can heal you through the power of God. I'm not telling you something I heard. I witnessed it for myself. It's true, Moe. He healed me. I watched as the Holy Spirit used him to heal a little boy the other day."

The nurse at the door bringing in fresh linen began to chuckle. Rufus walked over near the bedside to lay hands on Moe, but she held her hand up, shaking her head 'no.'

"Moe, please believe me," Malcolm begged.

"You've got to trust me." His eyes started to water. Vanessa was weeping too.

"Moe, I think Malcolm is right," Vanessa agreed.

"I've heard stories from my mom about Uncle Rufus laying hands on people, but I've never witnessed it for myself."

Moe whispered softly, "I believe God can heal me. I always have, but y'all, I'm tired." She looked at the sad faces around the room.

"Don't be sad for me. I'm going to live with my Father. I'm just ready to walk in peace. This is such a cruel world, people are mean-spirited and unforgiving. There's too much pain and disappointment."

Moe's son held his head down. Deep inside, he was thinking that much of his mother's pain stemmed from choices that he and his brother had made.

"Momma, please," Moe's son cried.

"Don't do this. I'm sorry. Give me one more chance."

Moe reached for her handsome son's hand. "It's not just you, son. Don't blame yourself. You go on with your life. Use the insurance money from my death wisely. God will take care of you, along with your aunts Carol and Gloria. Please don't disappoint me. I want to see you and your brother again one day," she squeezed his sweaty hand.

"My mind is made up, son. I tried my best to raise you and your brother right. I'm sorry I didn't do a better job. I'm worn out," she glanced around the room again.

"I'm going to sleep now," she closed her eyes.

"No Moe!" everyone in the room cried.

Steven walked into the hall. He needed a moment alone to talk to God. He grasped the locket of his late wife and son that he'd worn around his neck for years. The tears he shed now weren't tears of sadness, but tears of freedom. He stood outside the door in prayer for several minutes and finally he truly forgave himself. He put the locket in his pocket and felt a sense of relief as he walked back into the room.

"Moeisha," Steven called out, admiring her long eyelashes as they rested on her cheeks. Moe didn't answer.

"Moeisha," Steven called out again softly.

"I love you," Steven said.

"Yes, Moe, we all love you," Vanessa and all the others joined in.

"I love you all too," Moe answered with her eyes still peacefully closed.

"You don't understand," Steven said.

"I'm in love with you. Please don't leave me." Steven bent down and kissed her Vaseline coated lips.

Moe squinted with surprise, and then opened her eyes to wide stares throughout the room.

"Steven, are you on m-medication?" she stuttered.

"I said, "I love you," he said again.

"Let me take care of you," Steven implored her, taking her hand and holding it in both of his.

Malcolm couldn't help but wonder how Steven was planning to do that, judging from the dilapidated hovel he was living in. There was no way he was ready to take on such a big responsibility, but Malcolm promised himself he'd do everything in his power to help Steven get on his feet. Moe kept silent. She was exhausted and really wanted to be with the Lord. She smiled briefly at the hope of happiness.

"Momma," Moe's son made his way back to her bedside.

"I know you think you didn't do a good job at raising us, but you did. It's because of what you've taught me at such a young age that I believe right now God is real. I know Jesus can heal you. His power is real. I believe he wants us to witness his authority over sickness and death. This man is standing here telling you he's in love with you. Don't throw away a chance of happiness. It's not your time to go."

"Life and death are in the power of your tongue," Ivy said boldly. Moe's son had sparked something in him that he would never forget as long as he lived.

He winked at his beautiful wife Yolanda from across the room. "I love you," he whispered to her softly in the air.

Yolanda cracked a slight grin, for she felt his sincerity. Rufus approached the bed, waiting on an answer from Moe. Everyone in the room appeared tense. Moe smiled, showing some teeth. As tired as she was with this miserable life, something in her wanted her son to witness the mighty power of God and what better way to witness it than to witness her getting healed. She nodded her tired head toward Rufus and a room filled with believers. Rufus grabbed Moe's son by the hand and pulled him up closer to the bedside.

"Put your hand on your mother's head," Rufus said.

"No sir, I can't. I don't have any power."

"You're right, you don't, and neither do I," Rufus said.

"God has the power. The Holy Spirit will do the work, that's his job to guide, but he needs you to act and believe. The power of God works through three things...the Word, action and expectancy. That's it, it's that simple. Faith without works is dead. Do you understand me people? Believing in something but not doing anything to make what you believe happen will make it fail to happen. Faith without works is dead! Now let's go to work." Rufus pushed up his sleeves. "Now this is what happened," he said it in past tense purposely, as if he were telling it after the fact.

"You put your hand on Moe's head, God released his power through your hand and she recovered. Now when I prayed, you saw your momma walking out of here, didn't you?"

Rufus didn't wait for the boy to answer. "See her walking out. You got that picture in your head? If doubt starts coming into your thoughts, you cast it down."

"The weapons of our warfare are not carnal but mighty through God to the pulling down of strongholds, casting down imaginations and every high thing that exalts itself against the knowledge of God." Ivy quoted the Scripture, beginning to get excited at what God was about to allow him to witness.

The boy nodded as he kept the picture of Moe walking out of the hospital, healed and whole, in his mind and most of all his heart.

"Okay," Rufus said.

"You keep that picture there, don't lose it. Do you believe He can?" Rufus asked the entire room.

"Yes!" Everyone shouted.

"Now I need you to believe He will. Moe's son looked at Rufus intently and would not move a muscle. He starred into the old man's face, holding up his hands in the air, the boy broke down in tears, for he surely believed what was about to take place.

Rufus felt the Holy Spirit in the room waiting on the word so He could move, just as He did in Genesis when He hovered over the waters, waiting on God to speak His creations into the atmosphere. Moe's son placed his hand on the side of Moe's head where the brain tumor had been. Rufus placed his hand on top of the boy's. Everyone in the room stretched out their hands as Rufus called for the Holy Spirit to release his power. Everyone in the room had the same thought in their hearts and mind, Moe being healed. They began to pray on one accord in their Spiritual language as Rufus prayed aloud in an earthly language. Rufus's hand started to shake. He kept his fingers snuggly over the boy's until the shaking had ceased. A moment later, Moe suddenly sat up in the bed as everyone watched in wonder. Her face turned lighter, and energy shone through her eyes.

"I'm starving," she said brightly. Everyone in the room glorified God with the fruit of their lips. Ivy hugged Yolanda, Malcolm embraced Vanessa and Ray held a weeping Donae in his arms. Steven stood beside Moe holding her hand and, although she felt her healing had taken place, she was hungry and wanted to rest.

Moe's son asked Steven to meet him in the hallway.

"Thank you, Mr. Steven, for giving my mom hope to live again. I know in my heart she was giving up because of disappointment that was caused by me and my brother, but I want to be on God's side now."

The boy took off his colored bandana and reached into his pocket, grabbing the brass knuckles and the handgun, and handed them to Steven. He embraced the boy. His heart filled with the love he'd lost so many years ago. He thanked God in advance for a wife and not only one son, but two.

Ivy followed Rufus into the hallway and the two talked for a long time. Rufus confirmed quite a bit for Ivy. He knew he had been onto some biblical truths with his teachings from his former church, but they wouldn't allow him to teach it. Now he knew he wasn't the only one the Holy Spirit revealed it to. Ivy was convinced that the Lord had spoken in that hospital room through Rufus and Moe's son and he was determined that Mt. Emanuel would begin to walk and operate in the same anointing and power.

Exactly a month after the Code Red project had officially launched, Ray sat quietly at the oval office table, waiting for Blake Sheridan to enter the room. His knees were shaking. Amanda sat confidently across from him like an innocent school girl waiting for the principal.

"Nervous?" she asked Ray pulling out her makeup compact from a small designer purse and applied a fresh coat of lipstick.

Ray didn't bother to entertain her childish game.

"I guess you should call on your God to save you," she smirked.

"But can He?" she rolled her eyes.

"He couldn't save our baby, could He?"

"Amanda, I know I may be getting fired any second now, but as long as I've got Him," Ray pointed up toward the ceiling.

"I've got enough to start over again."

Blake Sheridan entered the room, carrying his Italian walking stick.

"Good morning, Raymond.... Amanda," he embraced his deceased brother's daughter with a friendly hug and peck on the cheek.

Mr. Sheridan took a seat between Amanda and Ray. "Well, well, well, let me see here."

He began leafing through a folder of papers that he studied through his gold rimmed glasses. "Looks like the Code Red Project is making me and our shareholders a lot of doggone money," he smiled.

"I surely like being rich," he smiled again.

"I like making money when I sleep, don't you?" he looked at Ray.

As Ray grinned in response, Amanda smiled in agreement. "Me too, uncle Blake. This project has made record breaking numbers, and we've already exceeded our top competitor."

"Yes, indeed. Yes, indeed." Blake's good nature and tapping fingers on the table showed how good he felt.

"Speaking of our competitor," Blake glanced over at Ray.

"How did that job pan out between you and them?"

Amanda smiled inside. She hadn't known Ray had stooped so low.

Ray bit his bottom lip, wondering how in the world Blake had found out. He wondered if he had enough boxes to clean out his office.

"What happened?" Blake asked.

"I declined the job offer," Ray confessed.

"Why?" Blake said harshly.

"I'm hearing they offered you a pretty sweet deal."

"Integrity," Ray said proudly as he lifted his head to meet the other man's eyes.

"Good answer," Blake smiled.

"You're quick on your feet. Well, here is my dilemma," Blake shifted in his seat, taking a more serious approach.

"I want to say this has been a job well done, but I don't know who to give credit to." He glanced first at Ray and then at Amanda.

"Amanda, tell me something, anything, in detail pertaining to the project Code Red that would persuade me to believe it was your idea."

"Uncle Blake, this is ridiculous. You've known me all my life. I've never lied to you, so why on earth would I start now? I'm the mastermind behind this project. Ray just jumped on the band wagon. I think it's absurd, you're asking me to prove myself."

"Boy! She's always been a feisty one," Blake chuckled almost to himself.

Amanda chuckled along with him. She had always been able to easily win over her good natured uncle.

"Ray, I'll ask you the same question." Blake leaned back in his seat.

Ray sat and thought for a moment. "I don't know where to begin, honestly. I can tell you how I came up with the name Code Red." Ray wished he hadn't said that, since telling how he came up with the name seemed kind of silly.

Amanda laughed, "Come on, Ray, is that all you can explain?" She glanced over at Blake, who wasn't smiling.

"You're pathetic." She folded her arms.

"Go ahead, Raymond, I'm listening." Blake watched Ray intently.

"I was at a leadership conference in Texas for Zanderbilt, and you were the keynote speaker."

Amanda shifted in her seat, rolling her eyes.

Ray continued, "You spoke about how your vision for the company was to be the best at what we do. You said you were a bit disappointed that we weren't living up to our potential, that our company and our product could be better. You mentioned that being number two in the industry for so long wasn't good enough. You had a dream about a project that would put us where we were supposed to be. This project would bring our company back to life, because at the time, being second best was considered Code Red, a critical place. You said you wouldn't quit until this critical time had passed and Zanderbilt Industries soared through the Code Red stage."

"Wow!" Blake smiled.

"You're a great listener." Blake stood to his feet.

He walked over to the window and opened the blinds to let in more sunshine.

"Ray, you're a bright man, and I have to be honest with you, blood is thicker than water."

"I understand that, sir." Ray dropped his head before watching Amanda as she gloated.

Blake continued, "Decades ago when I took this company over that was passed down from my great-great grandfather, I was a stupid, arrogant knucklehead fool. But twelve years ago when I was forced to sell over 40% of the stock of this company because of bad investments and I listened to greedy colleagues. A wise young man said to me, *"Mr. Blake, always remember, you never want to get into a relationship where you are unequally yoked."*

"I always thought, of course, that he was only talking about marriage in the biblical sense." Blake smiled.

"However, he was he talking about so much more. This guy was talking about business too. Don't yoke your business to something or someone who doesn't share your vision because it will cause division, Ray," Blake shook his head with a smile.

"That's what I was reminded of as you were speaking about Code Red. You've done an outstanding job running this company. I not only want you here, but I also realize how much I need a man like you. One who fears God and can lead this company to new heights."

Amanda jumped from her seat in fury. Blake held out his walking stick and pointed it toward the chair, signaling her to sit down. Amanda pouted as she collapsed in her seat, nearly in tears.

"As I was saying - when you have a man of God with integrity such as yourself running a business, you not only have happy shareholders, employees and colleagues, but you likewise have the blessing and favor of God on your business."

"Mr. Durrant," Blake cleared his throat, "if you'll agree, I'd like for you to finish out the remainder of this year as plant manager. The first of the year you'll be taking over the Regional position, overseeing our other companies. Run those plants like you've run this one, and make this old man proud."

He turned to his niece. "Amanda sweetheart, as for you, I always knew you had too much of your conniving mother in you. She manipulated my brother for years before his death. I can't stand for this nonsense anymore. You'll get a hefty monthly allowance in the mail. Honey, you're fired."

"Uncle Blake, you've got to be kidding. I thought you just said blood was thicker than water!" She questioned his reasoning.

"It is, sweetheart," he pinched her cheek as he walked by.

"I was talking about the blood of Jesus. You see. Ray and I here are brothers."

Chapter 33   *Ivy*

The marriage ceremony for Alicia and Spencer Gillespie went off with a bang. Deacon Bailey spared no expense in throwing his daughter a beautiful and costly wedding. However, there was a brief moment of tension before Alicia said 'I do'. Her pause was just a little bit too long for Ivy, causing him to perspire. Everyone knew Alicia still loved Ivy. Even her new husband Spencer had his suspicions, for he pulled Ivy to the side before the ceremony to warn him how important this wedding was to him, and that nothing and no one was going to ruin it. Ivy thanked God that Alicia had been wise enough to move on.

Ivy had been trying to contact Kevin for months, but each time he got his voicemail. Every message Ivy left was an apology for his stupid actions. Ivy quickly realized that Kevin had only been looking out for him, like he always did. Kevin's intentions always had been pure, and Ivy was downright ashamed that he had allowed his fleshly desires to come between them. He wished he could find out where Kevin had moved, because he wanted to apologize face-to-face. Ivy tried to contact Kevin's mother Sheree and his cousin Kimmie to see if either one knew where to find him.

The only information that Sheree could provide was that he was somewhere in Florida. Ivy was stuck waiting on Kevin to eventually come around. Ivy did show up at Mel's house that evening, but not for any hanky panky. After his altercation with Kevin he realized he was giving the devil access. He needed to get his flesh under subjection quickly. He immediately started to fast to get control of his craving flesh. He apologized to Mel for his actions and hoped she wouldn't hold it against him. Ivy knew Mel didn't want him. The night they were together never should have happened, but at the time the two of them were like wild animals.

The exhibition fight was coming up soon. Malcolm gave Ivy twenty free tickets. Ivy was really looking forward to the big fight. It was the talk of the town. Everyone from all over town was making plans to fly to New York City to support "Bone Crusher." They all had grown to love him. Although he was a big man, his spirit was humble and loving. He'd donated thousands of dollars to homeless shelters, local churches and many non-profit organizations. The community members were now his biggest fans and supporters of his comeback. From the local talk and news programs, it seemed like every person in Richmond wanted him to beat the pride out of "Hammer Hand."

Ivy signed himself up for a sex addiction management class and was in route of deliverance from his lifelong problem.

After Ivy's twenty-one day fast, he continued for 19 more days with fruit, vegetables and water. He ate no sweets, meat, or bread. Although Ivy had been craving baby back ribs like there was no tomorrow, the fast indeed helped him to keep his flesh under control. Once he realized he could deny his body the food it needed for nourishment, he could also deny it the sex addiction it craved. He'd been intimate with his wife, but it was only for her pleasure. He held back his desires to reach the mountain top in hopes that it would teach him discipline. His only thrill was holding her in his arms and her knowing how much he loved her, not just her body.

Finally he had learned the true essence of intimacy. Instead of craving Yolanda's flesh, he now held her hand and winked at her when she walked across the room. He massaged her head, and bought her flowers 'just because'. He placed love notes on her rearview mirror, inviting her out for ice cream while he ate an apple. Ivy wooed her with acts of love that had nothing to do with the physical act.

Ivy learned many things during his fast, and God revealed to him mysteries in his Word that he'd never seen. He taught him things about love, life and healing. The Holy Spirit guided him how to love his wife. Intimacy was an act that was much deeper than sex. This type of intimacy was a form of foreplay that touched the soul. The way God taught Ivy to love Yolanda ministered to her spirit. Several nights she went to bed expecting Ivy to touch her, but he didn't. Many nights she begged him to allow her body to satisfy his flesh, but, instead, he only held her in his arms until she drifted off to sleep.

Ivy asked Yolanda to meet him at her favorite restaurant with Dominic and Bryson. She gladly agreed, but asked if she could grab the boys some hot wings because they wanted to stay home and play video games, which for the most part was true. Yolanda had another plan. She wanted her husband all to herself. She bought a sexy, snug-fitting dress that flattered her curves. Yolanda smiled with excitement as she held up the lingerie she had purchased. This was going to be a night Ivy would never forget. Tonight she would make him explode. He wouldn't be able to hold anything back.

Ivy took a break from working on his sermon. Some of the Deacons and a few of the trustees were still hounding him about the building fund. Ivy had stressed to them that the building would get built eventually. They needed to be patient. The bottom line was that he was going to listen to God. He continued with the seminars of the debt free classes and was encouraged that a lot of God's people were wholeheartedly on board. He decided to go to the diner to visit

315

Moe. His stomach was growling and Moe's home cooked vegetable plate was calling his name. Ivy sat in the booth alone enjoying his carrots, cabbage and pinto beans. The watermelon Moe brought him was so delicious that he closed his eyes to savor every bite.

Ivy couldn't help but stare at Moe. Who would have ever imagined that 3 weeks later after being in the hospital on her deathbed that Moe would have walked out with her cancer in remission. Frequent tests were performed weekly, all with negative results. The cancer was gone completely. Her beauty was breathtaking. She looked twenty years younger. She'd colored her hair a beautiful light shade of sandy brown. Her makeup was flawless, and her smile lit up the diner. Steven's love had changed her and God's love had healed her. She didn't have to show off her new engagement ring. It sparkled in Ivy's eyes like the bright sun. Ivy felt like running circles when she proudly smiled as she flashed it in his face. He couldn't be happier for Moe or Steven. Now his concern was helping Steven get back on his feet. He couldn't help but wonder if Moe's ring had belonged to Steven's deceased wife.

When his cell phone buzzed, Ivy smiled when he looked at the screen to see Mel's name. She had had a change of heart and was working with him so he could spend time with the kids. He was delighted when she told him the twins wanted to come over to his house for a while. Ivy gladly told her he'd be there to pick them up after leaving the church. He'd spend some quality time with the kids and then drop the twins off at home on his way to dinner with Yolanda. The day was going smoothly, that was until Perry strolled through the diner doors wearing a crooked smile. Ivy braced himself, determined that he wouldn't give in to the enemy's trick. His spiritual fast had brought him too far to fail now. Ivy prayed for strength to help him get through this without giving Perry a big piece of his mind.

"What's up, Playa?" Perry's words rang through the air.

"How's my little sweet thang doing?"

Ivy took a sip of his water. "Perry," he nodded.

"Mind if your old friend joins you?" Perry sat down in the booth across from him without an answer.

"Sure, why not?" Ivy forced a grin.

"You'll be glad to know my project for Zanderbilt has been fulfilled. I'm leaving town in the morning to go back to my big, empty house, thanks to you." Perry helped himself to Ivy's scrumptious bite sized watermelon.

"Are you ever going to forgive me?" Ivy asked.

"Let's see," Perry smiled as he motioned for a female server to come and take his order.

"You, my old friend, are on top of the world, aren't you? You have it all, fame, a beautiful wife, kids, big house with a picket fence. What do I have? Nothing but a destroyed dream and a pocket full of money, thanks to you."

Ivy exhaled. "Perry, I'm sorry, man. It was an awful mistake."

"You hear that?" Perry said to the server who was removing Ivy's empty bowl.

"He's sorry. Give me the baby back ribs with potato salad and fries." Perry put down the menu.

"Ivy, you haven't changed. You're still the same no-good skirt chaser you used to be. The only difference is you've got a title. How many of those women in the church have you slept with?"

"None," Ivy said quickly.

"I doubt that," Perry smirked.

"I know you."

"You *knew* me," Ivy corrected him.

"You don't know me now."

The waitress dropped off Perry's ribs and refilled his drink. Ivy's mouth watered at the smell of the barbecue sauce that stuck to the beautiful ribs.

"I remember in school you holding a mirror under Mrs. Hopkin's dress, looking at her white panties," Perry blurted with a smile.

"And how did you know they were white?" Ivy chuckled.

Perry tried holding in his laughter, but was unsuccessful. He guffawed loudly, drawing the attention of nearby customers.

"Okay, what about when you poured red Kool Aid in her black cushioned chair? She walked around the whole day unaware, all the kids saying her period was on," Ivy reminded him.

"I hated that woman," Perry shook his head, recalling how she had his home number on speed dial.

"You remember when we were in middle school and you got mad at Mrs. Wilson for telling your dad you cut school?"

"How could I forget?" Perry said.

"My dad whipped my behind for days."

"You went and smashed her pretty red, white, and blue mailbox with a hammer, destroying it to smithereens. Then you found out it wasn't her who told on you, it was Mr. Grant, but you had already ruined her mailbox, the one her husband had made for her before he died."

Perry still felt ashamed over that. Poor Mrs. Wilson cried for years over that mailbox.

317

"Seems like everything I did to make her feel better wasn't good enough. I paid for that mistake until I was damn near twenty years old." They shared another quick laugh.

Ivy turned the conversation. "That's how I feel about us. I know I messed up, I messed up bad. I can never replace what I took from you. All I can do is ask for your forgiveness."

"I'd give anything to go back and make us right again. We'd still be boys right now if I hadn't have messed that up. I'm begging you man, please forgive me so I can forgive myself."

Perry sat in the booth, silent. "Is Ms. JoAnn still cooking up her famous chicken and dumplings?" Perry changed the subject.

"Nah, man," Ivy said tenderly.

"She lives with Yolanda and me. Her health isn't good anymore. She has dementia."

"Man." Perry felt bad.

"Mrs. JoAnn used to hook a brother up."

"I miss all that too," Ivy admitted.

"So tell me, man, why didn't you find love and marry after you left here?"

"I don't know. I was just too hard on myself. Truth was I could never find anyone to fill Cara's shoes. You only find real love once in a lifetime, and Cara was my mine" Perry shrugged it off, taking a drink of his Coke.

The two men didn't part the restaurant as friends, but they did end lunch with a handshake. Ivy told his old friend to live again, and that he hoped he would have a safe flight home.

****

Heading to the front door of a well-kept condo, Ivy rang the doorbell at Mel's house to pick up the twins. She answered the door wearing her spandex workout clothes.

"Daddy!" The twins raced to his side.

"Is Grandma going to know who we are this time?" Justin asked.

"I hope so," Ivy answered.

"You munchkins go jump into the car. I'll be right over."

"Hey Mel, you got a sec?" Ivy asked.

"Yeah, what's up?" She stopped doing her lunges to the workout video she was watching on TV.

"I hope I'm not overstepping my boundaries, but someone asked me where they could find you, so I gave them your address.

"Who?" Mel asked without alarm.

Perry stepped from behind the door. "Hi, Caramel," Perry loved the nickname he'd made for her so many years ago.

"God you're still beautiful.

Mel froze. Her eyes, mouth, and legs wouldn't move. It was Perry at her door, the love of her life, the man she was supposed to marry so many years ago, but they had never made it to the altar after Perry found out that Mel got sloppy drunk at her bachelorette party and slept with his sloppy drunk best man. Ivy walked back to his car, leaving Mel and Perry still standing in the door staring at one another. By the time he drove away, Perry had at least made it into the house.

Four hours later, Ivy sat in the game seat with his hat turned to the back, making his boys mad as fire. He kicked their butts on the video game, never having to give up his winner's seat. Jessica was on the phone with one of her little girlfriends, yelling for the boys to be quiet, while Yolanda was upstairs getting dressed for dinner.

"I quit," Ivy announced.

"I need a challenge. You guys suck!" they all laughed.

Bryson jumped on his back, with Nicholas, Dominic and Justin not far behind. Ivy had Nicholas in a headlock while Bryson called himself punching Ivy in the back. Ivy dragged all four boys from one section of the room to the other, throwing them around like rag dolls.

"Stop it!" Jessica yelled, getting annoyed with all the noise.

"I wish Ebony was here so I would have somebody to have fun with," she pouted.

"I'm sorry, baby. Ivy signaled to the boys for a timeout. Your sister couldn't make it; she and her mom and stepfather are out of town."

Jessica sulked in the oversized chair and decided to play a game on her cell phone.

"Ivy!" Yolanda yelled from upstairs.

"I'll be down in twenty minutes."

"Okay, baby," Ivy yelled back.

As he waited in the side, room that Yolanda often used as her reading area, he wondered what had happened at Mel's house. He started to wonder if he should take the kids back home shortly. Mel might just haul off and smack him. Ivy prayed and asked God for mercy, hoping his reintroduction of Perry to his ex-girlfriend didn't ruin his chances of spending time with the kids. Now that Ivy had thought things through, he realized it might have been safer if he'd just given Perry Mel's phone number instead of taking him there. The phone rang just then, and Ivy panicked when he saw Mel's name of the screen. He prepared himself to get cursed out.

"Hello?"

"Ivy, hi," Mel said in a normal tone.

"Hey there," Ivy tried to remain optimistic.

"Do you mind if the twins spend the night? I'm going out to dinner and a late movie."

"I don't mind," Ivy said, wearing a grin.

Mel laughed. "Thanks Ivy...you did good."

"Yeah, thanks Ivy, you did good," Perry's deep voice echoed Mel in the background.

"Is Perry still leaving in the morning?" Ivy couldn't resist asking.

"You need to mind your business, Mr. James," Mel giggled, as Perry tickled her from behind.

"You go, girl," Ivy said before hanging up the phone. His heart began to dance.

He prayed and asked God to give the two of them a second chance at love. If things with them worked out, he was certain Perry wouldn't ask him to be his best man again, which was all right with him. Ivy raced up the stairs to give Yolanda the good and bad news. Unfortunately he'd have to give her a rain check on dinner, now that the twins were spending the night. Ivy opened the bedroom door and his eyes found delight. Yolanda's curves were making him seasick. Her beauty had him mesmerized. He was speechless. She'd chosen to dress conservative ever since she got saved, so seeing her in a tight fitting dress was a treat.

"What's wrong, silly?" Yolanda smiled inside.

"Lawd have mercy!" Ivy closed his eyes, and then explained he had to cancel dinner.

"Meet me downstairs, and I'll tell you all about it," he smiled, needing to get out of the bedroom before he lost all self control.

Yolanda ached inside that her night was ruined. Ivy pulled the door closed slowly, savoring every peek of his lovely wife. He opened the door wide again just to get another a glimpse of his glorious gift from God. Although disappointed, Yolanda danced around the room as she slipped out of her dress. *It's only just a matter of time now*, she laughed to herself, *Momma 'bout to make daddy go pop!* She swirled around the room like she used to do at the strip club where Ivy first met her.

Chapter 34   *Malcolm*

Malcolm tried reasoning with Telese about granting him the divorce, but she refused. He considered sneaking in her house while she wasn't there and finding the documents, as he knew exactly where she would have placed them. The same spot she put anything else she used to hide from him. In the back of the framed Ali picture. Malcolm didn't have the heart to tell Vanessa that the papers hadn't been signed yet. The last she'd heard, Malcolm was on his way to sign them so they could be mailed. Telese was leaving Malcolm no choice but to file for a legal separation and wait the year timeframe.

Malcolm's soul was in turmoil because his decision to marry Vanessa was set in stone. Her ugly past had no bearing on his love for her, but watching her walk around jolly while making wedding plans was torture because of Telese's stubbornness. Malcolm couldn't enjoy the excitement of planning his wedding day because he'd started to feel stressed. Vanessa's house was under contract to be sold, and they were making plans for her to move in. Her wedding dress hung safely at Uncle Rufus' and Johnnie Mae's house where she visited everyday just to look at it. She was having a hard time deciding on bridesmaid dresses. Luckily for Malcolm, the date she'd chosen was eight months away. He hoped and prayed daily that Telese would soon come to her senses and realize how much he wanted Vanessa to be permanently in his life. He promised himself he wouldn't panic until they started looking at wedding invitations hoping by then God would have softened Telese's hard heart.

The Bone Crusher and Hammer Hand fight was just days away. Although Hammer Hand was the heavyweight champion of the world, he was not the champ in the eyes of people throughout the city. Once word spread that Bone Crusher was training in Richmond, people were surrounding the ring like crazy. Luckily the handlers were able to keep things on the down low until the last few weeks before the fight. When Bone Crusher was asked by local TV media why he chose Richmond as his training camp, his answer was simple: "God led me here."

Bone Crusher had given Malcolm additional tickets to give to his family and friends. Although the fight was scheduled in New York City, everyone who was offered a free ticket found a way to get to the big city of dreams. People were car-pooling to show their undivided love for Bone Crusher. If Hammer Hand won the exhibition, he was likely to get booed; that's how much Bone

Crusher had won their hearts. Everyone wanted him to beat the brakes off the champ, and Malcolm knew it would surely get done.

Telese pulled up at the "Glamor Girl" nail salon and spa to get her manicure & pedicure. She had to look smoking hot for this New York trip, as she was on a mission to win back her man. She'd already booked flights for her and the kids. Malcolm had graciously made hotel accommodations for them and two of KJ's best friends, who'd be bringing along their parents. The kids were excited to be traveling to a big city, and Telese was eager to execute plan *'Bring daddy home'*.

As Telese bounced toward the door, Lauren, Malcolm's sister, almost bumped into her on her way out.

"Hi, Lauren," Telese smiled.

"How are you?" she gave her a friendly hug.

"I'm fine," Lauren said dryly.

Telese instantly picked up on Lauren's nonchalant demeanor. "How are my niece and nephew?"

Lauren forced herself to smile briefly.

"They're okay, missing Malcolm, but the Lord will work that out," she said with a smile.

"Why would they be missing Malcolm? They see him all the time," Lauren said.

"They want him home," Telese responded.

"Do they want him there, or do you?" Lauren shifted to the side, allowing another customer to exit the door.

"We all do," Telese said, being honest.

Lauren pulled Telese close beside her. "Look, Telese, I know the kids probably do want Malcolm to move back in, but don't you think with the situation the way it is, that you should encourage them to know the relationship with their father is secure, no matter where he lives?"

"I know he's already stressed that to them, because he did it when he was staying with me. I just think you should support him, since Malcolm has tried so hard to move on. Telese, you crushed him when you left. Now that he's found happiness, let him be happy. No disrespect to you, but he's found a wonderful woman to spend the rest of his life with, so please don't stand in the way of that. He let you go when you chose to be with Morris. I would hope you'd do the same for him."

Telese suppressed her anger. "You don't know anything about Vanessa. She's not the angel everybody portrays her to be."

"She doesn't have to be," Lauren said.

"All I know is she helped my brother get through one of the roughest times of his life."

"And I didn't?" Telese put her hand on her hip.

"Who do you think supported him when he got fired from job after job because of his temper? ME."

"Who do you think helped him pay child support when he was out of a job? ME. Why do you think I stayed with him all those years when he beat the crap out of me? Because I loved him, so don't tell me about being supportive. I bent over backwards for him." Telese couldn't help but cry.

"Now, he's changed for the better and I want him back, now all of a sudden I'm the bad guy. That's not fair for you to judge me like that, Lauren. You act like it's a crime for me to still love him. He is still my husband."

"I'm not judging you," Lauren said sincerely.

"Honey, you slept with one of his friends, for goodness sake. He's a man. Men can't get over something like that."

Telese dropped her attitude. "That was a mistake. Morris was there for me when Malcolm was abusive to me. It just happened. I didn't plan it, Lauren, I swear."

"You don't owe me an explanation, Telese," Lauren said.

"All I'm trying to get you to see is that you chose to leave Malcolm. He tried telling you he'd change, but I guess you were tired of hearing the same old story."

"Only this time he really did change. I don't blame you for your choices," Lauren said compassionately.

"Putting his hands on you was wrong. Dead wrong, but when you left him, you told him to move on. That was your choice."

Telese was silent. "What about the kids?" She wiped her tears.

"It's not just me. They want him back home too."

"Don't use the kids as a way to try to get him back. You're only hurting yourself. You should want a man to be with you because he loves you. If he's there for any reason but that, you're deceiving yourself. Why would you want him with you when you know his heart is with someone else? You don't want a relationship like that!"

"You and he would be miserable. Don't do that to yourself," Lauren grabbed Telese by the hand.

Telese's tears flowed hard, her heart ached. She was saddened by the truth. She loved Malcolm deeply and didn't want to let him go. Lauren reached out and embraced her sister-in-law, realizing how hard it must be for her to watch the man she still loved love somebody else. Telese left the salon without getting her service. All she wanted to do was go home and eat and cry.

323

Malcolm and Vanessa had made plans to stay in New York a few days after the big fight. Neither had been to the city of dreams, and they were looking forward to spending time away to relax. Malcolm had Crystal reserve some places for them to visit and dine. He couldn't wait to walk through the city with his queen-to-be.

"Hello." Malcolm answered his phone after looking at the caller I.D. first.

"Malcolm, hey it's Sydney. I just want to say I'm sorry for everything. I know I hurt you and Crystal. I really want you to know it wasn't like Tony made everything seem. I left him and I plan on being a better mother and taking care of my child. I admit I made a lot of wrong choices."

"Sydney, I don't know what to say." Malcolm breathed heavily.

"I'm not going to judge you for what you did or did not do. I just hope that when you make decisions from now on that you think about what's best for the both of you, you and Crystal. As her parents, we should have worked as a team. I know it was part my responsibility to make sure my child was okay, but when I fell short you should have been able to pick up my slack and vice-versa."

"You should never depend on a man or anybody else to survive. Baby, you've got to be able to survive on your own. Your child should always come first."

Sydney agreed, sniffling and in tears. "I know you're right. I'm going to do better. You will see."

"Don't do it for me." Malcolm stressed. "Do it for yourself. And ask God for guidance. He's the key to it all."

Sydney dried her weeping eyes. "I see how you've overcome your struggles Malcolm and I am so proud of you. I know if you can do it so can I, and as a single parent I now understand, I can't depend on others to support me and my child. I have to do it."

"Once I get myself straightened out, do you think we can all sit down and talk about Crystal coming back home for good?" Malcolm paused a moment.

"Let's see how things go," he said.

Malcolm felt sorry for Sydney after seeing her live in misery after Crystal left. He'd given her a few tickets to the fight to let her know he was over the cruel things she'd done. He paid for Crystal to fly with him and Vanessa, but she'd return with Louise and Lauren since Malcolm and Vanessa had planned to stay longer.

Malcolm called Ray to let him know he had booked extra hotel rooms in case he and Donae needed one. Ray was living on cloud nine these days. His big promotion had promised to put a few more zeros behind some commas. He and Donae found out they were expecting another boy, and things couldn't be better in his world. Malcolm was delighted that Ray had been so blessed. He hoped Bone Crusher would lay Hammer Hand flat on his back, so they both would be sitting pretty. Malcolm had a gut feeling this fight was going to open up plenty of doors for his sparring, which was easy money, not to mention the job of his dreams. His headaches had cleared up, and the doctor had given him a clean bill of health to continue pursuing his favorite activities.

Pastor Ivy and Yolanda had already flown in for a couple of days of alone time. Ivy anticipated the arrival of the others to join them soon because Yolanda held him captive in the hotel suite for the first few days. She brought with her a bag full of lingerie and cashed $200 worth of one dollar bills, planning to make it rain.

Steven was the one Malcolm was most concerned about. He still couldn't understand why Steven was living in such a dump. It was obvious Steven was down on his luck, but every time one of the guys offered help, Steven politely refused. Malcolm wondered how on God's green earth Steven could take care of Moe and her two sons if he was broke. He had heard about the rock of an engagement ring he had purchased for Moe. Where had the money come from? It was just not adding up. Thoughts started running through Malcolm's mind that he instantly rebuked.

It was the day of the big fight, and Malcolm was nervous as all get out. You would have thought he was the one fighting Hammer Hand. All the crew had flown out to NYC except Moe, who'd taken a later flight because she had visited her son in prison earlier that morning. Hours later, every attempt Vanessa used to calm Malcolm down failed. He was more hype than a kid in timeout who had just eaten a whole bucket full of Halloween candy.

"Honey, will you calm down?" Vanessa sat on the king size bed, turning the pages of a bridal magazine.

"I can't, girl." Malcolm jogged in place.

"I should have had some business cards made up, you know, because I'm a business man." he flexed.

"I can see them now; Malcolm Stewart, Professional Sparring." Malcolm laughed at himself.

"Because when Bone Crusher makes his comeback, Malcolm makes his come-up," he patted himself on the back.

"We 'bout to blow up, girl."

"Boy, you are a true mess. Sit down somewhere," Vanessa laughed at his silliness.

"That's a good idea, don't you think?" Malcolm asked, being serious.

"Yes, baby, it's a brilliant idea. You should have thought of it sooner," Vanessa said, turning the magazine sideways to admire a beautiful full-length ad.

"Malcolm, have you gotten your official divorce decree in the mail yet? I'm not sending out invitations until it comes."

Malcolm swallowed hard. He surely didn't want to talk about that tonight. Steven knocked on the door lightly. Malcolm answered, boxing at the air, trying to play off his momentary discomfort.

Steven chuckled. "We're heading down to the Arena a few hours early, grab your stuff."

"Okay." Malcolm got his bag, glad to be getting out of the line of fire.

He gave Vanessa a big bear hug and told her to make sure Crystal, Lauren and Louise got there on time. "I'll see you ringside," Malcolm sang, still showing his silly side.

"Steven, can you please calm him down? Does anybody have any sedatives they can give him?" she laughed.

"You wrong for that, Vanessa," Malcolm said playfully.

Malcolm followed Steven down the hall to the elevator. "Listen," Steven said.

"There's been a slight change of plans. Bone Crusher wants you at the stoop with him."

"Me?" Malcolm was surprised.

"Why? I'm no trainer. I can't tell him what to do. I don't know about that one, Steven. I'm not too comfortable doing that. I think someone trained should be there."

"Mackie will be there too, but Bone Crusher said he wanted you specifically, and Mackie, no trainers."

Malcolm counted it an honor that Bone Crusher trusted him that highly. Although Malcolm didn't have much ringside experience, the trainers and Bone Crusher's manager felt Malcolm would be good for moral support and motivation. As Steven and Malcolm passed through the bar area of the hotel, they walked up on Rufus sitting at the bar with a crowd of people around him, having a discussion about Christians drinking alcohol.

'Oh Lord.' Malcolm dropped his head as Steven laughed at how countrified Rufus looked in his overalls. Rufus was a fun old man to be around. Malcolm overheard one of the men question Rufus, saying if the Bible says not to drink to drunkenness, "then why are you drunk?"

Laughter exploded through the crowd. Rufus laughed along with his new friends. "I ain't drunk," Rufus replied to the man.

"I'm tipsy," he joked.

Malcolm noticed a couple of people with a perplexed look on their faces, one that Malcolm knew all too well, the same look he had every time he got into a discussion with Rufus about the Word. Malcolm knew those people heard something Rufus said that caused them to think. Rufus had a way of revealing truth that reached out and grabbed you. He brought new meaning to the word "outreach."

"Are you nervous, buddy?" Malcolm asked Bone Crusher.

"You seem too calm."

"I'm good," Bone Crusher replied heavily.

"It's just a fight."

"Just a fight?" Malcolm looked at him sideways.

"What do you mean? This is your comeback. This is all you've talked about for months."

"The Lord says to be anxious for nothing." Bone Crusher lay back on the table to stretch.

"Besides, if I let my nerves get the best of me, I'll end up with diarrhea."

Malcolm tried to keep from laughing because Bone Crusher was serious. He turned his head so the champ wouldn't see him chuckle.

"Hey man, I need a favor," Bone Crusher asked.

"Can you step out for a few minutes I need to have a private moment alone if you don't mind?"

"Sure." Malcolm left the training room to give the boxer his time with God and prayed that the Lord would grant his request.

The Arena was filling up quickly. Malcolm watched Bone Crusher's every move. It was as if the prize fighter was in a daze. Malcolm noticed Mackie began taping up the Crusher's hands and kept patting him on the back. At least Bone Crusher seemed to be at ease. Malcolm, on the other hand, was as nervous as he could be. Soon the Arena was packed wall to wall with buzzing fans eager to see the big event. Malcolm knew no way to explain it, but he felt like he was supposed to protect Bone Crusher from harm, as though he were a bodyguard. Steven, Malcolm, Bone Crusher, his manager and Mackie, along with two trainers, stood in a circle as Steven led them in prayer.

"Dear Father, protect the fighters and give them strength. Show us Your glory tonight and allow your name to be glorified. We honor you tonight and we believe we will leave this place victorious."

Moments later Mackie stepped back, shaking his head, as Bone Crusher jumped in the air from side to side, waiting for the commentator to announce his name over the loud speaker. Seeing the concerned look on Mackie's face, Malcolm pulled his old friend to the side.

"Mack, be straight up with me. What's up? Why does it feel like something is wrong? Why are you looking like that?" he nervously chewed the cinnamon gum Vanessa had given him.

Mackie shook his head again. "It's that obvious?"

"Yeah, it is. What is it?"

"He's not fast enough to fight the champ. Sometimes, son, you've got to know when to call it quits."

Suppressing the sinking feeling in his stomach, Malcolm said, "I think he's ready, Mack. Look how calm he is."

"He's already accepted he's going to lose," Mackie said wearily.

"How many times did you put him on his butt?"

Malcolm looked away. The truth was he had often wondered the same thing, but then, Bone Crusher had improved tremendously.

"He's gotten better," Malcolm offered.

"You're right, he has," Mackie agreed, "but 'improved' and 'ready to fight the heavyweight champion of the world' are two different things."

"What about the trainers? Do they agree? What does Steven say?"

"We agreed that if he'd have picked up his speed, he might have pulled it off by wearing the champ down. But the trainers get paid to train, so they don't care if he's ready or not as long as they get their checks."

Malcolm shook his head in despair.

"He's out of his league on this one, son," Mackie said.

"Don't you worry, he'll be okay." The older man rubbed his grizzled chin.

Malcolm's heart began to race as he heard the commentator on the loud speaker say, "Are you ready to rumble?"

The crowd screamed and roared in anticipation of the history making match they had come to witness. Malcolm went to grab Bone Crusher by his arm, but Mackie jerked him back.

"Don't," Mackie said, "he won't back out now."

"He's going to get clobbered in there!"

"No, he won't," Mackie shook his head.

Malcolm was really confused now.

"The good thing about it is, it's just an exhibition match, not a real one. No one but us really knew that Bone Crusher was trying to make a comeback, so no harm done."

Malcolm digested this.

"Hammer Hand probably hasn't even trained a day for this fight; it's nothing to him. This is his way to make people think he's giving back to the community. Just enjoy the show." Mackie patted him on the shoulder.

"But Mackie, he really wanted this, man. He wanted it more than anything."

"Yeah, I know. As long as he gets in there and treats this as an exhibition, he'll be alright. No one was really expecting anything less than a good fight. They'll put on a great show. Don't you worry, son."

'That's why he said it's just a fight,' Malcolm thought as he looked around for a close-up. *No wonder he's so calm. He's given up on his dream.* Sadness filled Malcolm's heart for his legendary friend.

Malcolm prayed as Bone Crusher jogged into the arena while the crowd jumped to its feet, screaming his name. "Lord, give your anointed man of God supernatural speed and strength to see his dream become manifest. Let his blows feel like iron, and guard his body. Take the sting out of Hammer Hand's punch."

Moments later, Hammer Hand stepped into the ring, striding around it as though he were king of the world. He'd heard through the grapevine that Bone Crusher was planning to use him as the means to his comeback, but it wasn't about to happen: not today, not tomorrow, not ever, the champ boasted in his mind as he mean-mugged Bone Crusher up and down. The champ had trained a couple of weeks just to embarrass the washed-up wannabe. He was definitely going to enjoy this.

"You ready to go down, chump?" Hammer Hand said, showing no mercy.

"You're about to see the truth today."

Bone Crusher flashed a foul grin, talking a little junk to hype up the crowd. Malcolm's tension eased, and he kept telling himself that it was only an exhibition. Finally he sat back on the stoop to watch the match. The bell sounded and both men came out their corners, dancing. Bone Crusher threw a few light jabs, making no effort to bruise the champ, but the champ's hits were stinging him hard.

"Lighten up," Bone Crusher said between gritted teeth.

"It's just a worthless exhibition."

Pow! The champ smashed Bone Crusher hard in the nose. Blood dripped into his mouth and onto his teeth.

"What are you doing, man?" Bone Crusher felt his nose.

"You better come with it, Bro. I know your plan, but it ain't going to happen." Hammer Hand hit him again forcefully.

Bone Crusher started punching back, but he struggled to keep up with the champ, who in a matter of seconds had him on the ropes, beating him to a pulp.

"Get out of there!" Mackie yelled.

"Push him off of you, Bone!" Malcolm yelled as his fury accelerated.

"Fight him back, man, don't give up!"

The champ popped Bone Crusher another solid hit, and Bone Crusher fell face down on the floor. The ring announcers were in awe.

"Who made the champ so mad? Is this an exhibition or a real fight?" they asked.

"He's going to murder the man."

The referee rushed over to start counting: "1....2....3....4....5....6....7...."

Mackie asked the Lord to please tell Bone Crusher to stay on the floor. Bone Crusher got to his knees. His heart was telling him to stay down, but his pride kept saying this was only the first round. Malcolm shook his head. He too wanted Bone Crusher to stop now. He was really worried about his friend getting hurt. Hammer Hand

330

wasn't fighting fair. The referee made sure Bone Crusher was stable, coherent and alert before stepping back out of the way.

Like a fierce bull, the champ charged into Bone Crusher, knocking him down again on the floor. "Stay down, you weak chump," he yelled. He pressed his foot into Bone Crusher's back and held both arms up as if he had already won the fight.

"I'll say it again," the commentator said excitedly.

"Is this or is it not supposed to be an exhibition fight? I'm wondering if I'm in the right place."

Bone Crusher struggled to get up, but the champ had too much bodily force on him. The fallen fighter tried to push his opponent's leg off him, causing the champ to almost lose his balance. This infuriated the man so much that he kicked Bone Crusher hard in his stomach.

"No!" Mackie yelled as Malcolm came soaring through the ropes, pushing the champ backwards.

"Get off him!" Malcolm yelled.

"You okay, Bone?" Malcolm tried to help his friend to his feet.

"Get down there with him, punk!" The champ sucker-punched Malcolm in the head.

Malcolm lunged at him full-force, pounding his bare fists into the antagonist's head as the crowd went crazy. Everyone in the entire arena was on their feet staring in amazement.

"You are messing with the wrong one!" Malcolm wouldn't stop.

"Ding—Ding—Ding!" The bell sounded. Malcolm didn't relent. It took Steven, Mackie and others they didn't know to pull Malcolm off the champ. Malcolm was sweating like a beast.

"Let him go," the champ demanded when he finally got his breath and reared back to study his new opponent.

The announcers were in awe. Never had they witnessed anything like this.

"Somebody give him some gloves!" The champ shouted angrily as he jabbed and pushed at Malcolm, trying to provoke the newcomer into a serious match.

Malcolm didn't budge his main concern was making sure Bone Crusher was okay.

"Get him some gloves," the champ was striding around the ring like a rabid animal. Malcolm had embarrassed him, and he was determined to redeem himself.

"Get back in the ring you punk. Come get this whipping for your boy."

"Let them fight, let them fight!" the crowd chanted loudly.

Vanessa and Malcolm's family and friends were on their feet. KJ and his friends were so excited, they couldn't sit down. Telese stared in disbelief that her husband had just beaten the hell out of the heavyweight champion of the world.

"Can they do this?" one commentator asked the other, who shrugged.

"I don't know. I've never seen anything so crazy. I feel like I'm in a Rocky movie," the other balding man said.

"Let them fight, let them fight – fight – fight – fight!" the crowd wouldn't stop chanting.

"I say let them fight," the commentator said, and the crowd screamed approval.

Malcolm looked at Steven, and Steven gave him a thumbs-up. Mackie hurriedly taped Malcolm's hands and put the gloves on.

"This one is for you," Malcolm told Bone Crusher who was being examined ringside by a doctor as Malcolm jumped through the ropes.

The bell sounded for round 2. Malcolm danced around the ring, punching blows of destruction that matched the lightning in his eyes. While he was pursuing the bully around the ring aggressively, jabbing and punching sharply, the champ only could remain standing because of the ropes. When he tried to move from the corner, Malcolm pushed him back like a ragdoll.

Smack – punch – jab Malcolm wouldn't let up. The champ struggled to stay on his feet. His embarrassment kept him from falling, but he was quickly wobbling. The champ threw a hard punch and Malcolm stepped back, dodging his fist. Malcolm threw a quick upper cut that landed so quickly the champ saw nothing but darkness. Falling to the floor, the champ was knocked out cold. Malcolm stood over the man, waiting on him to get up so he could continue the brutal punishment, but the champ never stood up to make it to round three. When the referee signaled the fight was over, Steven, Mackie, and Bone Crusher, who had a bandage on his broken nose, rushed into the ring, lifting Malcolm high off the floor. Ray stood up, crying tears of joy, remembering what the Lord had said about his friend: "I'll make your name great. I'll seat you among kings."

"I'll bet we'll be seeing this newcomer again," the commentator said in amazement.

"Who is this guy?" He kept shouting over the cheering crowd.

"Malcolm! Malcolm! Malcolm!" the crowd chanted again and again.

Cameras and microphones were shoved in Malcolm's face. News reporters were asking questions in rapid fire succession. Malcolm tried to find Vanessa in the crowd, but so many people were surrounding him he couldn't recognize anyone he knew. KJ came rushing up with his buddies, but the cameras and reporters were everywhere, and the boys couldn't get through the swarming mob.

Vanessa got as close to Malcolm as she could, and he finally spotted her. She blew him a kiss and smiled. Neither could believe what had just happened. He had knocked out the heavyweight champion of the world in one-and-a-half rounds. Vanessa eased to the back of the crowd so she could wait on Malcolm in the trainers' room. Telese saw her heading that way, so she grabbed Layla's hand to follow. A few moments later Vanessa was rising from the floor after saying a prayer. She had thanked God for a prophecy fulfilled, and she blessed His name that He was no respecter of persons. If God brought Malcolm's word to pass, she knew hers was about to be fulfilled, too. All she had to do was believe it. She asked God to help her be a good wife.

"Wow! Isn't this so exciting?" Telese walked into the small room as Vanessa got firmly to her feet.

"Yes, it sure is," Vanessa agreed.

"God is so awesome, isn't he?" she added.

Telese didn't have time for small talk, so she cut straight to the chase. "You know Malcolm hasn't signed these divorce papers yet, don't you?"

Vanessa looked confused. "He hasn't?"

"No," Telese said proudly, pulling them out of her purse.

"See, I've already signed them. We're just waiting on him."

"I thought he came by to sign them months ago," Vanessa said.

"He did, but I think that after he found out your little secret, he started to doubt. Maybe he's having second thoughts about you, Vanessa. If I know Malcolm like I think I do, I'm sure he just doesn't want to hurt your feelings."

"Hurt my feelings? What little secret?" Vanessa didn't understand any of this.

"Vanessa, sweetie, you're a whore," Telese said, adding a frown. She pulled the envelope out, showing Vanessa the file containing her ugly past.

Vanessa opened the envelope and turned her head away quickly. "Where did you get these?" Tears slowly drifted down her cheeks.

"That's irrelevant," Telese said.

"The important thing is Malcolm knows, and now he can't marry you, Vanessa, let's be real. Technically, he's the heavyweight champion of the world. Won't it be catastrophic when pictures of you prostituting yourself hit the paper? He'd be the laughing stock everywhere."

"If you love him as much as you say you do, you wouldn't put him through that. His career is just getting started. Besides, my kids really need their father. This living in two places is not working for us. You should just go away. Malcolm and I have been intimate since you've been with him." Telese lied. "It was the day he found out you were a lesbian." Telese smiled smugly.

Vanessa's heart dropped to the pit of her stomach. She wanted to defend herself, but what was the use? She stood in the small, airless room, staring blankly at his ex. Telese couldn't read Vanessa, so she tried a different approach.

"Vanessa, I'm not judging you, honey. I know we all make mistakes. I'm no saint, but the truth is I still love him, and I want him back." She began her fake cry.

"I'm sorry; I didn't mean for anyone to get hurt, but Vanessa, please. I'm begging you, my children miss their daddy."

"Layla cries every night because he's not there, and she thinks he no longer loves her. She's a child, and she doesn't understand all of this."

Telese paused to let these words sink in before adding, "You may not appreciate all that a mother will do for her child because you don't have any." Emotionally Telese twisted the knife.

"I'll do anything for my children, and if begging you to give us Malcolm back is what I have to do, then I will. But Vanessa, you have to admit if he wasn't having second thoughts, why hasn't he filled these papers out?" She set the envelope on the bench.

"I'm begging you; please don't break up my family. This is tearing my baby up." Telese forced more tears from her eyes. She motioned for Layla, who was standing behind a door so Vanessa couldn't see her.

"Ms. Vanessa," Layla came around the corner and stood in front of her.

"Can you please let my daddy come home? I'll give you a dollar," she handed Vanessa a crumpled dollar bill.

Vanessa raced to the hotel room and packed her belongings quickly. Her heart ached with sorrow and she wanted to run to a place where no one knew her. She took a moment and left Malcolm a note on the back of one of her wedding invitation samples.

My Dearest Malcolm,

334

I love you with all my heart, mind and soul. You truly are a remarkable man and I am so proud of you. Malcolm, I can't be your wife. I don't know what I was thinking or who I was trying to fool. I don't deserve a man like you. You deserve someone much better than me. Go back to your wife and children they love and need you. Move on with your life. If you really love me as much as you say you do, please respect my decision, and don't look for me.

Vanessa

Two years later Ivy was awakened by a familiar aroma and the sound of old hymns of praise and worship music. "Who's downstairs cooking?" Yolanda asked as she looked at him and he at her.

"I don't know," Ivy shrugged.

The loud sound of the empty pot hitting the floor startled them both. They quickly wrapped up in their bathrobes and raced down the stairs, peeping around the curve of the wall.

"Momma." Ivy looked surprised.

"What are you doing?"

"Sorry baby, did I wake you up?" She pinched Ivy's cheeks.

"Ms JoAnn, what in the world? Collard Greens, pinto beans, fried chicken, and corn bread; it's 7:30 in the morning!"

"Hush up, child. Ma Jo feeling good this morning," JoAnn smiled.

"Sunday dinner supposed to be cooked and on the table before noon. Lord, Ivy, Momma gon' teach her right for you, son."

Ivy nodded in agreement. "You teach her momma," he laughed.

He couldn't believe his eyes. The Lord had cured his momma. "Has Mr. Rufus been over here?" Yolanda asked.

"Yes, he was here last night," JoAnn smiled as she dipped the fresh chicken parts in her special egg batter.

"Him and Johnnie Mae. I don't know why on God's green earth y'all wanted him to touch me so bad. I told that ole fool to go on somewhere. I wasn't about to let him put his hands on me."

"Hallelujah," Ivy shouted.

He and Yolanda smacked their palms in a high-five and ran a lap around the house.

"Call all my grandkids, Nicholas, Dominic, Bryson, Ebony, Jessica, and Justin and all the baby mommas too," JoAnn chuckled. "We gon celebrate."

"Celebrate what, Momma?" Ivy asked.

"Celebrate life baby, celebrate life." She kept an eye on the chicken now browning in the skillet as she started peeling sweet potatoes for her pies.

"Should I make room for Daddy?" Ivy asked, to make sure she was fully in her right mind.

"Jessie?" JoAnn paused.

"Boy, you know good and well your daddy gone to be with the Lord and have mercy! I can't wait to see him again one day." She started humming one of her favorite hymns.

Ivy called Courtney and told her the good news. Courtney couldn't believe it either. She told Ivy she was headed right over. Thankfully, she had recently moved back in town.

"What's this, Ivy?" Yolanda held up a beautiful party invitation.

"This house in the picture is beautiful. Whose is it?"

"I don't know, sweetheart." Ivy was sneaking into the pinto beans pot, tasting the juice like he used to when he was a kid.

"It says we're invited to a party three weeks from today, at this address. We're supposed to arrive promptly at 3 p.m.. My goodness," Yolanda added.

"It's a two hour drive."

"Mark it on the calendar. We'll go if you want," Ivy said.

"You can't tell who it's from?"

"No," Yolanda answered, unable to peel her eyes from the gorgeous photo of the house.

Ivy sat at the kitchen table like a school boy. JoAnn grinned at Ivy as he watched her peel sweet potatoes. He had to pinch himself to see if this was real. Yolanda walked over and stood behind Ivy and the two of them starred at JoAnn in amazement.

"So," JoAnn smiled, as she picked up the potato peelings to throw away in the trash. "Y'all two sure do love doing-it don't you?

Ivy and Yolanda both dropped their heads giggling.

JoAnn made her way over to Ivy with a serious face.

"Son, are you still having those bad dreams?" Ivy dropped his head and said a soft yes. JoAnn placed her hand over her sons head and pulled him into her bosom, whispering the word peace.

The next morning Ivy awakened from a peaceful night's sleep. He dressed for work and noticed two birds chirping away at his window. The sound was so beautiful it took his breath away. He hushed Yolanda, who was still in bed yawning loudly, so she could listen. As he watched the two birds fly away, realization came over him, but his spirit wouldn't let him cry. He walked into JoAnn's room and smiled sadly at seeing her lifeless body in her bed. Her face was still warm, and the smile on her face gave him great comfort. Her small black suitcase sat in the chair beside her bed, packed and ready for her trip. The note she left behind said, "I love you all, and tell S.P. I'm sorry I couldn't say goodbye."

On the day of JoAnn's funeral, bouquets of roses and lilies filled the sanctuary as the choir sang JoAnn's favorite hymns. Kevin was now a pastor under the leadership of Apostle Reed, and he'd come back home to preach her eulogy. He and Ivy had an opportunity to talk and embraced one another in brotherly love. It felt as though Kevin had never even left. Ray sat beside Donae, holding their toddler son. Donae tried to reach for a tissue, but her big belly kept getting in the way. The two got a big surprise when she went for her six week check-up. Donae admitted the mortuary had done a lovely job with JoAnn's body. She appeared to be simply resting.

Moe sat quietly beside Steven with her head tucked into his shoulder. "She looks so beautiful," Moe breathed, "and she's still smiling."

Malcolm sat beside Telese and the kids, praying for Ivy's strength. The pastor hadn't shed one tear since JoAnn passed. Malcolm was afraid that when it finally hit him that his mother was gone, he would lose it. Now Malcolm couldn't go anywhere without someone wanting his autograph. After the fight, Hammer Hand demanded a rematch, arguing that he hadn't properly trained for the fight. After the rematch was over, Hammer Hand had to give Malcolm his props, especially after going toe-to-toe with him and then knocking him out in the eighth round.

A quick glance at JoAnn's obituary program made Malcolm shift nervously in his seat when he saw Vanessa Reardon's name on the program to give comforting words of reflection. His heart began to flutter. He wanted to get up and run, but he had to remember he was attending a funeral. He hadn't seen or heard from her in over two years. It was as though she'd disappeared off the face of the earth.

The family walked into the sanctuary to say goodbye to JoAnn. Ivy was at the front of the line with Yolanda beside him. Courtney and all of Ivy's children followed as the music softly played. Jessica wept loudly as she looked into the casket. Seeing her grandmother laying there not moving just broke her heart. Mel and Perry jumped up from their seats and rushed to her side to comfort her. Courtney's heart ached. She never really concerned herself with life after death, but she was certain she wanted to see her mother again. She thought about her own life, and whether or not when she laid her eyes to rest if she would make it to the better place everyone was talking about.

Ivy had tried ministering to her for years about Jesus, but at the time Jesus was the last thing on her mind. Now, seeing her mother lying in a casket with a cold face and a smile caused her to search her heart for something deeper. She wasn't planning on getting saved and all that, but what she was wanting was for God to show her more of Him. Courtney couldn't understand how JoAnn could be totally healed one day and die the next, but she was grateful to God for giving her that one day with her mother where she was whole and in her right mind.

Kevin walked out into the speaker's area to take his seat. He spotted his mother, Sheree and Kimmie two rows behind Ivy. Sheree's tears touched his heart deeply for he knew it was at that moment Sheree wished she would have told JoAnn before she died that she forgave her. JoAnn would send her birthday cards every year up until she got ill, and Sheree never opened them. She had over twenty years worth stowed away in an old shoe box. When Ivy called to say that JoAnn had passed, she ran to the shoe box and allowed JoAnn to speak to her through the heartfelt cards. Sheree cried and cried until she couldn't cry anymore. When JoAnn loved, she loved hard, and her love was like the love of God. It had no conditions. Grace and mercy lived in her and never left.

Shortly after Kevin walked onto the platform, Vanessa made her way to her seat holding her Bible. Several close friends and family members stood up to speak about what a warm and loving woman JoAnn had been. The wall-to-wall friends were a clear indication that she was truly a much loved woman. Vanessa was the last to speak before Kevin preached the funeral. She came up to the podium, wiping her eyes. Silently she prayed for strength because she didn't think she could make it through without breaking down.

"She's gained some weight," Telese whispered.

"Be quiet, Telese," Malcolm shushed her so he could hear.

He longed to rush up and grab her, and run to a place far, far away. Vanessa looked out into the congregation and could hardly look at Malcolm or Telese, so she looked the other way.

"There are so many things I can say about this woman of God. It may take me more than a few minutes to say what I really need to say, so please bear with me as I tell you the story of this Angel who touched my life, Ms. JoAnn James."

"JoAnn was an earthly Angel. She knew how to love people. Her love wasn't based on what you did or didn't do. It didn't matter how messed up a person was, she was able to look past all that and see the real you; kind of like the way God does."

Sheree raised her hand and said "Amen," for she agreed wholeheartedly.

"JoAnn was good at keeping secrets. She protected those around her from themselves. She had a gift to minister to your soul, calling forth the real you. The one that you didn't even know existed."

Courtney began to cry, remembering the long talks they used to have when she first came out of the closet.

"None of you know this, but I met JoAnn long before I started caring for her." Ivy and Yolanda looked at one another strangely, for neither of them knew.

"I met JoAnn when I was eight years old. She dragged me out of a car where a confused man was about to molest me. She saved me that day. I remember asking her if she was God's wife. When she drove me home that day, I couldn't take my eyes off her; I'd seen her before in my dreams."

"When we pulled up at my house, I didn't want to go in. I wanted her to take me with her and keep me safe because I knew I was about to leave her safety to return to hell, a hell where my mother sold me and my sisters to men and women for sex."

Courtney shook her head, now understanding why Vanessa was so confused.

"I remember standing on the porch, tears running down my face, and her saying to me words that I have never forgotten.

She said, "This situation is a weapon formed, but I promise you, it won't prosper."

She also said, "You hold your head up baby, and live."

Rufus and Johnnie Mae began to weep, remembering how abusive Vanessa's mother had been to her children, for that was the reason why his Rufus' sister, hated him. He had shut her sex ring down by turning her in to the police.

"So from the age of eight, the only thing I knew how to do was to sell my body for sex, and even when I walked the streets prostituting my body, I could still hear her saying, 'Sweet Pea, you hold your head up baby, and live.' And even though now till this day, people still judge me because of my past."

Telese shifted uncomfortably in her seat.

"Today I can stand here, finally free from what people think about me. I am who God says I am. I may not have traveled down the same road as you, but I went through what I went through so that the Glory of God might be revealed."

Tears began to flow heavily down Ivy and Yolanda's face, because they hadn't been able to figure out for the life of them who S.P. was in JoAnn's note, but now they knew.

"I thank you, Mr. Steven." Vanessa looked through her red rimmed eyes.

"I thank you for walking the streets of one of the roughest neighborhoods in the area and handing out roses to us prostitutes, telling us how much God loves us. You took us to an apartment and paid us what we charged our customers to listen to you teach us

God's Word. I thank God for you showing us what real love really was."

Steven felt her pain, but was glad God had used him to help His people.

"I remember telling Ms. JoAnn when I grew up, I wanted to be just like her and save people, and in a sense, that's exactly what I did. I grew up to preach the Gospel of Jesus Christ, to save the souls of people who are lost. My job is to get them to Jesus. I know who I am, and no Devil in hell or on earth will ever again be able to tell me otherwise." Vanessa looked at Telese.

"But I forgive those who tried to keep me down. You only made me stronger." She paused and looked down a moment as though praying.

"When I got pregnant at the age of twelve and had to give my child up for adoption, I could still hear JoAnn saying, 'LIVE.' I even named my child after her: 'JoAnn' kind of spelled backwards, 'AnJoelina' with a J," she smiled.

"So you see, she's been ministering to me all my life, and when I saw her again, I had to take care of her when she was sick. That was God letting me give back to her everything she gave me. I'll miss you JoAnn James. Rest in peace, true woman of God." Vanessa broke down and cried softly.

Kevin came up to the podium and embraced her lovingly, wiping her tears with his handkerchief and escorting her back to her seat. Pastor Kevin James preached a powerful sermon. He turned to the Scriptures and preached JoAnn's life, the story of the Good Samaritan. Her funeral no longer was a funeral; it was a celebration of life. Kevin thanked his fiancée' Vanessa for her powerful testimony. Had she not come to Florida to preach Apostle Reeds women's conference they never would have become reacquainted.

Malcolm was numb, his heart ached at the thought of Vanessa being engaged to Kevin. She never gave him a chance to choose. She had chosen for him. The note she left on the bed that night along with her engagement ring telling him to move on with his life because she could not be his wife, still sat in his wallet two years later. The envelope containing her ugly past was thrown in Telese's face days after Vanessa was long gone.

Vanessa never even knew that on that night Telese left the divorce papers in the trainers' room, Malcolm walked in after the exhibition fight and signed them, mailing them the next day. The divorce decree arrived in the mail a month later. Malcolm didn't have the strength or the heart to tell Vanessa the truth. She was engaged now, and he didn't want to cause her any more pain. He watched as Rufus walked up to his niece Sweet Pea and embraced her with an unconditional love. He introduced to her Angel, his young neighbor, who turned out to be Vanessa's long lost child. Who would have ever thought that when Malcolm dropped the papers about Vanessa's child, Angel would see them and recognize her old address?

****

Ivy, Yolanda, Malcolm, Ray and Donae all smiled as they sat in the beautiful white chairs near the garden. The 10,000 square-foot mansion sat on 50 acres. Steven's beautiful bride rode in a carriage and buggy up to the end of the driveway where Moe's two sons walked a breathtaking Moeisha down the aisle to give their mom to the man of her dreams; one whom they both loved and respected. He'd given their mom everything she could have ever wanted. Neither of them had seen her frown since the day she left the hospital. Steven hired an attorney to reopen his stepsons case and he was released with time served. He purchased the diner for him, giving him his inheritance. Immediately after his release from prison, Steven sent the young man to culinary arts school, for he shared in his mother's passion to cook. Now Moe's Diner has two locations, one on the east and one on the north side of town, with talk of building another. Moe's oldest son kept his promise to God after healing his mother and submitted his life to the will of God. Steven's influence touched the lives of his stepson's tremendously.

When word got out about Steven's apartment being a safe haven, prostitutes and drug addicts from all walks of life began to show up, wanting to get their lives right. Malcolm and Steven together funded a non-profit organization to help get homeless and helpless people off the streets. When people arrived, they were fed and their basic living needs were met. They could go to rehab if needed. After rehabilitation, they enrolled in school to get GED's or to learn a trade. Some were offered jobs at either MBK Security or through the temporary service called Second Chance Agency, both of which Steven owned. Steven's younger son earned a bachelor's degree in Business Management and received his inheritance as CEO of Second Chance Agency.

Steven Hill was a humble millionaire. The investments he'd made with the insurance money from his wife and son's death all turned to gold. Everything he touched prospered, however, he chose to remain humble and continue to put on his security uniform from time to time, as owner of MBK (My Brother's Keeper) Security. He and Moe planned to travel the world for he surely had more than enough. His 40% shareholders stock with Zanderbilt had been doing nicely for the last ten years.

Steven had made some other moves that had congregational members calling the church left and right. The church secretary had people breathing down her neck, wanting answers. They had sent out letters in the mail asking members to make sure to come to church on Sunday morning, where everything would be explained after service.

Sunday morning after Ivy preached, he smiled as he addressed the congregation. "I know you're all wondering why many have received these big checks for thousands of dollars from the church. Members in the pew were nodding and a few loud "Amen's" were heard.

"Please don't be alarmed," Ivy said.

"The church is not doing anything illegal." The congregation hung on every word.

"The reason for the checks is this. For the last few years since we stopped the building fund, we asked you to bring food to God's house so we could store it up for those in need. The offering has been used for the upkeep of the church, but for the last few years your giving has been set aside and put in the bank, earning interest. We are giving what you gave back to you. God wants his people free from bondage, so take this gift and pay your bills so you will owe no man or woman. We've shown you through the debt-free classes how to manage your finances. Take this blessing from God and prosper in your lives."

People all over the sanctuary shouted till they were hoarse. Ivy shared with them how God had been dealing with him about building bigger buildings to house the church, putting burdens on the members that were not from God. The church made the front page news. Pastors from everywhere were rebuking Ivy from every direction. What he did went against everything any other church was teaching. He understood that he wasn't supposed to get rich off the Gospel. The Gospel was free. Things were about to change, but the change had to start with him, and his knowing and sharing the truth. The world couldn't dispute the fact that people walked into the church deaf and came out hearing birds chirping. The church grew because the power of God had become manifest. He told everyone, if the power of God isn't working in the church you attend, you need to find out why. Many Pastors are gifted with an anointing but power is supposed to abide with it, hand in hand.

Two years later the church built a beautiful three-story, sanctuary, debt free. Because the members were out of debt, they gave more and with a cheerful heart. No longer were they bound by a law that said for them to give a tenth but they were lead by the Spirit which prompted them to give from a Christ-like heart. For in their hearts they knew to do right. They helped their brothers and sisters in need, and no one in the church lacked anything. The ministry soared so greatly that Ivy received countless interview requests and even some external donations. As the popularity of the church and the pastor grew, Ivy stressed to the people not to follow him but to follow Jesus. His job was to get them to Jesus. He'd often ask them, "Why are you still here? Don't stay in this building looking at me."

Get equipped with what you need by the Word that I teach, and by what the Spirit will teach you. After that, go minister at your job, in your neighborhood, at your house or wherever the Lord leads you. The church is not this building; the church is you. The Lord wants us to be givers. It's better to give than to receive. Give to someone in need. God wants you to take care of the poor, the widows and the elderly. You couldn't do it while you were in debt. Jesus came so you could have life, and have it abundantly. Do what God said you could do and be the lender and not the borrower. He already showed you how to save a tenth.

****

After years of being angry and disappointed with God, Rufus Reardon forgave himself for not being strong enough in his faith at the time to lay hands on his own daughter and trust God to heal and save her life. He traded in his beer with, the exception of an occasional drink here and there, for a louder voice to minister in the community and evangelize the good news of Christ to the lost people in this world who need a Savior.

Sequel to "Picking Up His Pieces" - Unedited

God Please Don't Tell

Chapter 1

Press 1 for checking, Press 2 for savings, followed by the pound sign. Jada fiddled with her cell phone as she pressed option 1 and waited on pins and needles for the automated system to display, her account balance.

Your available balance is negative seventy-two dollars and thirty-three cents. Jada closed her eyes and exhaled deeply. Anxiety gripped her like super glue to paper; it just stuck. She called her husband Quinton to ask if he had any money for groceries because her son Kyle called to say all the cereal, milk, and oodles of noodles were gone. As usual, Quint was broke. His little fireman check couldn't put out smoke. He barely paid his share of the mortgage, leaving her the stress of keeping a roof over their heads, food on the table and clothes on their backs. Lord knew she loved that fine specimen of a man to death but he had about as much drive as a broken down parked car. She'd just days before mailed off one mortgage payment and now the mortgage company was still hounding her for two other payments that were still delinquent.

She had less than twenty-four dollars to her name that would have to last until she got paid with three hungry kids at home. She was stuck like chuck, not to mention the gas light in her Lexus had been on for nearly 8 minutes, and she had fifteen miles to go before she'd make it home from work.

God, I'm sick of this! She got angry. I'm tired of living paycheck to paycheck. I'm your child, I'm not supposed to be broke. Damn!

Jada called around to her family and friends requesting a hundred dollar loan until payday. She had to at least feed her three kids, but all her efforts were to no avail. Her sister Janet, had ,the money but she refused to help since Jada still owed her $200 from last time.

Feeling defeated she pulled into the gas station almost in tears, stopping at the pump. She rambled through her car for several minutes before finally heading inside, holding onto the front of her t-shirt as if she was protecting someone from harm. Standing in line she watched the doors closely, relieved that today the store wasn't crowded. But she quickly became annoyed with the well- dressed business type gentlemen that stood so tall in front of her. His indefinite choice as to which scratch off tickets he would purchase was giving Jada a headache. She prayed that he would hurry so she could get out of there quickly but when the fat stubbly man who reeked of strong liquor stood behind her with two six packs she wanted to scream. Because of his state she still kept her nerve up to see this through.

Lord will this man please hurry up, Jada thought, as her impatience and embarrassment started to overwhelm her.
  "Hi Jada," a friendly voice echoed through her ears.
  "Hi, Ms. Francis," Jada turned sideways hiding her disappointment.

We missed you at church on Sunday sweetheart, the bubbly, silver headed saint smiled.

I had to work. Jada lied, the truth was that she barely had enough gas to make it through the week. A twenty minute drive to church and back would have burned a few days worth of gas.

Well I hope to see you there this Sunday, the woman gave a friendly smile.

Jada responded with a polite nod, as she carefully watched Ms. Francis pick up a pack of chewing gum and a big bag of potato chips and stood in the back of the line.

Jada shifted her weight after hearing the cashier tell the well- dressed man to have a great day as he walked out the door scratching one of his scratch off tickets.

Looking into the cashiers eyes as she slowly approached the counter, Jada quickly slid out of the line and stood nervously in front of the potato chips pretending to decide which bag she'd purchase as the line dwindled down from customer to customer.

See you on Sunday, Ms. Francis waived goodbye as she dragged her wide hips out the door. Jada waited until the only two people in the store was her and the cashier.

"What's wrong honey?" The old white man asked. " Life!" Jada answered feeling sorry for herself. This good ole miserable life, she said as she reached into her t-shirt dumping the rolls of pennies, nickels and loose change on the counter. She sat a five dollar bill and four ones on top of the mounds of change. "Nineteen dollars on pump three," she said never looking up from her humiliated posture. Running out of the store in tears, she couldn't bear to watch him count all that change, especially as customers were starting to come in. Jada stood at the pump and waited for the attendant to turn on the gas pump in hopes that her nineteen dollars worth of gasoline would quickly pump, so she could drive away her shame.

Afterward she felt relieved, feeling no fear of running out of petrol on the highway.

"Hello," she exhaled out of frustration into her cell phone. She didn't dare complain, for the Lord only knew how long it would be before it would stop ringing due to' nonpayment'.

Jada's son, Kyle, called her back in a panic, "Hey ma, please don't be mad," he tried asking for forgiveness before telling what he'd done.

I've been checking the mailbox everyday, waiting on a letter from girl. I forgot I had this mail in my room for you and daddy.

"Okay," Jada said unalarmed.

One of them is from the power company. I can see red letters through the envelope.

"Oh, goodness," Jada thought. "Open it up and read it."

The boy opened the letter, Jada heard his lips chirp, which was an indication of bad news.

"Ma, please don't put me on punishment," her 15 year old son, begged.

"What does it say?" Jada heavily exhaled.

"You have to pay $160.99 before 5pm today."

Okay Jada said, hanging up the phone, she sat in her car at the gas station at 3:30 p.m., crying like a baby. What was she going to do, move her family in with her momma?

Jada walked in the house at 6:15 p.m. bringing in mounds of grocery bags. Hey baby," her husband, Quint, started removing his fireman uniform.

"Pastor Ivy and First Lady, Yolanda, just called and said they needed you to speak at a women's breakfast in a couple of weeks."

"Really?" Jada answered, feeling exhausted.

"You alright?" he asked, You look tired.

"I'm fine. I just want to lie down. Can you help the kids get the groceries out of the car."

"Yeah, you go get some rest, I guess you worked too hard today."

Jada walked upstairs and looked at herself in the mirror. The sadness in her eyes concealed up her beauty.

"Hello, she answered, whispering, on the first ring.

"Jade, baby you left your work keys in the hotel room. I'm still here. I'll make it worth your while if you make me smile again. I love it when you call me 'Big Poppa'."

Jada was disgusted with herself. She slept with her ex-boyfriend for money. Never in a million years would she have defiled her marriage by sinking so low. 'But God I had to', she kept telling herself. Nothing could make her feel better. The truth was she was no better than a hoe. She exchanged money for sex, but the lights were still on and her cupboards were filled. Nobody but her, God and Trent knew what she had to do to get it.